Farewell Fifteen

About the Author

Mari Howard is a painter and writer, who has also written poetry. She has a lifelong interest in the natural world, and in our social life as human beings. Mari grew up in London, studied in the North East, has grown to love West Cornwall, and lives in Oxford where she's raised a family.

Farewell Fifteen

MARI HOWARD

HODGE PUBLISHING

Other books by Mari Howard:

A Problem in our Cultures: Science; Faith, and Prejudice
(formerly *Baby, Baby*, 2009):
The Mullins Family Saga Book One

A Maze or a Labyrinth? Art, Science and losing your way
(formerly *The Labyrinth Year*, 2014):
The Mullins Family Saga Book Two

Live, Lose, Learn: a poetry collection (2019)

Life in Art and Culture: stories from my Younger Self (2022)

To Liz, with love and thanks.
Still missing you and your wonderful smile.

Copyright © 2023 Clare Weiner *writing as* Mari Howard.

Published by Hodge Publishing
10 Bainton Road, Oxford OX2 7AF

ISBN 978-1-7395372-0-3

British Library Cataloguing in Publication Data

A catalogue record for this book is available from the British Library

Cover artwork and design and book typesetting:
Rachel Lawston, Lawston Design

Acknowledgements

A short list of 'acknowledgements' for *Farewell Fifteen!* - which is both a stand-alone YA/crossover novel, and the third in a series of three 'women's fiction' type novels about the Mullins family. It can be read either way: for young women 13-18 probably as a stand-alone, for women who enjoy a developing saga, as the story of Jenny Guthrie and Max Mullins's older daughter Alice, who has her own ideas about who she is and who she is becoming...

I have dedicated this story to my lively friend Dr Liz Williams, who is sadly no longer with us, but who was such an encourager in so many ways as I laboured away with each of the three books: providing insights into medical conditions (especially the mystery of changes in Eliot's behaviour and physical abilities and the reason behind what how and what he does...) alongside wild shopping expeditions for retail therapy and super chats. Miss you still, Liz!

Huge appreciation also to my friend and fellow writer Anne Booth, whose insights led me towards making this a far more cheerful, light hearted book, and Alice a more delightful young woman. Thank you, Anne, for passing on your wisdom...

Thirdly I'm grateful to Dr Lianne Davis and Dr Anthony Morgan, good friends, and always ready to enlighten someone who is writing fiction which includes in its background the trials of being an academic scientific researcher dependent on funding.

Also, and as ever to Prof. Marsha Fowler with her knowledge as a minister and as child of a fundamentalist home, and for our long discussions as the Guthrie and Mullins family gradually evolved and grew into the next generation.

Finally, and not to be forgotten, the technical help: super cover and book designer Rachel of lawstondesign.com for not only the actual designing but also giving guidance on where this story fits, shelving-wise... and my excellent proof reader/copy editor/supporter who has laboured over the typos etc... And to all who guided and advised on the two earlier Mullins books and spent time explaining and enlightening me on the higher reaches of the science involved, making sure the life scientific come alive.

And to the family, who grew up in Oxford surrounded by, well, Oxford academic kids and teens...and remain our and each other's good friends.

Part 1

Chapter 1

I FIND A PHOTO AND GET AN INVITE

I was 15 going on 16 when I began wondering about the photo – Granny Caro, Mum, Aunt Hattie (Mum's sister), Zoe and me — in a silver frame. It lives on the bookcase in Mum's study. The five of us grinning like cats, *but no Daze.*

I turn it over and look into the five faces, all matching, big fat smiles in black and white, eyes, smiles, hair. Except Zoe's hair is black like Dad's. Us four blondes all have our hair up. I have a big silk flower stuck in mine. Granny has the same picture, in the dining area at Chapel House. Just to myself, I call it *The Perfect Ones.*

It was taken at a wedding. Someone related to us. Distantly.

And today, drifting into Mum's study, I'm curious: I carefully remove the photo from its frame. Turn it over and read the writing on the back. A list of our names, in Granny's squiggly writing, and then, *Eleanor's wedding* and the date.

Eleanor – one of Mum's posh cousins — we never see her family, so why did they ask us all to the wedding? And why leave out Mum's stepsister, Daze?

Suddenly the landline rings on Mum's desk, giving me a jump, and immediately she answers in the kitchen, 'Mum!' in her happy-to-hear-you voice, and begins talking: 'Yes, still writing that funding application... yes, and the Florence Jenkins Fellowship of course...'

So, if Mum and Granny are going to yatter on about Mum's work, I have time to carefully replace the photo in its frame, and stand it back where it lives, then bunk off up the stairs to my room.

Later Mum comes looking for me. She knocks and enters, saying, all smiley, 'Sweetie, that was Granny on the phone. She mentioned your birthday.'

'Oh – in what way? It's not for months. And it's in the middle of exams!'

'I know but...'

'Like, for medics you didn't plan me that well, mid-June birthday, GCSEs?'

'I'm sorry. These things happen!' Mum says, laughing. I notice she's gone all pink, which is embarrassing, but also funny, so I grin back, and she says, 'anyway, Granny's

inviting the two of you to stay over for a birthday treat at her flat, to see a show in London.'

'When's she thinking of? Can't be in the middle of exams!'

'Of course not! Just after your exams end, so she thought, as a sixteenth birthday present, and as you said you didn't want a sweet sixteen party...'

'I didn't want a huge gross one, paid for by Grandpa Guthrie, like what they do in America – and Canada, I suppose...'

'Ally, can you maybe listen?'

'I am. Now. Me and Zoe, for my birthday?'

'Yes, I know, Granny said she wants to see both of you... she's booked *Mama Mia*, because she knew you wouldn't enjoy *Les Mis*, which is the other show she's keen to see. I said I thought *Mama Mia* would be fun – all those lovely songs and costumes!'

'Okay: so my birthday treat has my sister coming along as well, and it's with Granny Caro in London... What's *Les Mis*, the one we're not getting?'

'*Les Miserables*... From a classic French novel. It's a rather serious story, so anyway I told her not that one. Not for a birthday treat... And another thing you'd like, Alice, Granny's flat's all 1930s, quite interesting. You have been there, actually, though you were – maybe only nine or so?

'Mmm, that might be. I remember her funny furniture and some art stuff. Lamps and – a set of horrible kitchen chairs... How come we've never been there again?'

Mum shrugs. 'I suppose another visit just didn't happen. It belonged to Great-Grandma Ianthe. My grandmother, Granny's mum.'

'Oh, her. Famous scientist great-granny.'

'Yes, her. So, a fun weekend to look forward to?'

I do slowly-considering, head on one side, then the other. Then, I get up and give Mum a hug, 'Yes, yeah, *Mama Mia! Grazie mille, Mama!*'

Mum laughs, 'Good, maybe you'd like to call and thank Granny Caro? And how come all that Italian?'

'Someone I know in the school orchestra – their Mum's Italian...'

To stop Mum questioning me about Fabian, I quickly change the subject: I have a question on my mind. 'You know that photo – all the women in the family, you, Granny, Aunt Hattie, me and Zoe — I wondered why Daze isn't included?'

'The people whose wedding this was, well,' Mum murmurs, like she doesn't want to say, 'Daze wasn't related.'

'I know, Daze is adopted. But isn't that – you can't not include a person who's part of the family just because they're adopted.'

Mum looks cagey. 'The Lavenhams are rather different to us. They've got a big place in the country — you know, green wellie types.'

'So? Haven't they heard of people being adopted?'

'Ianthe's family never approved of her being a scientist, and they were even more shocked by her relationship with Derek Bradfield, especially when that produced Granny.'

'But that was years ago!'

'Yes, well, I guess the wedding invite was the relatives of my generation trying to break the ice a bit. Granny was perfectly respectable after all, a country doctor, and so were we...'

'But Daze wasn't? And Des wasn't there either was he?'

Mum looks shifty. 'Um, no, I think he was on one of his art weekends...'

'And Daze wasn't up to their standards? God, Mum, what snobs! I wish I wasn't related to them!'

'You know, Alice, it was just after she'd had Rothko, so she'd probably not...'

'That's what it was then. Another single mum, very unsuitable at a posh wedding, and no idea where the baby came from!'

'Ally, we don't know that...'

'No, but I know the type. There're some like them at school, they only want to know you if you're their snooty sort. So Daze is a quite well-known weird artist, adopted, single mum, mysterious baby — she would definitely mess up one's fancy wedding.' I feel really angry on behalf of Daze. I'd like to get her views on it. And come to think of it, I've never really been told about where Rothko came from.

'So what about Rothko, anyway? Do you know about the father?'

'Ally, we've got a long way from Granny's invite. No, I don't know anything definite. Not our business. You know Daisy, she keeps stuff to herself. And now I come to think of it, it wasn't long after Ianthe died, and there was a long period of uncertainty about the London flat — some legal problem — I think the Lavenhams were quite interested in it, and maybe hoped that Granny Caro would be open to a deal...'

'They sound really sh—, sorry Mum, but they sound awful. Like they only wanted to be friendly to Granny and us to get what they were after...'

'Yes, well, people are strange sometimes...'

She looks at her watch, 'Forgot the dinner! Made a pizza, it'll be burnt!' And as she hurries downstairs she yells back to me, 'And you need to phone Granny and thank her, can you remember to do that?'

Actually, the subject of Daze, our aunt Daze who, when we were about seven and five, made sure Zoe and I never called her 'aunt' any more, feels more important than whether I call Granny Caro about the trip. I want to see Daze, I've got some questions to ask her, I remember what a fun person she is to be with, and now, I'd like to know more about when she was growing up at Chapel House, the family house in Cornwall, along with Mum and her sister. And — if I can — find out about Rothko.

It's spring term, 2007. GCSEs are like dominating my mind, but my sister has got the most annoying friend — her newest discovery. Zoe has a talent for discovering anyone new to the area or her class at school, to make sure that the person doesn't feel left out and lonely. Every day, well maybe not every, but it feels like most days, she brings Annalise home after school and they take over the house. 'We're cooperating on our homework,' she says. Or 'I'm showing Annalise how we set out our English essays, or our French translations, or our maths homework.'

Annalise, as far as I know, arrived with the label 'a gifted student', and I'm sure she could have worked it all out for herself left alone. They work it out tuned into the radio, and over making jam sandwiches and hot chocolate in the kitchen, then stomping upstairs to Zoe's room, next to mine, to work. Sometimes they include flute practice: both of them are at about grade 2.

Come the Easter holidays, Annalise still turns up almost daily, and I have massive revision. It gets to the day when I stick my head out of my bedroom and yell at them. Embarrassingly, Mum's key is already in the lock, so when she opens the front door she hears it all. Me shouting a second time, from the top of the stairs. Zoe and Annalise, making pancakes in the kitchen, have spilt flour on the floor, and on each other, and they have the frying pan out with hot oil in it, and Zoe is laying into Annalise for heating it before the mixture's ready to add. Annalise is giggling, probably embarrassed — her hand's over her mouth as she sees Mum in the doorway.

Mum is very much not impressed.

Once the mess is cleared, and Annalise sent off home, I say, 'I'll have to go and stay somewhere for the holidays if nobody believes that I can't concentrate without some silence.'

'Well I can't think where,' Mum says, 'Though of course there is the library.'

I picture the library, where I've seen old men, who look like they have nowhere else to be, reading the newspapers at the desk provided for people hunting things up in reference books. It seems to me a desolate place to revise, with not even a coffee machine or a loo. 'Not Mariam's,' I say, mentioning my best friend, 'she's away somewhere – and Nina's away, and – look, maybe Granny Caro'd have me, in Cornwall? She'd support that, here to do revising! It'd be nice and far away from the adolescents.'

And 'Anyone other than Zoe would know that I am under pressure!' I scream at my sister, who's casually hunting in the fridge near where Mum and I are talking, to make the point.

And then next day, Friday, a magical thing happens. The house phone goes and when I answer, a gruff Essex-estuary male voice says, 'Oh, that's Alice isn't it – how're you love? Is your Mum there?' without waiting to hear how I am. It's Des, my step-grandad, Granny Caro's partner and Daze's dad. Here's my opportunity. I ask, casually, 'You and Granny, are you around at Easter?'

'We'll be in Italy, love. I'd say come down and use the house, but we've got the decorators in while we're away. Yeah, getting a bit long in the tooth to do it myself so... your aunt Daze's down here though, house sitting for a friend, in St Just, if you girls want to see if you can stay with her. If your Mum's okay with that?'

'Daze?'

'You'll need to ask her. She's got Rothko with her of course. But that means it'll not be a retreat she's doing!'

'Hey, Des, thank you! I mean, I'll ask. Just for me. To get some school stuff done for my exams. I'll get Mum for you, OK?'

'All work and no play,' Des says, laughing.

Later, I put my plan to Mum. She makes her screwed-up, considering, face, 'Daze? Do you think that would be a better place to do revision than at home here — even though Zoe and Annalise...?'

'Yep. She's house sitting in St Just. Des told me. Des *suggested it*. Gosh, I'm fifteen, Mum. And I do know what I'm going there for. I do want to get good grades in my exams. And I haven't seen Daze – she hasn't been around – since whenever! Whatever have we been doing to not see Daze? A lost aunt – I like it – gonna stay with my long-lost aunt.'

Dad's voice comes down the hallway, he's been listening in, 'And Daisy can't lose a fifteen-year-old like she lost you in the Lafrowda crowd ten years ago.'

'Dad, the voice of reason,' I say, 'Listen to him, mother.'

Chapter 2

So, what do artists do all day? I watch the countryside rushing by, and try to remember as much as I can about things we did with Daisy. The train slows and trundles a bit once we're really near, and we glide along the coast. Grey sky, and the sea! As we draw into the station, I've already grabbed my stuff, I'm squeezing down the carriage, heavy backpack digging into my back (all those revision notes!) and suitcase weighing down my arm. Ticket in the other hand.

So, where's Daze? Across by the exit, a petite woman in black jeans and maroon baggy jumper, crazy hair tied back with a purple scarf, waves, and even jumps up and down: my arty aunt! I drop my suitcase a moment to wave back. When I reach her she looks over my luggage and asks, 'That all you've brought?' and takes the case off me. 'Can I say it? How you've grown – up... hell, how long's it been?'

'Four years maybe? No, five. Where've you been?'

'Good question. I turn around and my little nieces have turned into women, boobs and all... sorry, just adjusting to you not being the little five-year-old I took to Lafrowda!'

'Where you lost me!'

'Where I turned around and you'd disappeared! Vehicle's this way – across the car park... Listen, I've got the keys to Chapel House, and we'll be working there during the day. In the studio. The decorators have done the living area, they're only upstairs now. Family firm, the two guys that run it, they're twins, I knew 'em at school,' she adds. 'Little tykes!'

'Tykes?'

'Kids that mucked about. Nicked all my pencils one day, I found them behind the Wendy house in a flower pot. The pencils. Here we are...'

Daze's vehicle is a van, and once we're inside she explains how she shares Des's studio space whenever she's down here. Which seems to be often, but never when we're staying. Why not? Anyway, this is all so cool. We'll go there every day, and while Daze works I can revise either at the kitchen table or using a corner of the studio.

And now we're there! As Daze unlocks the front door, still Gothic-style like a chapel, but repainted a delicate green, not bright blue, I have a thought, 'They haven't changed things, have they? You said the living area – it's not all different, is it?'

'Not wallpaper or patterned carpets, you mean? Nope. They've bought a few antique pieces, a nice roll-top desk, an old wooden armchair, terribly un-comfy, an Oriental rug. Caro gets bored being retired now, so she goes off to sales and buys stuff.'

In the porch, there's a battered-looking surfboard that's been here forever — Daze's, I've always assumed. But there's also a long yellow one I've never seen before. Hmm. It looks kind of male. I wonder? And there's a blue body board, a bucket and spade bristling with sand, and shells and pebbles lined up on the window sill. My whole body responds, like a wave breaks over me, heart stops a moment. How much this house means.

Then Daze opens the inner door, and I smell paint and over that the homey scent of hot bread. Not that Mum has time to bake bread. Things are pretty much the same, though I can see Granny's new antique furniture dotted around. The oriental rug is being used for a railway, with a layout of wooden track and trains. On the coffee table there's a pile of books; the top one is *The Hobbit*. I love it all.

'Other people's stuff!' Daze says, picking up and folding a crocheted throw from a chair, 'and left-overs in the kitchen. Half-chewed pizza slices!' She turns and goes back to the kitchen, throwing conversation over her shoulder, 'Today you meet the domestic me. I had a friend of Rothko's here, he brought his Mum and little brother, so we've had the train out… the little one's left his blanky behind.' The bin clatters as she throws out the chewed pizza, then comes back to gather up kids' drawings from the table.

'It's nice, being here, though. I mean, the domestic bits. Maybe this house is a bit more you without Granny in it…'

'Just a bit!' Daze says. 'Though I am definitely not into chewed pizza crusts! We don't come here too much when the step-mum's here, frankly. When it's Wagner on the stereo and drinkies at wine o'clock it isn't, like, quite my style,' she says with a huge smile. 'Have one of these – cheese straws with a dash…,' she adds, doing a mock-high-heeled teetering walk across the room, imaginary wine glass in one hand and plate in the other, which sets us both off laughing.

'Great imitation of Granny! Though maybe a bit…'

'OTT? Actually, I mustn't. Houses have ears. Or eyes. Let's eat – I've put supper in the kitchen tonight – and then we'll get going to the cottage. Gotta pick up Rothko from the friend with the baby brother on the way. Better not forget the blanky…'

'I wondered where he was.' Actually, I'd been rather pleased not to encounter him right away.

'Holiday drama group,' says Daze, 'thank God for adults who can't get enough of children! He loves it. Most of the kids are at the local primary – where I first met your Mum – back then she was always called 'Four-eyes' — and they're totally cool that my annoying infant's a grandkid of Dr Caroline and let him join in.'

'Wow, Granny must be popular around here!'

'She is. Her being my step-mum opens doors for me, I have to admit. Either it's that or 'cos I was once a local.'

We eat vegan curry at the kitchen table, from where I can see my favourite view of the landscape. Daze wants to know everything about my life. When I tell her, she laughs and says that it's *typical private school teenage*. So I ask her about being at Cape Cornwall Comprehensive, where she knew those decorator twins, and from where (I've always believed) Mum got in to Cambridge. But she changes to asking whether Mum's still as bossy with me and Zoe as she was being a step-sister, back then when they were kids, and adds 'Your Mum did her A levels at private school – we didn't have a sixth form.'

'I didn't know that. Anyway, when did you last visit us? Did you and Mum have a tiff?'

'We go our separate ways, don't we? Scotland's a long way from Oxford. And Yorkshire. And here. I kind of move between those three, now. I'm in Yorkshire, mostly.'

'Well yes, but... Oxford's not Australia! Mum's other sister comes over...'

'Maybe she does. I'm busy, and as you see, I like keeping out of your Granny's way.'

'Gosh, you're saying mothers are that controlling even when you're – whatever age you and Mum are, with the kids and career?'

Daze grins, a big conspiratorial grin, followed by a laugh. She has a wide mouth, and a great laugh, and I join in. 'Comes with the territory. Don't expect to escape.'

'I'll have to pick some research that's really different from what Mum does, then! Assuming I get these exams,' I wave at my pile of revision, 'and get into Cambridge, of course.'

'Is that what you want to do, science research?' Daze asks. 'Or what your parents think you should do?'

'Well, I love what Mum and Dad do, I've always enjoyed hearing about it, visiting Mum's lab and stuff. And I guess there's a lot of good careers if you've got a science degree.'

'You ever had any alternative ideas?' Daze asks.

That kind of takes me by surprise. Because I also love arty things — slightly silly things — like the atmosphere of the Art Room, and the Lowry reproductions in the school corridors, and what you can see on the screen of your camera. But no one in the family has had a career in the arts — except Daze, and she's regarded as an off-beat exception.

'I guess so. I mean, don't we all have wild ideas about how we'd like to spend our life? But science subjects are my good ones...'

'You always been keen on science, then?'

'It was more animals when I was a little kid. Dad likes to tell this story, how when I was maybe four, we were on the canal path, and I watched a little mouse rootling about for food, and then I managed to pick it up!'

'I remember that,' says Daze, 'You were coming to see me!'

Here I am at last, I think, talking with someone in the family who's fun and yet serious. A person who'll talk to me about my plans for my life without assuming things. Am I doing what I'm doing mostly because it's what Mum and Dad assume I'd do? Here I can explore being me, and not being Mum and Dad's daughter.

Later, I lie in bed in the little stone-built terraced cottage in St Just Daze is here to look after, with one of the cats she's caring for sitting on my chest, and I'm picturing a career like Daze's. A bit like Daze's. Maybe in photography. What could I do in photography?

I want to know a bit more about Daze's life. Like how she gets commissions.

And who is Rothko's Dad? I mean, he has to have one — doesn't he. So, mystery man, who are you? Do you live here – or maybe he's part of her art community in Yorkshire? Or did Daze simply go to a sperm bank?

Whatever, Daze is mysterious. Does she have a boyfriend? A girl-friend? Anyone special? Whose is the big surfboard?

Next day, my mind is full of questions, but Daze is super-focused on her work. Whatever Mum said about being at Daze's wouldn't help my revision, she should see us now! Daze is finishing off an order (shoulder bags, made from some sort of felt fabric), sitting down the end of the scrubbed-deal table by the big floor to ceiling window in the studio. On the table is her sewing machine, but today she's using needle and thread to embroider what looks like a dragon on a piece of green fabric. I'm at the other end, browsing on some chemistry notes. There's silence, until Daze asks me, 'Pop or classical then?'

And I look up and say, 'Either,' and she puts on Radio Three, so we get Schumann. A piano quintet. Coffee time is everyone's break, and Daze includes us with the painters. We all sit outside, Daze discusses local stuff with the guys. She must come here more often than we know. Back to work, and she's obviously completed the dragon, as she's laying out more fabric and a template. My break extends a bit, as I watch how neatly and carefully Daze cuts out the pieces to make another bag. Her long fingers are so skilful as she fits them together, and I notice her forearms, slender but muscular over what must be quite small bones.

So now, on to History for me! Re-reading my notes underlines my determination that whatever A-levels I do, it won't be something that requires long essays. Did Chemistry interest me more? My mind wanders off to the question: do something different to the family, don't be caught in a dynasty? What should I choose to do forever? I think I'd like it to be practical, to have a practical side.

Chapter 3

LIFE AT DAZE'S: CO-OP AND CLIFF PATH

Rothko's now on a week's drama course, the performance's on Easter Saturday. The rest of the time, he either has friends round, or occupies himself, drawing, or kicking a ball about outside. Let's hope that continues! Daze promised me we could talk more when she's got her work done, 'I have to deliver this stuff to the shop ready for the influx of tourists over Easter. So, after that? I mean, you invited yourself, really, so – like I'm not saying I don't want you here, but I have to make my living...' Gosh, she can be sharp! 'So – no look, I don't mean badly, just that I have to. Money's quite tight.'

'Okay...' I wonder if I should ask about her career or not, later?

'One day it'll be a bit easier. Hopefully. If the Universe smiles that is!'

Today, my first Saturday here, we're off to St Just to deliver members' work to the artists' co-op shop. Making us a packed lunch for the trip, Daze says, 'I'd advise, bring a book with you, I've got business to discuss while we're there...' In the van, we pick up craft items from cottages scattered across several of the peninsular villages, me and Rothko squeezed together in front, alongside Daze, and everywhere we go, we all pile out to help each box, bag, or individually wrapped item to be safely stowed in the back, while I wonder what's in them.

Daze has put on a tape of old songs from when she and Mum were teenagers: on and off, she and Rothko sing along. Otherwise, Rothko keeps quiet. I'd thought he was being dropped off at one of the terraced cottages where we also collect some goods for the Coop shop, but no, he's coming all the way round on our circular route, and then to St Just. I'm watching how Daze handles the van on the blind bends and winding lanes, the driver's seat adjusted to her small frame. Her driving's same as her crafting: quick brained and skilful. Her slim muscular arms work in tune with the van, the steering wheel co-operates, the gears respond to her touch. Backing up for a big four by four beside a muddy farm entrance, she isn't flustered and swearing like Mum would be, she's confident and in control. 'Silly bugger,' she says, 'if he can't squeeze that into a passing place, he's probably the kind of tourist who normally enjoys driving his Chelsea Tractor around Islington – look at that surfboard on the roof, waggling away – that's not properly secured!'

I don't realise, as we drive off again, that I'm gaping at her, until — 'What're you staring for?' she says abruptly as we get going again.

'Nothing.'

'I've driven bigger'n this. Years ago,' She pauses: 'Hey, did your Mum ever tell you about my traveller days? She didn't, did she?'

It always goes something like that, our conversation. I love the way Daze talks, except of course when she's sharp, like when she told me I'd invited myself. Now, it's as if I'm getting to know her properly, not like when we were kids. Mum has always emphasised how different Daze was and that they have very few interests in common.

Actually, they do share one passion: photography. Des taught them both old-fashioned photography, using film and developer, there's still a dark room off the studio at Granny's. I'll ask Daze to show me how the old developing was done! Must've been exciting, the image creeping into view across the paper, in the bath of chemicals. A face, the branch of a tree, a boat on the lake... She might have an old camera somewhere – Des might – and even film? That'd be cool.

Next, I begin to remember how, back when I was really young, there was other stuff we did together. Me, or Zoe and me, with Daze. We were quite small kids. Helping with craft. Her making us magical things. Not just a costume for a school play. Halloween costumes. Animal masks. And visiting her narrowboat.

Those animal masks – or was their creator someone else? *Etta.* Etta is *Daze's birth mother.* Where is she now?

But for now, I want to know other things. 'So, were you a New Age Traveller? Was that before or after the narrowboat? Was it your boat, the one you lived on?'

Daze turns and throws me a quick grin. 'Chocolate in the glove whatsit,' she says, eyes back on the road. 'Break us off a couple of pieces each, can you? Yeah – lots to talk about later. When we've dropped this stuff off. You two are here to help when we do that!'

Rothko makes a groaning noise and complains, 'Do I have to?'

'Yes, then after that you get to stay with the shop guys and paint, while Alice and I do some boring stuff.'

'Yay!' Rothko punches the air, while I wonder, 'What boring stuff is that?'

We sweep round a bend, passing some cottages and a large bulky building, and St Just comes into view, familiar from so many holidays, a town that looks drear and grey in cloudy weather, but lights up in the sunshine. Like today: gorgeous spring, bright flowers, daffs, tulips, wallflowers, everywhere, like a carnival.

Parking the van outside the shop, Daze opens up the back and begins to hand us out suitably sized boxes and bags to carry inside. The shop's awesome. Brightly coloured clothing – jackets, trousers, dresses, and skirts hanging on rails, bags (like the ones Daze has been sewing) and hats hanging on pegs and stands. Knitted jumpers, crocheted shawls, beanies, scarves. Baby and toddler clothes, dungarees with appliqued dinosaurs, lorries, or flowers. Pottery – mugs, plates, jugs, teapots – arranged on tables and shelves. Paintings and collages and small boxes, little tables painted with flower patterns. A cradle. Mobiles hang from the ceiling, slowly turning in the breeze from the open door. Wow. And more of these kinds of things are in the bags and boxes we take through and stack in the stock room at the back.

A guy who'd I'd noticed as we unpacked a box of carefully wrapped and packed pottery invites Rothko to a game of snap: they go in the store room and play, sitting on wooden packing cases. This guy is wearing pale blue nail varnish, which flashes as he deftly shuffles the cards. Meanwhile, a red-haired woman in dungarees quietly supplies Rothko with a mug of hot chocolate, and some ginger biscuits placed on another crate like a table. A couple of the women open up the shop while we and three other coop artists retreat into the stock room. Coffees are handed out. The ginger biscuits disappear rapidly. While the whole sales group are there, Daze talks about taking some of the work for sale at a festival in Yorkshire. As I quietly put brightly coloured toddler sized dungarees onto diminutive plastic coat-hangers, I hear she may, some time, actually move back to Cornwall. It sounds as if someone else is involved. A partner?

No more on that topic, though: soon she changes the subject, and introduces me, as her step-sister's daughter, 'one of Dr Caroline's grandkids!'

And then, Daze fishes about in her bag, pulls out her keyring, and rattles it in front of my eyes, 'Hey, chance to bunk off to the van and get your revision out, then I can let your Ma know I'm keeping an eye on it. Okay?'

'Okay.' I'd rather stay and hear more, but obviously there's no option.

When Daze and Rothko reappear at the van half an hour later, Daze rummages around and produces a packet of sandwiches and a boxed drink and hands them to Rothko. Then she says, 'Right: Rothko's fine with Steve and the others, so we'll have bit of a free afternoon. Not here – down at the Lizard. There's an inn, we'll slake our thirst there, but the eating's expensive, hence the sandwiches. Picnic up above the inn, and look at the sea.' She turns to Rothko, 'Mouse,' she says to him, 'we'll be back around 5.00, okay? Look at your watch – five?'

'Yeah – I *know*, Mum, don't fuss...'

'I'll pick you up from here. Right here, outside the shop.'

And they hug. I wonder again if his dad might be one of that group. Even Steve of the blue nail varnish? Daze and Steve?

'We might talk about my bus now, a bit more,' she says, as we're speeding down a straight road towards Cadgwith. 'It was an old coach, the sort of vehicle they called a charabanc back in the day, to sound more romantic... that is, the day when a trip to the seaside was an Event. Not of course my day, just me calling it that for effect, probably it was a single decker bus or maybe a long-distance coach. But, you get the idea. And, yes, it was heavy, and it had, like, a steering wheel and a gearbox like a bus. And yes, I used to live in it, and I used to drive it around.'

Cripes, I think, trying to picture Daze driving a new age travellers' bus. Not beyond imagination, now.

I've never been to the Cadgwith Cove Inn before. It's cute, and it's really old. 'Are you a ginger beer woman?' Daze asks me, at the bar, ''Cos I don't buy alcohol for under agers.'

'I'm a ginger beer woman today!' I say. Daze chooses cider. We share cashew nuts. My stomach is beginning to crave a proper meal, or at least an added packet of crisps.

'So, my travelling days, yeah. After college – which was a blast after growing up at the end of the world down here – I went a bit uber wild. I got the bus off a guy I was with for a time, and I kitted it out – actually we kitted it out – but he – you don't need to know that bit... 'cept later I made some good women friends and we had a site outside Cambridge for a while...'

It's a nice story, but the extra memory-stuff frustrates me, as Daze includes a long description of her friends, their kids, and lots of detail which isn't about her life with that guy, who as he left her, and the bus, isn't relevant any more. He can't be Rothko's Dad, it's far too long ago.

At last leaving Cadgwith (I'm starving), we start off on foot up the cliff path. The gorgeous Cornish wild flowers dot the landscape: pink, blue and yellow, scabious and campion, trefoil, white and pink stone-crop. We find a sheltered place out of the stiff breeze, and sit on our folded hoodies. We unpack our rather untidy lunch: Daze-made sandwiches are large and overstuffed, and require you to eat holding on with both hands. The sea, turquoise where it's shallow, navy where it's deep, shimmers and dazzles. There are fishing boats looking more like toys than their real tough selves, and small white wavelets lap the harbour. End of the world? I'd just adore to grow up here!

'It's amazing,' I say, waving my half-eaten sandwich at the scenery. 'I mean, it's like eternity – or something.'

'Watch that slice of tomato doesn't fall out!' says Daze.

'Hey — remember that labyrinth? You drew one in the sand. Ages ago, when we were all at Chapel House on holiday. Not Granny Caro or Des. But Uncle David, Dad's cousin, was there.'

'Mm?'

'At Chapel House. For a holiday. You helped me and Zoe play ballet classes!'

'Did I? Yeah, maybe I do remember something.'

She doesn't say more. Over to our left, the sun shines on the sea, turquoise, dark navy. shimmering, dazzling. 'It's just so amazing. I'd rather be here than Oxford. For my forever home, I mean.'

'Mm?' Daze says.

'Don't you think it's amazing?'

'It's amazing till the wind changes,' Daze says.

'What?' My mind's on that labyrinth. 'It was before we went to South Africa, and we were there maybe two years? And then… then school got serious and I went to Headleigh Park.'

'Until the wind changes,' Daze repeats.

'How? What?'

'Life. Amazing till the wind changes.'

'I'd rather live here than anywhere,' I say.

She takes a breath. 'Yeah. You can see why it's so dangerous with all these rocks,' she waves a hand towards the cove. 'Anyhow, the labyrinth. Do you also remember when I was doing the labyrinth at St Hildegard's, and you helped me?'

'The St Hildie's labyrinth – yes. They've covered it up with a carpet now – my sister's friend told me, her mum works there. Did you know about the carpet?'

'No! They shouldn't have done that. Someone weird must be in charge, someone who has no perception. You had a piece of the action putting in some of the mosaics for me?'

'Tesserae. Gosh, I felt so important using real tiles, at school we just messed about with coloured paper. And, remember my Angel Gabriel wings, that I could move? You made those – there was a lot you did. Pretty cool to do all those, like, craft things. For us.'

'Never knock craft.'

'I'm not. I don't mean — you know I don't mean – whatever, I don't. Though I wondered why you stopped...' Daze cuts off my sentence.

'Painting? Doing serious art? If I thought that, I'd not let you stay with us, would I? I still paint. My craft might be a sideline, but I have to make a living!' She reaches into her backpack, 'Let's look at the map. It's not straightforward here. I want to take you to the Lizard. There's supposed to be a path, they advertised it as a walk, about two hours. Let's have another shufti at the map.'

Chapter 4

I LEARN ABOUT MY FAMILY

After that 'shufti', we go back to the coast path, and cross fields, from where we can see the sea. We pass the Lizard lifeboat station. The walk ends at the Lizard Lighthouse, where we lie on the grass, drink from our water bottles, and comment on how far six miles feels! I still think I could live here forever like this, with the sun and the sea and the breeze.

On our way back, through some rather boring fields, Daze begins to chat. 'So when d'you return to the slave-house?'

'Slave-house? You mean school?'

'Yeah, that. I mean, you can stay till my friends want their house back. And their cats. I wouldn't mind keeping both, of course.'

'When d'you move out?'

'We're off back to Yorkshire on the Tuesday after Easter, I could drop you off on the way?'

'Yeah, thanks, that'd be cool. I'd not need to catch the train and lump my luggage along.'

'Great. And maybe your folks would provide a bite to eat, though I suppose they'll be working.'

'I can give you something or we could go out somewhere?'

'Whatever, loo break's the main thing, meal's optional! OK now listen, where were we? I'd been living in Colombia a while, after college, where,' she pauses, giving me a look, and dropping her voice like a secret's about to be shared, 'do you know this bit? Your Grandad Guthrie had a clinic, where...' she gives me another look, 'Where – don't tell your friends, will you? — he worked on some very edgy stuff. Edgy *back then*; pretty normal now.'

'Wasn't he working with a group developing what were they called? Fertility solutions. I know a bit about it.'

'You won't know this part. Did your Mum and Dad tell you girls about how I brought them together after they'd split up?'

I shake my head. 'I didn't know they split up! When was that?'

'They got together when she arrived for her Cambridge interview, and then they broke up, after he wrote and told her he wouldn't be in Cambridge when she got there to study.'

'That was so mean! But didn't they study together, at the same time?'

'You telling the story or me? So, you need to know how I brought your Mum and Dad together. Listen. So, after your Mum had done finals, I was also in Cambridge, maybe looking to contact my step-sis. We bumped into each other at the market, and her eyes popped out on stalks, 'cos I had a bump – ha ha, I know — and wasn't planning to tell the family yet.'

'You were pregnant?'

'You could put it that way. Anyhow, what your Mum didn't know, that I didn't know either, was this: your Dad, Max, was back in Cambridge again, doing what's called paediatric rotation. A spell of working on kids, up at Addenbrookes. Look, this walk's quite long – you hungry? Have a fruit?'

We stop, Daze pulls a couple of apples out of the pocket of her hoodie. She polishes them and hands one to me. Casual, as if she hasn't just told me something really important. She'd definitely had a baby, way before Rothko. And something must've gone wrong, because there is no older child, none we've seen or heard of. Nobody till she turned up with Rothko in tow, when he was — maybe three? And I was ten? On a quick visit to ours. I'd not seen Daze for maybe five years. And after that, well, Daze hasn't visited us in Oxford, and she's never been in Cornwall along with us.

'You listening?'

'Yep – about Dad doing paediatric rotation – how did you bring them together?'

'Right, back to him and your Mum, want to know the details?'

The details are awful. That baby had so much wrong with it, she couldn't have lived more than a few minutes. What'm I supposed to say? I can only mumble that I'm sorry that this happened, but Daze kind of waves that away. 'The point is, really two things. First, your Mum and Dad met each other again, and they must've sorted something out, because – after your dad acted like really a decent person to me and sorted a lot of stuff so I could like say goodbye to the kid properly – after that...' The story is really weird. She says Mum and Dad moved in on that poor baby and tried to trace why its DNA was what she described as screwed. 'So, think about it, those two fell back in love over my deceased kid – not *any old* piece of research — in the pathology lab.'

I try imagining. This is my parents, Mum and Dad, aged about twenty-one. Dad a bit more. They have samples in a dish. A body. It's all very disturbing. Like a murder mystery movie, but it's not a movie, or a book. It's oddly spine-tingling. 'Gosh. Weird.'

'Don't forget your apple! Wasps will come.'

'I won't! And they won't, too early in the year. Anyhow, what happened next? I mean...' I lean towards her gesturing with the apple, now more like a core, 'and you better not be dissing me here.'

'Why would I?'

'I don't think you would. But hard to imagine it all happening – like that.'

'Nope, all true. At Cambridge they were that weird. Researchers are. Academic minds, different to you and me.' Maybe to her — but what about me? Certainly, my sister Zoe would be that weird, given a chance.

'Of course, there was a lot more than kissing over the slab or whatever they did. Your Dad had managed to get my baby – I called her Persephone, named after a girl in Greek mythology who was forced to marry the king of the underworld — back from the morgue. Really silly myth of course. Anyway, he got her all dressed up by someone and tucked up in a Moses basket with flowers.'

'That sounds like Dad.' It would be Dad, with his religious background. 'He has a lot of what they call empathy, which is better than sympathy because it means that you understand people from the inside, you don't judge them or look down at their feelings from the outside.'

'Yeah, that. And I kind of baptised her. In the name of the Universe. I don't think he'd have approved, or any of them would – but that made her like human, didn't it. I was probably a bit mad at the time. Anyhow, "He's a keeper," I thought then. About Max. I told Jen, your Mum, that guy's a keeper, treat him properly.'

This is like she's brought everything back to something ordinary, and expects me to. Which is difficult.

We walk on a bit. I don't know what to say, I don't want to cry, this couple are my parents, for God's sake, not people in a book or film. 'Thanks for telling me all that. I'm sorry – about your baby.'

'We had a proper funeral, they all came.'

'Who?'

'You know, the family. An' my traveller friends from the women's camp.'

'Oh. Okay.'

'And then, I made my experiences into art. It's what we humans do, or what we're meant to. Poems, novels, songs – mine was an installation. Have you heard of Judy Chicago and the other feminist artists in the nineteen-fifties? They did a lot of stuff showing what women's real lives are like. Art history's full of idealised women, women who don't have dead babies, or miscarriages, who don't bleed on a monthly basis. I was doing that kind of work anyway, so it wasn't odd. Chicago and the others forced people to look at the reality of being female. I carried on in their tradition. I'll lend you the book if you like.'

'Right. Thank you. But you aren't that now.'

'My paintings wouldn't be the kind that sell, not to people who want something nice and calm, to remember their holiday. Craft — and the co-op — came later, after your Aunt Val suggested I went to live at hers a while, in Edinburgh — you know she's a weaver and knitter? I got into craft, and then joined the Yorkshire co-op. And, of course, the one down here. And in between Persephone and going to Aunt Val's, I managed to work at a studio in London for a year, then bought that narrowboat and lived on the canal a bit, near your parents. But Aunt Val's was what got me off conceptual art and into craft – though I'll probably go back to proper art, as you might call it, some time. And that's it – life of Daisy Potter, in a nutshell! You know it all!'

Do I? I now know she's had a baby who was born peculiarly formed, and I'm kind of stunned. We walk on a bit in silence. I know enough about chromosomal abnormalities, from Mum's work, to imagine how that would have made her feel, so I can't say anything useful. And I know Rothko was born at Aunt Val's, and there's nothing weird about him.

I think somehow instinct is telling me to respect her privacy. Walking carefully through a field of maize, then around one of cabbages, I study the green-stalked veg and think.

Can I imagine Mum and Dad falling in love over a deformed human baby in a pathology lab? Thought of them *falling in love* is weird enough. The breeze has turned stronger, and a bit chilly. We pass an isolated church: St Grada's. It looks immensely old, and lonely, no cottages nearby. Daze doesn't stop walking, I have to run to catch up.

'Sorry,' she says, 'maybe I shouldn't have told you. My big mouth, gabbing, wasn't it?'

'No. No, I asked. Just a bit – you know – lots to think about?'

'After all that happened, it was like life was different.'

'Yeah. It would be.' We move on, and now I'm wondering what Granny Caro thought about it. I hope she was a bit empathetic. And I decide there's another question here: 'You know the photo Granny has in the living room, at Chapel House? All of us – I mean Mum, and Aunt Harriet, and me and Zoe, and Granny Caro, together in the photo?'

'What about it?'

'I wondered, why you weren't there? At the wedding?'

'Oh, why I'm not in the photo? I can tell you: I wasn't invited. I hadn't long had Rothko, and I reckon they didn't want some scruffy artist who was adopted and her little bastard crashing their super-posh county wedding party.'

'Des wasn't there either, was he?'

'Nah.'

'Why not?'

'Dad's not the type for high society, networking and stuff. Look, Dad and Caro are kind of – they're partners, and it works — that's the arrangement they have. Because he had the house, she could look after his daughter – i.e. me – better than he could alone. But he's got no interest in the rest of the snooty family and stuff!'

'But it is a marriage. I mean, that's obvious, isn't it?'

'Well, I'm officially adopted!'

Chapter 5

EASTER, ROTHKO'S PLAY AND SPILT MILK

Was I right to come here? I've learned more than I really wanted about Daze's life... things that Mum's not told me. How did Daze feel about that baby? She tells it like it wasn't a trauma, but it must have been! I've seen Mum's birth family through her eyes. I've learned some amusing but weird stuff about Mum and Dad's romance.

'By the way,' Daze says, 'not a lot of time to talk more about the family, and the other thing, we'll both keep schtum for now. Rothko knows nothing about it, so, everything kid-friendly, okay? I've got stuff you and he can both help me with.'

So, that's me told: and left frustrated and curious and wishing I didn't know all this. But, did Daze's baby, Persephone, arouse Mum's interest in working on genes which go wrong, and kick off her career? Don't people who have problem babies have to be really careful having another? Whatever, Rothko must have a different father, so, different DNA. But who is he?

But I let it go, for now. Each day's drier and warmer. I get on with revision, Daze gets on with her craft work, and Rothko's busy with his friends.

One afternoon we all go to the Chapel House studio, where Daze sets up her sewing machine, and unpacks felt in several colours, a couple of metres of brown velvety fabric, and masses of stuffing. 'Okay, you two are Santa's Easter elves – and you have to use these stencils' (she hands them out) 'to draw and cut out the shapes for applique. You know what that is?'

Well I do, from sewing at junior school, and I begin to see that this is Rothko's costume for the play we're making, in Easter colours — the applique might be daffodils, though the brown velvety fabric could suggest he's playing an animal? The Easter Rabbit? That'd be so un-cool for a boy his age!

Daze finishes at the sewing machine. She's made what looks like a sack. 'You need to try the whole outfit on, now, see if it's right.'

Rothko slowly pulls off his socks and jeans, and reaches down into one of the bags, 'First I have to wear these *tights!*' he says, holding up a pair of deep brown kids' tights for me to see. 'And guess what I put on next?'

I say, 'I don't know – what do you put on?'

'My egg-suit!'

'Hey, in the play, you're an *egg*!'

'Yeah, a boring old egg. We're in an egg-box – that was more fun to make. We could work on that, like carpenters, with Mr Mills, who's a woodwork teacher. An' in the play, us eggs all crowd into the box, and pull down the lid!'

When Rothko's in the egg suit, Daze adjusts the stuffing until the bag looks oval (the nearest it can), and pulls up the hood to cover his straight, blond hair. He's a chocolate Easter Egg. Yeah, it's pitched too young to appeal to Rothko's age group, and definitely not religious.

'See, it's the *most un-cool* play! Only I have a song, which is a solo, and someone may come from – what's it called, Mum?'

'Something like Young Singer of the Year?'

'Cornwall Young Singer of the Year?' I suggest.

'Yeah, that.'

I grab my phone for a quick photo. 'Wait!' Daze says, 'We've got to add the decoration!'

There's an argument about where's best for the daffodils, and when that's settled, she pins them in place to sew later. The last touch, the name 'Rothko', cleverly made in white fabric and looking like real icing sugar piped on, is added and pinned.

Rothko makes a face, 'Can I get out of this now?' and Daze nods. 'God, it's a stupid play – the drama group lady wrote it.' (Daze shakes her head, 'don't say that, not polite.')

'But my song is the best part, isn't it? Like I'm the chief egg or something.'

'Oh wow, your Mum is great at costumes!' I say, thinking of the ones she made for me. 'You remember, don't you, my angel dress with the wings that moved? At my school Christmas play, when I was five?'

'You were Gabriel, the messenger.'

'And Brianna, who was Mary, stuck her tongue out at me? And I stuck out mine back, so all the parents laughed... which was okay until it was kinda spoilt, because you spotted Dad's cousin David at the back, and you were having a fight with him about something so...'

'Over a building we both wanted to buy... don't remind me!' Daze says, and goes pink like this embarrasses her.

'David was a school governor...'

'Okay, all a long time ago, let's take that off now, Mouse,' she says, turning to Rothko, 'and we'd better hurry, you're supposed to be at your friend's house in ten minutes.'

We go to watch the play in the school hall on the Saturday of Easter weekend. It's really quite funny, a musical romp of kids dressed as Easter bunnies, Spring flowers, and chocolate eggs. There's a sort of country dance, making arches and all dancing along underneath in a line. And Rothko's song, and a flowers song (all girls!). But I can see why he hates being the chief egg. And the other kids must resent a visitor being handed the part.

Of course, Granny Fee would say 'Not much to do with the true message of Easter.' But it was, it was joyful, and colourful, and happy.

'So, celebration over, and Easter weekend'll be for the tourists,' says Daze, as we climb into the van and drive back to the cottage. 'Your Gran's quite house-proud and I like having the place to stay so we'll make it as if we were never here. A garden tidy-up to greet the returning travellers, and a good scrub of the kitchen, vacuum all round, and check the decorators have left everything that they moved back where it belongs. Sunday and Monday. Okay?'

'Aw — Mum,' Rothko complains.

'You've got Monday off!' says Daze. 'Sleepover Sunday night and Monday all day! At your best friend's!'

'I have to be organised,' she says, 'being a lone parent means I've got to think of everything, nobody else will cover my back if I forget and leave the cottage – or Chapel House – in a mess. Or don't make it back to Yorkshire until the early hours of Wednesday.'

Yes: that's kind of obvious, but I hadn't really seen Daze as that kind of person. But of course, I should've. All fits together, with the neat craft, the impressive driving.

I feel a bit homesick gardening, cleaning and tidying over Easter. I miss our tradition of going to the egg-hunt at St Hildie's, which I could've grown out of, but it's like, we've always done it, and we know the other people who do. It's a nice tradition. Not that I'm particularly religious. Not involved like Dad and Zoe. Undecided like Mum.

At teatime Rothko is collected by his friend's family (I'm impressed that they're having him to stay on a holiday weekend).

We eat a snack supper at Chapel House. Afterwards Daze takes out her craft stuff, felt bags with a dragon design already sketched on, and I get out my revision notes. Last proper evening here! There's a gorgeous sunset: stripes of cloud edged with gold stretch across the sky, reflecting on the sea like a golden path from the shore to the horizon.

Daze puts on some music, and we work silently, until Daze's phone rings, and it's Rothko, to say goodnight! I look up and notice that the sun's gone, and a thick sea mist's creeping up towards the house. For a moment, I imagine being marooned here by the mist. But then, I know

Daze is not going to let that happen: she'll happily take on the winding lanes in a mist.

'Jake's family — Rothko's known them forever,' says Daze. 'Since the first time I came down here with him? Jake's mum and dad were at school with me,' she says, 'we grew up together.'

'So you kept in touch like regularly, through college and beyond, and you've been down here lots, so Rothko really has kind of grown up with those kids?'

'Yeah, something like that.'

'That's rather sweet, old school mates.'

'They actually started the craft co-op. Yep. Entrepreneur types – who knew? Me, actually, since Geoff – Jake's dad – used to try selling stuff around our school when we were like nine or something. After A levels we all went off to art colleges — different ones — and then we met up here later.'

'So – I don't s'pose he was your boyfriend, was he, or Mum's?' I try to make it sound jokey, so she doesn't get why I want to know.

'Gosh, no!'

'Right.'

'You didn't think?'

'Nah! Not really! But, interesting, that you were all, like, allowed to go to art colleges. So were their parents artists?'

'Nope. Geoff's dad runs a fishing business, his mum works in the big hotel. Meg's dad is a Methodist minister. Down the coast.'

'Right. so, d'you think I shouldn't worry about whether the parents want me to be another scientist like themselves? That makes me feel I'm stuck in a sort of dynasty — four generations from my great-granny!'

'Maybe they just don't see beyond their obsessive medico-scientific interests! They love their subjects so much. If you believe in your own ideas, parents should take time and listen. What sort of thing would you do if you didn't do – that – the stuff you've been revising? And don't we need a bit of light? Can you actually see what you're reading?'

I get to my feet, which are now pretty near frozen, and flick all the light switches. 'Behold the dawn!' Daze says (irony or what?).

'The thing is, Dad dared to be different: he resisted Grandpa Alisdair's plan for him to be his successor as the minister at First Truly.'

'Look, I'm saying I can't make up your mind, or change what my sister and your Dad would like, and I shouldn't.'

'OK, I get it.'

A bit disappointing not to recruit Daze the rebel to help me negotiate with Mum and Dad.

'Anyhow, it was great hearing about some family background, and that you've always been, like, touching base back here with people. I'd love to hear more, some time when Rothko's not about, maybe.'

'Mmm... Meanwhile, these big glass windows don't exactly keep the cold of that sea mist out, do they?

The mist's almost crowding in the door. I sneeze, close my notes and watch Daze cutting the thread she's been sewing with, and packing up her work. I start clearing up my own things. I've opened up two stressful subjects, her family and her career. But we might be able to talk about the family, if she's a bit more relaxed?

Then I have a genius thought: I offer to make us both hot drinks. Partly so I can take what Daze would call a quiet shufti at the family photo albums. 'That'll finish up the milk from the fridge.'

'Go ahead, then!'

On my way, I creep into the living room: Granny Caroline's photo albums were always kept on the bookcase, and I know which shelf. They're still there. I carefully extract '1980s-1990s', slide it into my bag, and move into the kitchen, where I make enough noise finding mugs, and putting on a pan of milk, that Daze will be assured I'm doing what I said I would.

I put the cocoa into the mugs, then open the album carefully, while I wait for the milk to heat. I even turn it down low, to give myself more time.

Good: mid-1980s, here's a picture of Daze and a crowd of other women doing some kind of drama, tucked in loose among the pages. And here's Daze (stuck in nicely) celebrating Christmas in Edinburgh, with Grandpa's sister Val and Mum's cousins Harris and Lewis, who're named after Scottish islands.

But then, a loose photo falls out. I pick it up. Daze, Mum, Des and Granny Caro, even Mum's sister Harriet, are gathered in a churchyard. Around a little white basket covered with flowers: a coffin? Maybe this is the 'screwed' baby's funeral? There's a plump smartly dressed woman, maybe a minister? And some other women, in jeans or dungarees or long skirts (with toddlers clutching their Mums' legs) – they could be the traveller women who Daze said she shared a campsite with one time?

So, the baby had a proper family funeral? Is Dad there? No: where was he? The only man is Des. No sign of anyone who could have been Daze's partner...

I turn the picture over. Yes! On the back are details in Des's writing: *Persephone (granddaughter) laid to rest, Wed 29 June '88*. Oh, now I know... how terribly sad... Oh, poor Granny Caro and Grandpa Des...

Suddenly, a hand on my shoulder! 'Alice — sneak!'

Daze! I squeal, 'You didn't tell me all of it!'

'Because maybe it's my private business? Does your Mum tell you everything?'

'We don't do secrets!' Not true: more like, there are many secrets which have not been told. Am I meant to be ashamed, caught snooping? 'I'm sorry – okay, seems it's a mistake, but I just...'

'Yeah. People often just – but listen — all that's in the past.'

'Not necessarily.'

'Believe me, it won't happen to you, or Zoe. I'm not a blood relation – get it?'

'Okay – it wasn't about that baby you told me about – it wasn't I needed to know about why... I just wanted –' so we're now in a tangle.

'Look I'm sorry and of course I shouldn't have. It's like really awesome staying here and I'm grateful and everything. Can we start over?'

'Forget the whole bloody thing?'

There's a sudden hissing noise from behind us and the stench of burning.

Leaping to the stove, I shout 'Oh my god, the hot milk – I forgot about the cocoa!' The saucepan's on its side, burnt brown bubbly milk all over the hob.

'Teenagers, how I hate them!' Daze says. But then, as I squirm, she grins. 'Clear it up, Sherlock!' And she reaches into the fridge, and pulls out a tin. 'Let's share a beer,' she says, 'And I'll make cheese on toast.'

Well, I thought she disapproved of underage consumption of alcohol?

Chapter 6

A SHOCKING DISCOVERY

Easter Monday's cleaning and tidying day at the cottage. I hunt for the vacuum cleaner and find it upstairs. Rothko's looking inside.

'Ah, you've vanquished the dragon?' I say, joking.

'New bag,' Rothko says, obviously unimpressed by my kiddie remark. 'Bag's full, needs a new one.'

'Shall I ask your mum for one?'

He gets up from the floor, and gives me a look, 'I can find them. You're a guest.'

In a moment he's back, and expertly replaces the bag. I wonder if they actually live as a community?

I've learned an awful lot from Daze, nearly all unexpected. Mum's version of Daze, is 'a wild child, when we were kids.' She's told me how Daze led the primary school rebellion against uniform and compulsory team games, and later on, she'd climb out of her bedroom window to go into Penzance with older teenagers. She had terrible boyfriends and used to read her work at a poetry group.

Now I know wild kids can grow into adults who keep silent about things they don't want you to prod at: bits of their past; the things which hurt them. I'd feel the same, if I was Daze, and had had a baby which had died and got used in a research project by my recently graduated stepsister!

All difficult to think about. Whatever did Granny Caro think? She came along to the funeral – so she must've known quite a lot.

Shoving the vacuum cleaner's tube under the bed, I wonder how that part of Daze's life affected the rest of the family. The ones gathered around in the churchyard picture. What if working at Grandad Guthrie's clinic, where he did edgy research, connects with the baby? Chilling thought…. supposing it was – an experiment? No! Now my brain's feeding me a film-script!

And Daze calls out: 'Alice! You finished yet? You don't need to vacuum the carpet right off the floor!'

Waste of electricity! 'Sorry! Just finishing!'

I shove the gross thoughts away, finish cleaning my room, pack my stuff, and am ready to go into Penzance for a last visit. We go to the Penlee Gallery and look at paintings from the Newlyn school, then have tea and cake in its cafe. I'm staggered that one of the artists, Walter Langley, used watercolour for large paintings of life in West Cornwall fishing villages. I absolutely love the soft colours, muted brown, pink, and pale indigo, the colours of the working people's clothes, Daze says. And the diffused light in the sky. I envy him and all those other artists their skill, painting ordinary people living their ordinary lives. Just before photography became really popular, and people could take snapshots of each other, artists were recording the fishermen and their wives, daughters, and girlfriends, and the interiors of their cottages. One painting shows the seagulls dive-bombing the catch as the fishermen pull in the nets, with the shimmering fish imprisoned in them.

'I love the colours. The drawing's amazing.'

'Yes, but they're also disturbing. Putting life before our eyes. Just like modern art. In these pieces you can see real people, and read all the difficult bits, the traumas, in their expressions, their body language. They're standing all hunched up, they're looking sad, two fishermen's wives are hugging, a group of kids are looking curiously at something. I mean, they were poor people, fishing was — and is — a precarious life. A storm could wipe out all the men in a fishing family.'

I look closer at the paintings, and understand. 'I suppose. I mean, yes. I have to look beyond the colours and imagine the cottages cold and damp and, I dunno, fishy-smelling, and their lives unpredictable. So in a way, those make my brain work more than maybe some modern art?'

'Exactly. Not romantic. Some of the haves were waking up to the fact that the have-nots are human too, and trying to tell the other haves.'

'So what are artists in Cornwall doing now?'

'Up to the same thing, aren't they? We'd need to visit the Newlyn Gallery for contemporary art, but it's closed for updating.'

♥ ♥ ♥

My alarm wakes me at six next morning: only time for a coffee. We'll stop for breakfast somewhere on the way. Right now, Daze wants to get going. Rothko impresses me: he's packed all his stuff, pencils, drawing pads, clothes, books. Lego in tupperware boxes. His duvet in a linen bag. He drags the bag downstairs to the hallway, stacking it with Daze's things by the front door.

I add mine. Backpack, zip bag, paper carrier with presents: a book about Cornish wildflowers for Zoe, a bottle of wine from a local vineyard for the parents, a scarf and a ring each from the Craft Cooperative for Mariam and Nina. And a saffron loaf for tea back home!

We pile the luggage into Daze's van. We feed the two cats that live here an extra big breakfast and tell them their humans will be back tonight. We leave the keys to the cottage in the safe place where they asked us to, and set off. I soon realise we're on the road to Chapel House.

'Gotta collect a few things I forgot I left in the studio,' Daze says.

Lovely, I'll get a last look at my favourite place, and five minutes later, we're parked and Daze feels in her jeans pocket, and hands me her keys.

'In the studio, the end cupboard? Can you bring me the big tin of medium and that tube of superglue we used to mend the jug that ditched its handle in the sink? You can't miss them.'

'Sure.' I smile at Daze's description of when Rothko helped with cleaning some kitchen things, and managed to knock the handle off one of Granny's big jugs when putting it in the sink. As I let myself in, I realize that if Daze still has her own set of keys, then she probably comes here much more often than we know. I stand on the threshold, looking into the house. It's so quiet, so early, everything's still, and a big rectangle of sunshine beams through the open door and lies across the floor.

How can anyone leave this magical world – how could Mum have wanted to go away to Cambridge? I want to be here always, I feel pulled back, like the house is trying to swallow me. My legs go weak.

Then I remember I'm here to collect some things from the studio, not to have a sort of Cornwall-sickness in advance. There are two end cupboards in the studio, beside the door to the dark room, one above the other.

And the dark room isn't necessary any more, so the fun of watching the picture appear, or being in control as it develops, has gone. I imagine Des teaching Mum and Daze all the tricks of the old photography, and wish again I could time-travel, back to when Mum and her two sisters were all living here with Des, and Granny Caro, and watch them being my age, and know who they are, and who I am because of it.

Anyhow, back to earth again! I'm here to find stuff Daze forgot to bring away last night, and I'd better find it. So, two cupboards, which one? More likely the lower one: but, inside, there's only canvases, stacked on their sides like books on a shelf. What's here? Tempting to take a quick look at the paintings! I reach in and hope maybe there's some of Daze's work that she left behind.

I pull out one canvas, then another, far enough to see. Des's work. A couple of seascapes. Next a still life with Cornish wildflowers. A portrait: looks like it could be Mum as a teenager. Same smile, same look, almost same hair pulled back into a ponytail, just different glasses. All predictable. Then, *What is this?* An icon? The bright colours, the angular style, suggest an icon. A copy of an – oh gosh, not quite an icon — a spooky, weird, take-off of a religious scene.

I start shoving it back – then pull it out again. It is *like* a crucifixion, but it isn't exactly Jesus on the cross. The cross isn't a cross — it's — *a woman*. And the figure is *very much not* Jesus. A woman *with her arms held out horizontally.* A wooden-looking woman, arms outstretched and the attached figure *is a child*?

Oh my God, the artist can only be Daze... I pull the canvas right out, to stand it against the wall. I keep staring at it and don't let go. My arms shake as I stand it up, portrait-wise, against the wall. The drawing is amazing, the figures have life even though they are stylised like an icon.

Realise I've been holding my breath since I found this, and take some long, deep breaths. Trying to steady my thoughts.

I shut my eyes, and reopen them. The picture looks back at me. A girl child reaching up, stretching her arms, her head falling, or leaning, back. Her hands just touch the woman's. Huge sharp nails join their hands. So, *nailed together.* Their feet are bound with rope to the upright of the cross. The child is kind of *crucified on the woman,* facing outwards, enough for the viewer to see her face. I think recognize Daze's face, even as a child.

She's trying to look into the woman's face: but she can't. The woman's head hangs down, slightly tilted to one side. Her long hair falls across her face, like a veil. The child has huge tears, dropping onto her blue dress. The woman is passive. Or rather, her expression, what we can see of it, is unreadable. So, who is the woman?

I've found what I wanted, one of Daze's paintings, and I wish I hadn't. It's full of – whatever's been in her creative mind. Does it mean what I think? My brain zips back to my wish to time travel, to when Mum and Daze were growing up here: but is this how it really was? Is this how Daze felt – in this house? She must have thought this out long before she'd read about Judy Chicago and women's art!

Crucifixion.

A board creaks, footsteps behind me! Daze! And, of course, in this cupboard, there's no medium or tins of glue. Caught snooping a second time, by the artist, with a huge ginger cat grinning in her arms. It's the neighbour's cat that always tries to get into Chapel House. 'Can't you find 'em?'

Can't speak. I wait for a rebuke from Daze even more stinging than when she caught me last night, looking at the burial photo. But her voice is quiet and firm, as she says, 'Not bottom cupboard, top one. Didn't I say?'

'Yeah, wrong door – must be that top one?' I stutter like the idiot I know I am. Shouldn't have got myself involved. 'Don't – please don't be mad at me – I just opened the wrong cupboard first, and this was – in there?'

'Quicker to do it myself,' Daze says, trying to pull open the door one-handed. Then she gets emphatic. 'Bugger, bloody cat! Belongs to Evie next door. Always trying to get in the van or get himself lost. Need to shove him over the wall.'

'Can I help with the cat? Please let me have him. S-sorry – so sorry I looked at the paintings –'

She dumps the cat in my arms. Reaches up on tiptoe, and opens the top cupboard. I wonder if she set this up for me, so I'd see that painting? Now she's got down the tube of glue and the heavy, litre size tin of medium.

Why has she ignored what I did, and my apology? I know I shouldn't stick my nose into people's privacy. Though it is my family. A child crucified on a woman? Crazy. Seriously weird, and possibly significant. A shocking discovery, hiding among Des's super-placid seascapes, happy surfers and busy fishing boats. Safe pretty pictures to sell to tourists.

Daze says, 'The arts contain all of human experience.' I don't have a reply to that. Her remark makes me keep quiet and almost try not to think. She takes the painting and places it, rather firmly, back in the cupboard among her dad's work.

'Bring that cat,' she says, 'he'll not want to find himself locked in.' She holds out her hand for the keys, takes them from my now hot and sticky paw, says thank you, and locks the studio.

We walk through the house. 'Got all your revision?' she asks. 'Not left anything behind? Far as I know, nobody here's taking GCSEs this summer.'

'Yep – yep...' Please don't be sarky all the way home, I think. I didn't mean to go poking about. I only gave myself a shock, and now my mind's all jumbled up with thoughts.

'Let's go then!' It's so sad, and so awful. It's a horrible ending to my lovely time here: could I get a train, instead? To avoid being in the car with them, full of guilt and —shame, and discomfort.

'Would you – could I...'

'I'm not cross,' Daze says, taking care locking up the house. But something about her precision conveys displeasure or disapproval, or something. She indicates the cat, 'Please put him over the wall into his garden, next door, while I move the van so he doesn't try anything on. I'll park a few yards down for you to get back in. Got it?'

'Yep. I'm – sorry — it was...'

'Interesting. Yeah. I want to get you to Oxford before the rush hour, though. You got any problems with that?'

'No, of course not. I am – sorry.'

'As we'll have another long journey before we can go to bed... unless your folks are kind enough to give us a bed, hey?'

Give them a bed? It's that painting which fills my mind, leaving no room for other things as I settle into the car. We start off, and my mind is jolted back into my body, as Daze commands 'Seatbelt please!'

'Oh – yes – of course.'

A CD is playing, and this voice — quite a nice voice — reads us a story about trains, while Rothko chews on an apple in the back. We're flying along the lanes, leaving behind the amazing Cornish hedgerows bright with flowers. My mind goes back to the painting. The figures are styled like cartoons, but the child is Daze. Her wild dark hair is just the same.

The painting is something awful that Daze experienced. The bright colours, like illustrations in a children's book, contrast ironically with the grim subject.

'You saw it. I'm not asking whether you meant to, I don't think you did.'

'N-no, I didn't. But it, like, hit me in the eye. I had to look, properly.'

'Did it when I was a schoolkid. Long time ago. Let's not talk about it, right?'

A schoolkid? Not when she was the age of the child in it, about maybe Rothko's age! She couldn't have. I want to ask how old she was, but I daren't. The subject's closed.

The CD ends. Daze flips on the radio. Beethoven's *Ode to Joy* belts out. She adjusts the volume down. The music is so moving, so joyful, and I am – so indescribably not exactly confused, but too many things to name.

Daze says 'I Spy – Rothko, you go first, and remember we still have to be able to see it as we move along, so don't choose something daft like a bird or a flower, hey?'

I'm half out of their game, remembering something long ago. We were on Daze's narrowboat, and she showed me a photo of her birth mum. It was in a home-made frame, the sort of cardboard thing you make at junior school, and Daze had stuck wine gums on to decorate it with jewels – because her mum's name was Jewels. By then, the wine gums were dusty, sticky, and dull.

Was it then she said, to me, she hadn't seen Jewels since she was maybe the age I was back then, about five? Later, she rediscovered her mother, who was now using the name Etta – which was neat, as her whole name was Julietta. Etta was our mum's cleaner until she moved away to work in a women's refuge. That's part of the weird story of Daze's life, and somewhere in it is this picture. Is the painting about Daze's birth mother, Jewels?

No. I think the woman in the painting is Granny Caro. The wicked step-mother? The posh snobby woman who was with her Dad now? Like I know Granny Caro is okay, really, just a bit loud, and she expects you to know things which you don't, but if you were a kid, but not actually one of hers, you might be afraid of her. You might find her – like a wicked stepmother or a witch in something scary on TV.

I wonder when she framed the photo of her mother, edging the frame with wine gums? Was she in trouble for doing it? Whatever did Granny Caro say about her using wine gums as craft things? What did Des know about how Daze felt?

Much later we arrive in Oxford: I struggle out of my seat, wondering what happens next. We haul my luggage from the back of the van. Mum opens the front door, helps me in with my stuff (unnecessary), thanks Daze more than she needs to, and offers everyone a late lunch. She's taken the afternoon off because of me coming back, and because she could: 'Of course, Ally, we've all missed you! And there was nothing that couldn't wait back at the lab…', she says.

Daze produces Cornish Pasties from a cold bag I hadn't noticed when we packed the van. Mum exclaims, 'Ooh, you shouldn't have!', Zoe says, 'Yes you should, Auntie Daze!' If I hadn't seen that picture, this would be a lovely fun time, all together, Mum and Daze working on getting the pasties microwaved, a lettuce, tomato and avocado salad made, and opening a bottle of wine. 'No need to hold back, if you can stay the night, we've plenty of room!'

Afterwards, Mum and Daze walk down the garden, heads together. Zoe buzzes off to see Annalise. I go upstairs, dragging my backpack, and lean on the windowsill, looking out at Rothko, who's climbed to the top of our old climbing frame, and is looking over at the next-door neighbour's aviary. His life is still simple. Maybe Mum and Daze are getting along well, doing catch-up: I watch them a bit. Will Daze tell Mum what I did, sneaking a peep at that picture of her childhood? What would Mum say?

But then, I see them throw their heads back and laugh. Mum with the straight blonde hair, which she flicks back with one hand, and Daze with the wild dark mop, both wearing blue jeans and a sweatshirt. Talking about something that amuses them both. Sisters.

Well, step-sisters. How like a TV drama the three of them look, two women and a small boy: happy families in the spring garden.

Chapter 7

'Alice! They're leaving!' Mum shouts up the stairs. I don't know where time went, but they're not staying over. In fact, they didn't drink the wine, did they?

Daze hasn't mentioned my finding the picture again...it's as if it never happened. Rothko, then Daze, seizes me for a hug. We stand and wave the van off down the road, and then, we come indoors, and here we are, just us, Mum and me, in the house. Zoe's still out at her friend's.

What a visit! I might ask Mum more about what I've heard, when she asks about the visit. When she's not busy, that is. What's she going to think?

I might even look at Mum and Dad's medical and physiology textbooks, to see what could've gone wrong with Daze's baby.

Strange to be home again, knowing a whole lot about Mum, Dad, and Daze, I didn't before. I feel – is it older? I see them all differently. Daze opened up the years when Mum was maybe my age – and before. Once, I knew Mum's story (or thought I did) – now I know it how Daze tells it — I know it from both sides. My time with Daze has given me a different picture of Mum and Dad, it's opened up my mind to who they are besides being my parents.

And of course, they don't know what I now know, unless I tell them, so they'll act the same as usual. I still rather wish I hadn't seen the painting.

Mum cooks supper, Dad arrives. 'Nice to have my eldest home,' he says. He picks up the bottle of wine Mum and Daze didn't drink, and gives Mum a questioning look.

'Oh, I opened that for Daze, but in the end she decided not to stay over, so no drinks,' she says.

'Her loss, our gain. That's a rather nice one that Tim brought last time they came to dinner,' he says, pouring glassfuls for him and Mum.

'Celebration?' I say, ironically.

'Och no, just one more hard day done with!' he exclaims, cheerfully, and raises his glass, 'To you, Alice! For coming back from living with your crazy aunt.'

'God...' I mutter into my plate of spaghetti, which Mum's plonking down in front of me.

'What's that?' he responds to me, same moment as there's a sudden noise in the hall, and the front door bangs shut.

'Zoe,' I say.

And she rattles in, back from Annalise's, 'Sorry I'm late. Hey Alice!' She spends a while at the sink washing her hands, then sits down, 'Hey, Alice, what's Daze's cooking like?'

I watch Mum and Dad, trying to see them as they were in the pathology lab, with a tragic problem to solve, and so attracted to each other — and then I remember the painting Daze did — and I have to ask Zoe what she said, 'Sorry, mind somewhere else.'

'I said, is Daze is a great cook, or did you live on takeaways?'

'Food was okay, nothing special,' I say, 'except her sandwiches.'

'So what are those like? I mean, describe them?'

'Just – you know, big, thick, maybe floppy lettuce hanging out – but nice. Okay?'

Then I eat, and don't speak.

Mum kind of notices me being silent, and says, 'Alice, you are okay are you? You've gone a bit quiet.'

As it'd take a long time to tell her all the things I learned, and saw, and did, at Daze's, I say I'm fine, it's just the GCSEs, such a big thing. She says, she's glad I'm taking them seriously, but not to cut out all fun things.

Up in my room, after dinner, I phone my friends, beginning with Nina. Like me, she's just back from holiday. We arrange to go shopping in town tomorrow. Mariam has relatives staying (as ever!) so can't join us, but wishes she could. I go back downstairs, thinking about whether to share anything about Daze's weird painting with either of them.

The books I want to look for, to find out more about what can go wrong with a developing baby, will be in the study. But in the study I find Mum and Dad drinking coffee. They look up at me, Mum mid-sentence, 'shouldn't – or maybe we could – Alice! Sweetie, did you take lots of photos? I'd love to see… have you downloaded them yet?'

You look like conspirators, I want to say, so tell me, what's it about? But I don't, and Dad says, 'Your Mum's thinking about taking up yoga again – they've employed someone to give classes in the lunch break.' He grins at the thought of this.

'Yeah? What's funny?'

'I'm not going to stand on my head for you, Max, or anyone, anytime!' Mum bats him lightly. Dad makes a sad face. Mum says 'Maybe after a bit, a shoulder stand. Maybe not. But we'd love to see your photos, Al, if you have some. C'mon, I'm not here tomorrow evening, we're all meant to go to one of those awful bonding evenings, drinks and snacks at the pub… our lab and the other lot on our floor… so…'

Another thing's weird: I have defo grown concealment antennae while I was away, 'cos their funny-funny bright talk is, like, so irritating! I've never noticed its false, brittle tone so much before: my parents are hiding the real subject of their conversation, the one which I interrupted by coming in looking for a book. It's a façade to hide behind, the bit about the yoga classes, and all the happy stuff about what photos

I've taken. The subject of the 'wee talk' (as Dad might call it) is not to be shared with me. The antennae knew.

'Can we do this at the weekend?'

'Up to you...'

Whatever, probably it's work. Maybe it isn't a bad thing?

'Okay, I'll download them and then – yeah, Saturday when we're all here?'

'Splendid. And how was Daze, and that wee boy of hers? Rothko?'

'Good. They were good. He was in a kids' play. I might go to bed now...'

'Can you put your washing in the machine on your way up?' Mum asks.

'Utility room isn't on my way up, but I can,' I say. 'Where's Zo-zo?'

'Well, there's a problem – I can't be sure, but have you tried her room?'

Antennae again: they're putting on a silly act, because they want to get back to their conversation. The one before I interrupted them. Or, of course, they're still crazy in love and want to be alone (unlikely?).

My phone buzzes as I mount the stairs. My friend Mariam is very keen for a long catch-up after the Easter break.

▾   ♥   ▾

The next day, when Nina and I go shopping, she buys a very short flowery dress, and black tights. I'm flipping through a rail, and she comes up behind me and says, seizing a straight black garment with no sleeves, and holding it up, 'Yes! Perfect on you!'

'Really? How d'you know?'

'Because. Because Mariam told me.'

'You've seen her?'

'She rang about revision. And she said – she said that guy in the combined schools orchestra – the one everyone fancies – she said, Fabian Russell has the hots for you!'

'What? Mariam said that?'

'Not in those words. But yes. Her cousin — you know, Mahmoud, he's at the same school — told her. And if he asks you out, you'll want to look your best, won't you? Blondes should wear black. Actually, all women should, don't you agree?'

'Stop there. You're winding me up. How would Mariam's cousin know?'

'He's in the same class – they're friends?'

'So?'

Nina shrugs. 'We discuss them. They talk about us. I suppose.'

I'm not liking this. I do actually know Fabian, from the orchestra. He helped me when the string broke on my violin, he's one of those people who always have everything they need with them, and know about how to do things. Everyone likes him. But I didn't expect this: I feel threatened if this information's circulating about me, and in the holidays.

'My parents know the Russells. They go to dinner and come back laughing about stuff. Suppose...'

'C'mon, try on the dress. You don't have to say yes if he asks you out, do you? I would, but you have a choice!'

'Maybe. So hand it over.'

In the fitting room, Nina tries on denim shorts and the same dress in her size. As I wriggle into the little black fabric tube, she passes me a pink scarf through the curtains, 'Try this with it? It's that colour with the funny name, fucksia?'

'Fuchsia, you wally.'

In the mirror, zipped into that body-hugging garment, and twisting up my hair on top like Mum wears hers to work, a different person looks back at me. 'Yes!' Nina exclaims, holding the cubicle curtain back with one hand while she punches the air with the other. 'Stunning. Now,' she reaches over, 'if you take off your glasses?' she removes them, the vision in the mirror goes blurry, 'perfect!'

'Except I can't see!'

I throw one arm around her back, and we dance a few steps, realise we can't high kick in these clothes, giggle a bit and retire behind our curtains to get changed.

'Not buying it?' she asks as I pay for my purchase of skinny jeans and a top, 'Nope,' I say, 'not quite the serious scientist look.'

I really mean that. The thought of Fabian Russell actually liking me is amazing, the thought his friends know is somehow not exactly horrible, but, sort of like my life being owned by other people? The thought he *has the hots for me* is... weird. Nina can't see that at all, so I change the subject and we go down to Pembroke Street, to the Modern Art Museum Oxford gallery. At first as we walk round, I'm trying to picture Daze's Crucifixion among the pictures: it would fit, here, it wouldn't stand out the way it did in Des's studio with his tourist-friendly work. I could tell someone – Nina – a bit about staying at Daze's.

But actually, not about that painting. It would've been the same as I felt in the changing room, trying on the dress, when Nina told me about Fabian. It would be like people who don't know Daze sharing information about her private life.

Chapter 8

At home, I make a chocolate smoothie, grab a banana and a biscuit, and take this all upstairs to my room. Nelson's *Paediatrics* is a huge fat heavy book. I've chosen Dad's old copy, with his name and address in Cambridge, and at the Manse, written inside. As research is always ongoing, his updated edition wouldn't necessarily say the same as the edition they used back in 1988. So here I am, chewing on a 'Farmhouse hand-made' oat biscuit, and I've read up quite a lot about chromosome abnormalities, inherited and by chance. Then as I'm studying some quite alarming pictures and diagrams, Zoe bursts into my room. Just what I don't need. How'd I explain these images to my sister, and what'd Mum and Dad say about nicking the book and browsing this stuff anyway?

'What's that?'

'Nothing. What do you want?'

'S'not nothing. It's one of Mum's old textbooks.'

'It's Dad's. Okay?' I lean my elbow on the book, so my arm covers most of the worst on the page. 'So, where were you?'

'At my friend's house. Annalise.'

'Again?'

'Her Mum doesn't like her having anybody round – only me. So, can I see?' she asks, leaning in.

'It's about cells and genes – you wouldn't be...'

'I would,' Zoe says, leaning further over. I put my index finger in the place and shut the book on it. 'Actually, I was coming to tell you I'm back. We were just feeding Annalise's toad!'

'She has a toad?'

'In her bedroom. In a tank. Like a fish tank, but full of plants, gravel and stones. She made it a pond at Pottery Club. He's called Harold,' Zoe laughs.

'Harold Toad,' I laugh, 'Very pompous!' Keeping the conversation light. Though I'm curious about this new friend: it is odd that Annalise's only allowed one friend. Also, that their house, which I've seen from the outside, looks so neglected, with the curtains closed, and the front garden overgrown, you'd think nobody lived there.

'Today she showed me how she can pick up a mealworm from the box, in her tweezers, and hold it out and he comes for it. The tweezers look like a beak, so it's similar to a bird feeding its chicks. Toad – Harold – goes snap! And the worm disappears!' Zoe snaps her fingers in the air. I look back down, hoping to open the book once she's gone. But she doesn't. 'Her house is so cool. It was her Granny's house, and nothing's been changed. They've got – you won't believe their toilet. A chain you pull – like it's all Edwardian – well not quite, but defo 1930s, I should think... Can't I see that book – it looks interesting.'

'Listen. So Annalise has a toad in a tank. But I'm researching something, which for now is off limits.'

'Why should it be?'

'Because it is. Because it's – part of my life not yours. Actually, because I'm not sure we're meant to know.'

'That book's one of Dad's textbooks from med school, it's not part of your life! I might want to go to med school so maybe it's part of mine – don't...' She pounces, grabbing the book and snatching so my forefinger's twisted painfully, 'Ouch! Not yet!' I hiss at her, 'and not like that!'

'Well you were being mean! Gosh, it's only – what is it?' Zoe leans in, looking more closely at the photo. It is, actually, a photo of a baby with

Edward's Syndrome, and a diagram showing the problem on Chromosome 18, and possibility of inheritance – which is rare, it's not usually inherited, it's a mistake with the foetus and it's more likely to happen the older the mother is. But overall, it's rare. 'I didn't know,' she says, 'it's interesting, but very sad. Isn't it?'

'Yes. And that's a baby with a known syndrome,' I say. 'Sometimes, nobody knows exactly what's caused things.' Really, I'd prefer to be left alone. To consider what Daze has experienced, and how she got over it, and managed to have another child who's not — what they call these — dysmorphic. Rothko is like totally okay, intelligent, lively, perfect. But, I continue, 'It has the wrong number of chromosomes in its DNA. You know what chromosomes are? It has three copies of chromosome eighteen, but we only need two copies of each chromosome. Having the extra one occurs like one in five hundred thousand live births. If you don't tell Mum or Dad, I'll tell you why I'm looking.'

'Is it to do with Daze?'

'Partly. She had a baby – before Rothko – which had something wrong, and it died. I was looking at this paediatric book, because she also said Dad was really nice to her and arranged that she could see it to say goodbye.'

Zoe looks at me, like she's really dubious. And maybe a bit shocked. 'She told you? Why?'

'We were talking about when she went to the art college near Cambridge. She and Mum were both in Cambridge – though I don't think Mum knew — one day, they met in the market, and Daze was, like, obviously preggers. And nobody else in the family knew she was. That's all.'

'That's so sad, though. And she was on her own – like, no boyfriend?'

'Yep. It has a lot to do with why Mum and Dad got together, I think… Dad happened to be the paediatrician who was on-call when it was born. He made sure the doctors let Daze see the baby, anyway.' I thought a moment. 'He's very good at persuading people.'

Zoe flips the pages of the book. 'I hope it wasn't too – too much like these ones,' she said.

'I don't know.'

'I didn't know Dad was a paediatrician ever.'

'Just part of the training, you take a short time working in different specialities. It's called rotation... Anyhow, tell me about Annalise, and then, I've got revision to do. And I need to put this book back, before they see it's gone.'

I slip a postcard Nina sent from her holiday at their house in France inside the book, and close the page.

'Well, her house is so weird. I mean, everything's her granny's old stuff, like a set in a film about people back then. Back in, maybe, when our grannies were our age? Or at least when Mum was.'

'Granny Ianthe's London flat's like that.'

'But Granny Ianthe was old. Annalise's mum isn't.'

The front door opens and closes downstairs. 'Listen, I need to look like I'm working. I'm curious about Annalise's house, but not now, okay?'

I shove the book under my bed. Zoe bolts into her room and a moment later I hear scales on the flute.

I see that painting in my mind again. Do Mum – or Dad – know about it? How could Daze think of the idea? Was her real mum — or Granny Caro — so bad that Daze felt she was being – crucified?

❦ ❦ ❦

The next thing that happens is I'm breathing in the scent of floor polish mixed with school dinners (cabbage, greasy lamb) coming through an open window in the school library. I am so unsure about me – about whether I'm really happy to be a scientist or if being with Daze has offered me something else, something I hadn't seriously thought about before. How can I find out? A voice makes me jump. It's the deputy Head, Miss Swithinbank. 'Alice! Are you coming to the meeting about applying to Oxford and Cambridge? It's after lunch. I think you'd find it interesting.'

'Yes — I — would,' I say, wishing she'd not suddenly appeared, like a Dementor on a lonely path. I'm holding the prospectus for Central St Martin's, an art college I've heard of in London. She's leaning over me, her eyes gimleting into the booklet in my hand.

'I'd imagine Cambridge would be where you would thrive,' says Miss S, 'Oxford's far more humanities based.' She grimaces a smile, 'and of course, as you live here, it would be good experience to study elsewhere... Have you considered Imperial?' I wish I could get this booklet back in the rack without her noticing. 'Ah, Central St Martin's – yes, that's a very good art school, I believe – well, if you do think about Imperial, we have a speaker coming on Careers Forum Day, after the GCSEs...'

She doesn't finish inviting me to the Forum, though. We're interrupted by a humungous buzzing and hooting, chairs scrape across the floor as people abandon library desks, I drop the booklet back, and Miss Swithinbank announces (what we all already know), 'Surprise Fire Drill, everyone! Form an orderly line, then down the back stairs in silence, keeping to the left, and join your classes assembling in the playground.' Saved, for now.

On my walk home with Mariam later, my phone pings, and I get asked out! I feel my face glowing red, suddenly I wish I was alone. The great and gorgeous Fabian Russell has invited me by text to something very respectable: Haydn's *Creation* at the Sheldonian Theatre. At least, is he gorgeous? As a person, not just from afar, observed across our united schools orchestra?

'Hey, has – has *he* texted you?'

'Who?'

'You *know* who – *Fabian*, of course.'

'And you didn't know he was planning this, did you? Nina said you told *her* – and not *me* – how did *you* know?'

'A little bird – don't they say that?'

'Yeah, well, don't tell anyone else. *Anyone.* Okay? Was this a plot?'

'We love you – we knew Fabian wanted to know you. Aren't you pleased?'

'How did you know? Forget the bird!'

'My cousin.'

'So this is all over the upper sixth at the boys' school is it? Oh my God – d'you know what that means?'

Mariam grabs my arm, 'No! No, it doesn't! Fabian's lovely – he wouldn't do that.'

'Really?'

'Really. He's like really shy, but when we were all in Cafe Nero – remember, at the end of last term? Their crowd went by, and — I don't know it all but – they teased Fabian about – seeing you in there? Through the window? Like he must've said something – or, looked some way? And — *habibti,*' she leans in, and squeezes my arm, 'I promise, it will be okay. Fabian is okay.'

'Mmm,' I say. 'A concert at the Sheldonian.'

I accept. I'll discover what Fabian's like for myself. I don't tell any other friends. And not the parents (who I can now imagine trembling with attraction in the path lab, each pretending they're only there because of the research). I check the Family Organiser pinned up in the kitchen: they'll be Out. They have a lot of Out: college dinners, late surgeries, and experiments which need to be watched.

A concert in the Sheldonian. Haydn's *Creation.* I write that down in my rough notebook, with the date, which is a school night, and in a few days' time.

Chapter 9

CONCERT WITH FABIAN AND CHARLIE

So, I manage to sneak into town at the weekend, and holding my breath lest they've gone, find and pull out one of those black dresses without sleeves, the one Nina said I should buy, and check it's my size. Okay: I'd decided that if they had my size, I'd buy it, and if they didn't, I'd know I wasn't meant to, and go to the concert in my new jeans and top.

And now I have to buy – as long as it still looks good on me. In the changing room, I kick off my shoes, then my hands shake as I pull off my top and step out of my jeans. The fabric of the dress, as I pull it on, is slippery and cold a moment on my skin. It looks wrong with socks so I take them off too. Is it right for me?

Afterwards, I go into the covered market and buy the special olives Dad likes, which remind him of being small, in Cyprus, when Grandpa Alisdair was an RAF chaplain or something. I buy Mum her favourite chocolate. And then I buy what I said I'd gone shopping for, new pens and pencils for the exams, and thin tights for school summer uniform. As well as thin black tights. I take the clothes shop bag, and move its slithery silky contents, carefully folded small, into the bag with the tights, and I catch a bus home. They're all in the garden, and it's a superb summery spring day. Which is good as I'm all smiley. And that makes them look happy as well.

On the day of the concert, walking to school, I tell Zoe, 'Look, I'm going to *The Creation*, at the Sheldonian this evening — it's on the music syllabus. If the parents ask, which they probably won't, tell them I'm staying late at school for an orchestra rehearsal.'

'Who you going with?'

'Someone from the orchestra. You don't know them.'

She gives me a look, but thankfully decides it's better not to know.

'So, please don't hang about after school ends, don't go shopping. Go straight home, stay home. That way, you'll be safe. And if they find out, Mum and Dad shouldn't be too cross, because you did what they expect us to. If anyone's in trouble it'll only be me. I'll be back before the parents, okay?'

'What if I want to buy chocolate?'

'Today, please don't. I'll give you some, okay?' I fish in my bag, find a bar I bought yesterday, and hand it over.

Zoe gives me another look. 'It's the shopping, not the eating. Okay, it's both.'

'Sorry, today no shopping. And remember, I'm at a rehearsal. They're going to a college dinner, they might even go straight from work, they might look in on you. I'll be home first... and you've got my number, phone me if you need to... no, text – text, okay? Text.'

I'm changing at Mariam's where no one's home, and she loans me her posh jacket. It's black, like the dress. I wish it was cream, a contrast would look better. Mariam also finds a bright silk scarf, which I tie onto my ditsy across-body bag, and I stuff my money purse inside, while she puffs her sister's perfume over me. And, I catch the bus. My breathing's a bit shallow, thinking about the subterfuge involved in meeting this boy from the combined schools orchestra outside Blackwell's, where we arranged to catch a coffee and a slice of cake. It wasn't that I had to tell them, it was 'cos I couldn't get the words out, it was always the wrong time. And, this was what they call a school night, so they'd have said no... And, they know his parents...

Anyhow, it all goes okay. We manage a lot of talk about the music syllabus for GCSE (which actually I'm not taking), Fabian tells me what he studied for the exam, two years ago. When we get up to leave, I nearly forget to lump along my school bag, with my work and school clothes in it. We don't quite touch, we hesitate around each other. And then, he takes my hand as we're crossing the road towards the Sheldonian Theatre. The old Roman Emperors seem to watch us from their plinths on the railings. I give him a quick look, half a smile, as he lets go, and I fiddle in my bag for my ticket. Possibly it was only because there was lots of traffic, sweeping around the corner of Parks Road, and across from Holywell?

We enter the Sheldonian, show our tickets, and mount the steep stairs. We're high up, looking almost vertically down at the choir and orchestra. This building may be Grade One Listed, but not for comfort! When you're in the worst, cheapest, seats, the Sheldonian Theatre's about as comfortable as perching on a wall. No backrest, no leg room. Not so bad one way: not a cinema date.

Fabian has brought a score. He had it rolled up like a tube, in his pocket, and he pulls it out now we're settled, opens it, and flattens it out on his lap. 'Want to follow?'

He smells of cologne, a clean smell. No cuddling up, but I'm hyper-aware, though we're not touching. I can't not feel him next to me, in my brain I feel him, like a warmth down that side of me. All the same, 'Maybe not follow – I'll watch the orchestra,' I say. And I'm leaning forwards, craning forwards, looking out for the conductor to arrive. Kind of making some sort of a signal – I am interested in what we're doing, not just that we're here together – only of course, I am interested that we're here together.

It's now I see *Charlie*. Yes, it really is. My super-bestie from nursery and the first year of primary school. Grown bigger, but still stunning in a crowd. Wearing black and denim. It's definitely her. Tossing back her long brown hair. Her hair flips the old guy next to her in the face: he flinches a bit, adjusts his specs. Charlie. Thick dark mane, olivey skin.

So, the old guy – are those her grandparents she's with? They have silly names, which I remember. Though is he Jos, or Gussie? And the woman on the other side, her gran? Gussie, *Augusta*. He's Jocelyn. OMG, what names. Gussie's giving Charlie a sharp look. Charlie hides her face in the concert programme. Whatever, Charlie's here. Wearing something short and black, with a denim jacket.

Well, so'm I, in a short black dress, and a posh black jacket (not mine! I feel in the pocket: a train ticket, a folded piece of paper). With my blonde hair up, and a bright floaty scarf tied onto my cross-body bag, and an enviable addition: I have a boyfriend (I hope) as my escort. Charlie has her grandparents.

And everyone's clapping, I've missed the conductor's entrance. The orchestra starts up, the music grows until it fills the whole space. It blows me away. I mean, really. I'm somewhere else. I'm the only one here. My heart's thumping, I feel it banging around inside me. My foot is tapping. Is Fabian feeling the same about the music? And, about me? We reach out and grasp hands. Our hands are sticky when the interval arrives, and we let go, and we don't look at each other, hurrying downstairs among the shoving, pushing crowd, to breathe cool, dark, night air.

We're out on the gravelly space, and I open my mouth to say something to Fabian, when, out of the darkness someone — Charlie! — flings herself at me, arms wide. 'Alice – hey, Alice! It *is* you!'

This makes Fabian move back a step or two, into shadow. Charlie's hugging me almost to death. She jumps about, she offers me chewing gum. She's obviously shaken off the grandparents: 'They went off to have a pee and get some wine down them. God, when did I last see you?' she says, wriggling her feet in a little dance. (I remember Charlie's Mum, Shaz, used to dance about in the same way.)

It's sickening: the amazing music stunning us all into awe, my ears still ringing with *The Heavens are Telling*, and here's Charlie the Beautiful slamming herself right across my evening out. Obviously, she's not blown away by Haydn's amazing mind thinking up this awesome experience. Fabian stands apart from us, hands in his pockets, watch-ing. Charlie's stage-whispered question tickles my ear, 'Who's the guy?'

'Someone I'm in an orchestra with,' I say. 'School stuff? So,' I add, louder, more confidently, 'You with your grandparents?'

'Culture-vultures. They'd really rather be listening to Sinatra, I can tell.' We grin. I suddenly remember a lot more about Charlie, how she liked putting people down.

'*Char*-lotte?' Gussie's tight, super-educated voice across the crowd. 'Over here, darling. We brought you some Chardonnay.'

'Gotta run,' says Charlie. 'I'll Facebook you, look out for it?'

She'll have to look me up: I'm in no hurry. I watch her join Jos and Gussie. That skirt flares out under the denim jacket as she flies across the gravel towards her grandparents. And light streaming from the open door of the Sheldonian picks out a hole, just below the knee, in her leggings: intentional or not?

'So who was that?' Fabian asks, emerging from the shadows.

'Kid I was with, at nursery, and primary school. They moved away. I don't see her any more.'

'Not your type, now?'

'Defo not,' I say.

Inside again, me and Fabian shuffle crab-wise along our row, past coats and bags and feet, back to our seats in the gods. So, bum's on seat. Feet have no space, though. On the floor is my school bag, inside it my physics book, for revising, and my school uniform – shirt, skirt, navy jumper, rolled up and shoved down, under the book.

'Want to follow the score for this half?'

'Please.' I feel Fabian's arm lightly around my back. I am owned, possessed: and although I don't, like, want to be anyone's anything, tonight, with Charlie out there, it's a good feeling.

After the concert's ended, bemused by the music, we go to G and D's for ice cream. We discuss the music, we're buzzing, Fabian puts his arm cautiously around me again. I lean in to him. Spooning in ice cream, we glance: Fabian's dark eyes under that fringe of black floppy hair. Which is actually a bit like my Dad's in old photos? Do I want this? What is it? Who is he? A guy I'm in an orchestra with, hey?

I am not sure.

He doesn't come in the bus with me: but he waits with me until it arrives, and we hug, a bit awkwardly, before I step on. I can feel our hearts beating. I almost have the bus to myself. And then, at home, I hang my bag and Mariam's jacket on the newel post, run straight upstairs, and put my head round Zoe's door. She's sat in bed, wearing pjs, reading, safe, even obedient. I give her a thumbs-up, she does one back. Done, secretly, then, no parents, no fuss.

In my room, I hang out of the open window, breathing in early summer. The night's navy blue, warm, like velvet. What do I want? The honeysuckle's covered with flowers, its huge scent fills my nostrils and the darkness in the room behind me. It's only a plant, doing its thing to get the bees along, but... now I know what I want.

The music made me tingle. Fabian's eyes looked inside me. Is Charlie going to be back in my life? I wish she wasn't. Or Fabian hadn't been there for her to see. Or something. The feelings creep, under my skin. Signals down my spine. Quarter to eleven, says the clock by my bed. Noise of a car. Quickly, I get undressed, shove my dress and black tights into the cupboard, and I'm in the shower when they come upstairs. Can hear them, yawning, and talking college politics. Someone knocks on my bedroom door: I can hear the someone open it to look inside.

I know what they'll see: my physics textbook, lying on my bed. My school skirt over the back of a chair, my navy jumper. My school bag, open, revealing my pencil case and a pad of file paper. No problem.

Lying in bed, I think how Charlie is and isn't how I knew her before. Much less sweet and pink-spangly. The Charlie she is now might be interesting to see again. In a way. And then, a picture of something I'll have to explain away, burning behind my eyes: my tiny leather cross-body bag is hanging on the newel post downstairs. With an alien coat. Maybe I could sneak down, rescue it, and they'd think they imagined seeing it, all due to the ancient port consumed after the posh college dinner?

I was at the Sheldonian with Fabian Russell. I am not about to advertise this on Facebook.

Chapter 10

GRANNY CARO REVEALS HER PLANS

Coming in from school next day, trying to suppress yawns from my late night, I spot a dark Volvo outside our house. Oh no… it's Granny Caro's, and as I let myself into the house, there's her voice, speaking in that I-am-the-only-sensible-person, way: 'But sweetie, he doesn't know he wants to broaden his mind. Or that he will, when we get settled there. How could he not?'

'Who? Where?' I think. Granny's ranting, her voice even posher than usual, I know that voice. Drop my schoolbag, kick off my shoes, and creep along the hallway. She has come to get us on side for some plot she has thought up. So who's her victim this time?

'Oh *Mum*! You can't know that!' That's my Mum, edgy. 'And none of us want to see the house sold.' House? Whose house? 'I mean, how can you do this to us all?'

'*Me do this?*' says Granny. They're both shouting.

Then Dad's voice says, 'Caroline – Jenny – can we calm down a bit?' (Why's he come home early? Is it for whatever this is about?)

'I am calm. It's my mother who's…'

'*Moi?* I didn't expect you both to attack me.'

'Caroline, maybe if you didn't expect you could just explain. I don't think I know this – remind me – whose house is it? Do you have joint ownership? You are both on the mortgage?'

'There is no…' her voice drops, and at the same time, someone rummages in the saucepan cupboard, so I can't hear what she's saying.

So, what house? Chapel House? It can't be! Daze never hinted about anything happening to Chapel House! Surely Granny and Des would never leave! How could they? It's their lovely home, it was Mum's home, and Daze's house. And there's the studio, where Des works – and Daze when she's there. And I've just been there!

My feet are frozen to the floor. I shan't shout. What I need to do is keep quiet until I know they don't mean Chapel House. Or that they do. Surely they can't mean Chapel House? It's our holiday house.

And who needs to broaden his mind? Does she mean Des? There's nobody, only Des, she'd be settling anywhere with. So, it must be? My insides all tense up, can't breathe, but can't stop listening.

They're all talking at once, Mum shrill, Dad slow, all Scottish and emphatic, Granny Caro in her special posh voice, 'Oh for heaven's sake, it's a house! Yes, it was your home but that was years ago now and none of you – none of you – know how much I gave up simply so we — me and my children, Jenny and Henrietta, could live there and be a family together, after your father took off. I didn't know his plan was to stay in the States for ever, without us! What a bloody awful betrayal, when the girls were tiny!'

'We loved Cornwall, though okay, not at first…'

'You didn't have to think it all out, Jenny. You weren't the one betrayed. I'd kept that man while he finished his research degree, I'd worked all through my first pregnancy, as a junior doctor, in a hospital, you have no idea. Then the shock of it.'

'I was five, Hattie was three…'

'The shock of it. And relocating to that damp, draughty cottage we'd bought that was only liveable for short holiday stays.'

'And then – okay, along with Des *and Daze*, – came Chapel House. And now you think you can force Des out of his own home. Mum, you can't be serious.'

'Darling, I've worked my butt off down there, and put up with living in the sticks, no real friends...'

'Now, that's not true Mum! You've given amazing dinner parties, you've welcomed the village over at Christmas, there's the Endellion Festival, and the Minack Theatre... there's the what's-their-names, posh and intellectual, live up the road in Penzance, several of those friends...'

'Jenny... that's what I've put up with! And Des's hippie crowd... and you two girls picking up the local accent...suppose you hadn't made it to Cambridge...'

This is horrible. Hearing Granny swearing, and slagging off Des and Grandpa, and talking about Mum and Aunt Hattie like that. I cover my ears. But those words are in my head now, buzzing like flies. I can't, I don't want to imagine it all. Then ding! A text. I can hear that, pull out my phone. Fabian...? No, Charlie: can't look now, shove my phone back into my school bag. After what Granny's just said, Charlie'll have to wait. No idea if I want to see her again anyway. She looked a lot different. From when we were five.

Is Zoe upstairs, hearing the grown-ups' row through the floor of her bedroom? I creep further along the hallway, and position myself flattened against the wall, and able to see into the kitchen.

Suddenly I remember Daze's painting. Am I now experiencing a side of Granny that Daze put into that painting? If she can rant like this about her right to sell a house we all love, could she have taken important things, or friends, away from Daze? She's always been okay with us, full-on but nice — sometimes almost too much, with the perfumed hugs, the milkshakes with enormous dollops of ice cream, and staying-up-late to watch a kids' movie. I hate seeing her, now, in this aggressive mood.

'So I had a choice: either I and my poor deserted children stay in the hideous cramped terraced holiday cottage my wandering hubby and I had bought, or we take up with this hippie type and his abandoned child. What would you have done?' Granny turns, appealing dramatically (arms outstretched, oh what a gesture!) to Mum, 'Jenny?'

Mum sounds cool, now, 'I don't think that's a fair question. Not to ask me. Hattie and I had to take on another family, another sister. I can see – God, Mum, I know the sociology of it, but didn't you, weren't you, taking a chance with your own kids?'

'Darling, thank you for seeing into it,' says Granny.

Huh? I don't think Mum meant her mother to see it like that. Then, even I understand the irony of Granny's response. And 'Always the doctor,' Mum says, and a drawer slams. Is she getting dinner and having a row at the same time?

'That's cruel, Jenny, I am not. I wanted to help. With her mother gone, Daze needed someone to care for her.'

'Maybe that's exactly what I meant,' Mum snaps. 'Lady Bountiful – who gets a lovely house into the bargain.'

Can't take more of this. I walk in, talking like everything is normal, 'Dinner ready?' I stumble over words. 'Granny –' I try a smile, 'I thought you were in Italy?'

'Sweetie!' She opens her arms and descends on me, more like a hawk on its prey than someone who cares. Her perfume hits as her arms clutch, and her silver pendant digs into my boobs. 'Alice, darling, lovely to see you! And you've been with Daze, getting your revision done?'

'Yep.' I struggle and take a breath.

She frees me, holds me at arm's length like I'm a child, 'How are you?'

'Squashed!'

That makes them all laugh, like people who have to pretend everything is okay. (Antennae alert!) But then they begin again, Dad suggesting for some reason that I go and find Zoe, while Mum and Granny talk at the same time, bellowing more accusations at each other.

I can't listen to them. I cover my ears again, and shout 'Stop!' so loud even I hear it, through my hands, my own voice huge, horrible, and hoarse. They stare. Uncover my ears, my face blazing with embarrassment, and in a small voice I ask 'Please tell me what you're talking about, I mean, is this Chapel House? It's Daze's home, her base, her and

Des's studio. So if you mean Chapel House, Granny, you can't just sell it and leave! You mustn't!'

They keep staring. Mum says, 'And where were you last night, Alice, when we were out?'

'I said, this morning. Orchestra rehearsal. At the school.'

'School?'

'Yes. Why?'

'Because Sharon Parker Pollard — at my yoga class — told me you met her daughter Charlie — from primary school — and she isn't in your orchestra or at Headleigh Park.'

'It was at the boys' school.' I pause a second, that was a lie, adding another to saying it was orchestra rehearsal. Beginning a whole story now. I've haven't lied to them like this before. It feels like – like I'm not me. Charlie would tell this sort of lie. And she'd know what comes next — but I'm not that sort of person... But then, lest they pounce, I find myself carrying on, 'Yes, I know it was a school night, how couldn't I? But this was important.' Important? What kind of important? And did Mum notice my little across-body bag, hanging at the bottom of the stairs? I crept down and grabbed it once they were quiet in their room – maybe she saw it before that?

'And Charlie?' she asks.

'Charlie was on the bus,' I say desperately. 'To get back, I used the bus.' Okay, remember it was on the bus.

Dad raises an eyebrow. I actually notice he raises an eyebrow. Granny has sloped off to look in the saucepans steaming on the stove. Then my eyes are on my toes as I hear Zoe's voice, 'It was on the bus wasn't it Alice?' So now Zoe's joined in telling the story. I don't turn, but I say 'Yes, wasn't that odd? But maybe her term hasn't begun yet. At boarding school.'

Mum gives me a long look. 'Alice, where were you? It's a couple of weeks since term began, Charlie is definitely back, but she had an exeat weekend with an extra day – Founders Day or some such thing! I saw Shaz — Charlie's mum — today, I've been going to her weekly lunchtime yoga sessions at work. She bounced up afterwards and told me Charlie was at a concert with her grandparents, and that she met you there. Charlie said it was the only good thing about her evening.'

Something explodes in my mind. My mouth opens like a frog's – opens, gawps, and closes. They have no idea. My mouth opens again, my voice comes out, small, hoarse, raw, 'That's so unimportant. Keeping Daze's home is important. You grew up there. It's Daze and Des's home' (my voice is recovering its confidence), 'and Granny has no right, no right at all, to tell Des to sell it. Let her move, if she wants to.'

'And if she does, and Des stays, we shan't mind,' Zoe's voice says from the doorway.

'But Alice hasn't explained where she was last night, when she was meant to be here! Making sure you were both safe,' Dad puts in.

'At the Sheldonian, yes, if you must know! Amazing music. On the curriculum for GCSE, as if it matters to you!' I feel hot, and trembly, and my nose feels itchy and my throat's tight, because my eyes have started crying without being told. I grab my school bag and bolt out of the kitchen.

I can't take more of this. First they're hiding what they were discussing, now I'm hiding what I was doing from them. But I couldn't – absolutely couldn't – say out loud, in advance, that I was going to a concert with Fabian, whose parents are their friends. I imagine Dad, such an opportunity to grin, and make some embarrassing remark about me growing up and being attractive to boys! He'd say 'the hormones have hit and now we're in for trouble!'

Chapter 11

I FUME IN MY ROOM AND TALK WITH FABIAN

Upstairs, I chuck my schoolbag into my room, and I almost fall in after it, as it disgorges books, files, and my half-open pencil case. 'Granny, what a cow,' I hiss through my teeth, as I then bash the door closed with my bum so hard it hurts.

'All of them, *utter shit*', as I fling the curtains shut, wipe some furious tears away with my hands, and throw myself flat on the bed, knocking the breath out of me. Who cares about all the stuff that really matters? Who cares if Daze and her dad lose their home? Granny is such a snob. That's the only word for her.

Face in the pillow, I'm counting off all the great times Daze gave us when we were really small kids: the amazing angel costume she made for me with wings that I could move, the time she came over to us in her creepy Halloween outfit, and when she took us to the Lafrowda festival at St Just with her friends. All those memories we shared, in the studio at Chapel House, only last week. Even about the time they all got wasted, on holiday at the house. Daze, who'd slept on the sofa, woke up early and we played ballet class, my favourite pretend game back then, to the Nutcracker CD, while the other adults slept off their hangovers. How had I forgotten the great things Daze did?

And why really haven't we spent much time with her since? Once we'd been to South Africa, we came back and a lot was different: no

Daze times, no Etta (her Mum who used to babysit and stuff), and no Charlie (they'd moved away). Only posh Headleigh Park School. And soon after, Mum was firmly back in her career, even heading up her own lab in the science area. My mother, the successful research scientist.

I turn over and see the little cross-body bag hanging on the desk chair. It brings back the concert. The me that went to the concert with Fabian wouldn't react like this, would she? This is so self-pitying — I mean, would Fabian like me now? Behaving so dumb, crying and raging? I grab a tissue, and as I wipe away the remains of the tears (and the vile and demeaning snot) try to think about Charlie. Do I want her back as a friend? No, she doesn't fit. She's nothing like Mariam or Nina — or Fabian. Charlie belongs to when we were kids.

The exploding rage tries to pull me back. We have no say in family changes, because we're the children. They want us to wait until we have all the grown-up boxes ticked. Tick height, boobs, periods, even boyfriend (hopefully), but don't tick responsible adult, choosing careers, having a say in big family changes, actually being interested in how the world works, including the family.

Remembering the amazing music last night, I grab my phone, and text Fabian. About all this. He will see into it. Like my family can't. Like he likes me for who I am now, not what I was then? I press send.

I suddenly doubt that was wise. Mariam (but possibly not Nina) would've been a better person to share it with. Mariam is more serious, Nina is more daring... when I'm with Nina, I'm more daring...

And now, is that feet coming upstairs? 'Alice?' A tap on the door. 'Thought you might like something to eat.' Oh my god, Mum in caring mode.

'What's the food?' I call back. Rage doesn't seem to stop hunger, it seems.

'Can I come in?' She puts her head round. 'Macaroni cheese and broccoli, sorry it's boring.'

'Chilli topping?'

'Grated parmesan and toasted breadcrumbs. A touch of garlic.'

'That'll do.'

'Want to talk? You are all right?' Mum looks hopefully at me, while handing over a heaped plate of food and a fork. She begins to sit down on my bed, then hovers halfway. 'Can I perch here a moment?'

'How all right is a person who's about to lose something? I'm as all right as that. You can sit there, but you know she'll do it, she usually gets what she wants.'

Mum sits, cautiously, as if my bed might throw her off again. 'Is that fair? Look, Alice, this idea Granny's had is very far from a done deal.'

'But it is fair, 'cos it's true. And it's absolutely not fair about the house. She always wins out, what about us? What about Daze and Des? Does she care about them?'

'Give Granny some slack, darling.'

'And your Mum's bored now she's retired, and anyone can see it'd be easier to live in London and spend all her time going to plays and art shows and ignoring that other people want to stay in Cornwall — let's not talk about it, okay? Let's just not.' I wish Mum'd go away now, I can feel prickly tears trying to creep back out of my eyes. 'Can I eat this while I read some stuff for homework? I did revise in Cornwall, but there's a lot I still need to do.'

'You did say you worked every day. Proper revising?'

Ding! He's replied? Grab my phone. Glance at the screen.

'Darling?'

'Yes, Mum. I did shedloads of proper revision. Okay? And, we did loads of fun things and went to places we've never been to, 'cos you can't work all the time. And I met the cool people in her co-op, and did you know, Daze spends much more time down there than anybody ever said. And this is just a text.' I take a quick look: Fabian. Excellent.

'Whatever happens isn't going to stop Daisy doing her work with the co-op, you know.'

'Well can I know what's happening as it happens?'

'You know Granny. This is just an idea that's she's got at the moment.'

'Sounded to me like she'd got it all worked out.'

'I don't think she has. But she does need to make a decision about Ianthe's flat. Moving to London could just be an exciting idea.'

We are silent. I suddenly realize that there are other serious adult aspects to it that I hadn't thought about. So I'm still being a bit of a child, I suppose.

'You are okay now, Alice... Alice?'

'Yeah, okay now.' I do a quick grin. 'Hey, cool it Mum. I said, yes, I worked. Quite hard. Long hours. And, there's more I could do. If I want to... Oh, forget it. I'm a swot, I'm a Mullins. Okay?'

'Okay, then.' As she gets up from sitting on my bed, she touches my shoulder. She doesn't try a hug or a kiss. Thankfully, or I would cry, lots.

I turn back to Fabian, on my phone. *'Things fall apart, the centre cannot hold.'* Hum. A one-liner. From a poem we studied. By an Irish guy, Yeats.

'Everything all right then, sweetie? Macaroni cheese all right?'

'Yeah, yeah, everything.' I try hard, and manage a smile.

'Okay, kiddo,' she says, using that absurd name Grandpa calls her, like it's an intimate joke. 'And, could you maybe think about phoning Charlie. I think she's a bit lonely, she could do with an old friend.'

'Yeah, maybe. Maybe.'

'That's good. You may...'

'Okay, Mum, I'll think.'

Another smile. Each of us stretching our mouths in this signal that everything's good between us. And, she goes, shoulders a bit hunched. Crestfallen, slinking out around my door, and downstairs. I like that word, crestfallen. Like an exotic bird. Her crest is definitely down, poor Mum. Granny's got to all of us.

'Things fall apart... see yer soon, Al! Fxx.' They really do. But he cares about me. Doesn't he? Two xs?

I can't think about being nice to Charlie right now. Maybe if Granny hadn't turned up and told us her horrible plans. Before that, I might have done. I fish out some homework: going over stuff we've learned in order to reproduce it under exam conditions is boring and scary. Here's some moderately interesting Chemistry: immerse myself in it, learn to draw the diagrams from memory... presently my phone shrieks from next to me on the bed.

Grab it, stare at it: he's called me back! 'How're you now?

'Me?'

'Yeah. You. And that stuff you sent me, about your Granny's house?'

'It's too horrible!'

'Talk. I'll be an ear.'

'Okay. Granny's got an amazing house at the far end of Cornwall, the bit that's like a toe, sticking out into the sea?"

'I can imagine.'

'So you know it's magical there, and we've spent lots of holidays... when they aren't there – which is quite a long time in the summer sometimes, like a month — Granny and Des let us stay. And I was there a lot when I stayed with my amazing aunt Daze at Easter and we did such cool things... you see why we can't let Granny Caro sell up, don't you?'

He laughs. 'Okay. I know where you mean.'

'And you'd agree it's so right to keep this house in the family? Well Granny's inherited her mother's flat, which is in London, like in the centre somewhere, so she now thinks, as she's retired, she'll go and live in it! So she can be near the theatres, and art galleries, and things she likes to do. And to afford that, she's selling Chapel House!'

'Mmm,' says Fabian, so slowly I could kick him, if he was here!

Well, maybe not, actually. But, he doesn't say more, so I continue 'Granny may think it's part hers, but that's only because she shacked up with Des – Daze's dad.'

'Right. This is getting complicated. Daze is your Mum's stepsister, you said, so are they – your Granny and Daze's father — married? They might have made some legal agreement about ownership...'

'Whatever – I'll try and find out... wish I could show you what the house is like. Des is amazing. I mean, he envisaged what could be done with an old chapel nobody was using, and he made it happen.'

'Mm... sounds a special place. Des is an architect then? Or a builder?'

'He's an art teacher. I guess he employed an architect. Granny Caro put her savings in – so, legal agreement or not she can't really pull out now, can she? Doesn't that make the house part hers? I'd hate them to break up. Actually...' Explaining all this to Fabian has got me mega excited, I should really stop. I shouldn't tell anyone my dreams, not yet. Not even him.

'Actually?' Fabian asks.

'Oh, I dunno – Daze is Mum's stepsister, but Granny adopted her. Obviously Granny wanted Daze to become more like her own girls, but Daze's DNA is like super strong, and she's totally different. Granny Caro's a scientist, she ought to understand that! Something clarifies in my head, 'It's like Granny has to acquire things, isn't it?' I say.

'Maybe. So Caro's your granny, she was a kid in the war?'

'Yes, I guess she was born about 1940.'

'So, wartime childhood – figures. They're always making up for what they didn't have. Using that as a reason for acquiring material stuff, which to them represents security. Makes sense.'

'Yeah, fits. I didn't think of that: she's like hungry to eat up art and culture and she loves giving big generous parties to celebrate Christmas and birthdays, or even just life. And she's totally committed to feminism.' I don't tell Fabian about why Granny was raised in a single parent family, seems too intimate somehow. 'So going back to the old flat is about all that? About owning things?'

'Think about it. She's been left property in central London?'

'Yes.'

'So she'll pay inheritance tax, but she'll still have a nice investment.'

'And all the culture she wants is practically in walking distance, or a bus ride away.' I picture her, in our kitchen with Mum, glass of wine in one hand, stirring a sauce on the hob with the other. In the memory, I come running in and gabble something about being an angel in the reception class nativity play, something like that. An indulgent smile from Granny. And then, 'Wait and see what Des made you girls for your Christmas present! And I bought you both a little something to keep you going, because waiting for the present is so awful, isn't it?' Yep. That's my Granny.

'So to her this all makes sense. And she's not thought about how the rest of the family feel.'

'It's like that part of her doesn't care. And Des couldn't live in London. He loves Cornwall, and his arty friends.'

'Okay. Look, I have to go now, but, I hope it helped to talk?'

'Yeah, it did. I mean, it was like really kind?'

'Okay. So see you soon, don't revise too hard!'

'And I'm keeping in touch with Daze...'

'Yes, do that! Good idea!'

Chapter 12

MAX QUESTIONS ZOE, I PHONE DAZE

I'm determined to phone Daze tomorrow, and find out whether she's in on Granny's plans – and why she didn't tell me everything when I was there with her, in Cornwall, working in the studio?

So, it's early morning, I'm on my way downstairs, and Zoe, young, innocent, and thirteen-ish child-adult that she is, is chattering at Dad in the hallway. Dad is putting on his everyday, go-to-work tie, the one with turquoise paisleys on a navy background. Zoe is standing on one leg, holding the shoeless foot of her other one. Dad's cut into her diatribe about her friend's toad and begun quizzing her about my night out.

'So how did you get home? After messing about with that amphibian?' he asks. 'And was Alice here – shall I re-phrase that — did you notice whether Alice was here? When you finally arrived?'

That tone he's using gives me the creeps from my bottom all up my spine, like he hasn't forgotten anything about last night's revelations of what I was doing the night before, when we were both supposed to be here. Only I wasn't, I was at the Sheldonian with Fabian and Haydn's amazing *Creation* music.

'Stacey.' Zoe hops, looking down at the ground, where there's a muddle of shoes, and Mariam's jacket that I chucked on the newel post last night. Then she lets go of the raised foot, and replaces it on the floor. 'Do you need to do that?'

'Lost my other shoe. Under Alice's coat maybe? She drove me. Stacey. Annalise's Mum?' Zoe ends her sentence like a question.

'I know who you mean,' says Dad, impatient with her imitation California Valley-girl style. 'You know you shouldn't have gone home with a friend if Alice was...' He hesitates. Can't call it baby-sitting can he? '...in charge here. So was Alice here? When you got back?'

'Prob'ly. I wasn't late, I wanted to see Neighbours. After that, I remembered my French translation, so I did that. Then, I went to bed. With the radio. Well not with it, but with it – you know? There was a science programme, it was about ecology and caring for the planet?'

Virtuous try, Zoe! I think. While 'Och...' Dad says impatiently. 'And there's your shoe. And hang up that coat before you go? Whose is it?'

'Alice's.'

'So pick it up and hang it on its peg, please.' Zoe picks up Mariam's jacket. Reluctantly — because being told to do anything by Dad, in that voice like he thinks we're still little kids, is humiliating — she hangs it up. I'm still as a statue on the stairs, avoiding what I can see past them, in the kitchen: Granny sipping coffee. Dad (bad mood very likely brought on by her visit), then leaps into the study, grabs his jacket and bag, and bolts off to work, calling 'Safe journey Caroline!' as he slams the front door behind him. She riles him as much as she does me!

Zoe, foot shoved into shoe, grabs her school blazer and backpack, slings backpack on shoulder, reopens front door, half turns back calling 'Bye, Granny, don't suppose you'll be here when I get back!' and exits.

I go back in my room to find everything I need for school, thinking life would be better if I disappeared as well, mouse-like and without breakfast. But Mum and I collide on the upper landing, 'Alice!'

'Oops! – I'm gonna be late. Say goodbye to Granny for me?'

'Okay – but can you just *think about* giving Charlie a call?'

Why's she so keen I see Charlie again? And why this, rather than any mention of my misdemeanours? Is that shelved, for a long session later?

Whatever, I'll call Daze... If she knew about Granny's awful plans, then she should've told me! On the way to school, I pull out my phone and click on her number. Daze answers with a yawn, 'Yeah? Can't talk, call you later?'

'This is urgent!'

'So is the home-school trip to see this castle we're off to in half an hour! I'm responsible for making packed lunches for six kids and three adults – and driving everyone in the co-op minibus!'

'It's just about whether you knew about what my Gran's planning to do with Chapel House?'

'Alice, I do – I couldn't tell you when you were here because back then, I didn't. I've no more details. So, we're equally in the dark, and when I know, your family will as well. Okay?'

'Okay. She stopped off here to tell us, yesterday, and it was, like, awful, 'cos I walked in on her and Mum having a row about it.'

'Sounds like my step-mum. I'll keep your family up to date if she doesn't, that do?'

I'm about to say, it'll have to, and wish I'd left this until the end of school today, because now I'm feeling grouchy, when 'Alice Mullins! No chatting on your phone in the school grounds!' comes a heavy teacherly voice. Same time, a hand appears, held out, palm open. 'I hope you are going to give that into the office now?'

'Sorry – I was just,' I say, switching my phone off. I'd hardly noticed I'd walked into the school grounds, 'yes, of course.'

'Thank you. All phones to the office every morning, you know the system.'

Yeah, of course I bloody know it. Everything has a rule here doesn't it. Where is my smile? Better put it on. 'Yes, Miss Bevington. Sorry, Miss Bevington!'

'Hurry, it's nearly time for assembly!'

Chapter 13

DISCUSSION WITH MARIAM

Mariam's taking ages to come out from her piano lesson! I can hear her in the music room. Scales, and then that piece she practises all the time, with the mistake she always makes. She stops, and re-plays it. Now it's correct, but too slow. She plays it again. The music teacher will be tap-tapping with a pencil on the piano's lid, keeping her to time. My insides twist as I think about Chapel House being sold... part of me being taken away... I've been waiting through all the lessons and stuff to share this with Mariam. My closest friend. We met at the scholarship exam and stayed in touch. Mum knew her mum from work. Her parents are medical like mine.

I try to think in what's called the present moment... I sit on the wall near the school gate. The sun's been out all day, the bricks feel warm and comforting against my bum. Lush weather: everyone's saying we could have a long hot summer. Just right for a long stay at Chapel House. Graduate from body boarding to half decent surfing, or more likely get some cool shots of the real surfers. And the sunsets.

Downside is, Daze, I need to speak to you! I called at lunch break: no answer, and she didn't have a 'leave a message' on her phone. Whenever I remember Granny's visit, that horrible sinking feeling in my stomach comes back: her awful news, the unthinkable thought that she wants to sell up and move to London! My friends asked me why I'm so moody today: but I can't share the awfulness with everyone. It's like – it's like a bereavement. They mightn't understand that.

A plane drones overhead. An early ladybird settles on my hand. An eight-spot. Its life is uncomplicated, all it needs is to find the right plants to lay its eggs on… *Things fall apart* all right. Fabian sent a line from that poem, maybe he actually understands?

Does Fabian care about me? Could I be more than…an experiment? I remember his older sister from when I went to my ballet class, I was five, she was older, maybe nine? She wasn't at my school, I haven't seen her since… If me and Fabian were an item, I don't much want her to remember. She was the star in the shows we did, and I haven't really thought about her since then.

I don't want all my friends knowing about Fabian. Yet. It's kind of not their business. I know it was crazy to go out on school night, leaving Zoe on her own. Dad's already shown me what he thinks: last night he came to collect my plate after supper: it was obviously an excuse, 'cos didn't he hang about, he asked me straight out what I thought I was doing leaving Zoe on her own?

'I don't know,' I said, uselessly, 'I suppose I didn't think anything could happen to her?'

He said, 'You didna' think – you must think, when you're left responsible for your sister and this house.' And he picked up the empty plate, and the fork, and disappeared off with them, downstairs.

And his words made me realise what I'd done, and see it differently.

Suddenly, the world goes dark: I shriek, jumping up, 'Don't!'

But then, I realise, 'Hey, sorry…!'

This is Mariam, she's crept up and put her cool hands over my eyes. For a moment, I'd seen some vile stranger in our porch, and Zoe opening the front door, and it's dark, and he…

'What's wrong?' Mariam laughs.

'N-nothing…okay?'

'It wasn't.'

'Okay, it wasn't — I let Zoe be home alone last night when Mum and Dad were out, and went somewhere. You know where that was. And, I mean, I told her everything she mustn't do, and she's thirteen, old enough to understand and be sensible – but Dad had a go – and – now I'm imagining the what-ifs...'

'Yeah, my sister used to hate staying in watching me — there wasn't really anywhere she'd be going, but she didn't want to be responsible.'

'Was really stupid. I'm okay with being responsible – I really didn't...imagine... and as you did that... I did, I was imagining...'

'Yep. I get it.' Mariam gives me a hug.

'So now... Hey, let's go!'

I jump up, we grab our bags and walk out of school together, arms round each other's shoulders.

'Everyone's out at home,' Mariam says, ''cept my sister. Come back, we can revise together?'

'I don't know.'

'Why? Are you needed at home?'

'Not exactly. But, I can tell you this – Granny, that's Mum's mother, the granny whose house we can stay in when she's not there, like in the holidays? She was there when I got home yesterday. I walked in when she and Mum were in the kitchen having this awful row. Granny's inherited a posh flat in London, and she's stupidly, selfishly, wanting to sell Chapel House and move into that flat in — Baker Street, I think, or near there! It's like part of the family's being snatched away.'

For a second, I wonder why Mariam isn't as moved as I was. Then she says, '*That is so sad.* You've always talked about your family's magic house. With the art studio, and that you can see the sea from the garden.'

'Yep. So she'd come up from Cornwall to look at the flat, and on her way back she came to ours. She's selling her awesome house in an awesome place as if it's any old house, somewhere ordinary! And, listen, it's not even her house to sell.' I lower my voice, like a conspirator, 'It's really my step-grandad Des's house, his dream house he'd converted from an old chapel.'

'Can she do that?'

'I heard Mum saying to my Dad that she – Granny — is a bossy old bat. And she is. She'll batter her black bat wings on Des until he gives in. I don't know how much she would need to pay him off. There was a lot of shouting last night, I lurked in my room.'

'That was awful. Where was Zoe?'

'She had homework that had to go in.'

'What about your aunt – Daze, the artist? The one you stayed with last holidays?'

'She says she doesn't know any details... I can't think what to do. Except, maybe if we all went there, and had like a big family reunion, with Mum's sister who lives in Australia and her family as well – if everyone got together, having a great time, would that show Granny how important that house is? It's the family's house, it's not any old building with no atmosphere, no specialness.'

'Maybe you could suggest that idea?'

'I don't know. Like, it's — So. Not. Likely. Isn't it? This is becoming a bum year. Except for Fabian – who you mustn't tell anyone about.'

'Nina already knows.'

'Yeah, well, Nina got that from you, didn't she?'

'No, she didn't! It was from his crowd – Fabian's crowd? Someone asked her what you were like as a person. You know, whether you – had anyone else? Whether you were — Nina told me!'

'Whether I was what?'

'You know the kind of thing. It was Nina. Whether you were like her?'

'And?'

'Oh, she said, no, you were one of the quiet types.'

'And a nerd?'

'No. Maybe a half-nerd? Look, it's all gone fine, forget it. Forget them. Let's talk about the holiday house?'

'I think that's the problem – it isn't really a holiday house, it's where Mum and her sisters grew up – we've just thought we'd always go there?'

'You could begin by talking to your auntie Daze?'

'I tried this morning, she was busy! Taking some kids on a school outing... When I was staying, I asked her what it was like moving in, and she said that Chapel House belonged to Des before Granny was in his life, and how they went on making it into a home, together, though of course Des did all the designing and a lot of the hard work. Granny was working full time, and she did the easy shopping for furnishings bit. Now, her talking about selling sounds like a betrayal, seeing she got an almost free gift nice home out of having a relationship! Betraying Des.'

'If it was my family, well your step-grandad wouldn't allow your grandmother to sell – she'd not be allowed!'

'You don't know him. He'll give in. He's easy-going. Like too nice to other people.'

'I wish mine was. He's paying for my sister's wedding. So she has to have it back in Cairo!'

Mariam might not want to go to Egypt for the wedding, but I'm really more interested in my problem: it's only a trip to where she was born, and then she'll be back here doing other things. Losing Chapel House is worse, it'll change our lives. The wedding only changes her sister's life.

I said, 'It's like they're all conspiring to wreck my exams with the worry of it all.'

'Conspiring?' Mariam asks. 'I'm sure they're hurt as well. They're trying not to show it. My family are being so super-supportive about GCSEs, it's embarrassing.'

'Okay, not conspiring — of course it's accidental, but it feels like everyone's decided something that'll mess up our lives, and Des and Daze's lives, in what's called a done deal.'

'Aw, Alice!' Mariam says, 'But there's Fabian!'

'Yeah, well, I don't know he doesn't do that, too, do I? Listen,' I say, 'don't say a word to anyone here, we were only at a concert. Nothing *happened*. Except Charlie, like I told you?'

'Promise. I hope your parents like him.'

'If it gets that far!' So we part, Mariam saying, 'Talk to your auntie, Alice!'

'Well, if she doesn't answer her phone again, I can see if she's on Facebook. What I want her to know is that all our family'll support her in a fight to keep the house.'

Chapter 14

But when I get home, Mum is on the phone, wittering away to a friend and poking at potatoes boiling in a saucepan.

'Well, I can only ask,' she says, 'now I must fly, the gannets are gathering!' She swivels round as I drop my bag on the floor. 'Oh, there you are! Zoe's been back for hours.'

'Yes, well now I don't have to walk her home... I mean, when it's light and stuff...'

'Mmm,' says Mum, 'least said about that.'

Best to avoid more being said, despite she's implied not saying anything, so I turn to get my bag and wander off upstairs, but my eyes notice something on the table: a leaflet. *Sharon Palmer Pollard, Yoga for Scientists, Wednesdays 1.00–2.00pm, Thursdays 7.00 to 8.00pm.* So Mum knew when she joined... Did Shaz maybe get in touch with Mum, get her to join?

And that instant, Mum turns to give me her attention again, since the potatoes don't need it any more, and puts down the fork. Standing leaning her back against the kitchen counter, 'Alice, just a moment... I was talking to Shaz, you know about the yoga classes, and — you don't have to decide now — but there's a spa weekend for mums and daughters at a place she works, and as one of their teachers she got a double deal!'

Groan inwardly. Before I can interrupt ('No! Please not...!'), she adds, 'And thought of us. After you met Charlie at the concert.' She stops and looks at me, head on one side. 'What do you think?'

Before I even get round to calling Charlie, she's made a move. Without consulting me. 'I didn't *meet* Charlie, Mum. She bounced us in the interval and Fabian was forced to stand aside while she grabbed and hugged me. It was embarrassing!'

'Yes, I can imagine. But sometimes we have to put up with embarrassing. I had to when I... look, I think bouncing was, well, yes it was a bit rude, but Charlie was pleased to see you! You know they live out at Wormleigh now, and I expect she's a bit lonely.' She picks up that fork again, to give the potatoes another poke.

Wormleigh? A cute Cotswold place, the kind of village where Granny would take us for lunch when she's visiting... 'I don't see why she should be lonely. She must go to school somewhere and have friends. I don't owe her anything!' As I say this, Dad walks into the room, home early enough today to hear me and Mum on the edge of arguing.

'Of course you don't owe her, friendship isn't about trading,' he says, washing his hands at the sink. This annoys Mum, who's now queueing behind him, wanting to drain the potatoes, 'We all know that.'

'Ally, love, can you please call Zoe?' Mum says, 'and Max, can't you go somewhere else to do that? Here, we're ready to eat, and without soap on the veg.' They find this funny, and laugh. Adults... *parents.* Parents who fell for each other over a piece of research. Now *that's* embarrassing!

I know what I said was mean. 'But she was pressuring me,' I say at Dad, as he sticks his head in the fridge, then pulls out what he's looking for, and brings the half-finished bottle of wine to the table. Why do parents have to have an argument? And see it as funny? 'What was the other thing you were going to say Mum? You were embarrassed having to?'

'Oh, that embarrassment is natural. I was embarrassed when I had to give a paper at a conference where your Grandpa Guthrie was also a delegate. Suppose he'd attacked me with a tricky question, and I fudged up the answer?'

'Did he?'

'If he did I don't remember, so let's say my answer was okay. And I was embarrassed when I went to meet your Dad's family, because they're Fundamentalists.'

Dad makes a noise like, 'Ochhh..' to dismiss that, slopping small measures of wine into glasses for him and Mum, while I say, 'Those aren't as embarrassing as…'

'I know, I do understand. But, do it, come to the spa weekend, and you'll see, you'll make Charlie happy, and that's a way to feel un-embarrassed…you've done something…'

'For someone else…' I snap. 'Yeah, right! You're going to Shaz's classes – Granny's trying to move to London…'

'I know, and you have exams. But, this might be fun, something positive? Have a think? And do run and call Zo-zo can you?'

What I don't say is, don't treat me like a child – the child I was. So why, because she's enjoying doing yoga at Charlie's mum's classes, must we go to this spa weekend?

'Sláinte!' Dad exclaims, raising his glass, 'something positive: today we have appointed a new partner!'

Chapter 15

I GO TO THE SPA

Mum kept on, 'Hey, don't say anything now, but I'd like to go, a couple of nights, lovely relaxing massages in a country location? Before you start your exams? Could be just the thing?'

'Mmm,' I say, escaping after supper to my room and my revision. Or actually, to Mariam on my phone: a rumour has started at school that someone's had an abortion. An abortion sounds a pretty serious thing to happen when you're – possibly under sixteen?

I say 'I mean, obviously if she's had one, that means whoever it is has — had sex, like maybe more than once...'

'Or even just once,' Mariam says slowly. We pause, probably both thinking about that. 'Possibly incest...' Mariam adds.

'Or, she was attacked by someone? And — raped... that would be awful.'

'Or, just raped on her date,' says Mariam.

'Just?' I say, 'that's horrible!'

'It happens.'

'Mum said – I forget when – sex talk I expect, she was, like, very clinical about all the downsides of being women...like, the upsides can be downsides...'

What I said sends a cold shiver down my back. Mariam says again, 'It happens. Maybe even on a first date.'

'Yeah. I mean, well, like yep.'

We pause again. Then Mariam changes the conversation, 'But, talking of happy things, once we've done these exams it'll be the holidays! And then – we only have to study the subjects we've chosen to do!'

And Mum knocks on my door, 'Ally?'

'Yeah, on my phone!'

'Important?'

'Mariam.'

So, Mum sticks a hand round the door, and drops something onto my bed. 'Leaflet,' she says, from behind it.

'Okay.'

'Gotta go,' says Mariam, as I reach for it, and see it's about this spa weekend thing. 'Grandma's skyped from Cairo!'

Left with the discomfort of our discussion on the disturbing downside and possible consequences of sex, I read the spa website. Bikini clad women lie on sunbeds by a turquoise pool, under a blue sky. They laugh and sip fruit and veg smoothies. They lie under towels, wearing apparently nothing, being pummelled on their backs by pretty blonde white-uniformed women. Out in the grounds, there's a photo of six women, with Shaz as instructor, doing yoga, 'One of our occasional yoga weeks' it says.

The grounds of the place look lovely: trees, wildflowers, and more blue sky. Never mind the yoga – taught by Charlie's Mum.

Mind goes wandering back: I think how I felt, leaning out of my window, inhaling the scent of the honeysuckle. Just crossing the road holding hands. I wonder, then worry, about how far Fabian might want me to go, and how soon. How embarrassing, if nothing else – to mention – contraception!

I chuck that thought away, as very stupid and knowing we are sensible people. With broader interests.

There's the spa weekend: maybe getting Mum on her own we might talk some more about – things. A weekend away would break up the daily diet of exams, how we approach them, how we revise, how we need to relax. Like, I would learn to relax?

♥   ♥   ♥

So, here we are: a Friday evening. Mum picks me up straight from school, no time to change, 'Got to beat the school run and the Friday-night escape!'

The spa's a country mansion with a fancy name, run by the kind of beautiful people Charlie might want to become. We walk into the luxurious reception area and Charlie's Mum rushes up and hugs me as if we're all close friends. I'm drenched in her fragrance. She speaks from within the cloud: 'Hi Alice – looking forward to being pampered? And please, you can call me Shaz now!'

'And it's GCSE term, so I brought my revision.'

Shaz lets me go, to clutch her mouth and say 'Oops!' Oh gosh, it kind of popped out the wrong way, I heard myself there, sounding very sullen, giving my excuse in advance. I know I'll need a bit of time off with my books.

Mum gives me a frown, and says brightly, smiling at her friend, 'But we're both looking forward to a lovely break, certainly what I need, been much too busy this year.'

'Jen, you've also become a regular at my classes! That's so wise, to get some balance in your life!'

So, where's Charlie? I look around. The reception desk is huge, hotel-style, and on it there's a vase of white lilies which scent the whole area. The smell tickles my nose. I move away a few paces, and sit down on my weekend bag. Shaz explains she came straight here from teaching in the nearby village, Cudsmoor (which always makes me think of cows...). Charlie's supposed to be picked up from her school by her dad, and dropped off in time to join us for dinner.

The mums lean on the reception desk, as we wait for the receptionist to answer the silver bell Shaz tinkled for her attention. Yeah, I agreed to come, packed some revision notes, and several chocolate bars in case they only feed us on carrot juice, nuts and seeds. Mum's Aunt Val – where Daze used to live for a while in Edinburgh — apparently lives on those. I would really miss chocolate.

The sounds of a car on the gravel outside. I go to the window: there's a Range Rover parking. This'll be the test, will we want to be friends again?

But it's not them. A woman in a tracksuit – designer style – hops out and leans in to grab her bag, turns and slams the door. She doesn't come towards Reception but heads off into the grounds.

Then a small car approaches, and stops rather suddenly behind the Range Rover. The occupants — Charlie and Eliot, her dad – get out. They extract Charlie's bags, and walk towards the entrance. Eliot, limping, carries the larger bag. Charlie has a huge soft heavy-looking bag on her shoulder, and she's brought a tennis racket, pretty much twice the luggage I have. She's wearing a bottle green tartan kilt, possibly part of her school uniform, with a black cropped tank top and boots. She has a ponytail, but there are highlights in her hair.

They come through the door, Shaz steps away from the desk, takes the bag from Eliot, grabs and kisses first Charlie, then Eliot. They speak briefly. He comes over, remarks how nice it is to meet me again, compliments Mum on becoming what's called a Principal Investigator (only Eliot says, 'on your promotion': the promotion was, actually, three years ago – but he can't know that). And then, he gives Charlie a big hug, and me a wave, and leaves. What I notice most is, he's having trouble with walking.

'Ally! Oh wow, I didn't know if you'd make it!' Charlie's squashing me again, in a great big bear hug.

'Why wouldn't I?' I say, from inside. I see she's left Shaz with the two bags and the racket.

'Well, Mum said you might not. You've got exams, you're - you know, like, such a swot.' (Thanks, Charlie - but you are right.) 'Hey, it's gonna be great – massage, sauna, maybe tennis if we can find a couple of guys to make doubles?'

'Not sure if there's any guys here. Maybe.' Try to smile, try to be nice, I think. 'Let's see if the mums have our keys yet – dump our stuff in our rooms and get rid of the remains of school uniforms?'

'Gosh yes – this skirt is hideous! No time to change, Dad was in the school carpark, engine running.'

'What about me?' I indicate my track suit bottoms and T shirt 'in my PE stuff, last lesson was Rounders!'

'Rounders?' Charlie gasps. 'We don't play that after third year. Haven't they heard of lacrosse?'

'So, ladies, no more gossip, come and choose what you're going to eat,' Shaz hauls us towards the desk. There's a menu for dinner in the restaurant, and there's another menu for 'Treatments'. That's where Charlie's looking. I jab her arm to get attention. 'So, what's a Body Wrap?'

She leans over again to read the list. 'They cover you in mud and wrap you in cellophane for thirty minutes!' She follows the print with her index finger. Then clutches her mouth and begins to shake with silent laughter.

'What? *What…?*'

'Body Polish?' Charlie manages, between gulps for breath. Her chewed, but pink varnished, fingernail points it out on the list.

'Polished with what?' I try to suppress the giggles but it really is weird.

'Quote, Using salt, sugar, coffee, or even pecan hulls.'

'All very dubious from a scientific viewpoint!'

'Painful!'

'Yes, but what d'you fancy to eat?' Shaz interrupts us.

'Anything if it's not salad,' says Charlie.

I catch Mum rolling her eyes, and grin back.

Eventually we've all chosen, Charlie and I have room keys, and we go off to change. Guess what, we're each sharing with our mums, but in next-door rooms. We meet up again, and Charlie's in low rise denims, with a pink top showing two inches of her belly. The colour is perfect for her olive-y skin. I'm in my skinny black jeans, no belly showing, and feeling a bit frumpy as Charlie says that flared bottoms are coming in, 'Though that's a nice top!'

We decide to further investigate the treatments, and maybe find the tennis court. Mum and Shaz disappear leaving us to explore the premises until dinner is served. They return, chattering in whispers, wrapped in towelling bathrobes. When they see us they snap back into parent mode. 'Where've you girls been? We had a sauna and a dip in the hot tub.'

'Nearly time for dinner!'

The dining room has round tables, six or eight people at each – though we are only four. Starched white cloths, pale yellow walls, watercolour landscapes, and all the furniture's pine. Place smells fresh, maybe because there's no fried food? Charlie and I seize the menu card, because the treatment list is on the back, and we want to decide what we'll do in the morning. If we can bond over the treatment list, then maybe Charlie's almost tolerable — for a weekend. Dinner, based on salmon, is okay. The non-dairy ice cream sundae's delish.

Saturday morning we're booked to share a massage, two couches, two masseuses, one treatment room. Though waiting for the masseuses to arrive, stripped to our pants (Charlie in an electric blue satin thong), I have visions of the showers at school after a hockey match.

'Hey, I picked up the towel and look, what's this for?' Charlie says.

I pick up the towel on my couch, and there it is, a designed, intended, hole. 'Obviously meant to be there, part of the design of the couch.' I look again, and then at Charlie, 'You have to lie flat on your face with your nose through the breathing hole?' We burst into laughter. 'You could stick your tongue into it?'

'You could spit through it,' she responds.

I kind of knew Charlie would have done something like that, from when we were five. She doesn't actually try spitting though, she sticks two fingers through the hole and wiggles them, same time as someone outside wiggles the door handle, 'You ready? Can we come in now?'

We're bent double, shaking with laughter, but we manage to shout 'Okay!' while stepping away from the couch, where we've carefully replaced our respective towels to cover the source of our laughter.

The masseuses enter: two matching ponytailed people wearing white tops and navy trousers. Their tops have the spa's logo embroidered on the left, and their names – Michelle and Juliette – on the right. They soon have us on the couches like plucked chickens, and they spread warm towels on our backs. Oh, and they tell us they aren't masseuses, they are definitely Massage Therapists, which is different! Under my warm towel, I feel out of place: these treatments are for blushing bride types, not me. But then I wonder if Daze has ever had a massage at a spa? She's done all kinds of things that don't go together. Why not me having a spa treatment?

Charlie says something about next time I see Fabian... Her therapist (Michelle) looks meaningfully at mine (Juliette), and the two of them look meaningfully at Charlie, together. It's a *We're healthcare professionals* look. And that's what I think as well: this place really is weird, a cross between a posh hotel and a clinic, with fine dining and aromatherapy as add-ons. Juliette works on my shoulders, where there's tension. 'Exams,' I say. 'GCSEs?'

'Oh yes?' she says. She has a soft Irish accent. 'That's a hard year isn't it. So, remember, you're here to let all that go for a couple of days, and relax. Have you booked a head massage? They're so lovely.'

I can't stop feeling like I'm someone else. Do people become someone else when they do stuff that isn't them? Mostly, Saturday morning is for getting my weekend assignments done. Zoe sometimes goes swimming with Annalise. When we get home, I'll gratefully slip back into my real self, it'll be like putting on comfy jeans (less tight than the ones I brought along here), and going round to Mariam's to eat tabouli and olives with pitta bread, and lie on her bed listening to music. And revising. And talking about, 'Will it last with Fabian?' And her sister's wedding.

And maybe about the other thing: and whether we'll ever know who it was.

Chapter 16

SATURDAY AT THE SPA

'It was the best of times, it was the worst of times...'

'What?'

'Dickens – *Tale of Two Cities*, it's a quote. Maybe your year didn't read that – maybe it's off the syllabus, but ours did. Doesn't matter – but if you'd read it — it fits this spa weekend. Like, some of this spa's good, like the pool, which you can go in any time you like, and some of the food, and the massages, which are funny. But being with both our Mums, and Charlie...'

I'm chatting to my sister, who is full of questions. I'm outdoors, sat on a bench in the sun, wrapped in the towelling robe that was laid out for me on my bed, and my freshly-washed hair in an expertly-wound towelling turban. Like some celebrity. In front of me there's a huge chestnut tree, covered in white flowers, like a Christmas tree with candles. They gently sway in the breeze. 'So what's the food, was dinner nuts and seeds?'

'Dinner? No, it wasn't nuts and seeds with carrot juice! We had poached salmon and salad and the desert was mint non-dairy ice cream with chocolate chips, and, get this, Shaz and Mum decided we'd all share a bottle of prosecco! How cool was that?'

Zoe squeals into her phone. 'Awesome! You said, two days with Charlie, how do I survive? Okay, what else? You said something was funny?'

I tell her about the massage couches, and that we started today with a few lengths in the Olympic pool.

'I bet it's not really Olympic!'

'It is almost. Anyhow with a swim. Then we had pedicures, and head massage! And of course, the pedicurist ended up doing my toenails green and blue!'

'Like a mermaid. Like a selkie! Watch out — a gorgeous personal trainer might appear, and nick your sealskin!'

'Mm — Dad has a song about that, he used to sing it with his school girlfriend, he told me. A folk song. Anyhow, gotta go!'

That's it: I've stepped out of my normal skin like a selkie – a mythological Scottish creature that can shed its sealskin! But, take me back to the shore, let's find my skin and pull it back on.

Charlie, in her towelling robe and turban, is waiting inside by the reception desk. So funny, everyone wandering about as if they're at home, dressed in swimmers or towels or bathrobes. I suppose all spas are the same? 'What now? Do they do coffee here?' Charlie asks.

'Shall we look? Or rather,' I act out exaggerated sniffing, 'shall we see if we can sniff it out?'

'Like bloodhounds?' she says, doing a comic imitation she thinks looks like a dog.

'As coffee hounds? Let's see: can you smell anything?'

At the café, we choose iced lattes with coconut milk and huge slices of carrot cake. We sit at a little round table, wearing our drying swimwear with white towels as turbans on our heads. Charlie pulls out her amazing new iPhone to take selfies. She sends one off straightaway to her dad, and another '*To my bestie, Olivia* — that is, my bestie next to *you*, Alice.'

'As in, from your school? Is your boarding school okay then?'

Mum said Charlie might be lonely. Doesn't sound like it. Or does including me there tell me something?

'It's shit,' she says, 'GCSEs — aren't you worried? Didn't you go and stay with that aunt I met once – Daze? To work over the holidays?'

'Mum told you that?' I stop, something urges me not to share the Chapel House news. 'To escape my sister and her little friends,' I say, 'and to see Daze who is the coolest aunt.'

'I wish I had an aunt like that. Jos and Gussie are kind of cool grandparents, but they think now I'll get all these top grades, because they made Mum and Dad decide I'd go to this posh school, for my dyslexia. But dyslexia doesn't go away,' she snaps her fingers, 'like that. You're in smaller classes, you get given more time and stuff, but, it's not like magic, is it.' She puts down her cake fork, and bites on her thumb nail. 'My other school, they didn't expect anything.'

'So why not stay there?'

'Boring people? Bullying? Racism?'

'Racism?'

'Like they use the P-word?'

'Oh – gosh – but you're not!'

'Where you're wrong. *Of course* they were wrong, but not *totally*. You remember my dad's like quite dark? Like he has olive skin an' that?'

Eliot. As a kid, I thought he and Charlie were beautiful, exotic, their pale brown skin, and those deep brown eyes. 'And he's adopted? Well Mum and Dad got into family history. Mum loves poking about in the past, and then Dad thought he'd try finding his birth mother.'

'Wow,' I say. 'Did he find her? Did they get on?'

'She's Spanish. Like southern Spanish? She's from Andalucia.'

'That's not...' I'm thinking, well, some people want an adopted baby to match their own looks, but Jos and Gussie chose a Spanish baby, and I'm wondering if there's an interesting story. But Charlie's looking quite upset – or is she angry?

'Listen!' she leans right across the table. 'It's all more complicated! It's bloody well screwed up my family! It's probably why Mum has brought us here!'

I'm stunned. 'How? Why? You mean, to get away for a bit of perspective, like my Dad would say?'

'Not exactly... really not at all. Different. Look, let's just not talk about this!' She jumps up so fast the table shakes, over goes her glass of half-finished latte, the bent straw floating in the mess, and her plate of cake crumbs lands on the floor. I'm left to pick up the broken bits, and apologise to the cafe woman. Charlie is nowhere.

Chapter 17

LEAVING THE SPA

Left at the table, I pick Charlie's plate up off the floor, and pile it on top of mine, while the waitress mops the table. 'Your friend seemed upset.'

'School bullying,' I say. 'I'll go and find her.'

'That's right, you go and cheer her up.'

Actually, I go up to the room I'm sharing with Mum, and feel thankful it's empty. Pulling off the spa-owned robe (it has a little logo which is embroidered just over your left boob, with the name of the place and a laurel wreath in green) I dress as my normal self in jeans and a cheese-cloth shirt, a sort of ethnic-looking retro outfit, and brush out my hair. The cafe woman said something about me going to look after my friend, and I smiled back, trying to sound nicer than I felt about this friend who wants to be back in my life. I didn't want to help, but now I've begun to see further into her life, maybe I should? So, Charlie's been bullied for being mixed race? Of course, that's going too far. So, she's half-Spanish. Loads of people take their holidays or even live there… It's bullying, but it's rubbish, it's because she's a new girl. But what happened to give Eliot that limp? Why's Mum so keen to be friends with Shaz again, like she needs support?

Down at the reception area, I notice a board advertising Things to Do, with a list including a gym and tennis courts. You can hire a racket and buy a net of balls. Sounds more like fun than being covered in mud or having your face massaged. I walk over there, and watch a couple of women in tracksuit bottoms, knocking a ball about, so now I'm ready with an idea to offer Charlie.

People are moving towards the main building, as it's nearly time for lunch. I make a proper search for Charlie. There's a little protected yard round the back of the kitchen, where the bins are, and there's Charlie, with one of the chefs, more like an apprentice chef or work experience guy. He's leaning back against the wall, having a smoke, and Charlie, a smile on her face now, is still in the towelling robe. As I watch, she's about to share his ciggie (a second time, judging by the coughing I heard as I was on my way round). 'Hey, I wondered where you'd gone!'

'This is Adam,' Charlie says, pointing at the guy, and at me, 'she's Alice.'

I think quickly, and say, 'Hi, Adam, I've just seen they've got tennis courts here, I'm wondering if Charlie wants to play tennis?'

Maybe she did really want to, because she extricates herself from leaning on the wall with a sultry look. 'Sorry about the plate and stuff.'

'Yeah, well, all mopped up in the cafe, d'you want to play? It's like really casual, we don't need proper outfits.'

'Maybe.'

They crack jokes, while I wait. Voices and laughter pass by. I look out from around the bins: people are going towards the dining room, where folding doors have been opened out to let the air and sunshine in. 'Lunch,' I say to Charlie.

She hands back what's left of the ciggie, and the guy — he must be about eighteen, like Fabian but, let's admit it, I find him far less attractive – the guy grinds it into the concrete under his foot, and then – they cuddle up, and kiss. He tries to get his hands under that robe: she squeals. Oh God, she's as silly as I expected. She's so not my type!

'Lunch when you've finished,' I say over my shoulder, as I join the hungry crowd.

Lunch is a salad with small slices of nut roast, and no other carbs. I go up to the room I'm sharing with Mum, after, get out my sketch book, and draw the huge tree outside our window. I revisit my revision calendar. I flip through *Jane Eyre* reminding myself of the plot, and what bits I liked or didn't. I re-read my essay about what Charlotte Bronte was saying in her book. I consider the significance and symbolism of Mr Rochester's poor wife, who was assumed to be mad, and wonder whether *Jane Eyre* would be published these days. I'm not in the mood for Chemistry, so I close the textbook. Instead I look out of the window and sketch one of the pyramids of white flowers. Then I see Charlie crossing the drive, coming from the wooded area beyond.

Soon afterwards, there's a knock on my door. It's Charlie. I've got over the need to make a sarky remark about why I took myself off like a hermit, I ask nothing. We go down and find two girls to play tennis with. After the game I tell Charlie that the bullies only said what they did because she was new. 'You reckon?' she says.

Tomorrow, we go home! Not the best of weekends, but interesting to see into the way some people spend their time. Body polishes! Head massage!

♥ ♥ ♥

In the car, driving home, we talk about Charlie and the bullying.

Mum says: 'Did Charlie join her present school mid-term or in a form that doesn't usually have a new intake? Bullies are often fuelled by their own past, and when someone new comes along, that unsettles them and they seize on anything they can to upset that person.'

'That's so crazy though. I mean, why begin by being horrible?'

'To keep your place in the power structure?' Mum says. 'Suppose Charlie made a real hit with their friends, and those friends gathered around her as the new girl to follow? Can you see what she's got that others might envy?'

'Nope. Not really. Maybe her beautiful hair? Maybe even her interesting looks?'

'Yes. She's physically quite mature in a good way, she can have poise, when she's happy, I've noticed. Even in her school skirt and that ugly tank top, she moved well.'

I begin to understand. I've been telling myself not to envy Charlie her looks. To understand that it was much more than embarrassment which made me want her not to meet Fabian. Why I didn't introduce them.

'So she'd pull the guys... yes... I do see that. Though in that school there are only boys in the lower part... none she'd find interesting. But, she like bolted. After mentioning the bullying.'

I'd rather not admit my true feelings to Mum right now. She's got antennae, anyway. And she doesn't take it further, she simply asks, 'But the two of you got along all right, you did enjoy being there?'

'Kind of. It was an experience. Not really us, was it? Not, like, really me.'

'I loved the massage. I'm relaxed and ready to tackle those fund-raising forms. And Shaz said this morning that Charlie's definitely in a better place now, mood-wise. So, you've helped.'

I think: or maybe it was Adam in the woods.

'And you did do some revision.'

'If reading a set book in bed, and sketching a tree outside our window, counts!'

'Shaz said you'd explained something on the science syllabus to Charlie?'

'Yeah, it wasn't hard. She picked it up like she'd not been taught it before.'

'There you go then, complementary strengths.'

'Yeah, right: the beauty and the swot!'

'Sweetie, I didn't mean it like that!'

'Then don't say it,' I mumble under the noise of some opera playing on the car radio.

For a while, we're silent. Verdi's *Chorus of Hebrew Slaves* follows the other opera segment on Classic FM. Then, I try to quiz Mum about what's going on with us getting close to Charlie's family again. 'So, you and Shaz were chatting late last night. D'you know what's up with Charlie's Dad? I mean, the limping? Charlie said not an accident, it just happened. Limps don't just happen. And what're they so gloomy about? Okay, Dad's always meeting up with that bunch of other disgruntled GPs, worrying about the NHS, but Eliot's left general practice. In fact, medicine altogether, hasn't he?'

Mum's eyebrows draw together, she frowns at the road. 'We were talking about future plans,' she says, and reaches to switch stations on the radio. She chooses Radio Three, and Peter Maxwell Davies's *Farewell to Stromness* is playing. Which is okay with me. 'Oh wow, I love it!' she says.

'We all do.'

'Dad plays it on the piano sometimes.'

'Tries to!' I remember Zoe mentioning the selkie legend, and Dad's old girlfriend who he sang with. For a second I imagine, suppose they'd become an item and were singer-songwriters, and he hadn't become a doctor? What would that be like? Would I be me? Or someone else? Might I not exist? Back to Eliot, 'Mum, Eliot – Charlie's dad – any ideas?'

'Mmm?'

I wait. But as the announcer comes on with the News, Mum flicks the sound down and says, all emotional, 'Granny can't really mean to sell the house over Des's head and move to Baker Street... I must go down there and... try to talk to them...' And she takes her right hand off the wheel and wipes it across her face. Embarrassing me: evidently *Farewell to Stromness* has got Mum crying about Chapel House... I stare ahead, to stop myself crying too. I can't talk about this. Meanwhile a green local library van joins our road, and now it's leading us all towards the Oxford ring road, and ultimately home. Mum sniffs, and says 'I'm going turn off, and pop into M and S to grab a few things. That Stromness piece is so beautiful, sorry to react, Ally. While we're in there, I can toss in a couple of pairs of white socks for Zo-zo's tennis kit.'

And so it goes. Whatever's wrong with Charlie's dad, it's not up for discussion. Neither is Granny's scheme to retire to the big smoke.

Mum turns the sound up on the radio, a Mozart violin concerto, we reach the roundabout and head off down Banbury Road towards the shopping centre, for groceries and socks. 'What about those cookies you like, Ally? Chocolate chip with – what was it? Ginger? Cranberries?'

All cookies are okay when you have something on your mind. When you ask and parents don't tell. So, I don't even mumble 'whatever'. What I really want to know about though is the crucifixion painting, because that must be about something very important in her childhood. All their childhoods. For that, I need to get a bit closer to Daze than talking about the alterations which turned an old Bethel, or Bethesda, or whatever it was called, into Chapel House. I need to uncover these mysteries: Charlie's dad's limp (and the secrecy around it), Granny selling her house, Daze growing up with Mum and Aunt Hattie in that science culture. Also, who at school could've had an abortion. Four things, and my GCSE exams.

'Anything. Just let's get home,' I snap. I know I'm being what Mum calls a right cow. I know because I feel prickly inside, and no, I don't like myself much, today, either.

Until there's a ping from my phone, as we park near M and S, and that totally changes my day: Fabian wants to meet in town and 'we'll do something.'

Mum's saying something about me not needing to come in the shop with her. 'I think I will though,' I say, 'maybe I want to decide which of those cookies I want?'

She smiles, and says, 'Something good – that text? I don't need to know the details.'

'Something to make up for the dreary bits of the weekend,' I say.

Chapter 18

DAZE'S PAINTING AND A WALK WITH FABIAN

So, after that stupid weekend, maybe I've done my best to help Charlie by spending time with her? And I have a decent afternoon to look forward to. And then, after a snack lunch, as I run upstairs to get changed for my meet-up with Fabian, at last a message arrives from Daze! She'll be telling me something more about that creepy painting – here's the answer to how she thought of that idea — I'm almost shaking with excitement as I click to open the text:

'It's in a book I read, and it spoke to me. Like, this is my situation, same as the guy in the book.'

Book? In a *book?* 'Well, say what book!' I almost shout at my phone. No title, no author, nothing to help me find out more. And, can't right now, I've got to catch a bus, or cycle, and be in town in half an hour. Hastily I snap back a quick answer, typing *'what book? can I look this up?'* as I shove my feet into my trainers and decide there's no time to find the perfect outfit, I'll have to wear the jeans and top I put on this morning at the Spa.

Downstairs I hurry through the house, and get caught by Dad, 'Hey, where're you off to?'

'Out. Meeting Fabian. And maybe some other people? No time to chat, I'm late!'

'Wait – does your Mam know?'

''Course, he rang while we were travelling. Home. From the Spa?'

'Okay, just remember, we do like to...' I'm dashing out of the door, deciding I'll get a bus, as Dad calls, '...know where you are, and when you'll be back...'

Of course, I should've taken my bike, I think: waiting for a bus on a Sunday is stupid. So, I get hold of my thoughts and begin thinking straight. It's not like I can't send Fabian a text to say I'm on my way and got delayed (I do this). Waiting, eyes stretched down the road to any hopeful red object approaching that could be my bus, I think about what book Daze could've meant. Surely she either means something totally obvious I'd be able to guess, or she's trying to stop me knowing why she had the idea. I decide to share the details of that strange piece of art with Fabian, see what he thinks. I'll need to describe Daze a bit more, filling in the kind of person she is, and her sometimes sharp and evasive answers.

We've arranged to meet outside Blackwell's bookshop in Broad Street, because there's less chance of bumping into people from school, and because it's near all sorts of stuff we might want to do. Soon as we're together, I apologise for the wait, 'I had this text from my aunt Daze, the artist one who really should have Chapel House as her inheritance, and she was being super annoying!'

'Tell me? About the family row you walked in on?'

'No, I'd asked her about a painting she did – all she said was, she got her inspiration from a book. A book – no title, nothing! I mean what's that about? If she'd said, we could've hunted for it. They might have a copy here! But, no clues, so frustrating.'

'What's it like? The painting? There must be something to go on?'

'Religious paintings? Crucifixions? Icons?'

Fabian makes a face, 'That's pretty vague – contemporary? Renaissance?'

'I – don't really know where it fits. Icon-like. Only... this is really – look, can we go somewhere and I'll describe it? Daze is into this feminist artist – Judy Chicago – and her group, but you wouldn't have heard of her, I don't think.'

'No, sorry. Mum probably would. You could ask her about the painting?'

'Maybe. I mean, thanks for that thought.'

Would I feel okay asking Fabian's mother? She's Dr Francesca Russell — she's some kind of an expert in art, not just a person who likes looking at paintings. She knows Mum via the university... And I remember she's Catholic too... I suppose that means that Fabian is, officially. I hadn't considered that.

Blackwell's has a small corner upstairs where you can have coffee — expensive, but we decide to go there, not look for anywhere else. Here we are, all among the books, sipping real coffee, very hot and rather too strong for my taste, and eating cake.

'So — Daze's painting?' says Fabian.

I stop, lift up my coffee cup, put it back in its saucer. Take a breath, and look steadily at Fabian's face, which I know will change when I've said it all. 'It's not the style, it's the subject. It's – it's based on – it's *like* a crucifixion – but the person on the cross, it's a child, and the actual cross part isn't like a piece of wood, it's – a woman...'

His face is, like, 'Oh my God!' but only for a moment, then he says, slowly, 'Okay – this sounds like something really deep she wanted to say. Did she paint it recently?'

'No! She was like my age, she was sixteen, maybe not quite? It was done when she was still at school.'

'And it's – competent? I mean, she's a trained artist now, so – is it realistic?'

'Oh God, yes. I wish I had a photo.' For some reason, I feel so relieved to've told him and he's not shocked or anything, and he's interested, not making sarky remarks. 'And then, she tells me, she had the idea from reading a book!'

'Well, she could just mean the Bible of course,' Fabian says, shaking his head and giving a shrug. 'They're not religious are they, your mum's folks? She may not have – I don't know, Ally. The story of the crucifixion – the Roman way of doing executions... I don't know, what do you think?'

'I think, she'd have said if she meant the Bible. She's kind of blunt about naming things, usually.'

'Unless she didn't want you to know.'

For some reason I haven't told him that the child is a self-portrait and the woman could be my granny... It seems a bit too personal.

I drink some more coffee. It tastes better cold. 'So here we are, in a bookshop, and we can't know what she meant.'

'Seems so. If you've finished... How about we walk in the Parks a bit? Think some more about this?'

We do. We walk up Parks Road and past the University Museum. We discover that both our dads used to take us there to look at the dinosaur skeletons, and the fossils and interesting rocks. We go into the Parks, and walk all around the edge, and down a path through the middle where we stop to watch cricket practice outside the pavilion. We visit the duck pond, where two swans are eyeing each other up, and walk up onto the rainbow bridge where we stand looking at the river along with a load of early tourists. The trees are still in the pale lime-green of new leaves. Should we go down the other side and walk to Marston? Maybe another day. Fabian has no more ideas about what book could have inspired Daze than I have. We turn back, holding hands, and begin comparing Fabian's grandparents, the Catholic ones, with Granny and Grandpa Mullins. Their beliefs seem very different, though the do-nots are similar. 'But we're not bound by all that, are we?'

Which leads us to other things.

Until it's time to leave, and Fabian walks me all the way home, up Headington Hill, pushing his bicycle, which he'd left chained to the railings at the entrance, even though he lives on the other side of town, in Southmoor Road, with a garden backing onto the canal. On the walk, I go back to the subject of Daze's painting, and we agree, she can only mean it's the Bible.

So as I have one, a christening present, living on one of my bookshelves, I'll have a hunt through. But I can't yet, because Mum insists on inviting Fabian to stay for afternoon tea, which is such a conventional thing, and she's even made an impressive-looking cake, so we exchange glances, and grin across the room, 'so much cake!' which is nice. Later we encounter Dad crossing the hall, and I have this feeling that he's come out of the study just in time to see us saying goodbye. My instinctive response is to haul Fabian outside by one arm, and on the doorstep we kiss, under the prickly climbing rose which clutches at my hair.

I go up to my room, still feeling the warmth of him as we walked, and as we said goodbye under the flopping branches of the rose, and I read up the story of Good Friday to remind myself of the details. But that doesn't give me any clues: nothing about a woman or a child, nothing to connect with Daze's idea at all. I'm in the wrong book, obviously. And Daze doesn't message a reply to my further questions.

End of Part 1

Part 2

Chapter 19

GRANNY CARO'S SECOND INVITE

School is increasingly obsessed about exams. I've blocked out, on my revision calendar, that almost-six-weeks of abnormal life, and of course which days I'm actually in an exam. The calendar's stuck to the fridge door with magnetic letters, just in case the parents forget... with another copy in my room, though I'm unlikely to forget!

Though we do also need time off (thank you, Mum, for underlining this for me, on my calendar). So now's the time to spend with my first serious boyfriend, and yes of course my first what they call *public exams* – and try to work out how these things can work together and not crash? One time, Fabian and I (nice, that, 'Fabian and I'), well, we, with Nina and Jack, her guy, meet up for coffee at the Cafe Nero in the High Street after school. Possibly not Mum's idea of time off. But she should understand – she was crazy about – hum, yes – my Dad – though that was more helpful, they re-met *after* her Uni finals...

At present, I'm in the garden with a history textbook, re-reading what I already know, eating crisps, and waiting for Mum to get home and start dinner. It's such a gorgeous dry, warm, evening with the honeysuckle scenting everything, the kind of evening that makes me re-run in my head our walk in the Parks, and take it further, rather than imagining Elizabeth the First planning how to get rid of her cousin Queen Mary of Scotland.

Suddenly my phone leaps into noisy life. Hoping this is Daze, and she's going to tell me what was the book she mentioned, I seize it out of my pocket to answer... Big downer though – Granny Caroline has called me, direct, to schmooze: as if she can seduce us, after letting out that she's wanting to sell Chapel House! I was so angry when I heard about that, that I haven't wanted to think about her offer of a fun weekend in London to celebrate my birthday. 'Alice, darling,' she begins, 'I realise I should have apologised to you girls for the shock I gave you all about my future plans, so soon after setting up my little scheme for your birthday celebrations...'

I want to say, 'Yes, you should've — why didn't you?' But something makes me say politely, 'Yes, that was a shock, but...'

'I'm so, so sorry, sweetie,' Granny jumps in, 'I was so busy with this and that down here, and longing to let you see the flat and experience some real theatre...'

'We have two here, Granny, the Apollo's like the old fashioned formal type and the Playhouse, which is much nicer.' There, I've half-managed to be sort-of politely rude, and cold.

'Of course you do, darling. But this will be the West End! Anyway, thank you for accepting my apology.' (I haven't. It still hurts to be reminded she's planning to sell Chapel House.) 'And what I was about to say was, I need to check on a few things: what do you girls like to eat? You're the birthday girl, so I thought I might order a cake from the wonderful vegan bakery I've discovered. All you youngsters are going vegan these days, aren't you?'

'I'm not. Zoe might want to, she's totally into the environment, but no signs she's vegan, yet.'

'Well, their cakes are to die for. And I thought, as this will be a fun time entirely for you two, we'll go to the British Museum or the Vicky and Albert – whichever you like – and then it's *Mamma Mia* in the evening.'

'Mum said.'

'I had to ask her, which one of the two musicals I've wanted to see. So, all arranged, a birthday treat after your exams?'

But, yeah, I'm not taken in: she's invited both of us. It's a ploy, to make us happy about her selling Chapel House over Des's head. It's not going to work. 'Great, thank you, I mean, it's very kind, I love theatre,' (I notice Mum coming down the garden — what a relief, rescue!). 'But about exams, I've sort of got to go, they've given us a shedload of homework, revising...' I say to Granny, waving my phone at Mum, who gives me a questioning look. 'Granny,' I mouth, then 'Mum's right here, you'd like a word, wouldn't you?' I say into the phone.

Mum hurries up — she shakes her head but puts out her hand and takes my phone.

Zoe appears through the sliding doors into the garden, while Mum puts on a sweetie-type voice, 'Hi Mum, yes it's Jen here...' I take Zoe's arm and pull her out of earshot. Very quietly, I say 'Zoze, are you feeling much like going to Granny's for this treat she's arranged?'

'Not if she's still selling Chapel House.'

'That's Granny on the phone now, about our visit. I haven't said anything yet, but I wonder if we could get Mum to cancel it?'

'What about Dad though? He might say cancelling is rude.'

Just then I feel Mum's hand on my shoulder. 'So now I'd better be getting on with dinner,' Mum says, handing back my phone. 'But I know how you both feel, and Chapel House was my home, not just my holiday home.'

Zoe throws herself on Mum, with a big hug, 'So you're on our side!'

Mum stops moving towards the house to hold Zoe's shoulders and look into her face, 'Darling, we do have to allow people to be themselves and let them do what they decide. I know it hurts *us*, not only because we can't expect to stay for holidays. We might...'

'Buy a cottage so we can...' Zoe begins.

'... Zo-zo, I was going to say, it will be a treat to stay with Granny sometimes in London, explore the museums, go shopping, and catch some shows and concerts. It's something you'll grow to appreciate.'

'Big deal,' Zoe says, and she slumps off ahead of us. Evidently to the kitchen, as we hear the noise of the lid being taken off the biscuit tin. I pack up my revision, we go inside, close and lock the doors, and follow Zoe into the kitchen: she's eating a chocolate biscuit. She takes a bite, and then says, partly through the biscuit, 'I'd rather be catching lizards on the cliff path, and learning to surf properly.'

I add a thought, 'Yes. And where'll Des live?' Whether they've been married or living together for years and years, Granny not mentioning where Des would live is scary: not only where he'd live, but more how he'd feel, whether he wants this, and whether he'd still be part of our family.

Mum says, 'I don't know, loves. I don't know any more than you. We haven't talked about that. She's simply invited you both to visit the flat and go to a show, nothing to do with her future plans. And I think you'd better go. It will be nice for Alice, after her GCSEs. It'll be fun, you'll see. And the flat's all 1930s, quite interesting.'

'Huh, that sounds like you two planned it, together? Because I'd said I didn't want a big sweet sixteen party?'

'No, entirely Granny's plan, but she did ask which show, as you know, and I told her what I thought. Zozo, I'm cooking now, don't hog all those biscuits before supper!'

'Okay, but we had practice for Sports Day *all afternoon*, picking teams for stuff, and you know exercise lowers the blood sugar so I was *starving*,' Zoe exclaims. 'It's like I haven't eaten for a week! I *can't* like a place in London more than Chapel House.' Mum calmly opens the fridge and reaches inside. Out come eggs and a hunk of cheese, some salad veg. Zoe thumps her on the arm, 'Doesn't Granny know about the pollution? The air in cities is full of fumes from all the traffic!'

'I really have to make dinner,' Mum says, 'and then, there's an important meeting tomorrow, so I'll have to work this evening.'

'For what?' my sister asks. 'What's the meeting about? We need a meeting, a family one...' I'm shaking my head at her to try to stop her annoying Mum, while Mum says, busy at the sink, washing the lettuce 'That's why I need to read – hop it for now, and I'll call you to eat.'

'Can you just think about whether we don't have to go?'

'Let's leave Mum to it,' I say, moving towards the door, clutching my books, but Mum almost shouts at us, 'For once!' and then, a bit calmer, 'Look, I promise we'll talk another time, but please, can you put your disappointment aside for a weekend and try to enjoy it as a holiday treat? She wants you to get to know London, which is where she grew up. And Alice, you do like real theatre!'

'Yes, but...'

'Oh, and I've just remembered, Daze rang earlier and she sends her love.'

'Daze?'

'Yes, Daze.' So, Daze talked with Mum, but not to me?

'We shan't...' Zoe begins.

'Wait, Zoe – it's important – Mum, were you and Daze talking about the moving to London idea? What did she say? She almost lives at Chapel House, she sells stuff through the artists' commune — I bet she's against it!'

'Yes, we were, and no I can't say we decided to do anything.'

'Isn't Daze going to try to stop it happening?' says Zoe.

Mum shakes the lettuce in the colander, leaves the colander on the side, and kind of makes gathering-together movements towards us using her hands. I rest my bum against the corner of the table, books clutched in my arms. Zoe stands beside Mum. 'I told you, I understand how you feel, I feel sad too. Chapel House was my home, not only a holiday home,' says Mum.

'But now it's *our* holiday home,' Zoe says.

'Well, Zo-zo, that isn't true really – is it? It's Granny Caro and Des's actual home, and they very generously let us stay there when they're away, if our holidays coincide. You've grown up thinking that will always happen...'

'No, I haven't. Of course I know one day it won't. And I don't think Granny Caroline's invitation to London was generous of her, I think it was to – to get us to like her, and to think what she's doing is okay – which it isn't!'

'Your invitation to visit has got nothing to do with her move, her possible move, in her mind. She apologized to me that she'd turned up like that — we weren't meant to know yet...' she adds. 'As I said, Chapel House was my growing-up home, and I do miss it, I even sometimes miss Cornwall. But it's not a place I could live, and I understand my mother wanting to move away now she's retired.'

'Really?'

'Really? Listen. Cornwall mayn't be the least prosperous area in England, but it is one of them. Think about it: people there rely on tourism and farming... and fishing. Those don't bring in enormous wealth. Working on boats is a dangerous business. If I didn't know before, I learned that when the Penlee lifeboat went down with all hands lost. Some of the kids in my class lost fathers, or brothers. Or uncles. Even several members of their family.'

'Gosh – you knew these people?'

'They came to my school – it was the main secondary in our area — Cape Cornwall County Secondary. Granny and Des agreed we'd all three be educated alongside the local kids, even at the secondary stage, fitting into the community.'

''Cos they didn't want Grandpa paying after he went off to teach at CalTech?'

'It wasn't really so odd: Granny hated boarding school... Anyhow, yes, I was in the same class as some people whose families were on the Penlee lifeboat, when it was wrecked back in December 1981 – I was sixteen, done my first public exams. I left soon after that. We had to move on after we were sixteen...'

'To go somewhere so's you'd get into Cambridge.'

'They didn't have a sixth form, and I wanted to do A levels and try for Cambridge. Which is one reason why living in the far west of Cornwall has disadvantages, even though, yes, it is beautiful. It's is a hard life, mostly a hands-on life, with limited opportunities. All three of us knew that. If we weren't going to work in tourism or something to do with farming or fishing, what would we do? We wanted to see the world where there were opportunities to do all sorts of unlimited things. And we were lucky, we could.'

'I suppose you're right,' Zoe sighs.

'Yeah, guess it makes sense,' I say. 'But what about the lifeboat?'

'There was something like a force eight gale. The ship in trouble was a smallish cargo vessel called the Union Star. The lifeboat was called out into a huge sea, enormous waves crashing onto the shore. What probably happened was that the giant waves picked up the lifeboat and smashed it down onto the Union Star. Both ships were wrecked. Nobody survived...' Mum puts her hand across her eyes a moment, 'the crew were all from the little village of Mousehole, you know where that is?'

'Yep, along the coast from ...'

'The disaster changed Mousehole forever. You can imagine... People moved away to build their lives again... I remember it was a horrible Christmas, because that had all happened the week before, just around the end of term. When they put the Christmas lights back on again in Mousehole, they were only a couple of angels and a cross. It was that bad, we didn't really keep Christmas either. Some of those families were Granny's patients.'

The story made me think, if something like that happened to Dad – I mean, it couldn't, but I thought into how it'd feel.

I thought about the reality of living forever where most people aren't well off.

'Pound shops,' I say, into the silence.

'Exactly. And when I was at school, we were very aware of the fragility of life there. Cornwall gets quite a few subsidies, I think, from the European Union.'

'Mum's got work to do, remember?' I say to Zoe, 'shall we, like, help get supper?'

'No need,' Mum says, 'I'll be quicker on my own. You two do some homework, I'll call you.'

We go upstairs. I think the Penlee lifeboat has made us realise we are lucky to live here in Oxford among the academics and intellectuals. 'People aren't all well off here,' Zoe points out (it didn't really need saying), 'but would you say we are? Like quite well off?'

'I don't think it's so odd Granny let Mum and her sisters go to that secondary school. I mean, Granny's such a snob, but Des totally isn't. I think he made her.'

Chapter 20

After that conversation, sent away to get on with school stuff, we end up in my room, together, sitting on my bed. We don't talk about it much, but it goes like this.

'That sucks,' I say, wondering what work I should re-revise, and how long I have to settle down to it before we're called to eat.

'It was more than that. It was a cataclysm!' Zoe interrupts.

'Yep.'

'It was – a phrase our English teacher says we mustn't use too much – but that really *was* a perfect storm.'

'It was a storm which made it happen so... yeah, it was, it kinda made them all grow up before they—' I'm searching for what I mean here – not exactly 'take life seriously' (a Dad concept), or 'are really adult' (more Mum's thing) and 'ping! I'm interrupted by a text. Wish I hadn't looked: it's from Charlie.

And gives me a sinking feeling. Charlie, like me, is sixteen this year. And of course, being her, she's planning a Sweet Sixteen party. Whatever bullying there is, she'll have *some* friends from that boarding school, and they'll be her type — definitely not mine. I can imagine this party. I can hear the laughter, and the – banter, as it's called. I do not want to be invited!

Zoe taps my arm, 'Earth to Alice? You were saying, about what happened to the lifeboat.'

'Oh yeah, sorry. See this?'

She leans over, and I let her read Charlie's message, '*hey Alice, 10th July – save the date! (my actual birthday!) though we haven't totally firmed up – you'll be first to know – anyhow, best party ever! for my 16th! on a river barge with a band & dancing. sending invites sooooon. say you'll be there!*'

'So?'

'Listen, I think this party is on the same day as Granny bought those tickets for us to see *Mamma Mia* in London?'

'And?'

'I don't much fancy going to Charlie's party with her boarding school friends.'

'Why not?'

'You know the people in your year who talk boys, like, all the time? Maybe they even – send around pictures and stuff?'

'Yep. Does Charlie...?'

'I don't know she does. But, at the Spa, she was snogging with one of the staff – an apprentice. I mean, she didn't know him before or anything.'

'Right. At Base Camp we've talked about those things – I mean, when someone came to give a talk. Sounds horrible. And you can't – when you don't know someone...'

'Nope. And even ordinary people – not only churchy Base Camp people, can feel like that. So – do you remember the date Granny booked those tickets for? Mum told us, *July 10th, after exams are over.* My exams, and actually, the summer term. A weekend in London would be much more fun. Let's think now about– if we have to go, let's, like, at least enjoy the show?'

'And we'll tell Granny that although London is nice, Sennen's – more fun for us, now – only for holidays... we do understand?'

'We just learned why Cornwall is actually only – well probably only — magical for people like us, so yes. I suppose – we might apologise for being so angry as well?'

'Wouldn't that be a bit beyond apology? I'm still really sad. And for Des, it's not fair!'

'Dinner's ready!' Mum calls up the stairs, 'come on, what's keeping you?'

While we eat though a boring supper of salad, ham, and two kinds of cheese, I think a bit more about how Daze had told me, when we were on the cliff path, that Cornwall isn't always as kind as it all looked then, beautiful blue sea, dotted with boats. And in the Penlee Gallery: 'Look at their faces? Those women have a lot on their minds, a lot of responsibility to raise their kids, and see them go the same way – into the fishing boats, out on the uncaring sea?' (Daze's words, I remember, she can be poetic!)

I felt a bit got at. Or rather, ashamed: too old at nearly sixteen to be ignorant of the facts. And, as Daze went on: 'Hey, what is there to do here, for a career? 'Course I went off to Colombia to work for your Grandad Guthrie! Not having to do waitressing all through the summer holidays! Not staying here to do that all my life!'

I could've thought more about that. I could've thought sooner. I look across the table at Mum, quite ambitious as a teenager, now a research scientist working in the University, and I imagine how it would have felt to be her. *Four-eyes*, some of them called her, the GP's kid, head in her books. A swot, a geeky girl. Totally different types, like me and Charlie. She knew the other kids might be able to find work in Cornwall and be happy to stay, but she wanted to go further with her studies. When they had parties, did she feel like she didn't belong?

Chapter 21

A PUNTING TRIP

Anyhow, the clock's ticking: it's E-day, fifteenth of May, but we've made a plan. Last opportunity to enjoy ourselves before the exams begin, a kind of celebration in advance... Punting, on Saturday afternoon! Fabian and me, Nina and her guy Jack, Mariam and... Well, with her cousin Mahmoud actually, because we haven't yet found someone for her, and she's shy...

Useful having a calendar in my room. I've written *visit to Granny Caro in London* on there, now that we've given up on the idea of cancelling, due to Mum's revelation about the Penlee Lifeboat disaster, and that unwelcome text from Charlie. Which I have not replied to except to say thanks for thinking of me – not really true, I'd rather she hadn't!

So today's for punting. Though the weather's not quite so nice and summery as it was when we planned this. Zoe's off to an outdoor event at a nature reserve, with Base Camp, the Headleigh Parish Church 11-14s group. Mum and Dad are going to play tennis! So, our whole family's doing summer-type things.

Mum and Dad drop me off on their way to the tennis courts, and as I walk the rest of the way, through town, down the High Street, past Magdalen College, my stomach gradually fills up with butterflies. Am I wearing the right clothes? Is a tiny bit of make-up and a splodge of perfume the wrong thing for an outdoor date? Shall I look clueless if it is, and will Fabian mind if I don't look right for the event? I do think now that I have worn the wrong clothes: the few clouds have gathered together, and although I've got my skinny jeans on, my top is a wafty tunic, not terribly practical. And my long grey cardie is defo frumpy.

Anyhow, I can't change now! And they're all there as I arrive, and I get a hug from Nina and Mariam, and Fabian draws me into the group, and slips his arm around my back.

We've all brought snacks to eat in the boat. And Nina (who's wearing denim cut-offs with no tights despite the look of the weather), says, 'Look, it's an iconic day, guys, so we need souvenirs!'

'We don't,' Mariam, who's always practical, says, 'look at the sky! We should get on the river before it rains.'

The sky goes purple upstream as the sun beams out dazzlingly from behind a cloud. 'So, we go the other way,' says Nina, 'and avoid it.' She sweeps us girls into the kiosk, and begins raking through a shelf of different-sized beige-coloured furry teddy-bears, each wearing a navy T-shirt with *Oxford* across the front, all rather appealing. She picks one out, and holds it up, wiggling it at us, saying in a funny growly voice, 'It'll only be a shower, I can tell,' then puts it back on the shelf, and picks up a slightly bigger one, 'I'm buying this as a souvenir of – of the last day of my childhood!' We all groan. 'No, really – after exams we'll all be boring and serious, and have to think about careers and Uni and leaving home... so I'm buying my teddy bear in advance.'

'Advance of what? Will you need it when you're boring?'

'Shut up. Of course I shall. I'll be the one dragging everyone else out of boredom!'

Which is when Mariam decides to join in, selecting herself a smaller teddy, and I can't be left out so I look at what money I have, and buy one the same size, 'for my sister'. Nina also buys three 'Oxford' baseball caps in red, white, and blue, and once we're outside, where the guys are waiting for us making impatient noises, she slaps one each onto their heads, whether they want it or not. Fabian grins at me, like in some way we understand each other about Nina.

Next we hire our boat, assuring the people booking the boats out that we're over eighteen, and can punt, we've done it already, we live here. So we climb in, punt bobbing about under our badly distributed weight, sort ourselves out, and head off, down past the Botanic Gardens, following a kind of circular route. Punting looks easy, but it's not. No question of our boat being chauffeured by Punt Station people like some of the others going past, since the boys and Nina all think they're experienced from having grown up in Oxford. Our boat wobbles at first, then moves faster and a bit more smoothly, powered by Jack who acts totally confident until we collide with the riverbank. I let out a squeal but the other girls manage not to. Fabian takes over.

He is amazing. I lie back in the boat, alongside Mariam, supported by the slope of the hard seat, watching Fabian punting like it's natural to him, steering us back on course. Silhouetted against the greyness of the sky, his strong body making those smooth confident moves gives me a feeling I can't exactly define: a tingling all over, a desire to let go and sing (which of course I don't). There's probably a silly grin on my face. We've left the Botanic Gardens behind now. I close my eyes against the suddenly very hot sun…

Then I hear Jack's voice, 'Hey, Fabian…' and my name, 'Alice…' entwined in the words… something I can't quite catch, though I hear *watching out for Ophelia*.

My eyes fly open. Which Ophelia? Me? Fabian does a dismissive kind of laugh (about what was said?) but my face is burning, not because of the sun (which is back behind that cloud).

Is this the Ophelia who floated down the river in Shakespeare's *Hamlet*? The one who some Pre-Raphaelite painted, while his model had to lie in a bath full of flowers, and later died of pneumonia? (Did she really die of it?) Is this my fault, because I'm wearing this silly top? (It looked fashionable in the window of the shop, but is it suggestive? Does the thin fabric show my bra? Whatever, it's too thin for the weather!)

Maybe I can listen to the banter which is going on and defend myself? Maybe I would've done, only Nina jumps up, shouting at Jack,

'Shut up – Alice is my friend, for God's sake!' and almost clutching at his throat. The whole attack (as he retaliates) rocks the boat wildly, worse than when it hit the bank.

I curl my body up onto the seat to keep out of their way, Mariam's curled up against me, Fabian still has hold of the punt pole which he's stuck into the bottom of the river like it could act as an anchor. Mariam's cousin pitches into the fracas, trying to stop them, Jack hits out at him, his glasses fly off into the water, and — disappear. He shouts at Jack – flailing his arms, rocking the boat even more, and Mariam shouts at him in Arabic, so he calms down a bit, but then they start a big ding-dong. Nina and Jack sit back down, but Nina's ranting at Jack for causing all this chaos and the loss of the glasses.

All suddenly goes quiet, except for the argument in Arabic, with Mariam interrupting her rant to tell me that Mahmoud is using words which women aren't supposed to hear. At least Fabian works the pole back into use and manages to guide the punt to the bank, where Mariam and Mahmoud climb out first, still arguing (as it appears), and everyone else calms down a bit. I'll never know what horrid joke Jack made about me. Nina says not to worry, he was teasing Fabian, it was a stupid remark and meant nothing. We're all uncomfortable with each other now, anyway, sat on the bank eating our snacks to occupy ourselves, rather than because we really want them.

Fabian loops one arm around my shoulders, and pulls me in, so I have to snuggle up, which makes Jack smile and begin saying something. Fabian tells him 'Piss off, Jacob!' and he shuts up a moment. Then choosing to turn this into another joke, he wanders off, rather obviously, towards a group of trees.

The sun hasn't come out again. Someone wonders about the time. Mahmoud makes to look at his rather super watch, and regrets 'Without them I can't make this out...' Nina moves to read the watch but Mariam intervenes, 'We need to take the boat back,' she says, 'time's almost up.'

Jack returns ('feeling so much better,' he says), and he, Nina, Fabian and me get in the punt. Mariam and her cousin waver on the bank, talking rapidly. We all know that, whatever else, the glasses are lost forever, and that a huge purple cloud is up ahead. The expedition has failed irredeemably.

'Look, I have Applied Maths paper two on Monday,' Mahmoud says. 'We need to find an optician, if anywhere's still open.'

'I wish I hadn't persuaded you to come punting,' Mariam says, almost in tears. 'And the family'll blame me about the glasses!'

'I won't allow them,' says Mahmoud.

'Jack will write them an apologetic letter,' Nina adds. 'Oh shit!' she says to me, 'How do I make him?'

Tempted by my disappointment with our fun expedition, I say suggestively, 'You know how,' then feel that was mean. Even if Nina might well do it.

Mariam and Mahmoud decide to walk to Boots opticians to try and get temporary reading glasses so he can see to write his Applied Maths exam on Monday. So we push off from the bank, with Nina punting. Rain begins to fall in huge drops. At least we're on the home stretch. Though by the time we reach the boat station at Magdalen Bridge, we're all soaked through. I start typing into my phone, asking Dad to pick us up in the car. A wobbly text full of typos arrives back: Zoe's in the car already and asks, *Dad says how many?* Once we've handed back the boat, Nina and Jack unlock their bikes and pedal off towards East Oxford: 'we're gonna have a take-away at mine if my mum's out...' she shouts. I type back to Zoe-on-Dad's-phone, *two.*

At the boat station Fabian and I stand under what shelter we can find. I keep looking out anxiously for Dad's car. I have my cardie over my head and shoulders: Fabian did offer me his sweatshirt (maroon, *Geek Crew* in white across the back) but that would've left him nothing but a shirt against the rain which is falling in vertical lines. At last Dad's car appears and swishes to a halt. Heartsink moment: there are two little heads in the back, my sister and her current bestie, Annalise Thornton.

'Okay, Zo-zo, hop out, Alice, hop in, Zoe hop back,' says Dad, opening the nearside back door of the car. He's wearing his old waxed jacket (kept hanging in the utility room to wear when gardening) over his tennis clothes, which is bizarre. Thank God Fabian has seen my Dad, who's a friend of his parents, in his ordinary clothes!

Zoe doesn't hop out, she leans from her seat, 'That puts Alice in the middle!'

'You noticed,' says Dad. He holds opens the front passenger door, like he's a chauffeur. 'Fabian, good to see you, shall we have the pleasure of your company?'

Fabian hesitates a second, then accepts the invitation. I don't wait for Zoe to argue, and slide into the window seat, making Zoe move to the middle and cuddle up to her friend. Doors closed, seat belts sorted and secured, we head off, accompanied by giggles and squeaks from the youngsters beside me. It's obvious they rather enjoy having been soaked and now Annalise is wringing out her hair, having first flipped her plaits at Zoe, such long plaits that I got sprinkled as well. They think this is funny? To have been soaked in a downpour?

It's obvious that practical Dad has no plan to bring Fabian back to ours, as he takes us right round the Plain and back over the bridge into Oxford, before I can get a word in to ask if Fabian can come back for high tea. The giggling continues all the way to Southmoor Road. Plait-flipping and shrieks, and bits of adolescent humour.

Dad draws up outside the Russells' house. Fabian says, 'See you, Ally!' as if just – well, just any friend, as he gets out, thanking Dad for going out of his way to deliver him home. Well, okay, I do get a sort of hug, midway into moving to the front seat now it's free (and warm from him sitting in it!).

Now we've got to drop Annalise at her house. Where Zoe, of course, pointlessly gets out in the rain to accompany Annalise to her front door. Something overflows inside me, contempt and fury, once she gets back in the car. I turn round and hiss at her:

'I was so ashamed, you two behaving like little kids!'

'Yes, and we had to sit here sopping wet while Dad took your fancy boyfriend home!'

'Well your little friend didn't exactly help, flicking her hair over everyone!'

'Shut up Alice, we were having a nice time till you arrived!'

'Well lucky you, I've had a shit time punting and you've just made it worse.'

Dad looks hard at me, as water drips off his slicked-down wet hair, 'What are you talking about, Alice? This was a request to be rescued and I could've said no and taken those two home while you caught a bus.'

'Not the point,' I say, 'those two made me feel so ashamed. They giggled and fell around like nursery children, in front of Fabian. What'll he be thinking about me?'

'Nothing,' Dad says dismissively. 'Now let's away home to dry clothes and our tea.' He snaps on the radio very loud and jazz is playing — Dad's message that we finish our argument.

We are both pretty much silently crying. I am totally ashamed again. This time of my own behaviour. 'Seatbelts on, please,' he says, 'however emotional you feel.'

I bite my lips all the way home, not in anger but in total misery, to stop myself crying noisily, at the end of what was meant to be my beautiful day out. How daft is that?

Chapter 22

Of course, Zoe and I soon make up that row in the car. We were expected to apologise, and we do, both for being silly with Annalise (Zoe) and for flying into a rage (me). And Dad adds in that he is feeling fed up – partly with the rain cutting short their time on the tennis court, but mainly with the results of the General Election a couple of weeks back. He says mysterious things about the future of the National Health Service being in doubt now.

It's Monday. The 13th, how suitable. Two days till the Fatal Day: think about nothing but exams until half term. When I get back from school, there's this silver envelope waiting for me. Maybe a good luck card? Who with the carefully rounded handwriting sent this? Maybe my cousin Chloe, one of the saner Mullins relatives, who's already at Uni? Ticking off today on my revision calendar, dump my biology notes on my bed to read one last time, then sit and open the envelope.

The card's pink with silver writing. *'Charlotte Parker Pollard is inviting you to a River Party!'* Oh no! I rapidly skim read the whole thing: *Located on a river barge, sailing up the Thames, buffet supper, music and dancing, chocolate fountain.* Chocolate fountain? Never seen one of those – yet. Date and time: *10th July, 7.00pm, carriages at midnight.'*

Charlie said *probably* 10th July: and yes, it is! So, thanks to having already accepted Granny's invite, and persuaded my sister that we should, I can say no, sorry, to Charlie, without feeling at all bad about that! Sooo relieved: I'll explain that Granny had already bought the theatre tickets to take us to a show in London, on July 10th, so we can't disappoint Granny and waste her tickets. Granny asked first, which Mum's certain to remind me, and Charlie should understand, even if she's disappointed. Which she will be. Breathe again, no more threat of certain-to-be-awful party.

No chocolate fountain, but also no posh airheads. I don't hate airheads, but I'd have nothing to chat with them about. Only nerdish things they'd despise. Taking another look at the invite, I see a little arrow, added in blue pen, at the right-hand bottom corner. I turn the card over. *'Party will be lush!! And Mum says, after the Spa was such a blast, would you like to spend some of half term at ours?'*

Not sure I'd call the spa visit a blast. But help! I don't much want to be one-to-one with Charlie at her house! Can I escape this invite as well? Mariam's invited me for a revision stay-over, but it's only Monday to Thursday, 'cos they've got visitors. I need an excuse...

Meanwhile, biology notes: *in cell biology, explain the main subcellular structures... Explain the importance of cell differentiation...* I hang onto that card, I leave it in the notes to mark my place. I'll tell Mum that I'm okay about missing the party, so she doesn't try to start re-negotiating days and weekends with Granny. Adults are odd about things like loyalties to friends, but it's kind of dishonest, isn't it, to pretend you enjoy something when you don't, and that'll never change and be your thing?

After dinner, and final revising, studying the diagrams so I can draw them if necessary, yawning and with my head buzzing with biology, I go downstairs, hunting a snack. Mum's talking on the phone: 'I'm supposed to be getting away down to Sennen for a few days' half term break, from the weekend, with Max and Zoe...'

My ears tune in: hey, did we know that, at half term we're going to Chapel House? Don't think they told us, but lovely surprise! A treat in the middle of GCSEs!

Suddenly, I have a chilling thought: Mum only said 'with Max and Zoe' — what about me? Surely there isn't a plot with Shaz for Charlie to invite me to hers at half term?

But 'and Alice' is understood – isn't it? Don't be daft.

On my way to the kitchen I pause, standing back against the wall so that Mum can't notice me loitering in the hallway if she twizzles round from her desk. Prick up my ears to hear more of this conversation. Who is she telling about half term plans, and why? Might Daze and Rothko be coming from Yorkshire? I'll ask Daze more about that strange painting, and which book gave her the idea.

Of course, if we're going to Chapel House at half term I won't be able to accept Charlie's invitation to stay, excellent! Though it leaves me more vulnerable to her disappointment over the party. She could get really mean over that.

Mum ends her conversation and turns back to her computer. Tap, tap, tap – another journal article, another plan for an experiment, or funding... For a moment, I picture being small, before I could read proper books, and before Zoe could read at all. We had stories in bed. I'd listen sitting on Zoe's bed, wrapped in my duvet. I miss the cosiness.

Suddenly I'm surrounded by a wonderful waft of chocolate, a clinking noise like mugs on a tray, and Zoe's voice: 'Gosh, you gave me a fright, lurking in the shadows like that!'

Well, chocolate fountain this isn't, but my sister has appeared from the kitchen, with a tray, mugs and biscuits. Cinnamon biscuits she made to atone for the fight. 'Not really lurking, on my way to find... Ooh, one for me there?' I say.

'Nope. Mum and me... she's helping with my project on climate change.'

'That your coursework?'

'Yep. Mum's typing out a list of wildflowers and seashore creatures she used to find when she was my age. I'll research if you can still find them on the cliffs and the beach.' She pauses, 'It's hot choc with vanilla. I could do you one?'

Yum, I think, rejecting the idea of a banana. 'That'd be nice.'

'Zo-zo, this smells like heaven, darling,' Mum calls out, then swivels her chair and notices me, 'And Alice!' Patting the arm of the two-person sofa, inherited from Grandpa Alisdair's study, where it had been given a silly name, because people came over to discuss their weddings with him. 'Have a love seat.'

There's a pile of files on the oddly shaped sofa. 'Can I move these?'

'Careful. Can you dump them on the window seat?'

Five minutes later, we're all piled close together, Mum and me on the sofa, Zoe on one of its arms. Cosy with hot drinks, munching Zoe's home-made cinnamon biscuits.

'I don't think climate change has quite decimated the wildflower population of Cornwall yet,' says Mum.

'It will soon. And even if not climate change, farmers are using chemicals which are killing the bees!' replies Zoe.

'Okay, which wildflowers are we talking about?' Mum asks.

Zoe puts her mug down on the desk, and gets up to read the list from the computer screen, gesturing with a hand holding half a biscuit. Oh yes, let's be there for half term! The photos remind me so much of the gorgeous countryside. My brain instantaneously, and involuntarily, presents me with something that'd be amazing – but won't happen – that Fabian should be there too, to share all this gorgeousness with... But that couldn't, wouldn't happen, and it'd be silly to try it on: he'd not want to do it.

Instead, 'The flowers are wonderful: I mean, how gorgeous Cornwall must've been before industrialisation, how sad about the tin mining and stuff...how horrible to work underground in the dark, while the wildflowers are covering the cliffs above you.'

'And romantic scenery doesn't put food on the table,' says Mum.

'But the bees!' Zoe wails, 'they'd have been there, making honey!'

'They would,' she agrees.

We all go silent. Then, 'Mum, listen,' I say, 'when did you decide this? I mean, I didn't know we might be going, like, soon?'

'Dad and I need a break. Granny Caro offered. It was going to be a surprise.'

'Awesome!' Zoe exclaims.

'Yeah, amazing!' I echo, 'It saves me from a weekend with Charlie!'

'How's that?' Mum and Zoe ask at the same time, looking surprised.

'Oh,' I say, 'that card in the posh thick envelope that came today was Charlie officially inviting me to her sweet sixteen party. On a river barge. It sounds ghastly. Anyway, I can't go to that, because we'll be at Granny Caro's, thank goodness. But, the point is — and, this is awful, she wrote a note on the back of the card, inviting me to hers at half term. A whole long weekend with her! But if we're in Cornwall I can refuse that as well.'

Mum puts on a serious face, 'Have you told her yet, love?'

'Not yet.'

'Okay. Don't you think you should accept one of them?'

'But her party — I don't want to take Fabian, or meet her posh friends, she said she had no friends at school – but, actually she must have some! And obviously I can't go 'cos we've accepted Granny's invite...'

'Well, I suppose so, but what about half term...?'

'Please don't – don't say it? You know I want to go to Cornwall. I love it even if it isn't a magical dream place like I used to think. And you'd planned it before she invited me, you simply hadn't discussed it with us. I'll just have to apologise enormously to Charlie.'

I can't read Mum's face. I think she looks sad. Why be disappointed for Charlie?

'Ally,' she says, and Zoe tries to speak. 'No – wait, Zozo – Alice, can I see the card? Please? Could you fetch it?'

'I can tell you. One: posh sweet sixteen party on a Thames barge, after exams... but we've decided we're going to Granny's... Two: a weekend at Charlie's house, just me staying with her family in Wormleigh, which I've never been to, but is probably the same as all Oxfordshire villages. People stuck there farming, and second homes.'

'Probably. Some of my colleagues live in those. But — Ally, darling, can you fetch the card down? It would be easier for me to see exactly what Charlie says.'

When I've fetched it for her, Mum looks at the card, turning it over and reading both sides twice. 'Oh, chocolate fountain, dancing to a band. That's so Shaz, and I suppose Charlie, and I know it's not you. But Granny and Des only offered Chapel House to us last night quite suddenly, so —.'

'Right... so,' I say, hoping I can still pull off the argument, 'I can still tell Charlie no to half term. We're going away. I just didn't know because it was supposed to be a surprise.' I feel myself looking smiley, again, 'And Daze, might she be housesitting at those friends' place again? For Rothko's half term?'

'I don't know. But Alice, Charlie might be very disappointed, as you aren't going to her party either.'

'I know, but I can't help it she's planned her party when we go to Granny's in London.'

And just then Zoe, who's been waffling quietly through the last of a biscuit, sidles up to Mum, settles back on the sofa arm, and head on one side, interrupts.

'Listen! How about – no listen, Alice! How about – listen, it's very boring at half term for someone in a single parent family, I mean, when their Mum has to go to work. And they're just told that if they bring a book along, they can read quietly in the St Hildigard's library?'

I think I see what's coming. Zoe continues, patting Mum on the arm, 'Mummy, I thought, maybe we could ask Annalise to come with us to Granny's house? She'd love the seaside and all the wild life... And if Daze won't be there...'

'Oh my God...' I think, imagining. There's a pause. Then Mum, 'Mmm, Daze might be there, with Rothko.'

Brilliant. Zoe won't like that. Rothko, aged eight, is going to really annoy a thirteen-year-old, totally geeky, girl. 'I'll think about it,' says

Mum. 'For one thing, where would everyone sleep? And I've no idea about Daze being there.'

The idea of having Annalise at Chapel House, after that awful car drive with Fabian when Zoe and Annalise were giggling and being silly, is seriously off-putting. Am I beginning to change my mind? Even though Chapel House would be amazing as a break during exams, I can understand why Mum's questioning me about refusing both invitations. And if I did accept Charlie's invitation for half term, I'd avoid the early teen silliness.

'How long are you going to think about it?' says Zoe, slightly whiney now.

'Gosh, give the woman time!'

'Alice! Look, don't be a cow, love. We can work it all out. It could be fun, a big family gathering. We could take a tent and pitch it in the garden. If Granny and Des would be okay with us pitching our tent, and some of us,' she turns to Zoe '– maybe you and Annalise – could use it to sleep in? Because it's' (I join in here) 'hardly an elastic house, even with the studio.'

'Yes!' Zoe bounces off the sofa arm and punches the air. 'And that'll keep Rothko out of our things. I'll take a padlock, zip up the tent and padlock it: during the day, of course.'

'I hope that's just an idea, not something you're really planning?'

'Rothko sounds like a pain… Shall I phone Annalise?' And she gallops off, Mum shouting, 'Not now Zozo, I need to ask Granny! And Dad,' she says, quietly to me.

'Oh, God, please not,' I say in a groany voice. 'Listen,' I say, feeling a mixture of gloom and generosity. 'Never mind whether Daze is there, I'll go to Charlie's. I can't stand the thought of a weekend with Annalise!'

'Alice, love, that's a very generous decision — towards Charlie, I mean. You really think you could stay with the Parker Pollards?'

'Yeah. I've got revision. I want to come because it's so awful Granny might sell up, I want to be there as much as I can until it happens, even though I know it'll take months before they go. But, I need to do some revision, exams aren't over. It'll be all noise with those kids. You'll see how Annalise makes Zoe regress.'

'Let's see. Don't despair yet. Maybe Annalise's mum has plans for half term already. And we'll be at Chapel House again in the summer, and maybe even Christmas. It can take a year to sell a house.'

'I hope it does.'

'Thank you, Ally, for offering to be so generous to Charlie.'

'I'm not really, I just don't want to see my sister behaving like a total wally, because she's not really like that.'

'I know, sweetie.' Mum grabs me into a proper hug, 'I think this'll make Charlie happy, more than if you went to the party. I think she sees you as a more important friend than – well, the party-goers.'

'Gosh, you know that?'

'Old friends, good friends? I may be wrong – but thank you. You are getting so – so – you're moving along, you're behaving like – like we do when we begin to see what other people need. Gosh, let's not get too serious!'

'Thanks, Mum. That might also be why we decided to go to Granny's.'

'You'll enjoy the musical. I promise.'

We hear Zoe on her phone. 'Hey, ask your mum, yeah? Ask her now?'

Chapter 23

I GO TO CHARLIE'S

I naturally hope that Stacey Thornton, Annalise's mum, will get some time off at half term from her admin job at St Hildegard's Retreat House. Unfortunately not. Instead, she's really happy to have Annalise join our family for the week in Cornwall instead of hanging around St Hildie's.

Exams begin. Apart from the waiting in silly giggling groups to be let into the gym where carefully separated desks are laid out, and having to work in absolute total silence with the invigilator staring at us like she's a guard dog, and the rubbery smell of the gym mats stacked to one side, exams are okay. As day follows day, the damp greyness of everything outdoors, and the constant rain, add a solemn feel to what we're doing. When we hand in our papers from Eng. Lit., on a Friday morning, my mind flips back to my social life, and I wonder how Fabian's A-levels are going. We agreed to wait until this weekend to go out again. I like that 'we agreed to go out' bit, and wonder where to. Then Fabian texts that we might go to the Ashmolean on Saturday afternoon. The Ashmolean? A museum! Is that a date sort of place?

Actually, I haven't yet given Charlie a firm answer about whether I'm going to theirs next weekend. Dad tells me this is very unkind, and Mum adds that it's rude to keep a person waiting.

Before I escape to enjoy Saturday afternoon, Mum and Dad several times bring the conversation back to half term, and where I should spend its first weekend. 'Just go, Ally. We'd both like it if you go,' say the parents, each in their own way. 'You know that if you came with us to Cornwall, you'd have to put up with …'

'Annalise?'

'Charlie was your friend. Now she's lonely, stuck in a village. I'd hope that you wouldn't behave as if that friendship was nothing.'

'Give it a rest!' I mumble to myself, knowing what would be kind and is important to Charlie. 'How come I've got this invitation to Charlie's anyway? Is it because you two are so close to Shaz suddenly?'

'Listen, I'm only in Cornwall for the weekend,' Dad says (I notice he avoids answering my question), 'you don't need to be at Charlie's the whole week, you can come back during the week. But take a bit of time off revising. Get to know Charlie a bit better, she's probably more on your wavelength, you may find, than…'

'Yeah, right!' I recall her assignation with the trainee chef… 'I'll go. I might even find out why you're so keen on the Parker Pollards again — we never looked them up when we came back from South Africa and her dad left the practice. But anyway, Dad, I need to get back to Oxford on Monday early, because I'm going to stay over at Mariam's, so we can study together…'

This produces a parents' chorus, 'I don't remember you said anything to me…' 'When was this arranged?'

Braving it out, I say, 'She asked me at school, I hadn't told you yet. Fat chance I'd be able to do any work at Charlie's!'

'So, you'll spend the weekend at Wormleigh with Charlie and then go straight to Mariam's? Do her parents know?'

'Of course they do. They know we always do lots of our work together. They think we're good influences on each other.' Can't suppress a grin. Though it is actually true, we are.

Mum and Dad exchange a look. 'Mmm. I'll talk to Shireen about it,' says Mum. Shireen, Mariam's mum, works in Pharmacology, so they see each other crossing the science area.

'You don't have to… anyway, her dad said it's okay….'

'They need to know we'll be away.'

'They do.'

I spend the afternoon in the Ashmolean with Fabian and a bunch of wet and dripping tourists, though without tickets we can't access the special exhibition. We end up in the basement cafe, with him making special pleading (as it's called) for me to go to Charlie's and at least promising some texts while I'm there... and, I remember something Charlie said, that she has things to tell me.

γ ♥ γ

Saturday morning, half term week, and here I am waking up at Charlie's, in what she describes as their coolest old house. It is quite cool: mostly, it's two cottages knocked through into one, with a stylish extension on the back which needed all sorts of permissions and consents. Her dad explained it all to me, last night, while we ate. You must employ an architect. You must know whether it's grade listed. You must use compatible materials. As the builders remove any previous ugly extensions, you may discover exciting features: they discovered some scratchings on a beam which could've been against witches! Sounds like fun, like doing archaeology on your own house!

Charlie told me 'My Grandad's firm did the building — he's cool — not like my other grandad — the one you saw me with. At the concert that time.'

The builders took down a shambolic boxy bit (as Eliot — he said I should call him his name now, not Dr Parker Pollard, which is a mouthful — called it), on the end of the living room of one of the cottages. And they put up a nice creamy Cotswold stone extension which goes across the whole of the back, downstairs, and has a sloping slate roof, which cost an arm and two legs (he said). I laughed. My dad doesn't talk like that, I thought. He might come out with some Scottishisms, though. Like 'outwith', instead of 'outside'. I do like language, especially dialects.

I arrived on Friday, after school, to make the most of the two days, and Eliot bought Chinese takeaway for dinner, because Shaz has a yoga class she teaches on Friday evenings at the Women's Institute hut down the road. When Shaz came in she ate a salad with goat's cheese, and we chatted about exams in the kitchen, while Charlie was in the living room, hunting for some DVDs to watch. Shaz told me she hated exams at school, but she had to get some later and she did them at Further Ed college which was better. She told me she'd been a silly kid and wanted Charlie not to be like her.

Shaz talking to me like we're some kind of equals felt really strange. I mumbled something about being too much like a geek or a nerd. Then Charlie's parents went out for drinks with the couple next door. Eliot stumbled over the step, which is cronky, unlike the extended part of the house, you'd think he'd been having a few drinks already. Shaz wore her pink onesie. Could I imagine Mum wearing a onesie to go out for drinks next door?

So then Charlie suggested — insisted on — watching movies on her computer till the lights went out in the village street. Their eco-minded Parish Council wants to help save the planet by turning the streetlights off from two until dawn! We saw an *American Pie* movie and half a *Harry Potter*… tomorrow it's the other half…

The dog's on Charlie's bed, lying across Charlie's feet, sometimes she — the dog — makes a shuddering sigh. The sun woke me up, shining through a gap in the blue cotton curtains. Charlie's snoring (snoring!) under her duvet: she and the dog! The décor in here is spangly-pink and blue with white painted retro-style (or possibly 'Vintage up-cycled') furniture. I lie on my back: Miley Cyrus stares from a poster. The other posters are a pole dancer, and several boy bands.

I turn over. What'd it be like to dance with a pole and have men watch you? The men in my head look like Fabian. I let myself drift. When I wake up again, I have a thought: maybe Shaz telling me about herself at school was connected with Shaz and Mum getting to be cosy friends again, and the invitation to me to spend time with Charlie is all about me being a good influence? A person who studies hard and is going to Cambridge or wherever?

That could only work if Charlie wanted it to. Only if she was that kind of person already, which she isn't. Mariam happens to be, so we're fine, keeping each other focussed. Or, they think we are. I think we'd be friends anyway, and I like the differences in our families, which are interesting.

I look across at Charlie: she's still supine, immobile, her hair over her face. So I get up, use her private bog in her tiny ensuite bathroom, and look through her stuff in there. She has some nice things, Body Shop, top of their range. A Foot Spa, and very fluffy towels. The sun streams in through a tiny low-set window. The room's under the eaves: brown birds fly up and down outside. Martins? Do they have a nest up under the tiles? I can't see, however I twist myself. Somewhere downstairs, the radio's playing.

Suddenly there's knocking on the bedroom door, and Shaz calling out, 'Hey, there, Charlie-girl, Charlie-girl!' Charlie makes a shuffly noise getting out of bed, and they go whisper-whisper with the door half-closed, while I peep around the bathroom door and watch. Then Charlie makes a groaning noise like Shaz's told her to do something, and Shaz calls out, to me, 'You're okay if we tackle the veggie patch, aren't you, Alice? It's such an amazing morning, gotta grab the great weather while it's great!'

Well, sun's gone, though the sky's still blue between some grey clouds. The dog springs off Charlie's bed and bolts downstairs.

'Jump up, get dressed, come and look at the Task of the Day!' says Shaz, all up-beat and yoga-teachery.

Shaz shows me the veggie patch. It's huge. 'I grow all our veg now,' she says, as we stand outside sniffing the chilly morning air, clutching our croissants and mugs of hot coffee. I look down and see a slug sliding along the path by my feet. A white butterfly lands on a plant beside me, and opens and closes its wings. 'Hope you remembered your wellingtons, Alice.'

Shaz has the right clothes for gardening. Shaz always had the right clothes: Ugg boots in winter, a jacket with a fleece lining, and a pale blue scarf folded round her neck in Chelsea style (same as Mum, the scarf). Now it's green wellies and a waxed jacket. 'Hey, remember when you were tiny girls at nursery, and we used to go to the park, and you two had matching red wellies – do you remember that?'

I remember I had green wellies with eyes like a frog on the toe end, and a matching brolly. Maybe Zoe had red ones? I grin, over my mug, and then I yawn. And shiver, pulling my long cardigan tight round me. Though maybe I'm beginning to feel I could sort of like it here. That butterfly opens its wings again, then flies off.

'...manure. I thought I'd go down to the farm after we've finished eating and ... do you girls want to...' I realise Shaz's talking and I'm not listening.

'Pardon, sorry?'

'Mum's talking about collecting her yucky organic plant food from her favourite farmer, then we do the spreading while she's yoga-teaching in the village hall,' Charlie says, kicking at the ground.

'You're gonna begin and do a little bit for me, and then I'll take over,' says Shaz, 'because with the wet weather last week, we're all behind with everything outdoors. And Charlie's dad's always too busy.'

Or drunk? Has he become an alcoholic, and that's why he left the practice and got a desk job? And they live out here? I don't remember them being outdoorsy when they lived in Oxford. Probably not. They look like they're doing all right, though, don't they?

We ride down with Shaz in the Land Rover, we've left the dog behind 'because she gets overexcited around other animals'. It's a real country Land Rover, with a trailer bumping metallically along behind. I'm in my skinny jeans, with one of Dad's old shirts I nicked before it was thrown out for recycling, and the keffiyeh Mariam gave me for Christmas thrown around my neck like a scarf. And, of course, my wellies. I've borrowed an old jumper from Shaz so my cardie doesn't get spoilt. Charlie has on denim shorts, the kind Dad raises his eyebrows at when we wear them, with black tights, wellies, T-shirt ('Up St Bernadine's!' printed across the chest... her school is fundraising for a larger swimming pool, and an Arts Centre). That's so like Nina's style, except that, with the shorts Charlie's wearing a Barbour.

The farmer has a lad who spades the manure ('All nicely matured, Mrs Parker-Pollard') into the trailer. We hang about the Land Rover, Charlie making signs at me, and me trying not to laugh. It's hard not to. She's so classic. Actually this isn't a farm, it's a livery stables and riding school. Charlie rides here. She takes me to see the horses that make the manure. Horses aren't my thing: but they are wonderfully elegant, and smooth.

'So, d'you have one that's special, one of your own?'

'I wish. Gussie'd buy me one, but Dad's like, she can ride until she tires of it and then... "Tires of it", isn't that like distrusting me?'

I shrug. It's probably true. Both may be true. There's a kind of feeling I have about Charlie, from her bored face at the concert: maybe she does riding the way she said Jos and Gussie go to concerts like that Haydn's *Creation* — things you get involved with to fit in? Not things you can't live without. The girls who tease Zoe so obviously do that. But Zoe does eco things because she can't live without them. What can't I live without (excluding Fabian)? Science? Music? Photography and Art? What am I going to do about it? What would Shaz and Eliot say, if they were my parents?

Back at Charlie's, Shaz gives us rubber gloves, and we begin to spade manure onto the veg area. It stinks. It stinks inside your nose, and after a bit it's like we stink too. 'Oh, yuck the muck!' Charlie says, and then she sings it, and we begin to stagger around singing stupidly.

Laughing and staggering takes so much more breathing that we're inhaling the stench even more: this makes us stop, and lean on our spades. The ground's soggy after a night of rain, but the sun's heated up the air. There is a kind of fun here, even with Charlie. So, what's going on? Charlie seems happy, they seem happy. Why do my parents seem so protective of Charlie suddenly?

'We should take some photos and put them on Facebook.' Charlie pulls off her gloves and fishes out her phone. Her very special phone, a present from Gussie when she won an essay competition at her school... She can't be so stupid if she did that... I throw my arm around her back, she chooses video, we laugh and make faces. Of course, Facebook will ask us inanely, in small grey type, 'Where were you? Who were you with?'

'Muckspreading Cottage,' Charlie suggests, shoving the phone back in her pocket.

'Muckraking Cottage,' I laugh. I wish I'd brought my camera, now – but I didn't think I'd want to have photos. My Nokia phone doesn't have a decent camera: I could ask for one like Charlie's for my birthday?

Charlie's looking at the ground, poking at a bit of manure lying lumpily at our feet where Shaz wants to plant carrots. 'Mum and Dad've been doing some of that.'

'Some of what? Muckraking?'

'Isn't that a word? For, like, digging about in the past, looking for scandals? They're into family history.'

'Yeah, you told me, at the Spa? Then you wouldn't say any more. It's okay to say more. When we did a project on that in year nine, half the class had ancestors who'd been in the workhouse. Including me!'

Charlie doesn't laugh. Or tease me. She's totally straight-faced serious. 'No, it's not stuff about the workhouse. Dad wanted to track down his proper family tree. I wish he hadn't.'

'Why?' I ask.

'When Dad researched his biological mother — and of course you can't do that on the census and stuff, he had to inquire about the adoption — he contacted her, and then he found out some awful things...'

'Worse than the workhouse?'

'Granny — Gussie that is, Dad's adoptive mum, called it muckraking. Like he was going through all the fucking bad stuff in his birth family. It wasn't like that. It was — like I would want to know if I was him?' She waves her free arm, the one that's not holding the spade, 'To meet and talk to her. Calling it muckraking was horrible of Granny, like disrespect. If he wants to meet her, he has the right.'

''Course he does. I wouldn't want to stop someone doing that. It's who you are, isn't it? Part of your DNA.'

So is this all connected? It's genetics, then, inherited: but what?

'I don't think his Dad stuck around. Dad's not looking for that DNA. But he found her. He told me. She was like our age when she was pregnant.'

'So?'

'He wrote to her. Then he wrote again. Then there was a letter from one of her relatives. I think he did meet her, at theirs. Just once. Then he went silent on it all. I want to know. I think Mum does. But what about me? And what went wrong? Why doesn't he tell me?'

'Ask him. He might.'

'He won't. He's gone weird. Like seriously.'

'How's it going girls? Ready for smoothies? Or mint tea?' Shaz's voice gives me a jump, I was so absorbed in *Why doesn't he tell her?* Bad timing! Charlie was ready to talk more.

'Hey look at this!' Shaz opens her arms wide like she's about to hug the area of ground where we've been digging in the manure. 'You've done so well! Thank you! So, time to get washed and changed, I thought we'd go into Stroud? Have a snack first, then everything's about being beautiful! We're all getting our nails and eyebrows done, my treat. And a cream tea: a new vegan place, the cream's not dairy, but the whole thing, scones, jam, cream, is scrummy. How's that sound?'

I've never had a proper manicure. Or my eyebrows 'done'. As we eat our cream tea, later, my eyebrows do feel a bit odd. Shaz is sipping green tea, which looks hardly touched by any colour at all. Charlie and I both chose camomile, which is actually fairly vile, and tastes like boiled plant! But, the scone and the jam are delish, and the cream's good enough to be real.

Why was I invited really? Is it more than me being a good influence?

Chapter 24

Sunday, I'm woken by barking, and Shaz suggests the dog, Pandora, needs a proper long walk. She makes big hints that's a job for Charlie and me, and that the pancakes she's making for breakfast are to fuel our energy levels. They are pretty good: more like crepes than pancakes, and folded over and filled with blueberries.

So after that, we gather up dog, lead, and plastic poo bags, put on our shoes and start off through the village, past cottages with tiny front gardens or none at all, but plenty of flowers planted almost on the path. 'Yeah, it's called the High Street!' Charlie says, 'but don't expect Next, or Fat Face, or any of those!'

I was thinking how pretty it all was. But I'm beginning to see how living somewhere like a holiday place all the time might have drawbacks. At the end of this terrace of stone cottages, there's the village pub, called the Bee, with more flowers in window boxes, and a couple of benches outside. Next door is the one and only shop, this morning buzzing with customers. There's a small crowd gathered outside, mostly with dogs on leads. Pandora gets very excited by this, trying to get involved in the dog-style chat. The humans, wearing waxed jackets or cagoules, and stout walking shoes or muddy green wellies, clutch bulging paper bags, and newspapers. Charlie, trying to restrain Pandora from too much interest in another dog, gets involved in conversation with one of the dog owners, a woman in a gabardine rain hat and green wellies. As I stand back, a man, wearing striped pyjamas under his Barbour, emerges from the shop with a large size container of milk, jumps into a Land Rover Discovery parked nearby, does a three-point turn in the road, and roars away.

I notice that the friendly dog owner has started asking Charlie how her Dad is. I listen, hoping to hear more. But Charlie just says he saw another doctor and now they're thinking of booking a holiday but it won't be until maybe July or August. The woman sounds concerned, says she's glad they're thinking of taking a holiday (somewhere quiet and beautiful, she suggests, 'but where you can do your surfing, and have a bit of fun').

I've not learned much, though at least this doesn't sound like alcoholism. More like a debilitating disease. Could be what Grandpa Alisdair had, Multiple Sclerosis? Finally, Charlie detaches herself from the conversation, and we move on. Charlie gives the woman a wave and a big smile – she's good at smiles — so I wave too.

''Bye to the croissant run! Village tradition,' she says to me, 'The shop people heat croissants in their microwave on Sundays. Everyone queues up.'

'Not your parents though?'

'Sometimes. Mum wanted to impress you with the pancakes!'

'She didn't need to.'

'Whatever. Gonna show you our bluebell wood: a landmark blue haze of flowers as it has been called!'

As we turn down a lane, the church bell starts ringing for Sunday worship. I can see the bluebell wood, stretching all the way down. It is pretty good. Pandora finds a scent and presses forward, nose to the ground, 'Reading the news, Dad calls it,' says Charlie.

The sun's out, birds sing. I wish now that I'd brought my camera. As being here for the weekend wasn't my choice, I left it behind. But that was a mean thought, and mean to myself as well as Charlie. Now I'd actually like some photos of everything here. I'm beating myself up, disliking myself, and I can't record this lovely moment.

Charlie is talking: what did she say? 'Where've you gone? Listen!'

'Sorry?'

'The shop's all run by volunteers. Otherwise, there's no shops, like I said. Except, there's Wendy's Hairdresser's. It's really old fashioned. Passé, like Grandma Gussie'd say. Only old biddies go there! So, it's like the Universe intervened when I saw you at the concert!'

'The Universe?'

'Not exactly God. But – something,' she waves an arm about. 'Like, I don't know anyone here, properly. It wasn't so bad at first, when we arrived, 'cos I went to the village school. It's really small, and sort of cosy? But now, if I tell you about living here, you've got to swear not to tell anyone. Anyone. Not your Mum or Dad. Or your sister. Nobody. Are you okay with that?'

'I don't know what you're going to tell me though.'

'Things about my family. Nothing that affects you. Or yours. Just don't tell, right?'

I shrug a yes. Charlie tries to make me do the 'cross your heart' thing. 'No,' I say, 'l swear I won't split.'

'Okay. First, I hate boarding school. My Dad's parents have got some stupid ideas. One's about my dyslexia, another's about medical marriages – like the adults don't get much time to be together – and they decided, and told Dad – and Mum – that I should go to this school that's supposed to be good for dyslexia. And they said I had to be with other girls of our sort and make friends, and learn to mix socially. I mean, it's such an insult. I had friends. At the other secondary school. Even with the bullying, I did have friends.'

'So?'

'Gussie –my Gran, Au*gusta!*' she says, almost venomously, 'she said to me "You've still got the holidays, but sometimes your Daddy and Mummy *need time on their own.*" That's an insult, they *wanted* me!'

'But surely now he's not a GP he's around a lot more?' I ask.

At this point, however, Pandora, who's been straining on the lead, snuffling along with her nose in some grass beside the road, squats down to poo.

'We used to have lots of family time,' Charlie says rather thoughtfully, as she leans down to pick up the dog's poo, cleverly using a small plastic bag like a glove, and folding the thing inside. She ties the top up, then lets the dog off the lead as we turn into the wood. 'This place belongs to some posh person Mum knows called Margot, and we're allowed in,' she says. 'So, Mum didn't teach evenings when we were in Oxford. Not till they thought up the "we're going to make a new start" thing. Dad got the new job. We moved. It's a wilderness here. Nobody to know or go out with or have fun. They're all either working at sixteen, or so posh they don't want to know me. Too posh for one lot and not enough for the other!' Charlie holds out the plastic bag, 'Yuck!' she laughs. 'Am I too posh?'

'Ugh!'

'Or too stupid?'

'You're not stupid. Though that wasn't nice.'

'I was just being funny.' She looks at the ground. I think she was hoping for a reaction, something to change the subject. A fight, something silly. She was brought here, away from friends in Oxford, next thing, she's sent away to boarding school. Who wouldn't be miserable? What's going on? Why?

Charlie kicks a stone along the path, as we stomp through the bluebell wood and into an empty field. 'Good, Margot's taken her horse out, so if we turn right, down that side of the field, we'll come out by the church, and the village school, then we keep on going that way and we're home.'

I say, 'So that's the school you went to when you moved here?'

'Yeah, it was nice for a bit in the village school. But you went off to South Africa, your Dad's sabbatical or whatever. And your family didn't keep up with ours.'

'Not my fault. I mean, I changed schools too, and it was like — we got lots of work, and I dunno…'

'Dad calls what he does now a desk job, but it's still the NHS. I think it's something to do with complaints. He's home for tea. At my old secondary school, where I went first after being eleven, we'd all pile into the bus to go there and it was a laugh. Sometimes. But then came the boarding school idea.'

'And you haven't kept up with anyone from there?'

'Like I said, those kids are different. After they do exams – they're only interested in getting the basics, English and Maths, then they leave school and they're working adults. I'm not their sort. Like I've been out with some of the guys, but they've only got one idea!'

I kind of shiver inside, but I can see why they want to go out with her — she's what the fashion brochures call curvy.

'What about the girls? I thought you said you had friends there?'

'Don't you get it? They're growing up different. They have jobs.'

I'm stuck. Presumably Charlie's hoping to go to Uni? 'Doesn't it help, being somewhere they understand dyslexia?'

'No. Studying's too difficult. Anyway, Mum and Dad must have another reason to want me out of the house.'

'Okay, so maybe your Dad needed space and quiet when he gave up general practice? Maybe it was stress or burn-out? Was he ill and off work before?'

'No, he was like normal. I've heard about all the out of hours thing, that they all hate the new way it's done. That'd hardly be a reason.'

'It might. Mine's been going to these meetings where they're discussing the future of general practice, and he says one of the things is simply about surviving…' I pause, for effect, here, then add, 'Like a joke, of course – but it is a thing.'

'Grandparents are supposed to be nice cuddly people who give you things, but Jos and Gussie asked me to call them by their names, and are shit. It's not for them to say what school I go to, is it? That's being posh, for you! Mum's Dad's a builder, like he's got a building firm, her Mum's a secretary, and they're really nice. She makes great Sunday roasts and he slips me a fiver or even a tenner when we go there. How about yours?'

'Mine? They're all pretty weird. Cuddly grandparents are for inside kids' books... Back to you. Maybe your parents are just really keen that you get your exams and have a good career, and think that a school where the teachers understand dyslexia is the best way to get there. Got any ideas for a career?'

'Anything where you don't write stuff!'

'Are you into science? Art? Drama?'

'I was in the school play. I kind of like biology.'

'Do those for A-levels and see what happens?'

'So you'd just accept being there?'

'I suppose. You could leave early, and go to sixth form college, where you're like treated as an adult.'

'Great. You know you're talking like a teacher?'

'Didn't mean to. But I get what you said about being sent away. Our school has boarders, some of them come from overseas. They get effing lonely.'

'Overseas or bloody country village, same difference.'

'I guess.'

I am confused. Surely it's mostly to do with Eliot? They don't not want Charlie. Shaz is working hard to make me and Charlie friends again. That shows she cares. Why? There are secrets here.

We walk on silently. At least it's a sunny day, we're outdoors. The village is all so classic, and as we pass the church, they begin singing a hymn. *Praise my soul the King of heaven.*

But I'd not really want to live here, that's true. Cut off from cafes and the cinema, and G and D's to have ice cream (with Fabian), and Holywell Music Room, the Cellar (which I'm not allowed in yet), and even the stuffy Sheldonian for concerts (with Fabian). And bookshops. And places to buy clothes and that.

'Hey, you know the Truck Festival? Shall we go?' Charlie asks.

'D'you think our parents would let us?' Going to music festivals feels like a huge step, and Charlie's question gives me goose bumps.

'I'm gonna ask mine. We'll be sixteen. Hey, over the age of consent! You could go with Felix – is that his name?'

'Fabian.'

'Fabian, then. And I'll meet somebody fantastic,' she says, doing a few dance moves with a big smile on her face, passing the dog's lead from one hand to the other. 'And it'll be awesome.'

I'm not so sure. That's something else not on my mind, in reality, yet. And there are a lot more clouds in the sky, all grouping together to cover the sun. I hadn't noticed them before.

What Charlie said earlier, about the family history research, can that be the key to everything else? Why did the other family stop her dad seeing his birth mum again? Eliot might seem a rather good addition to the family. A good-looking professional? Or were they shocked, and ashamed of their mum, and their half-brother who was adopted? Was it that, before Eliot got in touch, they hadn't known she'd had a baby as a teenager, so that they felt shocked and deceived?

I'd feel so angry if I was his birth mum, and that was how my other kids acted.

As we get back into the High Street, the sky turns darker and darker, and we end up running the last bit back to the cottage in pouring rain.

The plan Shaz and Eliot had for the rest of today was to take a picnic lunch and go to Harcourt Arboretum, to gawp at the colourful azaleas and rhododendrons (which are which?), and the peacocks. Then back mid-afternoon to Wormleigh, where Eliot wanted to watch the village cricket match.

Instead, we eat the picnic at the kitchen table. How can we endure this long, wet afternoon? Shaz wishes the tennis was on at Wimbledon, so we could watch. Eliot points out that if it's raining here, it's probably raining there. I so wish I could go home as there's nothing to do, but we find an old movie and all sit round watching the TV in their lounge...

That night, we go for dinner at The Bee, which is apparently a well-known gastropub. It's crowded and cheerful. We all have wine. I watch Eliot. He doesn't drink more than a glass. He does seem to shuffle a bit, and maybe twitch? He's not very, well, animated. The dog sits on his feet, like she owns him. Back to watch more TV, except Shaz, who goes off to practice the yoga sequences she's planning to teach this coming week. Charlie and I end up watching another *Harry Potter*, in her room. And eating dried fruit from the packet, Charlie's idea.

Later, when I creep down to fetch a glass of water from the kitchen, Shaz and Eliot are snuggled up on the sofa. They look happy to me. I'm getting this feeling there's more mystery than I can understand. Is it that Eliot has MS? Why not say? I lie in bed, staring into the utter country night darkness of the room, and listening to the owls. I try to think myself into being Charlie. I have watched more movies than I normally do in a month, and had my eyebrows and nails done, I've tried to encourage Charlie, which hasn't really worked. I've had five texts from Fabian, mainly saying 'keep going, it's only...' and giving me the number of hours, minutes and even seconds... Well, he did also say he missed me, and has decided which Uni he really wants to get into... Durham, if not Cambridge. School says he has to put Cambridge first.

Chapter 25

LEAVING CHARLIE'S

On Monday I wake up, relieved to be leaving, bothered about being sworn to secrecy. It's more like she's *implored* me. I can't share any of what she told me with anyone. Not only because she asked, more because her imploring sounded so sad. When I try to imagine being Charlie, I think I know how she feels alone: like being inside a swirling nothingness, away from where everyone else is having a good time. Although, actually, we aren't. Not all the time. And how am I supposed to fill the gap for Charlie?

This all feels so uncomfortable. I don't want to talk to Charlie, because I don't know what to say. If I get up very quietly, and creep downstairs, I can avoid being alone with her. So that's what I do. As soon as I'm out of bed, I'm cold. I grab my clothes and sneak into the family bathroom to get dressed. I creep downstairs, taking my pyjamas which I shove into the pockets of my cagoule, so as not to go back into Charlie's room. I look out of the window and rain's falling on the soggy garden. In an hour or so I'll be shivering in that little concrete shelter, waiting for the erratic bus service to Oxford, and Charlie's going to be there with me, to see me off, she said.

In the kitchen, breakfast is laid. But Eliot's already left for work and Shaz is nowhere. Then the back door opens, and a draught of cold damp air blows in, along with Pandora and Shaz, who gives me a big smile. I saw her face a moment before the smile, but she doesn't know, and gets busy offering me muesli, yogurt, coffee, and the best thing, a ride home! 'I can take you all the way to Oxford, I've a meeting in your direction, at ten o'clock.'

'Ooh, yes, please!' Hope she didn't notice the big mood change when I heard that!

'Bag packed? And I've made a little treat for you and your friend – your Mum said you were staying with a school friend for a few days? Mariam?'

'Yes, we're revising together... I mean, we'll do other stuff, but, we're quite good at keeping each other on track, as Dad puts it.'

After breakfast, and now with my backpack straining at the seams with all the junk I brought with me, I'm in the hall, ready to go. Charlie, who came down really late, has been chomping muesli and reading a magazine. Now she sidles up to me. 'Alice – you should see this,' she pulls my arm, 'Mum mustn't hear,' she says, staying close beside me, so her breath tickles my neck, as we dodge into the living room, 'Okay, look. It's a card. I found it in the recycling.'

It's a tiny card, the kind which comes with a bouquet from a florist. She opens it up and sticks it under my nose. 'So read it – silently, to yourself!'

Darling Shaz, always love you whatever...XX. In neat, rounded handwriting. Hum: what do I think? 'Your Mum had a birthday or something?' (That's neutral at least.)

'No... I think she's seeing someone!'

I remember the way Shaz and Eliot were on the sofa last night. 'Doesn't look very likely to me.'

'Dad's writing's squiggly. That isn't.'

'But the shop person could've written that on the card.'

''Spose so. Anyhow, you know where she's going, don't you? She's driving you back home, and then, St Hildegard's, this spirituality place — it's near yours.'

'I know it. Daze made them a labyrinth. It's not a yoga place.'

'No, exactly, but Mum's been there a lot, they do poetry readings, and, I dunno, art talks? She's into all that. Though she's not religious.'

'So?'

'Suppose she's — really there seeing someone, and going to these events is a cover? Something nobody'd worry about? She could've met someone there.'

'I think that's unlikely. That writing's more like a woman's. I mean, let's not be sexist, but kind of carefully written letters? Maybe her mum, or her sister, does she have one?'

'I know Nana's and my aunt's – it's not them!'

'Okay – you're worried, but don't be yet.' I'm trying to act supportively, but really I think it's a dumb idea.

'Well, could you watch where she goes, whatever, and tell me?'

'Alice?' comes Shaz's cheerful voice around the door, 'Ready, love?'

'All done, and I tidied the bed! Okay, gotta go, I'll – Facebook you.'

Charlie's folding the card, shoving it into her jeans pocket. 'If you want to be cool, you should switch to Tumblr. And, when you tell your parents we're going to Truck – that you've got to come with me — don't say anything about what I've told you. Remember. Just between us.'

I give her a hug. She hangs onto me. I feel mean, disappearing, like I'm abandoning her to the village. I'm too quiet for a party person, which looks like what Charlie aims to be.

'And ask your parents about the Truck festival.'

'Yeah, well... I'll see what I can do...'

'Thanks, Alice, I knew you'd be up for it,' Charlie says. 'We'll have a great time. Truck'll be awesome.'

'Yep. *If we go.*'

'Good to go?' It's Shaz's voice behind me! I whizz round. 'Oh, did I give you a fright?' she says, with a grin.

'Nope, we were just – saying goodbye. It's been lovely, don't know what Mum'll think of my eyebrows!'

'And your nails! Turquoise!'

As we drive out of the village, I feel bothered. The things we did over the weekend were better than I expected. And the village is pretty and seems friendly — for grown-ups, who can escape to work, who know who they are, and are in control. But, what is going on? Charlie's unhappy at school, and her parents don't fit the pattern of people who'd send her away. But they have. There's something up with Eliot, maybe MS, or alcohol, or drugs. Is the mystery in his birth family? It might be some kind of shameful event, that's being kept hidden, or that he can't speak about – like have they made him promise, like Charlie did me? That part of my visit wasn't lovely. It did confirm my feeling that Mum and Dad are keeping something from me. Maybe because I mustn't tell Charlie?

Anyway, I've promised her. I shan't say a word to the parents.

Shaz begins to ask me about my plans for A levels, leading towards what Charlie wants to do. That's kind of uncomfortable, as she's comparing Charlie with me. But I don't know either, and I don't want to be a clone of my parents. When Shaz mentions the riding stables, I suggest what about working with animals, vet nursing, maybe? We manage some chatter about that. It's awkward keeping quiet about Charlie hating being at boarding school when Shaz raves about how amazingly the school understands dyslexia. At last we're turning off into Headington at the Green Road roundabout, and I take refuge in looking out for the sign, which I soon spot – *St Hildegard's Community and Retreat Centre*. Shaz asks where she should drop me.

'Mariam's is one of these big houses we're coming to. You could maybe leave me here – I'll walk the rest?' I feel a bit sneaky that I've deliberately asked her to leave me within sight of the turning into St Hildie's. I'll be able to see from here, and walk past and make sure the Land Rover's parked there.

Shaz slows, stops, we both get out. While I'm shrugging on my heavy backpack, she leans into the Land Rover to fetch something. It's a cake tin. 'Don't forget your treat: they're lemon cupcakes, Charlie's favourite!'

She gives me a big hug, then hands me the tin. 'Thanks for coming, it made Charlie's weekend.'

'Thanks for having me,' I say. It's like hearing my small self, as a kid, being polite. 'And for the beauty stuff, and the cupcakes.'

'You're always welcome,' she says.

Always, I think. The expectation sounds ominous. I begin walking, then turn to wave. So now, she's back in the car, and I cross the road. I'll be able to watch better from this side. I wave again (in case she notices me in her mirror), as yes, the Land Rover draws away from the curb, then a metre or two down the road, on goes the indicator and it turns left into St Hildegard's.

It's probably just a class, or what they call a Quiet Day. Or even, does she go there to talk about whatever the mystery is, like having counselling? Charlie really shouldn't worry that she's having an affair. I decide to walk slowly along to where I can glance casually up their drive as I pass on the other side. Then I can tell Charlie that I did.

The Land Rover is parked, driver's door open. Shaz is standing talking to a woman I recognise: denim skirt, long knitted cardigan (clutched around her as it's gone so cold today), blonde hair in a plait down her back: Annalise's mum. Well, I knew she works there, doing their admin. An innocent chat with the administrator. Here comes someone hurrying from the main house to join them, a man in tight jeans and an open-necked shirt. Then, *What?* It can't be – it is, *my Uncle David*, Dad's cousin. He used to be the Retreat Centre's Director, but now lives in Yorkshire. So, why's he back? They all chat, they laugh. Shaz shrugs on her jacket as she chats. David exchanges a word with her. Looks like he knows Shaz already – or is he just being what they call 'welcoming'?

Annalise's mum stands back, says something, waves a piece of paper towards the house, then turns and goes back inside. Uncle David and Shaz are still talking, then he raises an arm towards the new wing, indicating her to come along with him, and they go inside.

So where does he fit into this? If at all? He used to work at Hildie's. He's a priest. He's gay. What is he doing here today? Not having an affair with Shaz, that's for sure.

What I remember about that wing, the extension, is the eight-sided Livingstone Lounge, where Daze made the mosaic labyrinth for David. Where she let me help by putting some tiny tesserae in where she indicated. The picture has fish and the sea... I must've felt all tingly and proud, doing proper art with Daze. I was probably about five? And now they've covered it up with a carpet, and Daze was quite put out when I told her. So I don't suppose they ever walk it now.

Chapter 26

AT MARIAM'S

I turn down a side road, and work my way back to Mariam's house without having to creep past St Hildie's again and possibly reveal myself to Shaz. Who might be looking out of a window! Silly, really.

Now at Mariam's, I think like I always do, that the house is so like a dolls' house or a five-year-old's drawing: red brick, two sash windows each side of the front door, and four above. Balanced and square. The front drive's also tiled in brick, with standing for three cars. Two are out, but only one has left a dry rectangle of paler brick, the space where it stood all night in the rain. Two bay trees in pots standing either side of the large glassed-in porch complete the doll's house look. A rose tree climbs up the front wall, which I like, as it softens the boxy shape of the house. Yellow roses are in flower, if the sun was out I'd sniff their scent. Today they hang their heads, dripping from the rain, moving a little in the breeze. This really has turned into a weird summer.

I open the porch door, and step inside, where they keep raincoats, umbrellas, and wellingtons, all very tidy. Some of the raincoats are a bit wet, and a large black umbrella has been left open to dry. As I ring the bell, I'm shoving aside memories of Charlie's, I can't deal with them now.

Squeals behind the door, and it flings open, 'Alice!' Mariam catches me into a big hug. 'Oops!' I nearly spill the cupcakes out of their tin. 'Let me put this down! Present from Shaz.'

'Hey, love the eyebrows!' Mariam says. 'Who's Shaz?'

'Charlie's mum. Where I've been for the weekend.' I juggle the cake tin into one hand, and display my blue nails.

'Oh wow, amazing! So was that what you did – beauty treatments?'

'Just the two things, eyebrows and nails. Shaz took us – her, Charlie and me — and, she paid for it! Charlie is so much a make-up kind of person. I'd have liked my ears pierced, but I didn't have any money. Not enough. How's your weekend been?'

Mariam rolls her eyes. 'Busy. We've got cousins staying – but they're going soon. Anyway, come through!' Mariam seems to have an awful lot of cousins, I think to myself. But then, so have I, I suppose.

Inside, the house is warm. It wraps us with its interesting scents of spicy cooking, coffee, and cigarettes. Today the hallway's cluttered with suitcases, backpacks, and tennis rackets. It sounds like a whole group of relatives in the kitchen are all talking at once. We take my stuff upstairs, then join the party in the kitchen, which turns out to be only two male cousins and Mariam's sister Dina, drinking coffee. Dina presses a tiny cup of aromatic, thick dark syrupy coffee into my hand, waves me to a seat, and puts a glass of water on the table in front of me.

I'm grateful for the water, and I smile thanks, though I'd prefer a latte, coffee Arab style is so strong, and so sweet! What I love is the snacks we get here, all sorts of meze, in little bitesize pieces. And sweet pastries. Anyhow, no food in sight at present, and after introductions, one of the cousins (they all look like students: jeans, T-shirts, trainers) offers me a ciggie.

'Oh – no thanks,' I say, smiling at him, but waving it away.

He offers. I refuse again.

He offers. Mariam indicates I should accept.

Okay, I give in. He smiles and offers me a light. I have tried before, but it's not that nice: Dad told me he used to smoke... Dad (hard to imagine) was a rebel in his family. In Mariam's family smoking is what they all do, except Mariam, and I think, her sister. I try not to do more than play with the thing, and flick its ash into the saucer of my tiny cup. The cousin has black-framed specs, and is wearing a smart grey T-shirt with something written on it in Arabic. He and Mariam talk and laugh in Arabic, while the other cousin (called Sami, thinner, no specs, blue shirt) asks me how I know the family. Then I discover he's studying for a doctorate at Imperial College. I'd like to talk more about this – what's his subject, stuff like that, though I wish he'd not study my face so – so, *deeply*. I respond, when he asks, that I'm still deciding whether life science will be my thing at Uni, and whether it'd be wrong to do something my parents don't want me to.

Because, I realise, this thing is really bothering me. He kind of laughs, and asks what else I like to do, and says he went to see *Les Miserables*, but would've rather been at a concert. Here, I agree (it was the musical Mum advised Granny not to book for our treat) and mention Haydn's *Creation*. Which I went to with my *boyfriend*... (lest he should try to ask me out!).

And so, having finished my coffee, and drowned it down with water, I jump up to offer round the cupcakes. The little cakes in their frilly paper cups look so pale and somehow English, elegant sponge offerings so unlike anything that would go with that coffee. But everyone takes one.

And we politely escape, to Mariam's room, to do some schoolwork. Gosh, I hope the cousins aren't going to be here while I'm staying, it wasn't in the deal. 'Don't worry, *habibti*,' Mariam laughs, 'they're off to London later. They're both at Imperial. They're living in my father's flat, the one he bought when he studied here at Bart's. So, apart from the beauty treatments, how was your weekend with Charlie?'

I groan. 'How were we friends at nursery? That is weird. I mean, she is so – different. To me. Like she has no interests except boys and make-up. Well, and clothes. You know how it felt? Like I was having a break from being me.'

Mariam grins like she understands. 'So, what did you do? What did you talk about?'

'Stuff. We learned how much we have in common, which is like nothing. Nothing serious. We didn't talk about the biggest things that happened since we saw each other. You'd think nothing had happened. You'd think there was no climate change, and nine eleven and the London bombs never happened, and the world was safe and exactly how it was when we were five.'

'So, she doesn't know much. I mean, it wasn't safe for everyone when we were five, was it? The world's never safe... depends where you are... So, you had a holiday! I didn't work because we had visitors. So...'

'Yeah, that's true. About the world. But — I brought all my revision for next week's exams, so... How much will we get done, together?' We laugh.

'Let's see. I'll put the timer on, on my phone.'

'Wow, an iPhone now, you and Charlie both! You didn't say.'

'My American uncle bought it for me. He brought it when they came to visit. Last week.' I lean over to look at it. 'And, they brought my Grandma, who's staying with us a month!'

'You should've come to ours! Am I overcrowding your family?'

'No, we're used to visitors. And my parents like you and your family. So, we agree a time, and we work that long, and then, we go downstairs and make more coffee and eat baklava?'

Much later, we're absorbed in giving each other a test on history when my phone beeps. Not Fabian. Charlie. *Where did she go? Did you see her meet someone?*

Well, not the kind of someone Charlie means. I send her a brief message: *Yes. St Hildie's. No she chatted to a gay priest. Outside. I know him. No worries.*

As I press send, I wonder again what Uncle David was in Oxford for, at St Hildie's.

Mariam's face is a question mark. 'Fabian?' I shake my head, vigorously.

'Charlie – where I've just been,' I say, and give a sketchy description of Charlie's worries, without breaking my vow of secrecy. 'I wish her parents would explain — if there's anything to explain. Even I noticed that her dad has a limp, that he knocked into a chair when we were at the pub where we had dinner, and it fell over onto someone's foot – which didn't matter, but he wasn't, like, pissed or anything. We'd just arrived.'

'She thinks he's ill?'

'I think maybe he is. It'd be difficult, but couldn't she try and ask? She needs to know.'

'Her parents maybe don't want to worry her because it's our exam year?'

'Maybe. I don't know,' I say, unconvinced that Charlie's parents think the way Mariam's might. 'She hates being away from home. Even though she's in the drama club and all the sports teams.'

'It's the boarding school thing. Emily in our year, still cries when she comes back after the holidays.'

'I know. I don't understand why people send their kids away. I'd just make sure I had none if I didn't want them around.'

Mariam's mother is out, speaking at a conference in London, so Dina cooks supper. She makes a sort of lamb hotpot with spices and dates: I don't usually like lamb, but the flavouring is good and I swallow down plenty with the fragrant rice. We're seven altogether: Mariam's dad sits at the top of the table, grills us about the revision, then talks to the cousins and his mother about something on the news. I hear him say Amnesty International a few times, and the names of politicians, but the rest is in Arabic.

But, it's somehow happier here than at Charlie's. Mariam and I share the clearing up - even though people protest that I'm a guest. When her Mum arrives home from the conference, we make up the bed I'll have in Mariam's room. We stay in there, revising the circulation, which includes practising drawing a diagram of the heart. Mariam leans over and doodles the letters *FR* on mine, inside the left ventricle.

I add *'EE'*. 'What?' Mariam asks.

'You wrote *FR*, so I added *EE* – like I said, no kids to send to boarding school, so *free*, no kids?'

'Oh. Okay. Maybe. Or you'll change your mind.'

'Not about boarding school, I won't!'

In bed later, with the scent of that spiced lamb hotpot still in the house, I review the families I know: the ways they do things, the atmosphere in their houses. It's the atmosphere which defines a home. Shaz and Eliot cuddling on the sofa. Mariam's dad and the cousins relaxing in the front room with the beautiful carpet, her dad turning those large turquoise beads that live on the coffee table through his fingers like saying a rosary, all of them smoking, and watching a football match on the big flat screen TV. So where do her mum and grandmother sit in the evenings? In the other little living room upstairs?

Thursday early evening, we walk together back to my house, discussing the weirdness of parents: they presume they know who we are, but they so don't. 'Dad should be pleased to see me, anyhow. He'd be alone looking after himself otherwise.'

'Mine couldn't look after himself. You saw that. If Mum's on a conference he needs my sister to cook for him. The cardio-thoracic surgeon can't – or won't — even make couscous or boil an egg!'

'*If* Dad's not late back, if he's home before me, then I hope he'll make pancakes with maple syrup! He's good at those. But… I told you he, like, thinks I'm on this straight road towards becoming another of himself. Why be dynastic, when he was a rebel himself?'

'You'll do well in the exams, we'll all do well!'

'You think?'

'And then, he'll change his mind, and you'll become a famous photographer! And I'll just be a lecturer in pharmacology, same as my mother…!'

'No! A concert pianist! And I'll marry Fabian and end up home-schooling four children!'

'Never!'

Chapter 27

ME, DAD AND DAVID

I watch Mariam walk to the corner, and we wave. A watery sun suddenly pops out from the heavy grey clouds, lighting up everything. Maybe summer's coming back?

Then, I turn into our drive. If Dad's home already, we'll make supper together and chat. That'd be nice. What if he's late, shall I make something?, I then think, suddenly inspired by Dina.

Two cars are parked together, beside Dad's there's a white Renault Clio. Don't recognise it. I shrug off my backpack and ring the bell. I ring again. No answer. So, take out my keys, let myself in, and, hmm: house smells of fish and chips. 'Dad?' I call.

Silence. Dump my backpack and look into all the downstairs rooms: nobody. In the kitchen, two plates in the sink: fish and chips eaten? So, he's gone somewhere with the visitor? Did he even forget I was coming home? Nope, he wouldn't. He'll be at one of those grumbling GPs' meetings about their contract or whatever it was on the news. That's probably where he is. With the visitor, who's left their car parked here. I know Dad, he likes to walk to his meetings. And they had a scratch meal first.

Though why not leave me a note? Or send a text? Bit mean not to. Whatever, I think, checking the calendar on the noticeboard. There's a word I can't read, scribbled in pencil, on today and yesterday. And — a stiff white invitation card is pinned beside the calendar. *Mullins*

Family Reunion to mark the end of the Old Manse printed in black type. It's for the weekend of July 20th. And there's a Scripture verse at the bottom of the card, above the RSVP. And all our names, handwritten across the top.

What? We're all asked to go to the Manse for a whole-family meet-up? That's a first. And what's that about? Are Uncle Ian, Aunt Sue and family leaving the Manse where Dad grew up? OMG — if Mum and Dad's old homes are both being sold off, that feels a bit – weird. To me. I've always known those houses. Even if we don't visit the Manse that often. What about Granny Fee, what does she think about it?

But, hey, July 20th: that's me unable to go to the Truck festival with Charlie. Huge relief! This reunion thing doesn't sound like fun, but it will be useful for getting out of Truck with Charlie. A family reunion — an excuse she can't argue with.

Alone in the empty house, I can at least eat, so I open the fridge. Cheese is the only real option, so I take a big chunk, put it on a plate and add an apple and a bagel from the open packet that's in the bread tin. That looks a cold sad supper on a chilly evening, so I make hot chocolate to go with it, shove on my backpack, and head upstairs with the plate and mug.

Weird! My bedroom door's open — I always leave it shut — and a draught's blowing round the landing. As I go in, the wind flaps the curtains, so I dump my plate of food, and the mug, to pull the window shut, wondering why Dad didn't close all the windows before going out. Shove off the backpack. Look around. Sniff. Room smells perfumey. Someone's changed the duvet cover. Has someone been using my bed? The visitor? Why not give them the spare room? Have several people been visiting? And, looking round, how dare they use my desk, then tidy it all up, with a small pile of books – mine – at one end... I didn't leave it like that! So, anything else alien lying about? No slippers? No other things? Where's my fat revision file gone? What've they done with the clothes that were on the chair? And what else personal did I leave around? I don't remember. I had to pack clothes for Charlie's and Mariam's and my revision. But why the hell not use the spare room?

Hah! Suddenly, I think I know who it was — Uncle David must still be in Oxford – Dad's had *David* staying here – that perfume's aftershave, too much of it... He must have finished whatever he was doing at St Hildie's and come here afterwards.

Bed is all neat with clean everything (I sniff the pillows — smells of washing powder!), so at least they've thought about me coming home, and put it right. And he's leaving today. But how did Dad dare have David stay and not let me know! What's wrong with the spare bedroom? I'll take a look.

That is the biggest surprise: it's all been changed! Painted, even — it stinks of new paint. New shelves. Desk piled with books – Dad's medical tomes mostly – and a horrible thing – a skull, wearing a panama hat and shades – I remember he's talked about that, he used to keep it on his desk at medical school – why drag it out of wherever it was, to have it here?

Door bangs downstairs. I'm on the landing in a second, 'Dad? I'm back! Alice – remember me?'

I'm hanging over the banisters. He's in the hall, looks up, 'Alice!... Oh, Alice... back from Mariam's, oh, yes it's Thursday...'

'Right.' Well remembered Dad! I can also see David's head, but I can't hear what he says to Dad. He takes a few steps towards the front door... Yes, go, please... Dad takes a few steps, stops him. David disappears down the hallway where I can't see. To the study? Or the kitchen? 'Where were you? Why's Uncle David here? Why's he...'

'Alice – Alice, I'm so sorry, we went out for a walk when the sun came back.'

'And? You went to the chippy?'

'David brought fish and chips and we ate before our walk. I'm sorry there's none for you. I really am... Look, Alice,' Dad comes up a few stairs, I go down a few, 'Alice, dinnae worry yourself, but David had a wee problem to discuss, so as he was coming to Oxford it made sense… Och, it's taken a while and he's also helped me change the rooms around a bit, Mum wanted me out of her space so she can spread her work out…'

'Really? That's why you gave him my room and my bed? And moved my things?'

'Your things are all there, top drawer in your desk. Now, we've just to sum up our conversation and he'll be away home. Can you give us half an hour?'

'Maybe.' I feel a lot of things, all mixed up: they've split their work space, so we haven't a spare room any more. He's been so busy with David's problem that he forgot about me. He at least put my things in a drawer out of sight – but what were they?

'Then when I'm free we'll have a real chat, will we?' Dad says.

'Maybe. We seem to have an invitation to the northern rellies.'

'There's a ceilidh included —'

'Yeah. Okay.'

'Okay, canny lass?' he does a thumbs-up. I retreat up the stairs and into my room. The northern-speak or Scottishisms were to seduce my better side, to be forgiven. But, I can't help feeling *crabbit* about my room and my bed being used. Even if it has all been done to help some-one and it was done properly. And what's in the drawer? A jumble, some bits more personal than others. Fortunately, not too personal.

Okay, it was a surprise. I'll go down in a bit, make some noise so's they know I'm not happy and have my own life to lead. First, I dump everything out of my backpack in a heap, and sort out the tangle of books, underwear, and revision. At the very bottom are my muddy skinny jeans from going to the allotment with Charlie, tangled with a dress I bought when we went into Stroud to have our nails done, and wore with black leggings at Mariam's.

I'll put all the clothes in the wash. Leaving the books and notes on my bed. Open the window again, less wide this time, reposition the Anglepoise lamp David has been using to read (lying in my bed!) gather up the clothes, and tramp off downstairs towards the utility room.

The living room door's closed, and voices murmur inside. Not the time to put my head round to say hello to David — I'm not ready to do that yet. I wonder what the 'wee problem' is that's kept him here since Monday? Maybe not as *wee* as all that?

Suddenly, Dad calls out, 'Okay, Alice?' in that way that means *we're busy*, so I call out, 'Yeah, busy!' And through the door I hear, although he's dropped his voice now, 'so how did you...?'

'...a one-way exit....' says David, and I can hear no more.

The sun's really out now, it's a beautiful evening, so as I go into the utility room, I dump the washing and walk straight out into the garden. Still quite windy though. Clouds scudding about the sky like playful fluffy kittens. My phone vibrates in my back pocket: Mariam? Did I leave something behind? Please not Charlie... It's Fabian, he says *Any chance we can meet later?...F XX!* Two Xs? Oh, glory be, as I've heard Daze say, possibly ironically, but my heart leaps with serious meaning — as I think, When? Tell me what time, you idiot!

Try texting back. There's no reply. I want to know more! Back at the washing machine, I find it's full of damp stuff, my usual duvet cover, sheet, pillowcases! They might've taken that out and hung it up! S'pose they left it for days in there? I squat in front of the machine, hauling things out and dumping them in the laundry basket. Hey, there's a couple of my T-shirts and some underwear and pyjamas in that tangled pile! And as I wish Dad had not put my private stuff in, that wind blows a gust which slams the door between the utility room and the kitchen. And the next thing is, I hear Dad's voice on the other side of the door, talking loudly: 'Och, I think she's upstairs somewhere – or gone out again, leaving the house open, wind's blown this door shut... So, amicable?'

'Amicable,' says David's voice. 'We discussed the problem of social isolation being built into the system...and whether the calling – the vocation – is necessarily and unchangeably tied, through their obsession with keeping up appearances...' he lowers his voice a tad, 'to the tradition of celibacy.'

Oh no! They've come into the kitchen, which wouldn't matter only they think I'm upstairs or out, having left doors open (which I wouldn't do – would I?) and their conversation is about – vocations and sex? I can't walk out into that! Dad never thought I might be, like anywhere, and they're wandering about the house talking private stuff, without checking I'm not going to hear, like, did he even think? Damn, blast, b-word, fucking f-word, Dad!

Next, noise of cupboard opening 'What'll it be? Coffee, tea, lager? Better not a dram as you're driving.'

A murmur. 'Mmm,' says Dad, and I hear a clink, the alcohol's been chosen. So, has something extreme happened? *Unabashed*, let's say, voices continue. 'A one-way exit.' I've got one here! I've got no way out unless I go in the garden. And then I can't get in again without ringing the bell! But now I've heard a bit, I'm confused, embarrassed, and curious.

I may as well put my stuff in to wash, anyway, set everything up and start the machine. I'll have to wait here for them to go back where they were. But, they don't. There they are, I can imagine them, David elegantly sat on the edge of the table swinging one leg – I've seen him do that – and Dad, leaning against the counter, looking interested in what's being said, occasionally sweeping back his almost-fringe. Both sipping lagers.

The exit and the celibacy make no sense, so can't be combined in any way. The one-way exit suggests possibly a traffic accident, which David witnessed. If that's it, if he's a witness, or part of an accident, or helped in some way, they've got some reason to discuss it. I suppose. But celibacy and vocation? Hasn't there been (I've heard Dad talking about this) an argument about gay marriages in church? Maybe it's that?

Mumble, mumble… Dad's voice, 'And she…?' She? David's gay. Or is he bi? Strain my ears for the response.

'Of course, follow the tradition of celibacy. In effect, we are pretty much saying…' (David says with a snorting laugh), 'an ordinary person, a cis person…'

Dad, after a second, joins in the ironic humour. Then he says, 'Although I've heard Andrew F-P more than once embarrassing his congregation in a sermon about "the joys of Christian marriage", quoting from the *Song of Songs,* and adding in detailed descriptions!'

They also find that funny.

David goes on, 'Privately the Bishop may empathise with other views, but as Bishop he sticks, quite rightly of course, to nothing outside tradition. And how ever will the Synod allow something so outrageous? He doesn't think there is any way I can continue except by stepping back into the dubious gloom of a single, celibate, gay priest. Bi is not in his selection of options. I can continue as I am.'

Then this is about David himself, is it? Yeah, that would be horrible. No excitement. No daring. I remember, me and Fabian: feel us holding hands, poring over the score of Haydn's *Creation.*

So, it's even more embarrassing. It makes me sweat. That and the humidity. It rained all the days I was at Mariam's, which was half the week, so now the sun's making everything steam outside. It's beating on the window making the room stuffy. They'll know I've heard what they've been talking about, if I step out now saying, 'Hi, I was putting in my washing and the wind banged the door shut.' Better stay where I am.

Dad speaks up again, 'You said you didn't expect anything could change.'

David says, 'The worst part was, he may or may not have meant such an unthinking response, but the main thrust of his advice revealed what I have to forgive as outrageous insult... you won't – or rather you will – believe this. Questioning my orientation... the implication was – although you're gay, you desire to have sex within a relationship, so now you claim that you are bisexual, and therefore have decided to enter a relationship with a woman!'

'Unbelievable! How do they manage to consider that a pastoral consultation?' Dad bellows. And Oh My God... how horrible! And it is about David. I nearly die. I can't face them, not David or Dad. Could this woman be Shaz? No, impossible. I can't imagine she's his type and she's not religious. She must have just met him at St Hildie's going to these poetry things.

Whatever, I wish I'd thrown that door open as soon as it slammed! I'll go like a beetroot now, and look guilty. Whatever I do, they'll know what I've heard.

Dad says, 'How long will they manage to live in the past!'

'The imagined past – when virtuous heterosexuality was the norm — as of course it wasn't. Naturally, I emphasised that I would be making a serious decision, and it's not yet made. We haven't got as far as that yet.'

So, he's bi not gay? Can that happen? Maybe you don't become bi, you realise, it creeps up on you? Shall Google it: can a person become bi, how do they know? I move further from the door. If David is bisexual, did I want to know? Do I want to know what adult relatives do and think about in private?

Whoever she is, what haven't they *got as far as yet*? Murmur-murmur, now, really low voices. Water runs in the sink, and glasses clink. Sounds like drinks are over. More talk, louder voices. Then fading away, moving down the hallway. Very quietly, I open the door, a tiny crack, checking that they've left the kitchen.

Empty. Only our cat, sleeping in her basket. I creep out a few steps, and Dad comes from the living room, stops and looks surprised. 'Alice! Thought you were working upstairs...'

'Well I wasn't.'

There's a sound of flushing, and David comes out of the downstairs loo. 'Alice! Great to see you!'

I can't look at him. 'Yes...'

I try to escape, but he talks, 'Alice, I'm sorry we haven't got time to chat as I'm on my way home now. I really do apologise and I hope we can catch up soon? Maybe if you're all going to be at the Manse later on?'

'Yeah, guess so. Only just seen the invite.'

David moves towards the front door, and picks up some things stacked there: briefcase, man bag (as they call them), backpack, plastic carrier of books from Blackwell's.

'Well, I hope you'll all be there. And I know your Granny Fee would like to see you, Alice, and as your godfather I'd love to have a catch-up.' Hmm, might be embarrassing after what I've overheard.

And he leaves, pulling the front door shut very quietly.

But in a way, he still seems to be here...

Chapter 28

DAD AND I DISCUSS MY CHOICES

Me and Dad are left standing in the hall. It's like we both feel awkward — for different reasons, obviously. He says: 'Alice, so sorry about the muddle. I'm just away to the kitchen to clear things up, and then let's have a chat, will we? And you might like something to eat?'

I don't answer. I'm stunned by all I've heard. That conversation, things David was sharing with Dad, was way too intimate, and not what I wanted to know. And Dad giving my room – my bed – to someone without asking me hasn't helped. I need to process it all.

Now Dad's gone back into the kitchen, and I can hear him humming cheerfully as he washes up the plates from the fish and chips, and the tea, and whatever else they ate. And the whisky glasses. That humming is annoying. I plump down onto the nearest place to sit, the stair three up from the bottom. It feels familiar, from long ago: this used to be called the naughty step!

My thoughts are spinning like my brain's a centrifuge. I'm trying to handle ideas I don't know much about. OK, so I knew David was gay, that wasn't a problem. But now it seems to be all about him being attracted to women - or one particular woman — as well? How exactly does this work? And would that be a reason that a bishop can throw him out of his job? If that's what bishops can do, don't they know that orientation isn't a lifestyle choice?

Seems I've sat here a long time: my bum's gone numb. But, I've come to a conclusion: my fury and disappointment isn't really with Dad, something's happened to me. Like maybe my understanding of grown-ups has expanded, and I'm seeing that they aren't the massively poised and sorted-out people we think they are when we're kids. They try to project that in their relationships with, well, *us*. So, when I overheard Dad and David talking, I didn't want to hear any of it because they were discussing something they found difficult, which made me feel that grown-ups are not all-powerful, or in control, of everything in their lives. That is, like, scary. I shan't be, either...

David's had a revelation as well: must be scary to find your sexuality mayn't be the way you thought. When you're already – well, way into being a grown-up.

And he was trying out this revelation on Dad. Like telling someone and hoping you'll going to be accepted? Like Zoe might confide in me about something she's not sure about. Like when Zoe asked me about her period, because she started when Mum was away – she knew what it was, but she still asked me... and, that's it, telling and asking to reassure yourself.

Anyway, where is Dad? Still in the kitchen? Or maybe outside, in the garden?

'Alice?' I don't answer, I'm not quite ready to. Instead I move up a few stairs. Dad comes down the hall and stands at the bottom of the stairs. 'Alice! How was it, your week, did you have space to revise?'

Of course, he doesn't know I've just had a kind of life-changing revelation. I'll talk about what he wants as if everything's the same. 'Well Charlie's doing GCSEs as well – though we didn't work much... I did at Mariam's, we mostly revised.'

'I hope you took some time off!'

I try something. Being calm like him. Calm and determined. 'And I hoped we'd have fish and chips but you'd eaten them with Uncle David. Did you forget about me, or what?'

'Could you come down from there, so we can talk?'

'I could. Could you, maybe, not offer any more visitors my bedroom when I'm not here, or not until you've asked me?' This is negotiation, which he says we should learn to do.

'Yes. I'm sorry about that.'

'You forgot I'm not a kid now?'

He looks a bit bothered, then, 'Maybe I did, for a moment. David needed a place to stay at short notice, and your room wasn't being used...'

'Not being used? But everything in there is mine! I was only away for a few days!'

'Och, it was a slip of the mind. As you say, more than once, you and Zo-zo aren't parcels we care for... I'm sorry, am I forgiven?'

'Next time, ask, can you remember? It's not like I'm away at Uni, and if I was, I still live here! And we do have a spare room. We did... What exactly happened?'

'I got it wrong because, well, because David had something to discuss.'

'So – did he, like, say he was coming or just turn up?'

'What matters is he needed somewhere to stay and we've always believed in offering hospitality, haven't we, Ally?'

'S'pose we have.'

'Ally, David is family, it's not a stranger I'd put up in your room.'

'And I've got a phone!' I wriggle my phone out of my pocket and wave it at him, 'see?'

'Och,' he says, hand across his eyes, then flicks back what remains of his sort of fringe, and looks up at me. 'Och. Ally. I didna' think, and I'm sorry.' A pause. 'You know, this happened to us at the Manse, when I was growing up: hospitality sometimes meant we were moved about to accommodate some needy person, or a visitor. I really didna' think.'

'Look, I know the stuff you say in those relationship talks, how you go on about it's not only sex and boyfriends, it's other things. Like having private space – and then, you let someone use my bedroom, which is my private space and full of personal things. Like,' I wave my arms, 'books and cards and clothes and everything that's me. You didna' think, actually you seem not to understand.'

'Aye,' he says.

'Right. But why change our spare room?'

'Yes,' he says slowly, so it sounds like he's thinking, 'so another thing. Your Mam and I decided we've way too much clutter in our shared study, so I volunteered to make her a proper one upstairs. So that she could spread out all the admin she has to do these days. All those forms about funding for her lab.'

'Oh. Right. But hang on – you and Mum decided — did Zo-zo and I hear about this? What about when people – when Granny Caro and Des come to visit?' Here, I stand up quickly, and nearly trip off my stair. So I step off it, and descend properly into the hallway.

'It was only a wee change for us. The futon shop had a sale. I bought a sofa bed, so the room can still be used for visitors.'

'So why couldn't David sleep on the futon?'

'Because it arrived after he did. And by then your Mam had decided she wanted to keep her cave, she knows where everything is, she hadn't the inclination to go through it all, so it's me that moved upstairs. David being here was a help with humping files and books and furniture.'

I'm about to tell him what I think about that tasteless skull in the hat, but he seizes on something else, something he maybe doesn't like.

'Alice, something's different about you. You've done something to your – eyebrows?'

'Great – you've noticed. You've actually looked at me.'

'Come and have a proper look at the spare room then – see what we've done?'

Up we go. And as we enter the ex-spare-room, I say 'I looked before, like I said, I didn't like it – much.' A second look doesn't make any difference. Especially not to that skull with the shades and the hat. 'What do you think visitors are going to think about *that*?' I point at the skull, with its shades sticky-taped on, and its panama hat, and the little red bandana scarf where its neck should be.

'Och, my old revision buddy!'

'You mean it was on your desk when you were living in college? It's kind of – I mean, how could you?' He makes a disapproving face. 'Sorry, but... I get it, though I wouldn't want it in my room – I wouldn't want to sleep on that sofa bed with a skull watching me!'

'I'm sorry you don't like him.'

I was thinking now that I'd try out my revelation on him: how my brain kind of rushed forward and I saw into being a grown-up and how it might feel not so different to being, well, not one. 'Growing up is weird... anyhow, I just don't like the skull, is actually what I think. It's a bit too Goth to have in here, were you a Goth ever? I mean, it doesn't seem very you somehow.'

He stops me there, saying, 'I could put him away... If I say I'm sorry, and we'll not allow visitors, anyone, to stay in either of your bedrooms again, can we put all this behind us? Can we have a coffee or even – shall we go down to G and D's and have ice cream?'

'Because I'm not a kid,' I say quietly, hoping maybe that'll sink in, 'I could drink a coffee. Not out though. I only just came in, I want to be here.'

Dad stands up, 'That's true. You're not.'

'Zoe might still be, a bit, inside?'

'She might that. Would you like your drink up here, then? On your own?'

'Not really.'

'Okay. Then, you wanted to discuss A-level subjects before half term began. So how about now? With coffee and...'

I remember my food — the cheese, bagel, and apple — and the hot chocolate, left in my room, and my disappointment about the fish and chips. That door banging, and their coming into the kitchen, deprived me of even that supper!

'You get a coffee if you want one.' I say, a bit spitefully, as the feelings tear round inside me. No proper welcome home. Someone using my room.

'Still something the matter?' Dad says, sounding confused.

He's surprised. He doesn't know why I'm cross. Of course he doesn't. 'Just – well –– I walked in and smelt fish and chips and I hoped you'd bought that for me – for us. Then I found the plates in the sink — so I took some stuff upstairs to eat. And made myself a hot chocolate. It'll all still there. I could eat it now? While we talk?'

'I could make you a new hot chocolate?' Dad says (looking brighter, though what will he say when I tell him my ideas)? 'Might even have one myself, less caffeine. Would you like a cheese on toast?'

'I'm okay with what's in my room.' This is difficult, I'm about to disappoint him, so I shouldn't make him do stuff for me, should I? 'I suppose,' I say, 'maybe you could split the bagel and toast that?'

I fetch my plate, and hand over the bagel. Dad goes off downstairs. Sam the Skull regards me through his shades. I suppose, for a medic, having a skull on your desk isn't such a bad idea for personalising a college room. Boys' rooms would be different: I haven't yet seen Fabian's, now what would that be like? And what'd we be doing in there? Nina says there's nothing to it – but does she really know? Dad's feet are on the stairs, I hear him coming before my thoughts are sorted and ready.

He puts the tray down in front of Sam Skull, takes his cocoa and sits on the office chair, twizzling it around with one foot to face the sofa bed.

He's put cheese on the bagel and toasted it. He's sliced up a tomato. And made two hot drinks. 'Oh wow,' I say, 'thanks for doing all that.'

I shan't think of this as a bribe, I shall still tell him my thoughts about A levels, I decide, as I take my food and perch on the sofa bed — it's really hard as a sofa, I hope it's better as a bed. Suddenly, I picture myself on Dad's lap on the proper sofa downstairs, my arms round his neck, long ago when he and Mum had both been away, and we had our childminder stay over, and I'm saying 'I want to live with you always!' I just wanted to keep him there, and never have them both go away the same time, ever again.

Then I remember that that time he'd been at Granny Fee and Grandpa Alasdair's, and I seize on the subject of the Manse to delay getting into A levels. 'Hang on – that Manse invitation – what exactly is that about?'

'Granny Fee thought we'd all like to say goodbye to the old home. They're going to build a new more convenient Manse on the same site.'

'So you mean they're going to pull down the Manse? Uncle Ian's got a million kids so why not keep the house? It was big enough for all of us to stay. We loved the garden, and the tree house. Granny had her veg patch, with poles for runner beans. This is like Granny Caro and Chapel House, why does everything have to change at once?

'I know, I do know how you feel. The Manse is huge but Ian and Sue haven't the time to keep an old house up like Granny did, it's expensive to heat, it needs a lot doing. A new house will be much easier for everyone. You weren't fond of the old Manse, were you?'

'No, I just think it would be nice if we'd all known about it together.'

'You know now.'

'Not the point, Dad.' Is that look what's called 'sheepish'? A sort of half-grin? 'Look, I'm sorry we didn't talk about the Manse sooner. This reunion idea is new, I didn't know, I didn't have anything to do with it.'

We're both silent. I think Dad is actually a bit sad about his old home being knocked down. He drains his cocoa, and puts the mug down carefully with a concerned look on his face.

'I was glad I managed to get to the parents' evening: your science teachers said they're impressed with your work, which is always great news,' he says, as I take a sip of hot chocolate, and nibble a slice of tomato.

'Mmm, but, beware teacher smarm. They might've been sucking up to you, in your capacity as School Doctor for the boarders!'

'Well, no, I took that as genuine praise. You are very focused and you've picked up everything they've flung at you about some quite complicated facts and processes.'

'Okay, point made. It's easier with any subject if your parents know it all.' I chomp some bagel, hoping he's prepared by that to hear me out on not being a science graduate in the future.

'That said, I'm sorry I haven't been as involved as I could be in your studies. I realise that. It'll be helpful now, if I know how you're thinking about the future?'

'What does Mum think? Were you both at the parents' evening?'

'Unusually, I was there, alone. Mum was busy with re-writing an important piece for *Nature*.'

I raise what's left of my eyebrows, 'The big science journal?'

'The big science journal. I usually don't get to those evenings because...'

'I know, your surgery isn't over in time. It's better if both parents know what a person is thinking about at the same time, isn't it?' I know I'm interrogating Dad, but it feels better to confront him now, than to risk them thinking I have no opinions. 'I mean, you both need to know who a person is, where they want to be. In their future.'

He considers. He's brought the biscuit tin up with him on that tray, and now takes out a chocolate chip cookie. Then he says, wrinkling his forehead a bit, 'It probably is. I thought we did – don't we?'

I consider this. He told Grandpa Alisdair he did not want to become a minister, and he did want to study medicine. So he should, in theory, totally understand what being oneself and not being the same as your parents, feels like. Even if the science teachers have told him how good I am at their subjects. 'We've had a lot of career talks at school, and I – find them all interesting. I've enjoyed all the science I've done, but we heard about lots of other things.'

'And?'

'And, I want to explore a bit, about what's out there. Maybe, I want to do something nobody in this family is doing.'

'Have you talked to your teachers about this?'

'I got them to show me where the prospectuses are kept. I found the ones about courses that look interesting, trying to think what I'm good at and enjoy, besides the things I'm doing now. Well, as well as. They encourage us to, you know?'

'Go ahead, I'm listening.' He picks up his cocoa mug, looks in it, and puts it down again.

'Then you know, what I like doing, away from science – well, using a bit of science – maybe a lot of it – there's ecology.'

'I know Zoe...'

'No, this is me. And it's gonna be sooner than Zoe. There's also music, but as I'm not doing GCSE in that, it's only what I like doing. There's art and design, which can go either way: making things, or art therapy? Or, photography. I really would love to do that.'

'Art therapy? Why not clinical psychology or even psychiatry?'

'You're not listening! I don't want to be – I think I may want to get away from where I'm defined as another of you and Mum, and Granny Caro, and Grandpa who's a fertility specialist, and even great-granny Ianthe! I mean, right away, and like, find out about other things, and be me? I mean, take Fabian. His dad is a historian, and his mum studied art history. He's applying to Cambridge to do sociology.'

'We've come a long way from – what did you say you were thinking about? Ecology?'

'Yes. I'd not want be the next David Attenborough though: I'm not that into it. It was, like, something I might look into. So many aspects, all useful. But probably not that.'

'And is photography the most likely, then?'

'Maybe. Maybe not. I could do – with art and design of course – two science A levels? That would fit. Physics would be one. And, sociology or psychology?'

'So, where? After school?'

'Uni.'

Dad just looks thoughtful. I think, he's never considered the idea of me not following the dynastic route. Another thing about grown-ups: it seems hard not to see your children, if you have them, as an extension of yourself?

Chapter 29

ME AND FABIAN CATCH UP.

Another learning point: sometimes a person you think knew all about you actually knows only a bit, and that bit is way past its sell-by date, or it's in their head and not your real life. He knows I'm doing GCSEs and that like him and Mum I am better at science than writing essays – although I can write those okay enough. He knows I enjoy music and play in the school orchestra. He knows that unlike my sister, I am not in any of the school swimming teams, and I don't attend Headleigh Parish Church's 'Base Camp for Teens'.

So now, Dad's looking confused, or amazed, or – something, and he says, 'Oh. Well. I didn't know you were — thinking of —' and kind of waves the half-eaten biscuit in his hand, to demonstrate the unsureness of his knowing (or understanding). That hand gesture he makes is like Zoe does.

'It's not unusual,' I say, 'I mean, if I took, say, physics and chemistry – suppose I did – then if photography doesn't work out...'

He shakes his head, 'This is all news to me. You haven't spoken to Mum about it - or have you?'

'Does that matter?'

'Och, I wondered what she'd think. I mean – I could imagine you taking a gap year, after A levels, to do something creative? And then, med school, maybe? Or —?'

'*Dad*...that's absurd! Or you think it'd be okay, but this is my life, not yours!' I say.

Basically, this is going wrong. I need to talk more about my ideas, and I need time to absorb how little he knows about what's going on in my head. My very vague ideas are based around looking at Daze's life and Fabian's mum's work – which I've only really heard about — and reading up about what careers are available to photography graduates. Dad's written his own script for me on the basis of the courses I'm doing well on, without asking me what I'm interested in. I get to my feet, pick up my mug and plate, and move towards the door. 'Can we talk again when Mum's here maybe?'

Pathetic ending, but a get-out clause until I can think up better arguments for blazing my own trails. 'I mean, maybe she'd see into this. I don't really want to do ground-breaking research and,' I know I could get angry, and I don't want that, 'and I'm not into being a carer, medical or otherwise. I don't think... I could do it,' I say, and hurry downstairs with my supper things, stick them in the dishwasher, and lock myself in the downstairs loo.

There is no sound of feet descending the stairs overhead. Good. I creep out, realising it was daft to run downstairs like that to avoid showing how I felt: though the memory of hugging Dad at about age five and saying I wanted to live with him forever is like a warning, like a reminder not to appear to be ready to do whatever he suggests with my career choices. So, has something broken between me and him?

Then, the best thing happens: another text from Fabian. It's already eight-thirty, but am I free to meet in town?

Why not? Maybe I could slip out without Dad noticing? I really don't want to have to ask, and go through the conversation about it being late, making sure I'm careful, remembering my bike lamp, wearing my helmet, letting him know where I am, being back by... whenever... blah, blah.

Boldly (but careful to be as quiet as I can) I slip out through the back door, unlock my bike, and cycle into town. It's a beautiful evening, the wind's dropped, the grey clouds are gold-edged and shimmery — and that's brought out crowds of tourists and students, surging down the High Street and over Magdalen Bridge. I'm heading for Little Clarendon Street, where Fabian is waiting at the corner, outside Taylor's delicatessen: he grins, I grin, jumping off my bike, and we hug, one-armed, each clutching a bike with the free hand.

Defo (as Charlie would defo say), a big spontaneous Welcome Back Alice! Quite different from earlier, at home. We fasten our bikes together for safety outside the cafe, I like that, it's kind of, nice. Symbolic. Inside we take a while deciding on which flavours of ice cream. 'And a coffee?' Fabian asks.

'Ooh, yes, a latte!' And, he pays for what I'm having. More nice warm feelings about being wanted. Balanced on the high stools by the window, side by side, our shoulders touching, we chat about our half term activities. Which is remarkably easy.

Though it worried me when I had to say I'd been at Charlie's. 'That girl who jumped out on you outside in the interval at the Haydn concert?'

Gosh, suppose he fancied Charlie? Anybody would, just the right height for weight, curviness, strokeable dark hair, lips which ask to be... But, listen, I think inside, this is me you've asked out. 'I had to. It's a bit weird, but my Mum has cosied up again to hers. I only spent the half term weekend at theirs, though. That is a family I'm glad I'm not part of,' I emphasise, 'What about your expedition — the cottage in a wilderness in Norfolk?'

'We checked out Aldeburgh because we always do, the parents are Britten fans. More than any of us. Me, and my sisters. Dad insisted we go birding.'

'Birding?'

'His other obsession. Birding is a bit like a religion. It's something I don't talk about — and neither does Dad at college.' (Where Dr Russell is a fellow and tutor in Modern History.) 'Actually,' Fabian says, looking serious, 'birding can be cool. You might like it. I could take you. Not to Norfolk, but Otmoor, maybe?'

So, us in an isolated bit of countryside — though miles of flat Norfolk farmland stretching to a misty horizon, or the cliff tops in West Cornwall, covered with heather, would be even better! But even Otmoor, with binoculars, and a better digital SLR than my present camera, and a picnic, and a rug, and… a bit more.'

'Sounds amazing. Are there red kites – or more like smaller birds? Whatever, I've never done that. I'd like to try it.'

It's funny how you can be with someone and just spend time looking at them. Saying not very much. He has the best eyes, which look straight into mine like I am really interesting, and I don't care if people do think we're a pair of nerds or geeks or whatever, we are us. My whole body is kind of fizzing. I know I'm falling over words when I talk, so I decide to slow down, and spoon in some of my now-melting ice cream as we agree about *carving out* time. This is Mum's theory that when you have important exams, at half term it's sensible to *carve out* time for fun stuff, leaving the revision on one side. This is fun stuff.

Though when Fabian asks what else I did, and I say, 'Oh, I went to Mariam's and we revised!' he teases me that I am 'a little bookworm', which opens up the whole horrid conversation with Dad, and not being welcomed back as I wanted. It brings with it a scratchy feeling inside my head, like wanting to hurt myself for expecting a big 'welcome home, Alice', and ends up silencing my chatty mood.

Fabian asks me why, 'Hey, Alice! Where've you gone?'

'Nowhere. Well, somewhere. I had a row with my Dad when I got back. Not a shouty row. One of those conversations that go wrong, about my A Level choices? Like he has no idea who I am, what I want, how I think? Also, he'd had a relative stay over and use my room!'

'That sucks.'

'Yes. And the A level choices. He's been thinking all the time I'd be doing the same as he did – all science, straight into another Mullins working in life sciences or medicine.'

'He wants you to do something he and your mum did? I get it.'

'You don't exactly. The irony is that although it's not the same subjects, I do want to do something that he, actually, did. If he could see that, it'd almost be funny: at least he should totally understand. Grandpa wanted him to be a church minister, and take over as the pastor when he retired. But he'd already decided on medicine. He just stuck to what he wanted to do, until Grandpa gave in. And now, I'm not getting through to him even though I'm really doing the same as him. You'll hardly believe this – Grandpa believed that the minister idea was what God planned for him, but in the end he let go of that and was proud that Dad went to Cambridge and became a doctor!'

'Guidance from God – that was a powerful tactic. Back then.'

'Grandpa told him okay, do what you want – but you will be doing God's second best!'

'Oh, so God had a kind of back-up idea. Clever of your grandfather!'

'Nobody would say that today, would they?'

'Well, my ancient great-gran in Italy might have wanted me to be a priest – old Catholic thing really — but probably I could persuade her that today sociology is a better choice. Anyway, you?'

'Anyhow, Dad was like shocked, even suggested I could take a gap year to work out my feelings about doing something creative, something he obviously thinks is a waste of time. Which it isn't. Even though I hadn't prepared right, he could've listened, and been interested. Basically, Dad still thinks of the me I was as a kid. Or raw material he can, like, mould.'

'So, you've got to convince him that you're serious. You know — that you've talked to the teachers, you've got hold of all the prospectuses, researched the courses, stuff like that.'

'Yeah, I know. Would you believe – he was talking psychology, even psychiatry – I'd hate to be a psychiatrist!'

'You might make a good one... psychiatrists are needed...'

'Oh yeah? Can you imagine?'

'I think so. You'd have this wonderful couch, an oriental carpet on the floor, low lighting, silk covered cushions...'

'That's a psycho-what's-it – an analyst! Like Freud!'

'You wouldn't want to hear my dreams?'

'Shut up!'

We look at each other, and laugh. We kiss across the empty bowls and the coffee mugs. We go silent, and it's like the cafe is holding its breath. Then we realise that the buzz of people is done with for another day, only a few are left, someone's wiping the tables. A little group around the door is hassling each other about who goes out first. The bell tinkles as they finally leave. Outside darkness has crept up, and the street lights are on. I pick up my bike helmet from the counter. Fabian turns his wrist and consults his watch. 'Look, I have to go – but if we leave now, I could walk up to your place with you?'

'Really? I mean, I've got my bike, but...'

'I can still be home by half past...'

Walking down St Giles's, suddenly my phone screams from my pocket: oh my God, let it not be Dad!

But it's Mariam, 'Disaster! My parents talked to Mahmoud's, they all say Nina must pay for new glasses, as it's her fault they fell in the river!'

'They can't do that!' I text back. 'Nothing to do with parents.'

'They can, she didn't need to tip up the punt!'

'Was an accident!'

'Was stupid...'

I close my phone down and put it away: pointless to argue with Mariam in the road, I need my hands to wheel the bicycle. At least, I need one of them.

'What?' Fabian asks.

'Mariam. Her parents are making a fuss about Mahmoud's glasses that he lost in the river.'

'Well, glasses are expensive.'

'Yeah, but...'

'Are they making Nina pay?'

'Her family's less well off than them.'

'Doesn't work like that though.'

''Spose not. Can you be on my side?'

'I am. You should ignore it, it's their battle not yours.'

'So how do I do that? They're my closest friends!'

Fabian *says* nothing, but puts his arm round my back, and pulls me in so that our sides totally touch. Hip to hip, only he's taller than me. We walk on, silently, each guiding a bicycle with our free arm and hand. It's a clumsy arrangement, and difficult when crossing side-roads. I am debating whether or not it's patronising. Whatever it means, there's one person who believes I should stick to my own decisions, not give in like Mariam has done, and do what the family decides.

When we turn into my road, we slow down. I make sure we stop before we reach my house, and not under a street lamp. We totally stop, and then — then somehow we both think the same, because we kiss, properly, still holding the bikes so they don't crash to the ground. A long sloppy kiss, the most exciting, clumsy, thing.

It is a powerful feeling, to be wanted.

Chapter 30

MAX IS DISAPPOINTED AND I MAKE A CAKE

From the garden, the house appears totally dark, so I lean my bike against the kitchen wall, lock it, walk as quietly as the gravel allows around to the front door, let myself in, kick off my trainers. Sitting on the stairs, I wait a bit, wondering where Dad is. I look up at the door of his new den.

Surprisingly, that door doesn't open. Upstairs, I sneak by and into my room, where Radio Three (left playing) is offering me something by Philip Glass. I open the window as far as it goes, and hang out. A perfect evening, deep indigo sky, even speckled with stars. I've a lot to think about, too much and too many things. Suddenly a bright glaring rectangle appears on the lawn. Dad must have gone into his new den and turned on the light. I quickly pull my head in, shut the window, and move to close my bedroom door.

But Dad's voice suddenly calls out, 'Alice?'

I shan't reply. He calls again, and adds, 'I'm a bit disappointed with you.'

Disappointed? That's a nasty thing to say. Dad's becoming Grandpa Alisdair, who everyone says was gloomy and strict. Because I went out? Or really, because I want to do some A level people in our family don't do! Thanks for reminding me, and ruining my lovely evening!

Now I hear him from the passage, 'Alice, I don't need to know where you've been, but could you think before you disappear another time? I'm happy for you to visit your friends, but we like to know when you're out, where you're going, and agree a time you'll be back. Try to see it from our point of view: we want you to keep safe.'

He couldn't have done better: those words hit me hard with all the imaginings I don't want to imagine. Out of my messy feelings comes my voice, 'For God's sake, I only went to a cafe with Fabian! I am safe, he walked me back, I'm home — okay?'

'Okay, though I'd prefer to hear that without the swearing.' He takes a breath, waits a moment, then says 'I'll see you in the morning, then?' What for? A pause. His door closes. Will he now prepare a proper rant for tomorrow?

Door opens again, 'Mum's home tomorrow!' he calls, as if nothing was wrong. 'And Zo-zo!'

Click, door closes. I'm sweaty and sad now. My two best friends are fighting, Fabian and me have kissed long kisses, and Dad has handed me a guilt trip.

Everything's so messy, doing my head in. Back to exams on Monday... Exams were making me tired, maybe that's why the mess. Should've gone to Cornwall for half term... would have been easier, even with Zoe and her immature friend. I should go for a shower but lying face down on my bed, crying into the pillow, is easier. What a wimp...

In the morning, I wake up, look at my phone. I've slept until ten thirty! So relieved I don't have to see Dad, he's gone to work. A note on my bedside table says *Mum and Z home late afternoon, why not make them a cake? D.*

Why'd I want to do that?

Downstairs, I make a very milky coffee, and sit at the kitchen table forcing myself into doing some revision. A headache sits behind my eyes. Outside, a blackbird sings its amazing song, the sun shines, the garden's full of flowers, all is far too beautiful as a backdrop for my life! A tear forces its way out and splashes on my notes, blurring the words.

It's joined by another, and another. I've nothing to mop it up with, so let's let it all out again. My life has got too complicated, with Mariam's cousin's glasses falling in the river, visiting Charlie to help her cope, David sleeping in my bed, me actually telling Dad I don't want to be railroaded into a science career, and Dad disappointed because I went out with Fabian. Is that enough to be going on with?

There's also the two unexciting invitations — Granny's one to stay in London, and the Northern relatives' 'family retreat', whatever that is. And what about my birthday, which nobody has really talked about?

My chemistry notes are now a splodge on damp file paper. To save them from added snot, I'm heaving myself up and fetching a wodge of kitchen roll. Something is wrong with you, Alice – this isn't who you are!

Right: what did the Griffon say to the Mock Turtle? 'Up, lazy thing!'

Have mopped up the table, rescued what I can of the notes, swallowed down a painkiller for the headache, and begun to weigh out the ingredients for a cake. It's a nice idea after all, especially if Mum can mitigate whatever's got into Dad. Oh, and she might explain to us about not wanting the spare room for her study. Why didn't they mention it before we all went away?

Now someone rings the doorbell. There's a parcel to sign for: the postie gives me a funny look, like they've never seen a person in their pyjamas with a floury apron over them at nearly lunch time. All I'm doing is some baking mid-morning on a Friday!

The parcel is smallish. Its customs label is smudged, but the stamp is American. It's addressed to Mum, so probably it's work stuff, and not interesting. I'll leave it in her study. The cake I'm making is an Angel Food Cake, which is quite difficult, and if it works, it's a celebration of Mum replacing the one that Dad's naughty brothers stole and ate in their tree house long ago. If it doesn't – I'm not thinking about that! The video on Google about how to make this cake was a wonderful way to find something equally difficult to my life, and think about that instead... I now have to get into proper clothes and go to Waitrose to buy Cream of Tartar, whatever that is!

Coming out of the supermarket, I spot Nina and her mum, weighed down by bags of shopping. Do I hurry across and express my thoughts about the unfairness of Mariam's family? Two steps towards them, I hold back, rooted to the ground, and watch as they cross the road and disappear into the Oxfam shop, after browsing its window. Abandon my idea of giving myself retail therapy in the Headleigh charity shops, and hurry back home to my partially begun cake.

Mixed and ready to go into its tin, it looks so white and smooth, so retro and unhealthy! But, it's a memory cake to maybe make Mum and Dad overlook my disappearance last night: to say I do understand their concern for our safety, and that women haven't reclaimed the streets. Though once I'm at Uni they won't know what I'm up to. Did Granny Caro know about Daze being pregnant — did she know about her giving birth with Mum as her labour partner, almost grabbed off the street to be there? Did Granny Fee and Grandpa Alistair know about Dad doing illegal research, unsupervised, with a non-religious girlfriend? (I have the cake mixture in the tin, now, and smoothed down. Concluding thought: everything came right, didn't it? Or nearly everything.)

So, check the oven's hot enough, and slide the cake onto the middle shelf. Set the kitchen timer. Ready for another coffee and some toast – cheese and tomato on toast because, by the clock, this is lunch.

And while eating it (realising I'm having pretty well the same food as last night!) I re-read the invite from the Northern rellies. It's signed by Dad's much-younger brother the Revd Ian Mullins. The signature looks handwritten, but it's printed too, that must've cost more. He's one of the twins who nicked that cake, but now he's the Pastor of First Truly Reformed Church. At the top he's scribbled all our names: Max, Jenny, Alice and Zoe.

Uncle Ian's so pernickety I'd expect he'd even use Dad's first name, which is James. Dr James Maxwell Mullins. Or write 'Jennifer' not Jenny.

Anyhow, he didn't, and the text's not what you'd expect on an invite to a weekend with a party: we're invited to 'come away to be together' (illogical, or what?) at a *Mullins Family Retreat*. 20th July for four days, a long weekend.

How ironic: when this invite arrived, I first thought, I'll have to find an excuse not to go to it. But when I saw the date, I realised this was in fact good news. 20th July is the first day of the Truck Festival, so I've been handed a way of not giving in to Charlie's demand that we go. Life does work out! I don't think God planned it (as the rellies probably would). But Truck would or might have involved Fabian, and dealing with more than just Charlie making a play for him. It might mean the stuff which could be, like, expected, and which, I don't know, I don't feel ready for. It might be forcing us to do things we hadn't decided about. Maybe neither of us is ready? We've only just begun going out.

Me and Fabian, where next? My A levels. His Uni, possibly Cambridge. Or Durham. Stomach drops at the thought of those, as well as the other thing. I dunno. Nina says it's nothing, it's not commitment, it doesn't change you. But she doesn't really know. And surely it does? How do we know until we've done it?

Dad using that one word *disappointed* hurt. How can I be myself, do what I decide? I only wanted not to have to talk about my future, right now in the middle of exams and — and when I've discovered I'm sort of *desirable* to someone outside my family who finds me important.

So, it could feel like commitment? Even if it's not?

Dad's always said, don't be led only by your feelings. But, he got together with Mum and broke all their church rules. Mum chose the dynasty thing, Dad was the rebel. What does that say?

I'm staring out the window over my coffee mug, elbows on the table, imagining what I can't know until I've done it. The sun's shimmering on the garden. And the room smells of cake. And the timer's screeching at me!

I have the oven off — the cake's out, still in its tin but upside down on a cooling rack — when my phone bursts into life.

It's Nina.

I hit the off button: can't deal with her quarrel with Mariam right now.

Chapter 31

I GO SWIMMING AND THE CAKE IS SERVED

It's mid-afternoon, and June has become what it should be, summery, warm: maybe there'll be no more grey, cold rain? I'm revising on the sun-lounger, in my shortest denim shorts and a vest top. I've done more revision. The cake is cooling upside down on the kitchen table. Now, there's the scrunching sound of a car on the gravel out front.

Two voices: Mum and my sister. They mustn't see the cake yet. I scoot into the kitchen, throw open the cupboard where we keep dry groceries, and start shoving aside packets of biscuits and bags of flour to make space. The cake looks so fragile I don't dare let anything fall against it! Just done when they clatter down the hall. Apparently, no Annalise in tow. I do a twirl and lean casually against the cupboard, as Zoe gallops in carrying the cold bag, open, full of their litter from a picnic lunch. 'Didn't miss much!' she says. 'Only bodyboarding in wet suits in the rain! Only visiting the Eden centre and St Michael's Mount where we missed the tide, couldn't walk back on the causeway, and had to take the boat!' She grins. 'The sea was up and the boat ride was awesome! Sorry you weren't there?'

'Nope. Where's your friend?'

'We dropped her off. Gone to the dentist, why we came home early – her mum phoned and told us to, check-up they'd forgotten about. Your friend's outside, Nina?'

'Nina?'

'Something about swimming?'

Mum and Nina come through together from the hallway, Mum with a paper carrier from a shop in Penzance which I know sells yummy stuff. She begins to unload Cornish pasties into the fridge. Nina is swinging her swimming stuff in a hessian bag. 'Cool shorts, Al!' she says.

'Alice, darling!' Mum says, after the pasties are stacked away. 'Did your week go okay, love? We missed you!'

'Yeah, though Dad had Uncle David staying, and...'

'Yes, and I told him you wouldn't appreciate that, but apparently it was an emergency visit, something work-related.' It slipped out, I hadn't meant to blab to Mum about the bedroom thing. So, I'm thankful she's still talking, more so that she's on my side. 'Anyhow, Nina's wanting you to go swimming, she said she's come as you didn't answer your phone.'

'So, hey, are you gonna come with us? I've prised Emily out of her dark den of revision, and Mariam's actually allowed to go – her grandmother was the only person at home to object, and she didn't. We just need you!'

Do I want to go swimming? Sounds like the thing about the cousin's glasses isn't a problem? 'I was revising.'

'I wondered. You swots even shut off your phones to revise?'

'Go, darling: we can talk later?' Mum says. 'Look, I've brought back pasties, your favourite.'

'I saw.'

'Go. You look like you need a break.'

'Chemistry...' I say, rolling my eyes.

'Go!' she says, laughing. 'I can wait for the news and the hug!'

'Sorry – welcome back!' We hug. 'Promise you'll not look in there,' I extract an arm and point at the grocery cupboard, '*at all*, till I'm back?'

'I wasn't thinking of it,' she says. 'I could do with a coffee, or tea – but you go, skedaddle, as Grasndpa Des would say. I'll make it.'

So grateful to Mum! It's a great escape from the house, it's respectable with girlfriends, time off from eyes-down on the pages.

We collect Mariam, and then get Emily from her boarding house at school. The Matron has to make sure she's signed some book and she's told the time to be back. She's dead grateful to be allowed out to spend an afternoon with friends seeing she had to spend most of half term with an aunt in London. 'My auntie's a violinist. She has this tiny basement flat, underneath a family who adore her practising all day, can you believe it! And nobody else's back from half term until tomorrow!'

'Your aunt must be good though,' says Nina. 'I mean, she must be like Nicola Benedetti or someone, to play professionally? When my kid brother practises I cover my ears! Anyhow, ladies, I have a surprise for you!'

Now we're at the leisure centre, standing in the queue for tickets. It's hot and humid, and stinks of chlorine. People are shouting in the pool. Nina pulls down the neck of her T-shirt, and pushes aside her bra strap. 'Look.'

'You got one then!' Just where the strap goes, below her shoulder, there is a tiny fern leaf. A tattoo.

'Shush — for your eyes only!' Nina says, covering herself again. Wow. Over half term Nina's got a tattoo. And placed so carefully that school will never know.

'Unless we have naked showers,' I grin.

'Oh yeah?' says Nina. 'Never again. Sixth form, no compulsory team games,' she says, punching the air. 'No hockey. No rounders. Tennis doesn't count. Or badminton, archery, and golf!'

'Golf?' Mariam queries.

'Why not? For the networking, of course!'

Yeah, Nina would network. Nina's not afraid of sticking out, and putting herself forward. Maybe her family aren't as bothered as I imagine mine would be about Nina causing trouble? Our families are completely different. Nina's family are what Dad calls 'bohemian'. Nina's sporty, as well as arty. She was my friend at primary school, and then we both went to Headleigh Park on scholarships. Oddly, she's an approved kind of friend, the sort where the parents go to each other's dinner parties, and come home laughing and smelling of wine.

We're all keen to get into that shimmering pool. Mariam seems to have forgotten about Mahmoud's lost glasses so I don't mention them. I'll ask her more about it when Nina isn't around.

Instead, when we're out of the pool again, I look at myself in the changing room, outline emphasised by my damp swimmers, and wonder about how Fabian would like that. 'Defo sexy, babes,' says Nina, giving me a shove. 'With the dripping hair!'

❦ ❦ ❦

When I'm back from swimming, I check that Mum and Zoe are still sitting in the garden, and sneak into the kitchen. I turn the angel cake the right way up and shake icing sugar through a sieve over the top, then arrange raspberries, which I bought along with the cream of tartar, around it in a circle on the plate.

That evening, Mum, Dad, Zoe and me are back together around the dinner table. We've eaten up the Cornish pasties with a salad. Then, I produce the angel cake from the groceries cupboard, with a flourish of course. 'Ta-da! Here is what I made earlier!'

So satisfied when Mum gawps, then exclaims, 'Hey, Max, remind you of something? Look what Alice has made!'

'Isn't that – remind me, isn't it — this looks like that cake that my brothers ate in the tree house?'

'Right, Dad! Daze told me the story... Only you didn't see it because they'd eaten it already!'

Mum goes pink. Dad says, 'Well, and this one, are we going to eat it? I think your Mam should do the honours...' he says, pushing back his chair and leaping to the cutlery drawer to find the cake knife. He presents it, handle first, to Mum, who rises, does a ceremonial curtsey, and accepts it.

Zoe tops off all this by beginning to clap, and then we all clap, and we laugh. And we eat cake.

I get hugs from all of them, and this is the best part of half term, because I made that cake. I guess sometimes it's really worth doing something someone else asks you to?

Dad is on the landing later, when I go up to bed, about to shut himself away in his den. I feel a bit weird about it, but I sidle up and say, 'Thanks for the note – it was all your idea really.' And he gives me a hug and says, 'Oh I just thought it might be what Granny Fee would've suggested. But thank you for agreeing.'

I think we are okay again – for now.

End of Part 2

Part 3

Chapter 32

Saturday, and now half term's almost over, it's warm, and dry, and summery. I'm being dazzled by the sun as I pack the lunch plates into the dishwasher. The parents have wandered into the garden with mugs of coffee.

I say to Zoe, 'You seen this?' and point her to the Mullins Family Retreat invite on the noticeboard.

'That's bonkers!' she says (Zoe loves old-fashioned slang). 'Retreats are religious events, I know this from Annalise's mum, of course. People do retreats at St Hildie's, personal, silent, or in a group. This,' she says, taking the piece of thick card off the noticeboard and waving it around, 'is not a retreat... Unless of course we all stay silent! Our whole family couldn't be silent together for a long weekend, could they!'

'Maybe Granny Fee could – but no, I don't think anyone else. I'll take a book,' I say. 'a long one. And my camera.'

'There'll be nothing to photograph, people everywhere meditating, no talking.'

'I'll photograph what people find to do! I'll take pictures of them meditating.'

'No, listen. Bring your violin, we can say it's not talking, it's music. Hey, we'll sing everything, like an opera – the idea of a retreat is not to speak,' and she warbles, 'don't come near, do not dare, you must not speak!'

'Dear Uncle Ian, if you dare, please pass the vinegar!' I trill in reply.

'Have some cake – our Granny loves to bake!' Zoe giggles. Then, 'Why vinegar?'

'Because it rhymes. And because he's so – not exactly sour, but, so serious, like Dad says – "my brother, always the pastor". He wouldn't want to understand why we're singing.'

The Family Retreat sounds so dreary that it flits through my mind whether going to Truck with Charlie would be worse. But I wouldn't really want to spend a weekend in a tent with Charlie. And there's the other thing.

'Alice! Can you two come here and sit back down again?' The parents are back, looking like they've been plotting something. Grins on their faces. 'We're doing some holiday planning!' Mum says, as if this idea's only just struck them.

'Planning what? Can't we just go to Chapel House again? If Granny's moving, we *neeeed* to, before we've lost it!' Zoe exclaims. 'is this somewhere more exciting?'

'Come and sit down. Dad's been working on a plan to go on from the family retreat and show you some of the wilder parts of Scotland. So yes, exciting, places you've not been to before.'

Oh no, Dad's enthusiasm for a cold holiday up north looms up in the room like a big grey cloud. And I was hoping that maybe Saturday afternoon would be a good time to try to tell them my thoughts about A level subjects and career choices, doing it better than the mess I made of it with Dad. Like possibly Mum might make the whole discussion easier? Now we're stuck with another subject, holidays. Not going to Cornwall might be okay if Chapel House wasn't under threat of disappearing, or we were going somewhere warm, sunny, and interesting. Like maybe Italy, like Fabian's family do. 'Scotland?' I say. 'Must we? Aren't the highlands and islands cold and misty and murky, with lots of midges everywhere?'

'Hey, don't rubbish Scotland till you've seen it. Sit!' Dad says. You'd think he was an only child, not the second of five, the way he's taken charge of what we're all going to do without finding out what kind of holiday we might want! He's now unfolding a large map and laying it out on the table. Why's he gone into teacher mode? He's demonstrating how after the weekend, we leave the Manse early (good!), and drive on up to Edinburgh, where Mum's Aunt Val lives. It could be interesting as she's into craft with wool and once kept sheep on one of the Western Isles.

Dad is very lightly tracing a route across the map with a pencil. The pencil moves from Edinburgh across to Glasgow, and up the east coast to Oban, then makes dots in the sea from Oban to an island, representing a boat trip.

Mum is still thinking about Edinburgh. 'Aunt Val says she's looking forward to meeting you two again, "all grown up" she says'!'

'I hate meeting people who last looked at me when I was really small,' Zoe says. And I make a groany noise, then feel mean and wish I hadn't.

'Well, I think Aunt Val's actually interesting enough that you won't mind. After all, she did give Daze and Rothko a home, and not just for a few months! But we'll be gone before the culture vultures arrive for the Festival, because Edinburgh's far too crowded then.'

'I thought you were a bit of a culture vulture, Mum?'

She smiles, 'I can do without it, though. It'll be lovely to be away from Oxford!'

Dad joins in again, repeating the pencilled-in journey. 'Then cross country to Oban, the ferry and the Western Isles. Back possibly via the Lake District,' (pencil slides down from Carlisle and circles Windermere) 'but possibly not, as it'll be crawling with tourists.'

'What is wrong with you both?' I ask.

'I think Dad wants a real get-away for his main annual break this year. We thought you two'd be up for a change, now you're older.'

I just catch myself in time before saying something obvious and rather unkind: that I suppose it's seeing sick people all day that makes him, like, want to disappear so far from civilisation. Zoe makes a huge sighing noise, 'Bor-ing...I mean, I love nature but... the summer holidays are supposed to be for being on the beach.'

I remind Dad: 'Cornwall would be warmer, and at least we might visit Chapel House, I mean Des might be lonely on his own without his culture vulture.'

I get a look from Mum. One of her 'Don't say things until you've thought about them' looks. I stare at the table, knowing I have to work harder on how to say things unhurtfully. And remember something worth telling them, 'Dr Russell — Fabian's Dad – is a birder, Fabian said. They do birdwatching in Norfolk. We might even, like, go and do some, sometime.'

Dad nods, grins, and continues displaying confidence in his holiday plans. 'Good. Well you can start in the Western Isles, and maybe have some pictures to show off. And as for the family retreat, it will all be fine. What you have to remember is, this is my family. I do want to see them, even if you think they're a strange bunch. Now, Zo-zo, it's not all silence, or Bible readings and hymns. It's called a retreat because we're all supposed to've left everything else we do behind, and spend time on catch-up with the family, doing things together. Everyone will be there, several cousins your age.'

'Okay,' she sighs. 'Who?'

'Becky, Martha, Isaiah – he's a bit young for you of course – and Uncle Alex's little ones.'

Zoe rolls her eyes and mouths the name 'Isaiah' at me. I grin.

Mum adds, 'And there's Cameron and Chloe – Erin's two. Who're at Uni now, as you know. And it's only for a few days.'

Dad says, 'You need to show interest in the other members of the family. Be careful what you talk about, keep to safe subjects, don't provoke them, smile and try not to use extreme language. Then we'll be off to our next stop.'

So, being stuck in Northumberland with the weird relatives, to celebrate the demolition of the old Manse where Dad grew up? Depressing.

And before that visiting Granny Caro in London. Now we've made a temporary truce after her charm offensive.

Maybe I could do a charm offensive, and persuade Granny to keep the house and sell the flat? At least I have a birthday celebration some time in the next few weeks, and at least going to a show in London should be fun. And if summer's arrived at last then life after exams will be good, wherever we are.

Chapter 33

I WORRY ABOUT MY SUBJECTS

First school day after exams!

The time after exams was the dream we looked forward to. As we scribbled away at subject after subject, emptying out our knowledge onto the page, the sun began streaming in through the windows, and we believed summer was arriving. But then everything changed. Since half term, it's been totally un-summery, and now it's more or less rained every day for a week. I'm walking on a damp pavement, umbrella in my school bag, tennis racket in my hand in case it doesn't rain this afternoon. Breathing in air as humid as the saunas at the spa.

One dream came true: my birthday present! That little parcel with the American stamps, the one addressed to Mum, was Grandpa Guthrie's present for me. Grandpa sent me an iPhone! My best present! And, we went out for dinner, very posh, and the parents made that a surprise: they'd invited Fabian, as well as Mariam (whose partner for the evening was her cousin Mahmoud again – they can't be expected to get married some time in the future, can they? Absolutely not!) And Nina (so we had the annoying Jack there, but he actually talked sensibly with Dad and didn't embarrass me). So, a lovely evening. Celebrated ten days late, but no problem, my friends were all invited and there were sparklers on my cake!

Anyhow, today is for discussing our future plans, which I don't really have, since Mum and Dad have too many doubts about a career based on anything creative. Dad is disappointed and refuses to see into my sense of irony about how I'm now in exactly the position he was at this stage of school: I have an idea about what I want to do with my life, and my Dad has a very firm conviction about something entirely different! Mum even spent some time describing exciting developments in cell science and gene therapy, saying how amazing it would be to be involved, and why didn't I think that was a creative career?

When I get to Mariam's house, we might talk about this. Mariam and her whole family headed off to some weekend gathering after the birthday evening. So, no chance to compare how we'll deal with choosing subjects. If I have to have an awkward conversation with the science teachers, I know she'll give me a bit of support afterwards. They'll talk about wasting my talents, or throwing away my advantages, or something like that. Mariam isn't terribly keen on medicine, she says she'd rather work with things than people, a bit less terrifying.

I turn up the drive to their house. Two of their cars are gone, leaving dry rectangles on the gravel. The third – her older brother's — crouches by the bin shelter as usual. Mariam's not waiting outside, so I try the door into the large glass porch: it's locked. This hasn't happened before: she always waits for me on the drive, unless it's raining or very cold, and if so, that door's left unlocked so I can come inside the porch. I ring the bell.

No sound of feet. I'm staring through the glass: inside the porch, umbrellas are in their stand, folded neatly. Outdoor shoes and wellies sit in pairs. An advert for pizza delivery rests on the toe of one shoe.

They aren't here, are they? What has happened to them all?

They can't have gone away: it's still school term, and Mariam is required to be here. And I need her here too! I'm dreading the part of Orientation where we divide into groups, meet our subject teachers for next year, and 'have a chance to talk about why we have chosen these subjects'!

I ring the bell again. And try the door into the glass porch. It doesn't open. My insides twist with a kind of loneliness. It's not that I'm dependent on my bestie when we all talk futures, but it would be nice to share my thoughts.

I press the bell one more time. No-one appears. I have to accept there's nobody home. Mysteriously shut out of the house where I had a lovely warm welcome only three weeks ago, I abandon hope, and walk on to school. The long dreary road, the big houses with hedges and small trees in front gardens, or pink and red and yellow roses bursting out over their fence, looks twice as blank and miserable as the dark clouds already made it.

At the school gates, it's Nina, wearing a dandelion from the school field behind one ear, punching the air and arsing around. 'Hey, sixth form, no more uniform!' she cries, 'hey Alice, aren't you excited?'

'Why should I be?'

Nina grabs me and begins blathering something.

'What?'

'We're free! Time to celebrate!'

A sudden anger makes me tell her to shut up. Immediately I feel that's mean and want to bite the words back. 'God, what's happened?' she says,

'Nothing, except how to hack our 'few days' Sixth Form Orientation', when I've no idea what groups I should go to?'

'Aw, c'mon, what we study isn't the most important thing. Life is more than school subjects.'

'Yeah, cool, I'm sorry. Only I'm not sorted like you, I'm really worried about my A level subjects.'

'Maths, physics, chemistry, everything boring and...'

'That is the whole point. I might do those, *and* art.'

'Okay. If you want.'

'Or I might just *not do them* at all.'

'Really?'

'Really. I talked to mum. That was *so* not helpful. Now there's this doubting voice, like an alien living in my head, and it, like, asks, 'Do you believe in yourself? Can you face the parents if they're really, really disappointed? Should you do what they want to please them? Or do what you want, and find it all works out like they said, and be a total failure, chances to make a difference in the world gone?'

'God, I wouldn't know. Don't they get that they don't own you? Art, Drama, and Eng. Lit., my decisions?'

'Okay, well, our families are different. Look, where's Mariam? Is she here? Her house looked all kind of closed up. Any ideas why?'

'She'll be here. She knows what she's doing – like you, maths, physics, chemistry, whatever.'

'That is not like me! She's accepted her parents' suggestions. She's hoping she'll train to be a pharmacist. I know she doesn't agree with me questioning Mum and Dad's ambitions for me. And, up to now, I didn't think Mum and Dad thought like they do, did I? I mean, they've planned a holiday in the Scottish islands, and the weather's going to be like this,' I wave one arm at the sky, and the first raindrop of the day falls onto my face, '– that is not a holiday!'

'Aw, Alice, don't worry!' says Nina, putting an arm around my waist. 'You've always got me to talk to – and Emily – and Fabian of course.'

'Yeah, I've got you! And, don't say anything, but, I got – my Grandad in Canada sent me – guess what?'

'I can't. A ticket for the Centre Court, men's finals day?'

'Better. I mean, more long-term... he sent – in a parcel addressed to Mum so I thought it was work stuff – an iPhone!'

'Oh my God, I wish I had a grandad like yours! So, show me?'

'I'll have to keep this hidden, but, one look.' We stand close, and I pull out my new, sleek, precious birthday present. 'Camera's great, good focus, useful to have one with me all the time. Almost all the time.'

The rain intensifies. I fumble in my bag for my umbrella. Nina's still wanting to examine my phone.

'Show me everything. Can you stream music?'

'Nina Lewis! Alice Mullins! Ready for Orientation?' a cheerful teacher-voice comes up behind us. I drop the phone into my bag as I swivel round, putting on a smile. 'Arts this way, Nina! Science' (she grins at me, she's been my maths teacher, from when I joined the school till now), Alice, you're over in the Tennyson building. But, wait, first you're all together for registration and a few general points, in the library!'

The library. A cool dim room, where they've already switched on the lights. A breeze blows the rain against the windows. As the Head drones on, and a slew of teachers talk next year's subjects, I decide I'll do what Granny Fee calls 'grasp the nettle': I imagine grasping it firmly, crushing its stings before they have time to hurt. I'll find a suitable teacher – maybe the deputy head? – and explain why I haven't yet written my three chosen subjects on a form, or gone to join the science group in the oddly misnamed Tennyson building. It'll be easier to discuss options with teachers than the parents: they should have no particular ambitions for me except passing A levels with decent grades. Parents will be convinced by teachers, maybe?

The deputy head, Miss Swithinbank, is standing just outside the library as we file out to our subject groups. Very quietly, I ask her whether it's possible to discuss my options. And 'Please, please, can you not let my parents know about this conversation?'

'I can do that, for now, but you should share your thoughts with them, Alice. They deserve to know – after all, what you want to do with your life is part of who you are, isn't it? They might simply assume you're happy to continue with sciences, but I agree, they need to know that you have other ideas. And you'll need them to support you whatever further education you choose.'

Well, why didn't the staff take more time to help us before now? Apparently, the parents' evening had revealed I was happy to carry on being a Guthrie-Mullins clone! Eventually they decide I am 'distressed' about the subject choices (odd way to describe my thoughts!) and I have permission to spend some time researching among the prospectuses and leaflets in the library.

And so, instead of going to the Tennyson Building, I spend a quiet morning browsing the careers folders.

Chapter 34

ZOE SPECULATES ABOUT ANNALISE

At the weekend, Zoe gets to go to St Hildie's with Annalise. 'Base Camp' at the church has closed for the summer, leaving them at a loose end, but it seems they must see each other all day Saturday to replace that! I've been trying to find a space to introduce my parents, both together, to my sixth form study plan, so this seems a good moment, with my sister elsewhere. But first one, then the other is too busy, or not at home. Mum dumps shopping from the supermarket on the kitchen table, 'Alice, could you put this away for me, love?' and rushes off to the lab to check something vital. Dad holes up in his den to write an article for some other GP's blog about the state of primary care. The three of us meet again at lunch, which I lay up in hopes of maybe seducing them into a nice chat over coffee afterwards, about the courses I'm aiming for at Uni.

But no, turns out this was a quick lunch and they are both off out again. Mum's going back to shut herself in the microscope room all afternoon. Dad, intriguingly, mentions that he's going to see how Eliot Parker Pollard is. That arouses my curiosity about Charlie's family again, but no chance to ask anything.

I drag myself back up to my room to continue browsing prospectuses, lying on my bed with some music on my iPhone. Can't really text Fabian while he's birdwatching with his Dad on Otmoor. I'd better get 'forearmed', as Miss Swithinbank suggested.

I must have dropped asleep, because I'm suddenly woken by the front door slamming. Next minute, Zoe knocks and enters my bedroom, 'Alice –?' She gives an exaggerated look around, like I'm invisible. 'Alice...' Then her whole body barges in, and drops onto my bed. I've a moment to close the booklet I was reading and shove it under my duvet. And turn off my phone.

'Um?' I say.

'Listen!'

'What?'

'We were at St Hildie's. They took the carpet off the labyrinth! It's awesome, like all these turquoise, brown, grey and white tesserae, they're in a pattern of fish swimming all the way from the entrance to the centre, and in the middle three fish intertwine to form a kind of triangular design. It's like really mysterious and magical. Did Daze really do all that?'

'You were too small to remember, but actually, I made some of it as well. Well, she let me help her.'

'Really?' Zoe stares, her eyes slightly distorted by the long-sight lenses in her glasses.

'Yep.' I remember the thrill of being allowed to help. Feeling all grown up, holding those tesserae, setting the tiny tiles into the pattern Daze had drawn out. 'I put the tesserae into the picture where she showed me. Real tiles, real labyrinth, not like at school, where — you remember this? We used to make pictures with those little sticky-backed, brightly coloured, squares, set out on that thick paper? You did do that?' She nods. 'Well, I laid about twenty tesserae one day when Daze was working on it. The idea was partly, if the labyrinth was made of mosaic, then people with sight problems could feel their way through their feet? I don't know if that worked...'

Zoe says, 'Anyway, Alice, listen, the labyrinth, the rug was taken off and we walked it. Stacey – that's Annalise's mum – dragged us along to this event, because she said we couldn't be left alone in the house while she helped at it, as we aren't fourteen — so we had to walk the labyrinth with everyone else. When they arrived in the middle, people were hugging like that was part of whatever we were doing. We didn't do that, though Annalise wanted to. And, you know who was there? Uncle David! Who used your room while you were away at half term? I thought he lived in Yorkshire.'

'Uncle David?' I say. 'He does.' I think back: that unsettling conversation I heard. 'You know he used to be the director there, so maybe he was running the retreat, or whatever it was?'

'Listen Alice, I don't know why, but *it was him*. I think he knows Annalise's mum...'

'Hang on – so he keeps coming here, and you think he knows Annalise's mum? So what's the problem?'

'Not a problem. Just, that he, like, obviously knows them – Annalise's family — quite well, I think.'

'If Stacey's interested in retreats, why shouldn't they know each other? Anyway she's the admin person, so of course she knows him from him doing stuff there.'

Zoe looks thoughtful. 'And I thought, do you think maybe – Annalise and Stacey, and where's Annalise's dad? I thought, suppose it's David? Only – he's gay so...'

'So, if he is, he isn't her dad.'

'Or they got divorced because, well he came out – and, like left...?'

Well, I know that's impossible. Though I heard David telling Dad about being bisexual, and mentioning a woman he's attracted to now: but that wouldn't make Annaliese's mum his partner thirteen years ago! 'Do you need him to be her dad? Does she even look like David?'

'I suppose not. She's blonde and she's a good swimmer, but she doesn't look like him. Not really. Pity, 'cos then we'd be second cousins or something. Related, anyway.'

'So – anything else you need to ask me?' She looks a bit crestfallen (a word I rather like, having had to look it up the first time I found it). 'Are you really disappointed?'

'Not really,' Zoe says, getting up, and fiddling with stuff on my desk. 'Maybe a bit. They're weird, whatever. And she's allowed to keep that toad in her bedroom.'

'Does she get it out in her room? Let it hop around?'

'No — it lives in a glass tank. I told you before.'

'So she isn't a witch, then. And neither is her mum.'

'She keeps her bedroom curtains closed all the time. All the curtains are. In every room!'

'*That* is weird. Though maybe they rush out in the morning and don't have time...'

'No – they keep them closed to *keep to themselves*, Annalise says. And, she says she's not trying for the county swimming team, because her name would get in the papers.'

'Right. I'd wonder about that too. They're hiding something. But it's not something to worry about – I don't think. When did they come here? When did they move into that house, do you know?'

This has become intriguing. How well does Annalise's mum know David? When I saw them, along with Shaz, in the drive at St Hildie's, it looked like she'd popped out, being the admin person, to say something administrative. Waving a list about signing into lunch or something. But maybe more?

'It's her gran's house. It was. It's so old-fashioned. You should see their loo.'

'Just never got updated. You told me before... So, about your theory: David can't be your friend's dad. But they keep the curtains closed. That's more significant. Anything else?'

'No. Don't think so. Only the first time I was there, Annalise didn't want her mum to know. Today we met at the park. Stacey brought a picnic and then we went to St Hildie's.'

'Was the picnic weird?'

'No. Ham sandwiches, apples, Diet Coke, and cake.'

'Not mealworms?'

'Yuck!' She giggles.

'So a bit boring?'

'Yes.'

'Can I get on now?'

'What were you doing?'

'A lot of nothing. Checking Facebook, I expect.' I chuck my pillow at her. We laugh. She slinks out around my door.

Annalise's family are definitely different, Zoe's right about that. Deviant even. If the woman he spoke about can't be Shaz, and if he really isn't gay but he's bi – could it be Stacey? He obviously can't be Annalise's dad, that's just Zoe's fantasy – but suppose they recently met doing some retreat type thing, and she's why he's hanging about around here?

Though again, if I was him, would I go for her? A bit weird, and she doesn't look at all – stylish.

Car scrunches on gravel. The front door's opening. Voices. So Mum and Dad came back together? So at what point did they meet up? I wonder if they both checked up on Eliot?

Maybe I'll go down and corner the parents before they find something else to do! For now, I know the subject I might study, I'll have to do an undergraduate degree and then two postgrad years. Medicine would be at least that long and expensive.

Chapter 35

GOING TO GRANNY'S LONDON FLAT

It's the day we have to go to Granny's. I'm on the landing, outside the bathroom, about to go in to brush my teeth, and my phone's buzzing. I grab it. Charlie!

I'd kind of forgotten to let her know that I couldn't go to the Truck music festival. And she's bought me a ticket and wants to know: 'Deffo are you coming, Alice?'

Quick thinking: the Mullins Family Retreat, same weekend! 'Which weekend, remind me?'

'Starts July 20th. A Friday?'

'Right... Okay, look, I'm sorry.'

'Don't say you'd forgotten?'

She sounds just like when I left their house after my half term visit. Desolate and miserable. Makes me feel so mean, but – I actually didn't want to face all the complicated stuff (especially if Fabian was involved), apart from having to convince Mum and Dad... and life's too difficult to explain all that to Charlie.

So thank you, Uncle Ian, for your invite, and for planning the family meet-up to begin on 20th July!

'You still there?' Charlie's voice, rather small, asks.

'Yeah, I'm here. It's just that — I'm sorry you bought the ticket without asking me, 'cos I'll be in Northumberland.'

I hear a little gasp, then she says, 'Where?'

'Northumberland. There's this big extended family thing, and...'

'God, you could've been decent enough to tell me! Why didn't you think to call me and explain – like, when did you know about that – the family thing?'

Yikes. The invite arrived before I got back from Mariam's, at half term. What shall I say? 'Look, it's not that easy. I mean, I've – we've both, haven't we – been doing exams until almost now. And school is leaning on us to decide our sixth form studies, and – I don't know, do I, I just got under all this *stuff* – I mean, haven't you had to make all these decisions as well?'

'Me? I'm going to the sixth form college in Oxford or maybe another one. My school doesn't do A levels. Thank God, no more boarding. It seemed quite simple to me, tell them what I want to study, and buy my festival tickets.'

'Well it wasn't here. Mum and Dad are wrapped up in their bloody work and I needed to talk with them. And lots more going on.'

'You think there isn't for me?'

'No. But that's why I wasn't thinking about you.'

'Fine. Well, I'm going whatever. I'll find someone who's less of a geek next time. I thought I was doing you favours.'

'When I'm going to upset my parents over the subjects I want to take, am I likely to get them to let me go to a music festival in a field?!'

'You could've said you were staying with me, here!'

'I'm already in trouble with Dad for not telling him when I went out. Listen, I said I'm sorry. After I'm back maybe...'

'Fine. Festival will be over!'

Her phone goes quiet. I switch mine off. She isn't fine: I could hear she was almost crying, and she was furious. Both are totally right for her to be: I have let a friend down by not telling her straight off. It was cowardly: I didn't want to hear her being disappointed. In her eyes, I am a betrayer.

Only, the whole friendship thing was set up by our mothers, which is crazy now we're almost adults.

So, here's me, toothbrush in one hand and phone in the other, on the landing. Mum yelling from downstairs that we'll miss the train to London for our visit to Granny Caro and a show. A text arrives, Charlie again: 'After you're back I shan't be here. I'll be in Cornwall! We've been lent a cottage.'

'Cornwall?' I reply, then delete it and close my phone down.

Whatever's up with Charlie's family, I can't solve it for her. And she's got the holiday I would love... Or has she?

Then, I get packed and ready. Folding clothes into my bag, I have to remember Granny Caro's style, her emphasis on elegance, and not only choose something suitable for the theatre but pack it so it doesn't arrive all creased. I choose the black formal dress I bought to wear to the Sheldonian concert with Fabian, and a little ditsy turquoise blue cardie to wear over it, with black low-heeled pumps and black tights.

Mum has silently appeared beside me, smiling approval. She tries to pop something into my sponge bag.

Whatever's she up to? 'What? Mum...!'

'Ssh, that's some fragrance Dad bought for my birthday – no, it really is very soft, not at all crass and tacky.'

'Okay, can I decide?'

She laughs, and sprays a bit on her own wrist — thankfully, not mine. 'Okay, that'll work. For the theatre anyway.'

Aren't mothers peculiar? Once, I was probably nearly twelve, when she was getting her stuff ready for a conference, she came into my room with a pack of *Always* sanitary pads, in case my periods started while she was gone! I suppose it's a universal thing, they're always watching us with their antennae out, when we're not even thinking about something, or not sharing it with them. Everything we know about being a woman. I gave Zoe her first period stuff.

The perfume is actually rather nice. I kind of wish I'd had it to wear when I went to the concert with Fabian.

'Hurry Zo-zo up, could you,' says Mum, running back downstairs. I go to the door of my sister's room. She's reading a book while packing her bag. 'Train, Zo-zo!'

'Thought I was waiting for you. Only got to put this book in.'

❦ ❦ ❦

So now, anyway, off to Granny Caro's. The news has been talking floods in the south for a week, and we watch through the window as our train trundles through a watery landscape. Rivers and canals are full, meadows have become lakes. Dreich weather, as Dad would say.

To entertain Zoe and take our minds off the rain, I pull out my iPhone where I've stored all the photos Daze sent me of the conversions Des did, or the builders did, following his ideas, to make Chapel House the amazing place we've always known. 'Daze wasn't old enough to take these, but now she's scanned them so we can see.'

Zoe looks through, scrolling down all the pictures. 'Oh wow, look what they're doing here! And making the – what d'you call it?'

'The sanctuary, I think.'

'That – into a kitchen. And having his studio be the whole height of the building, with glass all the way up.'

'And all the bits out the back – the old kitchen and the minister's office, they've became part of the studio, with the old loos being his dark room – where he used to develop his photos. You had to use chemicals, and then wash them.'

'I remember! He had a piece of string, like a washing line, and pegged them up. Mum showed me, and she said, she once climbed out of the window after Daze locked her in there!'

'You know, I think some of this, like putting in floors to make bedrooms where there used to be a balcony, was seriously complicated engineering work, really. And if it was partly financed by Granny, then maybe we do have a problem. She could part-own it, if she invested in it.'

'So, we have to make Granny Caro keep it, don't we!' Zoe says, scrolling through a second time.

We rehearse how we're going to talk to Granny Caro about the awful idea of selling Chapel House. 'What we say has to be sensible,' I tell Zoe. 'If we get shouty, she'll say the *childish* word.'

'Which we aren't. We're supporting Des, our step-grandad.'

'Absolutely. And Daze, because she should inherit the house.'

'And we're not just selfishly wanting it as our holiday home.'

'So, look, let me go first and get Granny talking about when they were doing the conversion of the old chapel. I'll tell her I've seen Des's photos. Hopefully she'll feel relaxed. Then, you can talk about how much you love the house.'

Chapter 36

GRANNY CARO IS UPSET

Granny Caro's at Paddington to meet us, smiling, waving. Wearing a cream-coloured trench-coat style mac, over smart jeans and a blue chambray shirt. Pearl stud earrings, hair in a chignon with a black bow behind. Scented with whatever's expensive. She has to hug us both, which wafts her perfume into our hair. And then she leads the way to the taxi rank, where we catch a cab to the flat.

I feel a bit nervous, being in London and remembering all the awful stuff about the bombs almost two years ago.

In the taxi Granny asks us if we thought about the London bombings when we were on the train, so we discuss them. Zoe's memories are a bit vague, but I say I'm glad it isn't an exact two years since that happened. And it all comes rushing back, so I tell them what I remember. 'Everyone at school was in a panic, about their parents or other people they knew. Some of the boarders were scared their parents might've arrived in London for a holiday before collecting them from school. Others were afraid about their flights home being targeted by terrorists. My friend Emily and some of her friends — they live in Hong Kong —were all crying in the cloakroom, so some of us took them out into the school garden, right down the end, where teachers wouldn't find us. They didn't want to see the teachers, I'm not sure why. Maybe they were afraid of what the teachers would need to tell them? Or of crying in front of the teachers? My friend Mariam's dad was at the BMA building when the bus blew up: he did a lot of first aid, I know, and after that he sent a text to the family, saying he was okay. But it was so long before he did that her mum was already terrified he'd been hurt... Mariam said he came home with blood on his shirt, which made her scared, but it wasn't his...'

'Mmm,' Granny says. 'A lot to remember. Well, I think London has settled down now, because we have to get on with our lives, and live alongside each other, but we do, I think, look out for each other. It's all we can do. I hope you're excited to be here, despite the memories.'

'Oh yes!' says my sister, grinning.

'It was awful, though, wasn't it? The day after, there was a sort of guided discussion about it, at school – before we all went home for the holidays — the teachers seemed to think we kind of needed to express our feelings. Actually, that's probably why people wanted to avoid the staff. A lot of people didn't want to discuss motives and stuff.'

'Mmm. With boarders from across the world, it might possibly have been wiser if the school had set aside an organised day for considering such an emotional event,' Granny says. I suppose Granny's looking at it as if she were the school doctor. 'Anyway, London has settled down, though we're all alert in case we see anything odd. And here we are, let's think about what we'll do this afternoon, shall we?'

The cab pulls up. To one side there's a large red brick block of flats, very solid and old-fashioned and obviously built to look grand fitting into the style of the surrounding buildings. On the other side, there's a small square garden, with trees, and dark painted railings. It's all like something in a movie, or a novel, about people in the nineteenth century! Reminds me of books we've read in English this year. The sun comes out, for a moment, as we get out and go up the steps into the building. It's very, very quiet inside. You'd almost expect a guy in uniform at the door, like the one outside the Randolph Hotel in Oxford.

The main hallway has a carpet, and a wooden lift cranks us slowly upstairs to the third floor. It all sticks in my mind, and I'm realising how fashionable our great-granny Ianthe must've been. Mum's mother is more posh than I thought.

So, Granny's put us in her spare room. It has a mahogany bed, dressing table and wardrobe all matching, with silver backed brushes on the dressing table. There's a chest of drawers with a little shelf of books on it. She leaves us 'to unpack', even though we've only really brought backpacks.

'Granny Fee has bookends like this,' I say to Zoe, who stops looking out of the window and comes over. 'They're in the spare room, they've got a carved squirrel on each end. There's a Bible there, of course, and these paperbacks by Grandpa Alasdair and Uncle Ian. One's called *Living with Uncertainty* and the other's called *Hard Questions*. Let's see what Granny Caro's got.'

'Hey, these bookends are carved to look like books,' says Zoe. 'And the books seem to all be scientific, there's two by someone called Derek Bradfield FRS.'

'What's this thin green hardback, it's lost its paper cover? Oh look, Ianthe M. M. Lavenham: *What Every Girl Should Know*! It's by our great-granny!'

Zoe pounces on it, extracts it from the bookends, and flips the pages. I look over her shoulder. It's about how our bodies develop, with photos, diagrams and labelled parts. 'And it's about how to get pregnant, and how not to – see?'

We look at each other, and then we put it back. 'For later,' I say, 'once we've said goodnight and gone to bed?'

On the dressing table, along with the brushes, are portrait photos. A teenage girl who must be Granny. Does she look like us, do we look like her? And a man who looks like a movie star. Perhaps Granny's mysterious dad, who is never talked about? Zoe picks it up, to look more closely. I take it from her, and turn it over: do I dare remove it from the silver frame, to see if anything's written on the back?

Clip, clop, clip… Thankful that Granny's wearing heels, I put that photo back on the dressing table double quick, relieved that I haven't yet prised the frame open. 'I see you're looking at the photo! Do you know who that is, Alice?'

'Not sure, he must be important? So, if the other one's you —' Her face registers a big smiling Yes. 'Then he's — your dad, maybe?'

'That's right,' Granny says, and picks up one of the books we've just looked at. 'This is a popular science book from the 1950s, *Genetics from Mendel to Watson and Crick*. See the editor's name, Derek Bradfield FRS.'

She turns the book over to show the photograph on the back cover, picks up the photo, and holds them side by side. Same person. 'He was my mother's boss, but also — her partner, you would call him these days. But he did have a wife as well... So, that's why I wasn't Caroline Bradfield!'

Zoe gapes, her mouth partly open, her eyes serious. I wonder what to say. I knew there was secrecy, and I'd sort of made up a story a bit like this, but I've never properly asked Mum if I was right. I remember our great-grandma Ianthe as a little old lady in a grey skirt and jacket, with a white blouse, a mauve floaty scarf draped around, and a hat. Like Granny Caroline, she was powerfully scented with perfume. I only met her once. She looked at me, turned to Mum, and exclaimed, 'So this is Alice!' rather loudly. We all sang Happy Birthday. I don't remember more.

'Come and hear family history! And I'll only do this once!' Granny Caro exclaims, and herds us back along the parquet floored hallway to the kitchen, where she makes coffee milkshakes and sets out a tray with our drinks and three Danish pastries on a delicate, flowery, china plate. We go into the living room, we're invited to perch ourselves on the sofa. There's a small table at each end of it, and Granny offers around the plate of pastries and gives us each a small matching porcelain plate along with a silver knife to cut up our pastry and eat it politely. It's almost as if Granny had decided to set the scene, back in the days when she was growing up!

Granny now explains that Ianthe was one of Bradfield's research students. He took an interest in her work. He took her out to tea. He took her out some more. He was a well-known university professor, and didn't want the scandal of a divorce. Eventually, he agreed that she could have half of what she wanted. Even though she was a leading member of the campaign to make contraception available to all women, not just married ones, Ianthe wanted a baby with him. It was no to a wedding ring, but yes to a baby.

How weird, I think. I mean, he wanted to pass on his genes without having to support her – like being a prize bull or something.

'Did you – mind?' I ask her. 'I mean, was there prejudice because your dad wasn't, like, around to do stuff like school parent evenings, watching the school play, and sports day and – stuff?

'Mind? Mummy was assumed to be a widow. Divorce would've been bad for both their careers. And of course, people may've gossiped behind her back, but nothing was referred to in front of me – the head-mistress, of course, may've known. He paid my school fees.'

'Golly…' says Zoe. (Another old school-story word her crew have taken up using!) She takes a breath. 'I suppose then they couldn't publish a book together, could they?'

'Their work took them in different directions,' Granny says, killing that cosy idea. She pauses, then 'I suppose you'll be surprised that I was a wanted child?' As if we need to know that. 'I was very wanted. You may not imagine that a dedicated research scientist and contraceptive campaigner would've had time for me, but she was a wonderful mother. Always came to school sports days and plays… made sure I aimed for Cambridge… and as the daughter of a rather interesting widow, of course the school awarded me a bursary. Cambridge was wonderful.'

I don't like to think this, but the way Granny talks seems awfully posh and snobbish. It's a bit too much like the worst side of Headley Park. I feel kind of stifled. It makes me less keen on studying science subjects at Oxford or Cambridge, if it means fitting in with these atti-tudes. And it's kind of weird that Granny talks like this now, because when all this happened it must have been absolutely wrong and shocking and only done by people who were very advanced in their views and counterculture, and not posh at all.

I say, 'He was happy for Great-Granny to give him a child... I wonder if he had any others?'

Granny Caro obviously doesn't want to get into that one, she changes the subject, and suggests we might eat a snack lunch a bit later, and 'hurry to the Tube station to spend the afternoon at the V. and A.'

I would've preferred the Royal Academy summer exhibition, but Granny's been there already, 'with a friend...' She hoped we'd vote for the Science Museum instead, but Zoe says that was her end-of-year school trip. I am just about to ask how much Derek Bradfield was part of Granny's life — whether, for example, he ever took her there when she was growing up, when Zoe changes the direction of everything, saying, 'D'you know whether they teach Environmental Studies at Cambridge, Granny?'

'Environmental studies?'

'Yes. You see, our holidays at Chapel House are so perfect for exploring the environment. Finding lizards on the sand dunes, that kind of thing. It's what I most want to do when I leave school.'

'Lizards?'

'And other wildlife. And plants. How it all fits together to make our planet habitable. Or not.'

Granny gives her a look, 'Really? Well, why don't you write off for a prospectus?'

'I thought you might know,' Zoe says, 'if you've studied the local wildlife – where you live, I mean.' I feel we are getting near dangerous ground, and try to signal 'don't go there,' but she continues, 'Mum was telling me how much she loved walking the cliff path from the house, and about how all of them spent the summer outdoors, and we love that too when we're at yours — and we can't let you sell up just now, when we're...'

'I'm sure your parents will still take you to Cornwall,' Granny says, 'and then there's the Scottish islands, a different kind of wildlife but still fascinating, I believe you're off there for your holiday this year?' and she gathers up the plates and turns to leave the living room. Zoe moves after her, 'But, Granny, your house is so perfect, you can't want to move here, where the air's full of pollution, and there are no birds!'

'Darling, I can want a stimulating environment, where there's culture a step away from my home, and a proper retirement where I shan't be meeting my patients whenever I pop into the nearest small rural town to buy basic groceries at the Co-op!'

'*Granny!*' Zoe wails, 'does *Des* want to move to the *smoke?*' I smile a moment at her use of that term. And I try to help us out of this subject, by talking about how I love different places for different things, but it's too late.

'Zoe, this is about grown-up decisions, and when you're older you'll have learned about why people may not always want to be together because they've moved on and want to live in ways the other person doesn't want. Remember I told you about your great grandmother? If Des prefers Cornwall, that's entirely up to him. He's welcome to find a cottage, and remain.'

'A *cottage?*' Granny is clip-clipping down the hallway, Zoe in pursuit. 'Des is our step-grandad, you can't. And Chapel House is his amazing house, that was adapted from a chapel! I've seen pictures of all the stages!' Granny is in the kitchen, with the radio on, so Zoe shouts the last bit, 'He designed it – it's *all for Daze*, it's *not yours to sell!*'

I follow on, catching my sister by her arm. She hasn't stopped to let me put a reasonable view on this. 'Zo-zo, can we leave it?' I say, using a stage whisper, 'we agreed: tactfully, over supper? Or tomorrow, after the show...

Chapter 37

MAKING IT UP WITH GRANNY

I stop my sister rushing into the kitchen, holding her by her upper arms, both of us taking deep breaths. Over Zoe's shoulder, I see Granny Caro standing by the sink, holding onto it. Her shoulders are heaving like when you cry really hard. How terrible, how embarrassing. What can I say to stop this? We're all frozen, and in the kitchen, along with Granny weeping over the sink, the radio yammers on, something about the rain, which has been coming down almost daily for weeks.

I turn Zoe round and, hauling her by one arm, drag her back down the corridor into our bedroom, shut the door, and lean on it. 'What?' she says.

'What made you do that?'

'It's not her house. It partly belongs to Des.'

'Maybe, but we're here for a nice weekend, and you've made Granny cry. What d'you think will happen now?'

'Oh, *pigs!*' Zoe says. 'Granny's *really* crying, because of me?'

'Yes. She's really, really upset. It gave me a fright, that we've done that.'

'Golly... I didn't mean – I didn't imagine...'

'You didn't think people Granny's age could feel hurt by what we say?'

'How could I know?'

'You *didna' think*, as Dad would say. You have to think.'

'Oh help, what can we do?'

'I don't know,' I say. But I sort of do know: apologise. Make Zoe apologise? 'Wait, for a bit.'

And then we go silent, looking at each other. I creep to the door, open it a crack, and we listen.

Down the passage, the radio murmurs on. At least Granny hasn't stormed after us. But I'm stunned. Zoe lies flat out on her front on the bed, hair over her face. What I can see of her face is red as a tomato. She's biting her thumb. I have a falling feeling in my inside: this — making adults hurt — is a power we didn't know we had. How many times might we have done this but they've hidden their hurt feelings from us? Now we're becoming more like part of their world – or I am... How can I put things right?

I creep down the passage until I can see into the kitchen. Now the radio's off and Granny is talking. On her phone. To Mum and Dad? No. Someone else. She says, '...entirely reasonable,' and stuff I can't hear. Then she says, sounding normal, '...would be lovely... When are you here?' There's a silence, then she says, 'I'll look forward to that. A lovely idea. Yes! Bye.'

Whoever that was, Granny Caro's not crying now. She's dabbing at her face with a tissue, looking in a little mirror she has on the kitchen windowsill, and then, riffling in her handbag (on the kitchen table) and pulling out a tiny pink bag. Adjusting her make-up. Okay, time to creep back to our room.

Zoe is still on the bed, now curled into a ball. I sit down, wondering if I can do this, feeling I've been thrown something incredibly awkward to deal with before I've learned how these things are done. What would Mum do? There must be something. Is there something Dad has tried to teach us, something Granny Fee would do? Zoe doesn't move. I gently touch her back, 'Okay, Zo-zo?'

'No.'

'Listen, remember what Dad says sometimes? We all make mistakes, that's why when someone makes one...'

'We have to forgive them? But I wasn't the only someone. Was I?'

'Yeah, well, I get why you did what you did, she provoked you, but you didn't quite get it right either.'

'So if Granny's made this huge mistake, and she's sorry...'

'I'm not sure why she's upset, but if it's you and Granny both, that does make it kind of equal. But the other bit's saying sorry. Someone has to start that.'

''Spose.' Mm. This is not easy. Zoe curls up a bit tighter, resistant to the idea of apology. Are we going to spend a terrible day, stuck here, wanting to escape back home, and miss the show?

'Zozie, I know, grown-ups usually, well, they quite often, don't do the starting bit.'

'They should. Do what I do, not what I say, that stuff?'

'Yeah. But...' Suddenly my brain clears. 'Listen, we can't wish ourselves back in time, or back at home. So, we have to settle this and – and get to where we're in that tube train, off to the theatre. I think Granny crying may be a bit like a kind of sorry – for something, maybe about the house even, I don't know. If that's how it works, then if we say we're sorry, that should make sure we know each of us is. And possibly she'll say sorry back to us?'

Zoe uncurls a bit, 'Do I *have* to say it first?'

'I think that might help Granny?'

Well thank you, Granny Fee for putting that into my head. Or God, if that's who it was.

Zoe uncurls properly, stands up, and brushes down her rather nice new top, which she bought on-line from our local Green Party, and whose emblem slightly emphasises she's grown up fast since Granny last took a good look (as was said when we met at Paddington!). She reaches for a silver-backed hairbrush, and watches herself brushing her hair.

I say 'So, I am going to talk to her first, and then, you come and apologise? It'll work, I think. I think we have to, even if we believe that we're really right.'

She nods agreement. I take a deep breath and go down to the kitchen. Very quietly, I tap on the kitchen door. Granny turns from doing something on her phone, and looks up sharply like a teacher. 'Alice!' she says, as the sharp look becomes a smile.

I take another deep breath. 'Zoe has something to say. Could she come and say it to you?'

'Darling! Of course she can. I am just so sorry I allowed myself to be carried away, it was wrong of me to react. You girls love Chapel House, of course you do!' For a moment, I think she is about to descend like a dove, or more like a red kite, and give me a huge, boob-crushing hug. Her perfume is already stifling me, but no, she moves to put her phone back into her handbag. 'Darling, you are totally forgiven, I love Zoe's enthusiasm and commitment to causes. Send her to me, and I'll make sure she feels it's safe to stay with this silly old dragon!'

I go back and find my sister is now staring into her phone. 'Annalise?' I ask.

'Nope. I have other friends. What did Granny say?'

'Okay, Zoze, she seems to've realised we all made mistakes. It'll be alright. Careful, she's still a bit emotional. But in a good way.'

I leave them to it, and stand at the living room window, breathing, watching people in the street below, listening out for raised voices. A quiet murmur is all there is. I've climbed up the most enormous learning curve today.

We all agree that we'll leave the museum visit to another day. A bit trembly, we eat our snack lunch, soberly, in front of the TV, watching the men's finals at Wimbledon which Granny has videoed for us, 'in case you were doing something at school last weekend.' I thank her with what's meant to be enthusiasm, and I am pleased she did this: we all need to not talk right now, and recover. Federer and Nadal are fighting it out, but I can't totally concentrate, and not only because I already know who won the championship. I'm suddenly far too aware of how my life is changing, not only my life but my place in the world. I hear Dad's comment the night I went to G and D's with Fabian... *disappointed with me*... because I sneaked out, after I'd refused his invitation to go there earlier on. And when he invited me, and wanted us to get coffee or ice cream together, was he thinking of me as his child, or more like an adult? To take out for a snack and sort our disagreement?

Oh *God*, it's difficult. Was that a prayer? Maybe. How can I know what to do and say and when? I hope I did the right thing with Zoe back then. It seemed what I had to do? I think Dad would be pleased, this time.

I offer to make a pot of tea: Granny accepts this, and shows me where everything is. We nibble shortbread biscuits with the tea, and behave as if nothing's happened. Zoe looks at the tartan tin with the biscuits in, and comments that it's a pity that isn't a Guthrie or a Maxwell tartan. Granny says maybe we could look it up to see if it's a genuine one at all! Zoe says, 'Well, we're going to look at Scottish islands, after we've been to see the northern relatives.'

'Sounds lovely,' Granny says. I'm on the edge of my chair: don't let's get into the subject of Chapel House again, or even Cornwall! But Granny suggests we get changed ready for the evening while she prepares supper.

So now we're wearing our smart clothes. Our supper, salad and smoked salmon, is all put out. We're standing by the table about to sit down and eat. Oddly, just like at Granny Fee's before she says grace. Granny's holding the back of a chair she's about to pull out to sit on, looking down at her hands — wedding ring, engagement ring, deep pink nail varnish: she won't say grace though. I wonder why she's hesitating like that?

And something else I notice: she always wears heels, and even her slippers have wedges maybe over an inch high. But with her shoes on, standing behind her chair, Granny is still shorter than me. This is growing up: me without shoes dominates her in slippers, and it feels weird. I didn't notice that happening. Now both Mum and I are taller than Granny, and Zoe soon will be.

Suddenly as if she's changed her mood, Granny says, 'Come on girls, let's sit down and dig in or we'll still be in the Tube when the show begins! Zoe, I've slathered those new potatoes in unsalted butter, and sprinkled on chopped coriander, so you're going to enjoy them, aren't you? Ginger beer this evening, the next best thing to wine!' We sit down and 'dig in', and no awkward subjects are mentioned again.

We get to the theatre in good time. The show, *Mama Mia!* is amazing: noisy, colourful, and fun. We travel back with the Abba songs pounding in our heads. They're so singable! And, in the pink, posh, but old-fashioned bathroom, we hum and jiggle to them brushing our teeth.

We're sharing Granny Ianthe's huge, high, mahogany double bed, with eiderdown and slippery rose-pink *counterpane*. I can't sleep. The music pounds on, an unstoppable earworm. The window's open a crack and people pass in the street, laughing as they go home, or on to a night club after whatever they've been doing. Zoe wriggles and turns over. Soon we're chatting, talking about our great-granny. 'D'you think she was *like* Granny Caro?'

'How? I think she was modern, like – well, like the Bloomsbury set.'

'Who were they?'

'Writers. Artists. The main one was Virginia Woolf who wrote *A Room of One's Own*, and other stuff – *To the Lighthouse*. Fabian lent them me. His family have first editions of them, but he lent me the paperbacks from his sister's bookshelf. And, she – Virginia Woolf I mean — had an affair with another woman, called Vita. Vita Sackville-West.'

'That could be where Tolkien got the name of the Sackville-Bagginses from!'

'It could be. I don't think they were his kind of person... but they had an amazing garden, which Granny Caro sometimes raves about, you can't grow a garden like that in Cornwall of course – there's too much salt in the wind...'

This makes Zoe laugh. I cover her face with the rough, hairy, 1930s-style blanket, and she squeals. 'Don't! It's made of sandpaper! It smells funny.'

'Okay – let's not wake the sleeping dragon – Granny, I mean... I think that smell is moth-repellant...'

'Which is probably bad for us...'

'It is for moths.'

'So — Granny Ianthe – she wasn't a widow, but she said she was, and that's a lie.'

'You couldn't get away with being a single mum, never married, back then. But we don't need to go into all this now.' I give her a hug. 'Thanks for apologising to Granny.'

'She was okay about it. She said maybe I'd learn about these things when I was older, and to trust that Daze won't miss out.'

'Okay. Maybe we should try to sleep now? It's gone quiet outside.'

Interesting: have Granny Caroline and Des got a plan they're not telling us? And then I see more vividly what it would be like for Daze to be brought up by Granny Caro. Does that make it more likely that the woman in that painting was her step-mum?

Chapter 38

IANTHE'S RING

Sunday morning, I wake and wonder how Charlie's river party went — or whether it happened? With all the rain there's been, perhaps they haven't let any parties happen on the river? Granny's radio in the kitchen is blaring out the news: widespread floods in the Thames valley. Oh, poor Charlie!

This morning turns out to be for lounging about in our pyjamas. We're all gathered in the kitchen, where Granny (in a kimono dressing gown, silky fabric, printed with flowers), is making strong coffee, heating up some croissants. She passes us the magazines out of her *Observer*, and as she turns to get the croissants, I notice a wonderful dragon charging down the back of her kimono. Zoe screws up her face at the coffee, and I ask if we can slosh in oodles of milk, which is permitted, with a smile and an 'Of course you can! Should've done lattes for you girls!'

Granny then goes behind the newspaper, catching up with what the *Observer*'s been observing and commenting on. She reads bits out: a huge headline telling readers 'lock terror suspects up indefinitely', which doesn't please her. 'Narrow-minded and unrealistic,' she murmurs, shaking the paper as she folds the page to read the article properly. I catch Zoe's eyes. We grin. I'd love to capture the scene on camera, or make a sketch, Granny Caro with coffee in one hand, holding the folded newspaper with the other.

There's also a piece about an oil spill threatening the coast of Dorset, which makes Granny tut, and Zoe leap into talking about the effects on marine life, but she's learnt something — it doesn't lead to mention of Chapel House. It's peaceful, all of us relaxed and not talking about Ianthe or family tensions. I wonder if Granny Caro will miss us when we go home? Will she be alone here? Whatever, she and Zoe are totally over the problems of yesterday.

After breakfast, I take photos of the flat which, as Mum said, is all 1930s style, while Zoe makes friends with somebody's cat which has sneaked in.

Later, I'm cleaning my teeth, with the bathroom door open a tiny crack (what a mistake!) and Granny puts her head round. 'Alice! So sorry, sweetie. Are you thinking of having a shower?'

'Yes, but not if you want to…'

'Not right now, dear. But, a word. We were talking about Mummy, as I called her, your great grandmother.' She pauses. Like in honour of Ianthe. 'You're growing into a lovely svelte young woman.'

'Thank you,' I say, feeling her eyes all over me and wondering what this has to do with Ianthe. I hope not a sex talk. From Mum's descriptions of growing up with Granny Caroline, I'd begun to expect one.

'And possibly another life scientist? Have you thought about following your mother to Clare College?'

Wanting to avoid any clumsy mistakes, I've the courage to at least give her an honest answer about this. 'I don't know yet.'

'Oh?'

'Well, I might apply to Cambridge – but I've also thought of looking at other options.'

'What do your parents think, dear?'

I'm telling myself to be really careful. Of my words as well as of the toothpaste on my brush, so it doesn't fall off onto the bathroom's fluffy carpet. (Why do well-off people carpet their bathrooms? To keep their feet warm? The loo, by contrast, has its own safe area of marbled vinyl around its feet – or more like, foot.) 'I hope they'll be okay about it. I think Mum will understand I might not want to be the third generation in science research, after her and Grandpa. Though I think it'll make her a bit sad too.'

'Can I ask what this alternative is that you're exploring?'

Looking at the ground won't impress her. I'm trying hard to look her in the eye, as I say, 'Well, I thought of some kind of therapist,' (she gives me a curious look, I can't read it), 'I mean, it's useful, it's helpful, lots of people need therapy, and that includes, you know, kids with learning problems?' I don't mention what I discovered from the prospectuses —that you can train to do art therapy.

A pause, then Granny says (settling her expression a bit, so that it's positive), 'Well, darling, good for you! If that's what you feel you could make a career in, then have a stab at it! I always wanted to be a doctor, you know – not a researcher like my mother. And certainly not a campaigner!'

The relief is huge, not quite what I deserve. I accept the boob-squashing hug which she now bestows, holding my toothbrush aloft so it doesn't stab either of us or dump toothpaste on the carpet. Granny of course deposits her scent in my hair and on my pyjamas, but that's more than okay.

But then, she produces a small cube from the pocket of her flowers-and-dragon kimono, and holds it out to me. A box with a hinged lid. 'Well, I have something your great-grandmother Ianthe left for you, sweetie. And I think that now is the time for you to have it. Open it, dear.'

The box is lined with blue velvet. The ring lies there, glistening gold. Momentarily I think 'One ring to rule them all' and I'm hit by the irony, after telling her I'm trying to escape family traditions. *Hobbits in science*? But this ring has no inscription, and a single diamond – I think a diamond — set into the wide gold band. 'She wore it on her left hand, of course. Shall we see if it fits? Hold your hand out, dear,' she says, reaching for it.

She threads Ianthe's ring – the one she had for being a non-widow – on the middle finger of my right hand. Ugh, like a creepy marriage to the family tradition. I take a long breath. 'You really want me to have this?'

'Mummy – Ianthe — oh *yes*! She told me very firmly, *For my oldest great granddaughter.*' I can hear Gollum gloating over the Ring, '*my Precious.*'

'Why not – Mum?'

'It was left to you, dearest. So that's what we do. Right. One more thing: I'm sure you've started – your periods, haven't you? And your Mum mentioned a nice young man from the school orchestra?'

Oh God, I think. I run the tap, swish cold water into my mouth with my hand, and spit in the basin, hoping this signals: 'Please let's not... I'm busy.' But she stands there, right in the doorway, talking.

'Alice, I know you young people all go to festivals in the school holidays with boyfriends and girlfriends – well, if you want to make sure you're safe, you know can just ask me. In fact, I could give you a prescription now?'

What? 'I'm only just sixteen,' I say, 'It's legal, but – I – have lots of stuff I want to do. It can, like, wait?'

'And your periods don't give you any trouble?'

'They're a nuisance – but no, no trouble. I know some girls take the Pill for periods – but I don't need...' I don't. I kind of think maybe I'm not quite up to — whatever Granny expects. Of course, I do want to, but also I don't. And I'm going to a family retreat, not the Truck festival, and I'm not about to look for another festival this year.

'Don't forget the offer's there, sweetie. Now, I'll let you get on with your shower.'

And so I set the hot water running. Who told Granny about Fabian? Who else thinks I need guiding into my own future, and assumes I need their help?

Maybe us pushing at her to change her mind about the house – in a bigger way – gives her the same feeling? Do we feel the same things about being pushed, when we're – whatever age Granny Caroline is now?

So, after that discussion, and when Zoe's said goodbye to whoever's cat that was, and we're all dressed and packed, Granny Caro hands over the video of the women's Wimbledon Tennis final, so we can watch at home. We pile into a cab, the rain begins as we start out, and is running down the windows as we jump out at Paddington.

Chapter 39

We catch a mid-morning train. This time, Zoe's got her nose in a book, and I begin thinking about Granny's awful snobbery about her family, like a sort of dynasty of scientists. Then suddenly Zoe's nose is out of her book and into my life. 'Hey — what's that you've got there? That ring?'

'This? Granny gave it me. It's Ianthe's pseudo wedding ring. I'll take it off now – now she's not here to see — I think it's kind of weird to wear it.'

'Yeah, and it's like something Victorian. With that great big stone in it.'

'Well, something 1930s.'

I slip it off, and my finger feels normal again. I pack it away in its box, and stash it inside my cross-body bag. 'I don't want to tell Mum I've got it, until we can talk about it properly and she can tell me if Great-granny really wanted me to have it. So just don't say anything. I'll also tell her all the stuff about Derek Bradfield, paying school fees and sort of dynastic stuff. Inheriting that ring is embarrassing, wearing it would be like we're some sort of academic aristocracy. It'd be, like, offensive to everyone else.'

Zoe agrees. 'Blimey, I'd hate to have to wear a ring like that one. I'd probably try to lose it!'

Dad meets us at Oxford station, and suddenly some instinct makes me give him a big hug. He's kind of surprised, of course, and I say 'That's for being an ordinary person, and choosing your own career.'

'So Granny's lifestyle at the flat didn't impress you then?'

'Would it impress you?'

'Och, probably not so much. But you enjoyed the show?'

'It was amazing!' Zoe interrupts.

I say, 'Apart from that show, I think I might prefer staying with Uncle Ian and co.! Well, not with him but – you know?"

'I think I do.' We laugh.

It's now a week until we set off on our northern holiday, and there's still no sign of what I'd call real summer. Anyhow, the next morning I'm off to meet Fabian in town: at least his family haven't yet disappeared out of Oxford for the whole holidays like most of my friends have. I walk past Mariam's house. It looks from the street like nothing's changed since I last called there. I walk up the drive to the porch, and lean my head against the glass to gaze through. Everything looks just the same as when I first realized they were away, the only difference is piles of letters on the mat. I think about this disappearance as I wait for the bus. I knew about her sister's wedding, the relatives who were gifting the celebrations but insisting the wedding must take place in – where was it? Cairo? California? But surely the date would fit with school and Uni vacation time? She didn't mention anything, and then, she simply wasn't back at school after the last exams.

The bus appears and I get on, but the thought is creeping me out and lurking quietly behind everything that's good. The sun's less certain about shining, as I get out, and I am hustled along the pavement by impatient tourist passengers.

And there's Fabian, loitering, as Dad might put it, under the clock tower at Carfax! He has a huge black umbrella (still furled) and is using it as a stick to lean on, comically, as I wait to cross St Aldates. He even attempts a few steps of a silly little music-hall style dance with it, as I'm hurried across in a crowd of people. I get a proper welcome hug, after nearly two weeks apart.

Fabian says his dad hauled him off to Norfolk for birdwatching after A levels. I roll my eyes. He says, 'Because Dad had to go to East Anglia Uni anyway, for a conference, he insisted we all went, and of course had to be – to watch birds... You know my parents actually met birdwatching?'

'Okay, mine met – or at least re-met — watching my aunt Daze have a baby. No, really! My dad was the on-call paediatrician!'

This makes us laugh in a friendly kind of way, like 'how Oxford is that?' Fabian slips one arm around my back, and we stroll straight up the Cornmarket, sweeping tourists before us, and swing into HMV to browse CDs. I decide to buy one of Haydn's *Creation*, and while I'm paying, a very quiet voice speaks into my ear, 'So, is our song somewhere on there?'

Kind of ironic, but funny. I reply, 'If you say so!' Feeling fizzy all over, and that I'm defo past being a child.

Next, we go down Broad Street to browse books in Blackwell's, then buy and drink expensive coffees. I pull out my phone, my lovely birthday present from Grandpa Guthrie, to show Fabian the great photos I took illicitly from the windows at school: squirrels in the beech trees, the rounders teams practising, the Head haranguing a couple of teachers clutching armfuls of books, one holding a file over her head to keep the rain off! There's also some of Nina and Emily making comic faces at each other. Our heads together, we laugh.

By now very hungry, we buy filled baguettes in a sandwich shop, and decide to eat them in the Botanic Gardens. Appalled that we have to pay! I've always visited with Mum or Dad, and taken no notice of the cost. Not too many tourists about, and the air is warm, and damp, and still. The river is high but not in flood. You can smell the scent of the grass. We feed baguette crumbs to the sparrows around our feet. I am so happy, inside, except when I think about Mariam, or about the house in Cornwall.

Then we visit the hothouses. Under some hideous and fascinating vine-like plants with huge red flowers there's a crowd of teenagers blocking the narrow passageway, gawping at a pond where waterlilies with enormous leaves are floating. They turn their eyes on us, and all start saying hi to Fabian. Evidently friends of his.

Fabian says, 'Hey, this is Alice, from the orchestra.'

'So, another string player?' says one of the boys. He seems to eye me up, I suppose he's checking that I'm okay to be with his friend? Though I fantasize that this could be some male code. What might a string player be – except a violinist? Being strung along...?

One of the girls asks if I've been to Oxford before. I respond (feeling embarrassed but trying to sound cool) 'Loads of times – like I live in Headington?' The whole thing's very awkward. At last someone says that they have a punt booked, and do we want to join them. To my relief, Fabian says 'Another time maybe. Thanks.'

So now, I begin to see all the downsides of being what Mum calls an item: your partner's friends summing you up – noticing your clothes, your hair, how you speak, whether you are worthy of their friend spending time with you. Asking the two of you to do stuff with them. Having to get to know the partner's friends. 'So, are you two coming to the Truck festival?' another girl then asks. 'Begins Friday! All of us'll be there!'

'Sorry. I'm going to be away with my family. I – I would otherwise. I mean, it's an Oxford thing, isn't it?'

We walk back through town. The air's heavy with moisture, the traffic stinks of petrol, the clouds huddle together overhead. If they all join up, then we'll be using the umbrella. Briefly, we consider the possibility of visiting the University Museum.

'To see the dinosaurs! We did that all the time when we were little. We threw all our pocket money away on plastic dinosaurs, and things with dinosaurs on them!'

A raindrop lands on my nose, two more in my hair. Huge raindrops fall, like polka dots on the pavement, and Fabian stops to put up the umbrella. We snuggle under it.

We decide to head over to Fabian's, so we keep walking, past the old Radcliffe, and up Woodstock Road. A sharp breeze agitates the trees as we turn down Walton Well Road, around a corner, and into Southmoor Road. He leads me into one of the tall, gothic-style, houses.

It's such a thing, that first time in a friend's house. It may tell you things you didn't know, or it may help you to understand your friend. And the other people who live there. Fabian stands in the doorway, silhouetted, shaking the huge black umbrella, then folds it down, and brings it indoors. It's dark in the hall. I can make out a stand with hooks and coats hanging on them. A small table, with letters laid out. On the wall, a portrait — perhaps a Russell ancestor? And then, something standing in a corner: a double bass.

Everything is silent, except the tick, tick, tick, of the pendulum of a huge grandfather clock. We hear the sound of hail rattling on the windows.

We go through to the kitchen. There, everything is light, with a big window onto the garden, where washing flaps in the wet. A large table under the window, with chairs round it: six chairs. 'There might be some cake in the tin,' says Fabian.

But he puts his arms around me, almost like when Granny gives one of her boob-squashing hugs, and he kisses my neck. I shiver with the surprise. We stand there, with the grandfather clock whirring in the hallway, and begin kissing. As we lean into each other I am totally quivering inside. But also, very slightly worried. In a pause to breathe, I say, partly to take both our minds off this, 'So what are you doing next year?' I'm struggling here: where exactly are we going?

'Sociology at Cambridge. The trains and buses are atrocious from Oxford, but the great thing is, I'll have a car.' He strokes my back, his hand stays where it is, on my behind. I can't breathe. Well, I can, but my breath is short, and kind of difficult, and my thoughts whirl, as out in the hallway, the grandfather clock starts to chime. This is actually funny, it makes me laugh, nervously, and we break apart, just as a voice booms from the hall, 'Anybody in?' It's Fabian's Dad.

'Mio caro, are you home, darling?' calls his mum. Fabian shakes his head a moment, then calls out 'Mum, Alice Mullins is here. We're looking for cake?' I, momentarily, think it's amusing that Granny Caro's name means *Darling*, in Italian, only in the male form.

OMG, I have met them, but not – not recently, not as part of, well, an item with their son. More like, as a five-year-old, when Fabian's older sister had the same ballet teacher, and we were doing a show.

Whatever. 'Alice,' (his mum has a huge smile, as she extends a hand for me to shake, while studying my outfit and my hair) 'you must stay for dinner!' And, well, I eat with them. Another scary thing. She insists on giving me a ride home.

In the car we talk about holidays. Mum's told Francesca Russell that we're going to the Scottish islands. That must have been at the last academics' dinner party. Their house is full of pictures, not just of the Russell ancestors. Many painted by people they know. I ask her about them: some are in the big breakfast room where we ate.

At home, I lie on my bed, listening to the rain, and occasional rumbles of thunder. I hear Mum and Dad going to bed. Charlie phones, but when I see it's her, I don't answer. I am surveying the past day, and thinking what everything we did means. The dial on their clock has the sun and the moon on it...

Maybe if I had answered, things might've been different for Charlie?

Chapter 40

ZOE IS UPSET

I wake suddenly, it's still dark. I turn over, remembering the delicious, scary time in Fabian's kitchen, before his parents interrupted us. And then, I notice the odd noise. What is it, what's making it, where's it coming from?

Sitting up, and reaching for my phone: ten past one? Why am I sleeping in my clothes?

Oh, because I simply keeled over and dropped off, thinking the same as when I woke just now? And suddenly, my door's opening and the noise comes nearer. I lean over and switch on my bedside lamp. 'Zo-zo?'

'Ally?'

'You okay? Didn't see you last night, you must've been out too. So, d'you need something? D'you need a painkiller? Or something else? I mean, I know it's a pest but periods are normal – you'll get used to it.'

'Not that!' she hisses, shaking her head so her hair flies over her face, then pushing it back, snuffling, then rubbing her arm across. 'Can I borrow – have – a tissue?' she says, half falling over something on the floor, bashing into my desk, then locating my box of tissues and dragging out a handful. Then she collapses onto my bed, and snuggles her face against my back. 'Hey, you've got your ordinary clothes on!'

'Yeah, I was thinking, and I fell asleep.' She grabs my shirt, to wipe her face. 'Oy, you've just grabbed a bunch of tissues, don't use my top!'

'Alice, *they... chucked me out!*' she wails.

'Who? What? I thought – Mum said — you'd gone to a Base Camp holiday thing.' Properly awake, I try hugging her. Feel how she quivers, while gulping her words into my chest. 'What happened? Can you be a bit quieter, unless we want Mum and Dad in here?'

'Annalise! I went to Annalise's house to collect her for the barbecue, and she came to the door – but their car was outside stuffed with things, ordinary stuff, not like for a holiday – and her mum came out, grabbed Annalise by her arm and shoved her aside, and told me they were off – and not to bother coming by again! I said, but it's the Base Camp barbecue, I came by so we could walk together... and then, she – Stacey, her mum — pushed me out of their garden!'

'Gosh, that sounds wild. And weird. You weren't home when I got back. It was late because Fabian's Mum asked me to have dinner with them. Anyhow, where did you go, what did you do? The parents would've gone insane if they knew Stacey did that – why didn't you call them to collect you... if you didn't feel like walking back after being – well, attacked, by Stacey?'

'I was at her house *earlier.*' Big sniffs, and she actually uses some of the tissues. 'In the morning. We were talking. We climbed into one of the trees in their garden, and we were talking about – families and stuff. It's a school project — we're supposed to do something on family history in the holidays.'

'And?'

'She was kind of angry about the project. She said that was enough about families. Why didn't I go home, and say nothing about our talk. And she'd see me at the barbecue. I came back, I put my bike away, and when I left for the Base Camp afternoon, about five maybe, it wasn't raining any more, it'd been dry and sunny a while, and I thought, why don't I collect Annalise and we'll walk together? So, I did – and *that* happened!'

'What?'

'What I *said*. They chucked me out. Her mum did. Annalise didn't try to stop it happening. Maybe she couldn't, maybe she was scared. I – kind of thought, I didn't want to go back and blub to Mum and Dad – I did the pulling-myself-together thing, and went on my own.'

I give her another hug, 'Oh Zoze! I'm so sorry.'

'Yes.'

'Didn't you tell whoever it is that runs the group what happened?'

'Nope. I joined in with everything, to forget for a while. The place we went to – in the minibus – had shelters and benches, and we ended up round a firepit singing choruses – you know – that almost made me cry. 'Cos it was a perfect evening, and there were even bats in the twilight, and the moon all misty in a cloud. Anyhow, then the cloud covered the moon, everything got really dark, and Dad turned up in the car, and brought me back.'

'And you didn't confide in him either? Was he surprised you were on your own?'

'Not really. People go off on holiday before this, some go as soon as school term ends, don't they?'

'So you allowed him to bring you back, and you pretended nothing was wrong?'

'Yes. And they looked busy, so I – asked where you were, and they said, out, at Fabian's place, and I – went up so I didn't have to talk about it. I suppose.'

'If you'd said, they'd have listened. Even if they had looked busy.'

'Well they looked like – maybe I didn't want to talk right then.' More tears, more quivering.

'Zozo, they would. Why didn't you?'

'Because. I told you. She said not to.'

'Okay, she said not to talk about families. But not – not to tell them... what did you do?'

'I – had a bath. I lay in it a long time. I put music on, and read, I wrote Annalise a letter about it all, a letter to go in the post, not a text or an e-mail. Mum and Dad came upstairs, and I called out I was in bed. They were in Dad's new study. They *called out* was I okay, and Mum put her head round and asked if I'd had a nice evening. I said, "'Yeah...sausages and a fire pit. And bats!'"

'And?'

'She said, "it's a lovely group, isn't it?" We said goodnight. Then I rang her — Annalise. A lot later, when I knew you'd come back. When I knew everyone was asleep. Like, it was about twelve?'

'Did she answer?'

'Yes. She told me not to talk about her family *ever* again. She said *we shouldn't be friends any more*... Then she turned her phone off.' Zoe sniffs, shakes, and burrows into me, soaking the front of my top with tears. I remember how Fabian had crept his hand under it to touch my skin, in their kitchen. I feel so sad that I was with him, only aware of him, while Zoe was being treated like dirt by her friend. I shiver with the memory, and the chilly damp of my sister's grief. 'Alice, *now she hates me!*'

I don't ask more details about the family talk. I let Zoe cry, and then I peel off my top and my jeans, and snuggle both of us under my duvet together.

Holding her, with my brain full of memories about my afternoon and evening, feels weird. Intense. When I wake again, it's very completely light, and quite late. Mum is looking around the door, her expression like a question mark. 'Alice? Zozo? Better get up, you've missed half the morning! Is this the sleep of teenage exhaustion? I won't ask more, unless you want to say.'

'Nope,' I say, untangling myself from my sister. 'We had a chat in the night, but now, we're possibly both okay. Well, I am,' I said, looking at Zoe.

'Right. Good. Something was up, but it's okay now?' Mum's giving Zozo a chance. She doesn't take it.

Her eyes are swollen though. You couldn't not notice.

Mum picks up my clothes, and, taking a moment to stand and look thoughtful (feeling my shirt is damp?), puts them, folded, on my desk chair. 'I'm home today, the lab meeting's cancelled. I'll be around here making sure we've got everything sorted for our trip. You two can help: collect your things together — wellies, sun cream in case this weather ever changes, enough underwear in case the campsites have no washing facilities... warm clothes... that kind of thing. And so, if anyone wants to talk, I am yours today. And tomorrow.'

'Okay,' I say, remembering Granny Caro's little talk about contraception. *Oh, mio caro!* I'm hearing Dr *Francesca* Russell: '*Mio caro, are you home?*' I shall wait for him to call me, though.

And, that's odd, I think, Mum's in charge at her lab, so, that meeting, she cancelled it herself, didn't she? Possibly she thinks there is a problem here, and, as Zo-zo slept in my bed, that it's Zoe's problem.

I shan't mention it to Mum. Shall I try to get Zoe to talk to Mum about it, though? 'Ally? D'you think you could do yourselves breakfast – well, it'll be brunch now won't it – while I pop to the shops for a few things?'

'Huh?'

'Could you and Zoe get yourselves something to eat while I go out for some grocery things? I'm only popping to the Co-op?'

'Yeah, yeah sure – you go, we'll do it.'

'And, I'm glad Frankie Russell asked you to stay over for dinner. They're a nice family, aren't they? He's a bit scary, but she's lovely.'

I smile. That's to hide that I'd rather this relationship was with someone who's not part of a family that happens to be friends of my parents. Four pairs of eyes, who can compare notes, will be on us! 'Yeah. She's cool. You go, Mum, we'll eat. Promise we'll eat!'

Zoe slides out of my bed, and ducks under Mum's arm (Mum's swinging on the door handle, as Dad calls it, not gone but not staying in the room either). Zoe's going into her room, 'I need to look something up on Google, first!'

'Something I can help with?'

'Moon rainbows. Remember we saw one?'

As Zoe dashes off, Mum raises her eyebrows at me. 'No, I don't know either,' I say. 'But I can look after Zo-zo for you. I know what the problem is. She probably will share it with you, later. It's not something really worrying. For us.'

'I'll bring the bags down, before I go, so you two will have somewhere to put things you want to take.'

At last, she leaves me alone, and I grab my phone to see whether Fabian's tried to get in touch. He hasn't.

If Mum asks me about yesterday (supposing Francesca mentions walking in on us) – I shan't say that it was in their kitchen, and that it was what's called a *sexual awakening* by our English teachers. As in 'Romeo and Juliet is about sexual awakening... But what else is it about?' We all sit like we know nothing, waiting for somebody else to make a suggestion. 'Anyone want to answer this?' Well it's actually a whole-person thing, though that's not the answer the woman was looking for – she wanted to talk about tribes and rivalry in medieval Italy. And no, don't worry, Mum, we didn't do — anything.

But Stacey grabbing Zoe physically – after shoving her own daughter behind her, back into the house — I do think my sister should tell them both about that.

Mum's still banging about in the attic, shifting stuff around, finding the bags and cases for luggage, and I suddenly know I'd love a bacon sandwich for breakfast. But down in the kitchen, hunting in the fridge reveals no bacon: not really a surprise but disappointing. 'Zoze?' I call up the stairs, 'It's brunch time, could you eat scrambled eggs?'

She appears on the landing, still in pjs, and yawns. 'Anything. I don't care. Mind.'

'Look, we have to eat, whatever. I'm doing us eggs, okay?'

'Whatever.'

Ten minutes later, she comes downstairs wearing pj bottoms and a T-shirt. I've made scrambled eggs, wholemeal toast, and grilled tomatoes, and warmed the plates. I've also made milky coffee, set it out nicely, and even cut a couple of roses from the garden and stuck them in a vase on the table. I have slotted my new CD of the *Creation* into the old boom-box we keep in the family room, and the amazing music fills every corner of the whole downstairs.

It's supposed to cheer her up: actually, it's supposed to use up my fizzing energy: a superb day out with Fabian, doing nothing special I wouldn't do with a girlfriend (well, almost nothing, just a tad out of the ordinary stuff I'd do with a girlfriend), but it felt special. I've actually already described some of it to Nina, who phoned wanting to go shopping, and for Nina I included the extra bits. Nina squealed as I told her, and is very thumbs-up about it all, and said she'd send me some music that's more suitable for romantic encounters, Haydn being far too old-school and religious.

Zoe patters across the room in her bare feet, saying 'Wazzat on the player? Can I turn it down?'

'Up to you.' She turns it down until it's whispering. 'Please, that's my new CD, and I'd like to hear it – quietly, but loud enough?'

'I'd rather have a recording of the *Mama Mia* stuff.' She slumps into a chair at the table.

'We don't have one. We do have—,' I flourish her plate of brunch onto the table in front of her, 'Ta-da! Eggs scrambled in unsalted butter, tomatoes grilled to perfection, and un-burnt wholemeal toast!'

'I might go into town then and buy one! A CD of *Mama Mia* songs. An' I do like what you made, thank you for doing that. 'Cos when the smell came up the stairs, I knew I was starving, whatever. An' the roses.'

We eat almost in silence, Zoe obviously still in shock from being, as she called it, chucked out as a friend. Like a deflated netball. 'Zoze? Zo-zo? Nothing was your fault. You don't need to feel it so hard: if Annalise's family are behaving randomly weird, that's entirely them.'

'I suppose,' she sighs. 'Only I really tried to make Annalise feel at home, I mean at home at school, right? And she liked Base Camp. She liked it more than I do, because they all made an effort about being friendly. It's what we're taught there, welcome the stranger?'

'I know.'

'They are strange, aren't they?'

'Mmm, very.'

'Mum said Stacey goes to the lunchtime yoga class – the one Shaz runs? For the science area?'

'Interesting.'

Zoe brightens up: piece of toast with egg balanced on it, on the end of her fork, she stops with it halfway to her mouth, eyes full of interest in what I said, 'So she might know where they went, and why?'

Actually, I only said it to sound friendly. 'Well, she might. But Shaz puts up notices and advertises in the Uni Gazette or somewhere, so anyone can join if the class isn't full. Which it probably isn't in mid-July, everyone will be away, all the academics buzz off on conferences, or they go to France or to Italy – Fabian's family are off to Italy.'

'Oh. And we're going to Scotland.' She deflates again. I pick up the plates and put them in the dishwasher. 'Where it will rain again. Listen, I looked up moon halos.'

A plan begins forming in my head. 'Look, I think today we should do a few things that aren't packing for the Mullins retreat and Scotland. Why don't you get ready, and I'll tell Mum what we're going to do, and we'll go out?'

'What about moon halos? Don't you want to know?'

'We'll talk while we walk. That'll – save the bus fare!'

Chapter 41

ZOE AND I LOOK AT ANNALISE'S HOUSE

There's a way you can walk to the bus stop which takes you past Annalise's house. It's through a narrow lane, left over from when our bit of Oxford was still a village. Then you turn down a road leading to the bypass, and their house is on the right. From there you can turn back and down Mariam's road and reach a bus stop. I'm taking Zoe that way, today.

'Why're we going down here?' she asks, as we pass a short row of pretty terraced Cotswold stone cottages, with hollyhocks growing outside. The sun has decided to visit today, so it all looks cheerful, even if we aren't. The hollyhocks, loud with bees, bow in a light wind.

'You'll see.'

'Are you taking me past Annalise's, because there's no point, I told you, they don't want to see me and anyway they've gone.'

'Well, I thought we might make absolutely sure they've gone, and maybe, could they have left some clue to why they went? It's this corner, we turn here, right?' We're crossing a road now, and the houses are boring semis which match. Even so, there could be traffic, but Zoe slows down, and stops in the road. 'What're you doing standing where the traffic goes?'

'There isn't any. Remember this is Oxford, school holidays? There's never anything happening round here, everyone goes away.'

This reminds me about Mariam's disappearance and I get slightly irritated. 'Well, it worries me, and I'm responsible for you, so don't stand there.'

'I don't know why I agreed to come. I was looking up moon halos, and you said, let's go now, and let's buy whatever, and I had to get my shoes on, and read that up later.'

'I let you finish!'

'Yeah, just about!'

'Tell me what you found.'

'As if you care about anything I like!'

'That is not true. It's appalling exaggeration!'

'You hate science – I heard you talking to Dad about how Mum's obsessed with her lab work, and about playing a part in a scientific dynasty, and your A levels.'

I am really upset by this, I had no idea anything I said sounded like I hated anything. But maybe I did? 'Look, that was between me and him, and I didn't use the word *hate*! So – come out of the road and tell me more about moon halos. Did you look them up?'

Zoe sniffs, and pushes her glasses back up her nose, and begins in a very quiet voice as she steps onto the pavement, 'Well, when we were in the wood, and it got dark, the moon was extra bright – or it seemed to be, and it was a huge, full moon and it had a rainbow round it. We wondered what made the rainbow. I said, 'It'll be formed something like normal rainbows — the light shining through thin clouds or something.' Rick – that's the youth leader – wasn't terribly interested, more in herding us back towards the shelters, and the benches, and the fire-pit, to sing. So, this morning, I looked it up. On Google.'

'And?'

'The rainbows are refraction of light off ice crystals. Apparently, this can predict unsettled, stormy weather. But if the rainbow is like a kind of haze touching the moon, without a gap between it and the moon, which is more like last night, it could just be shining through thin clouds. Which it probably was, and that's light through water droplets, like a daytime rainbow.'

'Refraction rather than diffraction,' I say, as I happen to know.

'And if it's a proper rainbow, unattached, then it's bigger ice crystals. Or simply, ice not water droplets. Yes.'

'Depends whether the light waves are being bent around or through an object. Whether they're bouncing off or bouncing through. I actually do like science, I just don't want to live off it. And not physics.'

'Physics is my worst subject – in science, I mean. Annalise was better at it. She even liked it. I mean, we aren't bad at it, but we don't like it – I don't much.'

'What *do* you like?'

'Things which are alive? Animals, plants, insects? People who stay as friends?'

We're nearly at Annalise's house by now. I decide it's time to share something which might help us both. 'Zo-zo, listen, I've got a friend problem too. My friend Mariam?'

'The one you walk home with?'

'Yes. She's disappeared. She didn't come back after exams. There's a rumour she's had to go somewhere with her parents. I really miss her. We used to sit together in the physics lab, so we'd already have a partner to share with, when we did experiments. It's hard, losing a friend, I know the feeling too.'

'But it's not the same. She's only gone away. She may come back. Annalise said we *mustn't be friends* any more.'

'Yes, that is different. But Mariam didn't even tell me she was going away.'

'Did you try phoning her?'

'She didn't answer.'

'And now you've got Fabian.'

'That's – very different.'

'So because you've got a boyfriend, you stopped trying. That is so mean!'

'That's not true!' Though, actually, it does make me feel a bit guilty, having forgotten about Mariam's disappearance, because I was so happy being with Fabian, being the chosen one, as Emily said (I know a few other girls would've wanted to go out with him), and feeling – stupidly I suppose – grown up.

What is it that makes us all rivals, and makes boys so important? Hormones are just mating prompts, like animals and even insects have! I hope Fabian and me have a bit more than only hormones...

'So try her again. Text her, and keep phoning and sending texts. If they went somewhere, they might have come back by now.'

At that moment, I nearly collide with some branches sticking right out over the pavement, and I realise that we've reached Annalise's house. It's the only neglected house in the road: it's got bushes the size of trees at the front, waist-high grass, and a cracked path. A couple of steps and we're at the gate. 'You see, the gate's shut, and they've left the boxes out for the recycling binmen. It's true, they've gone...'

The dreary house looks like something from a fairy tale or even a horror movie. I look up at the windows: every one is closed and behind them, the curtains are shut tight. I think of Harold Toad in his tank. 'Zo-zo, how did you – I mean, what was it like inside? Really?'

'It was actually okay. It didn't smell, it wasn't dirty – inside. It was old and the furniture was strange. They didn't have a stair carpet, but the inside was kind of normal. Everything was clean. And tidy. It was a bit dark, though. We had to put lights on.'

'Maybe it was a squat – like they didn't own it, they simply moved in and occupied an empty house?'

'They had all the things though. Water, electricity, and everything. Fridge, though it was quite small. Cooker. It was like normal inside? A TV, Annalise had a laptop in her room.'

'But not totally normal.'

'Okay, not totally.'

We move up the path. At the edge of the porch, two rectangular boxes, piled with paper and card. Zoe notices something else, 'It's Harold Toad's tank! They've left his home behind!'

'Oh – so they didn't take him. I hope they let him out.'

'Maybe into the pond in the park? I don't think they'd...'

At that moment, the breeze gusts suddenly, sending rubbish whirling into the air and on to the long grass, and something — a coloured leaflet from one of the open recycling boxes – lands on my trainers.

I pick it up, slightly surprised by what it is, while 'What's that, that landed on your foot?' my sister says, leaning to see.

'Flyer. For Shaz's yoga classes in the science area. Stacey must've joined because this came through her door.'

We hunt in the box for anything else that might provide a clue about why or where they went, in such a hurry and so secretly. Mostly it's dreary stuff, adverts for pizza outlets, or flyers for plays and concerts, and charities asking for donations.

Zoe says 'Try texting Mariam again!' So I go and I perch on the wall to type a text, while she searches through the other box, kneeling on the cracked concrete path. 'Christmas cards – to Annalise from everyone in our form. Some leaflets I've seen at St Hildie's advertising quiet days and stuff. An old diary but everything's in initial letters, almost everything. And cardboard biscuit packets and things, all flattened. Her mum was kind of fussy about tidiness. It really wasn't a squat – it was like a house that hadn't been lived in, but it wasn't – how you'd expect. Did you text?'

'Yep.'

'What'll we do now?'

'Go round the back, look from the garden?'

'We could try the back door?'

'Maybe not...'

But, when we try the side gate, that stops us. It's locked, and unclimbable.

'Where, then? We've tried everything!'

'We'll have to give up for now. So, I know what we'll do. It's called retail therapy. We'll go into town, what we said we'd really do, and... Mum gave me some extra pocket money for us to share – we'll buy stuff...'

'How much? Is it half each?'

'It does happen to be. It has to be sensible things, she said! Clothes, or books?'

'The new Harry Potter! We were going to queue for that, then Annalise wasn't allowed... I wonder why, really? And I am sad we can't have a look from the back of the house...'

'Well, I know. But, Blackwells or Waterstones for the book, yes? I'm going to Lush for bath bombs, and... maybe look for a top?'

'How much did she give us, then?'

'More than you'd think. But for sensible things.'

♥ ♥ ♥

We get the Harry Potter. I find myself an art book about Young British Artists. In the Fair Trade shop, we buy chocolate to eat, because 'It's sensible not to be hungry,' Zoe suggests, 'and my blood sugar says I am!' A collection of small wooden painted cats, in several sizes, catches our eyes. Orange, blue, or white cats, with dark stripes and tiny flowers among the stripes. They have lovely happy little faces, and their tails go straight up, indicating they are indeed happy cats. 'Oh, how sweet! I'm buying one of those for... I can't though, she's not my friend any more...'

'I'll buy you one for you, if you like?'

My phone suddenly shrieks three loud rings into the shop. So embarrassing and intrusive! I grab it. 'Mariam! Where are you?'

'Phoning you!'

'Hey, where've you been? You didn't tell any of us!' Suddenly, I think, I shouldn't talk as if I know she's happy. She might not be. 'Are you — okay? All of you?' I'm walking out of the shop to the little hallway where the stairs go up to ground level, as I'm talking.

'Alice, I can't talk now. We're in London, at my Uncle's place. Tomorrow we fly to California for my sister's wedding.'

'What?'

'*Habibti*, I told you, my Uncle is paying for the wedding. And it's in California, now, not Cairo, and my sister's transferring to do her research there, for her PhD?'

'Why – why — is this all new?'

'Alice, her fiancé is studying there. He's – his father is my dad's best friend, and – you see, it's been arranged.'

I take a breath. Mariam's sister, who's a sophisticated twenty-something scientist, is being married to her father's friend's son, and sent off to a different country. Just doesn't fit. 'Can they do that?'

'Don't think I deserted you. I shall be back, I think, next term. I shall be. It's just –a family thing.' She sounds about to cry.

'Mariam?'

'Sorry, I have to go now.' She sniffs, and recovers. 'Dress fittings. For all of us.'

'But...'

'I have to go. Don't worry about me, *habibti* – I will be back. *Inshallah.*'

I click off my phone, and sweep my hand across my eyes. My sister's come into the hallway, and she puts her arm round my back. 'What's happened?'

'Her sister's going to be married in California. To the son of one of her parents' friends. They'll all be there all summer.'

'So, she's coming back then?'

'I don't know. She says she's coming back. It's not like Annalise, but – she's calling me her best friend, in Arabic, and that got to me. I felt like – you know – like, actually, I *don't* know. We seemed close, but we'll never be that close?'

'Yeah.'

'I'm sorry. You and Annalise were really close.'

'Yeah. We were. And her family — I was told not to talk about it.'

'And Mariam and I are close, but we'll never be... We're divided by culture. C'mon, let's go and – let's go. *Yalla, habibti,* as Mariam would say – let's go. But first,' I turn back into the shop with all its bright things for sale from every corner of the world, 'I'll buy us each one of those cats? And then – River Island, White Stuff, where's cool, d'you think, to find a new top?'

'That place by the bus station – it's new...'

Chapter 42

MUM AND I HULL STRAWBERRIES

When we get back I go straight into the kitchen, where Mum's doing something at the sink. Then we both hear Zoe's feet pounding up the stairs. Mum spins round, looking like she always does when she's worried. 'How'd it go? Is Zo-zo all right?'

'Zoze wants to put on the top she bought, and show you. She seems okay – I mean, a bit quiet, but... we – went past Annalise's house, it's all shut up, with recycling left in the front. Annalise wasn't at Base Camp yesterday, and Zoe and Annalise have had a bit of a bust-up. I think Zoe's really upset. But it's down to her to tell you about it when she's ready to.'

'Oh dear, it's been a bit of a highly-charged friendship all along, hasn't it? I kept feeling I ought to know a little bit more about the family, with Zoe spending a lot of time there, and I should have made more effort to talk to Stacey. So, maybe it's a good thing my meeting was cancelled?'

'Oh – yes – that's why you're here, doing packing.'

Mum grins at me, as if this'll be something really big, as she holds up a half-empty plastic punnet of fruit, with a smile like strawberries can heal damaged trust and hurt feelings, which of course they can't, though they are nice, and I shall enjoy them. 'No meeting, no crouching over the microscope in a tiny darkened room, or contacting suppliers who haven't supplied. I'm hulling strawberries! I thought, these'll be gone soon so we'd better have a bit of a feast of them. Cheer you both up a bit, before we go north? Cornish cream in the fridge. So, sure I shouldn't ask Zo-zo about anything?'

'No. She'll talk when she's ready.'

We sit at the table and both start working on the strawberries.

'So, how was your day? What did you find to do?'

I wonder about Mum cancelling a lab meeting just to be here for Zoe. It was nice, but, is there something else? I wait for it to emerge. I shan't ask – yet. I have other news.

'Shopping, like you gave me that cash for? Had a great browse, Zoze bought the new Harry Potter, we bought new tops — can't think why it's taking her so long to put on hers, — we had lattes in the Costa, we went in the Fair Trade place for chocolate and bought these little wooden cats,' I say, getting up to fetch mine and place it on the table.

'Aw, sweet!' Mum says, picking it up and looking at it. 'That's the sort of thing I used to do when I was a bit down at Uni. Only it was under-wear I used to buy – not too expensive but I always felt if I indulged myself, then what I bought had to be useful!'

I kind of smile imagining Mum browsing the underwear in Marks, and buying something small, 'Were there thongs back then? Did you buy one?'

We giggle, 'There were, and that's a secret!' she says. 'Actually, one day I met my friend Maeve – you know, the seriously religious one? She was buying silly knickers, black with red bows, if I remember!'

'No!'

'Yes, she was. Anyhow, you bought cats today.'

'Yep, and a really good thing was – in that shop, the Fair Trade place – my phone rang, and it was Mariam!'

'Oh good. Have they sorted out the wedding?'

'If you mean, is it happening, it is. In California. Venue change. But — Dina's marriage seems to have been kind of arranged. I didn't realise that they were so traditional.'

'I know. It does seem strange in a way. But it shouldn't. I mean, remember what I discovered about Maeve? I don't think religion should make people sad and gloomy... We're all different, and if Mariam's sister's happy, that's the main thing.'

'Well, we don't know that, do we?'

'I suppose we don't, and we probably won't... we can't change what other people do though. That is, we can't make them change.'

'I just can't get my head round the idea of somebody — parents — choosing partners for their grown-up kids, I mean, now, in the modern world.'

'Well, it does happen, and not just in other faiths.'

'How d'you mean?'

'Well, there are Christian groups that believe in guiding people to a suitable partner. It was a bit like that at Grandpa's First Truly Reformed Church when I met Dad. There was a redheaded nurse who Granny Fee and Grandpa liked very much, and thought was God's choice for your Dad. So they tried to bring them together.'

'No!' I must've exclaimed loudly, because Mum says, 'Sshh!' and turns back to taking strawberries out of their plastic punnet and pulling off the stalks, before she replies.

'Dad had already told his father that's not how it works these days – and certainly wouldn't for him. So in the end she found someone else.'

'Or — someone else was found for her?'

'Yes, pretty much. And that's another whole story. Anyway, Dad thought we should visit his family, so he could show them that he'd made up his mind for himself... When we turned up, there was a very frosty atmosphere over Sunday dinner, and then, Grandpa Alisdair decided to pick the relationship to pieces. All while we were supposed to be eating the lamb and vegetables.'

'Oh my God...what did you do?'

'Wished the ground would open and swallow me! Nobody knew where to look. It was all so embarrassing. Long story, I can't tell you it all now – but, here we all are. And that's what some faith groups are like. Might give you insight into Dad's family when we're there!'

I've never heard Mum's take on Dad's family before. I need to think about it. But actually, it makes me a bit angry on Mum's behalf, and that stirs up my feelings about Dad's attitude to my subject choices.

'So if Dad stood up to him, he should know what it feels like when the family wants you to be somebody you're not. So, don't you think that, like, when I said I wanted to make my own choices, over subjects, he behaved a bit like Grandpa Alisdair.'

'I don't think it was quite the same – but you do have a point there. Dad can be like his father. I can tell you, though, he doesn't want to be, and he'll stop himself when he notices. He tries to be more like Granny Fee. But, Alice, there's something else we need to discuss, so after Zoe's shown me her new top, we might try to find a time? It's not about your subjects. It's just about Charlie? Okay?'

I feel pricks of anxiety in my bottom. 'Charlie?'

She finishes de-stalking the strawberries, steps back, moves to the sink, runs water over them to wash them, and gives the colander a shake.

'Charlie, and it has nothing to do with the Truck festival, or staying at theirs, or asking you to do anything for her. Don't worry. Can you winkle Zoe out and persuade her to come down and show me the new top. I'll come up and find you when I've chatted with Zo-zo, love.'

Oh dear – Charlie. How can't this be anything but worrying? If I'm not invited to theirs – suppose she's been invited to join us on our northern trip? Suppose we'll have to squash up in the back of the car, and share a room with her at the Manse, and stuff like that? She wouldn't fit in with the northern rellies. And she said she was going to Cornwall...

I go upstairs. Zoe is on her bed, reading, flat on her stomach with her music on, buds in her ears. She's got her thumb in her mouth, which is rather regressive, but then she's had the shock about Annalise. But she has on her new top, which is actually two tops: a black fitted short-sleeve T-shirt, and over it, a waistcoat in grey denim. She's teamed these with a short gathered skirt she already had, and ballet flats: one of her shoes falls off as she bends her right knee and waves her foot in the air behind her.

'Zoze?'

'Yeah?'

'Mum's done with me for now, and she's asking if you're okay.'

'Yeah, I'm okay.'

'I think she'd really like to see what you bought with the money she gave us. I showed her the cats, she loved them.'

My sister very slowly gets onto all fours, on her bed, kneels up, and takes the buds out of her ears. 'Does she want, like, something particular?'

'She's just hoping you're feeling okay. She does care about you!'

'Has she ever lost a friend like this? Like a betrayal? Annalise could've told me they were going – but she didn't. She said *nothing!*'

'I know. You could tell Mum that, and how it makes you feel?'

'Mum isn't there when we need her, and then she wants to *catch up!*'

'I suppose. But can you, please, go and find her now? And show her your new clothes and – and then, maybe tell her exactly how you feel, being betrayed? She's bought the last strawberries of the season, and cream from Cornwall…'

'Okay, I'll go,' she says, hopping off her bed, and putting the ballet shoe back on. 'See me? I'm going to find Mum.'

'Okay, thanks. And tell her how you feel?'

'Okay!'

'I know how you feel, whatever she does. Dad said – something horrible to me by mistake, and I felt like that. We all – well you know, nobody's perfect, as they say.'

'Shame they aren't, isn't it?' Zoe says.

'Yep. We'll be the same.'

At the door, she turns, holding the handle, standing up straight. I notice that Zo-zo's lost her puppy fat, and now has a rather good figure. And that suddenly makes me feel protective, as she asks me, 'What did he say to you – Dad? When?'

'He said he was *disappointed*. I'd been out to meet Fabian but I hadn't told him I was going. It was when you were at Chapel House.'

'Right... Concerned in case you disappeared? Can you close my door when you leave my room?'

'Of course I shall. I'm going now.'

Concerned in case you disappeared? I see into it, with what seems to be a parental eye. I would be concerned, if Zoe'd gone to meet a friend, and not told any of us who or where, simply gone. 'Be nice to Mum – she does care.'

'Whatever!' Zoe's voice comes up the stairs.

Closing Zoe's door as instructed, I go into my room. I dig out what's left of the chocolate we bought, a couple of squares, and put them in my mouth. I pick up my phone and my camera, walk downstairs and through the kitchen, ignoring my sister and Mum sitting on the family room sofa, and go into the garden.

It rained earlier, but now it's actually a sunny evening. Bees buzz in the dripping wet lupins and roses. I watch how the lupin flowers are so cleverly made to hinge open and let the bees in to find the pollen, and try to catch them on camera. I take a chocolate box picture of a water-beaded pink rose, wondering if Daze would rubbish that as 'tat'. A bird is singing, probably a blackbird – its lovely song adds a whole dollop of sadness to that thought. It even makes our old swing, at the end of the garden, look desolate and empty. I go and sit on it, kicking the ground just enough to move the swing, and thinking about Mum and Daze, and Mum's birth sister, Aunt Harriet, growing up in Chapel House. A musical phrase is in my head, a few notes, where from? I hum the phrase: isn't that a piece called *The Protecting Veil*? But what is it, what's a protecting veil? And where's the tune from? Pull out my phone, and text Fabian: 'What's The Protecting Veil?' I ask. 'Heard of it, like the sound of it, don't know what it is, except music?'

He texts back, 'Tavener. Orthodox religious piece. Cello... Xx'

That's not the answer I was looking for, but never mind. I feel slightly better. Xx. Remember kissing and stuff at their house. Feel the feel of him. He does like me, a lot. One thing is going well for me, even if Mum is about to tell me that once again I shall have to be a friend to Charlie. I could be generous. I shall try.

Chapter 43

MUM EXPLAINS ABOUT THE PARKER POLLARDS

But what exactly does it mean, to be a friend to Charlie – and why is this important enough for Mum to be pushing it?

Zoe takes ages talking to Mum, and she's unusually quiet and thoughtful during dinner. And after dinner she kind of pushes me upstairs and into her room. We sit on her bed. Zoe turns very serious eyes on me behind those big glasses. I'm wondering what's coming.

'Mum told me why Stacey went away like she did. It's awful. I wish I could talk to Annalise.' She looks a bit like she's going to cry. 'It's all to do with her dad — Annalise's, I mean, obviously. Like Annalise told me her mum and him were separated. And she told me she hated him. But I wasn't allowed to tell that to anyone, not even you. I couldn't really imagine it, I mean I thought, how can you hate your dad?'

'No, even if he says he's disappointed with you, I mean you still —'

'Yeah, well listen, it's millions of times worse than that. He's practically a criminal. He used to beat her mum up, so they ran away to Oxford. I think the house belongs to some old lady they know. That's why they had all the curtains drawn, they were trying to stay secret. But somehow her dad's found out where they are, and Stacey's terrified that he's coming after them, so they've gone somewhere else. And they're not telling anyone where, so I can't even text Annalise...' Zoe's glasses look all misty and she's sniffing and wiping her nose. I want to put my arm round her, but something tells me not to.

'How does Mum know?'

'From Shaz at her yoga class. I dunno how it happened but she thinks maybe they saw each other at St Hildegard's and she told Shaz, Mum doesn't know why.'

'That really sucks, Zoe.'

'Yes, it does, and I want to help Annalise and I can't do anything...'

And then Zoe does come for a hug. A long one. And we spend the evening just chatting about stuff to help her feel OK, and go to bed.

♥   ♥   ♥

So now the talk with Mum's happening today. Again she isn't going to the lab. Instead she's busy baking something as a contribution to take to the relatives. As if Granny Fee and Aunt Sue don't spend half their waking hours baking! I suppose Mum has to show them she's a proper mother too.

I lurk in my room, music in my ears, waiting for her to stick her head around my door. To look useful (well, to be useful to myself, really), I'm sorting out clothes and stuff to pack. I make them into piles on my bed, and imagine what I might be asked to do for, or with, Charlie. This is like turning a compost heap — thoughts and memories, all half-remembered or half-forgotten — turning it all over in my brain. Some of these memories don't smell so nice. Such as: when she bounced up to me and Fabian outside the Sheldonian, what she said about her boarding school and living in a village, the incident of the apprentice chef. I'm sorry for her, but she must be able to tell that I'm a reluctant friend.

I've checked weather maps: the weather's stuck in a groove, foul, damp and wet, everywhere. Glastonbury's happened even with all the rain and mud, and now it looks like Truck will be the same. I am so happy not to be going to that festival! Even if it's courtesy of the family retreat! Dad's actually a bit dubious now, about camping on the Western Isles. He's noticed that Scotland's already had some flooding. You could see his enthusiasm drop from about a hundred per cent optimistic to about maybe twenty-five per cent – and that was only because he wouldn't admit being completely defeated by my fact-check. What we do after the Manse celebrations I don't know: maybe hang about in Edinburgh at Aunt Val's? Could be fun, she's an old hippie...

The piles of clothes and stuff grow. A mix from my wardrobe and drawers, and from the coat hooks in the hall, and the cupboard under the stairs.

Bathroom things... Shampoo! Uncle Ian and Aunt Sue are sure to buy the 'family' kind, which is disgusting. I remember Charlie's lovely bathroom, proper shampoo and conditioner, amazingly fluffy towels.

Then there's a knock on my door, but for some reason Mum doesn't open it and stick her head round as usual. Instead she calls 'Alice?' from outside. Has she got stuff to tell me that she knows I won't like? I'm feeling distinctly edgy. I won't mention the Stacey business, it'll just complicate everything.

I open the door. 'Okay. But first, I have a question.' I take the buds out of my ears and turn the music down: it continues, a tinny whisper, on my desk. 'You said I need to be a friend to Charlie: I want to know if I'm right about something,'

She looks taken aback: that is, she actually takes a step back from me, and looks at me, all kind of penetrating. Like examining my mind, and sort of – shocked? Then she quickly changes that expression to more like a smile. 'You can ask anything, love. Except I hope they're not unanswerable questions.'

'Nope. It's about Charlie. And her family. And, it's about Dad.'

'Right. Can I sit on your bed? I won't move your things.'

'Yep, just mind my clothes?'

'Oh yes. Good you're getting those sorted.'

'Yep! Packing. Doing what you said!' I grin.

'Zoe hasn't started.' She perches on my bed-edge, and looks expectantly at me. I sit on my bean bag across from her. It scrunches under my weight. 'So what d'you need to know?'

'I was thinking,' I say, and I get up off the bag realising that down there, I am actually on a level with Mum, or even slightly below her. And I need to be higher than she is. It's just an instinct, but approaching the question feels better if I'm on the desk chair. 'Charlie told me they were going to Cornwall, and it's the same time as we're going to Granny Fee's – and I know this is entirely random, and probably not true, but I thought, they aren't actually staying at Chapel House, are they?'

Mum looks very shifty, as she says, 'Well, love, actually —'

'They are, aren't they? That is so...'

She holds up a hand, like Stop! 'Can you listen to what I have to say first?'

'Why do they need to stay in Granny's house, when there are loads of places they could stay in Cornwall? It makes it even worse to have to go on this dreary trip north and stay with our boring old relatives, knowing that Charlie's family are enjoying Chapel House! And anyway, who plotted all this, and why couldn't Zoe and me be told?' I turn away, putting my back to her, not wanting to show my emotions. 'I thought I was getting used to the idea of going north for our holiday. Then I find out that you and Dad have planned this!'

From behind, her hand comes in contact with my shoulder: I smack it off. She says, 'Darling Alice, it's not like that at all! It wasn't some kind of a plot. We had all our plans in place, and then, well, Shaz and Eliot are having a crisis, and this was all we could offer to help.'

'So, are they breaking up?' I jump up from the chair, 'What fucking good,' I throw at her, almost spitting the words like a cobra, 'would a holiday do?'

'Alice,' (Mum has grabbed my arm), 'Ouch!' I say, 'don't hold onto me! I'm not going anywhere!'

'Darling, I hear you're very angry, but can you listen to me?'

I flop back onto the desk chair, and Mum perches back on the bed. 'Right, tell me more, all of it,' I say.

'Ally, a few things. I know Charlie asked you about going to that festival...'

'I told Charlie it'd be unlikely. It's a bad summer. Glastonbury was filthy with mud, Truck would be the same.'

'And now you know Charlie won't be going, anyway. And they need to spend time as a family, which should be helpful.'

'Helpful? It won't help Charlie, she'll be well devastated.'

'Yes. But no, they're not separating.' Mum gets up and looks out of the window. In the garden, Zoe is knocking a tennis ball against the back of the garage. You can't see Zoe from this angle, but I hear the ball, puck, puck, puck, bounce and roll and swear word. More puck, puck, repeat. 'Ally, I know you've been curious about why I joined Shaz's yoga class and why we've been seeing each other again.'

'Look, I thought, she's not your type. I mean, for a close friend. Like Charlie isn't mine. I know Francesca's in Shaz's yoga class with you, but Francesca is your friend – in another — academic kind of way, and Shaz was to start with – just a mum you knew at the school gate.'

'I know – Frankie and I – well Shaz designed the class for people associated with the University. Anyhow, she's looking to offer more classes...you'll understand why...' she pauses, turns around, and stands leaning against my desk, back to the window. Whatever it is, she's about to tell me. 'You noticed, when you stayed over, Charlie's Dad didn't seem quite the same now, you commented on it, that he has a limp, and he's a bit clumsy?'

'Yep: so...'

'Eliot Parker Pollard has developed an autoimmune neurological disease, which is causing those disabilities. It affects his movement, and it will – actually it already does – affect his brain. Shaz is having to – they're all going to have to – adapt.' This makes my stomach flip. It's not divorce, it's – worse. I'd hate Dad to get ill like that. Autoimmune. Creepy when your body works against you. 'So, we thought – Dad and

I thought – as Granny Caro and Des are away all summer, and wanting to let the house —'

'Hang on Mum, you suggested they go there? While we spend our whole holiday in freezing damp Scotland? I mean, I can see this is all dreadful, but still, Cornwall is full of places to stay…'

Mum ploughs patiently on. 'As Granny and Des are away, and had asked us for any friends we could recommend to house-sit, Dad and I decided they'd be suitable tenants – for a month anyway – so they could have a good, long break in a beautiful place by the sea. And you're not missing out, as I'll explain in a minute. And we have to be in the north for the Mullins family get-together, we can't let them down. There's Granny Fee, looking forward to having her whole family there, even Uncle David's coming. You like your cousins – what about Chloe? And Cameron?'

'Yeah, well they're OK…'

'And we'll go on to Val's in Edinburgh. You'll love spending time with her. But the point is, Charlie does need to have a proper holiday, and they're – well it saves them the expense. And the good news is, we may still be able to go to Chapel House, because Daze says she's hoping to do some kind of deal with Granny.'

'Daze is? What about Des?'

'She hasn't told me everything, love. I don't think she knows if it'll work yet. But about Charlie's family, Shaz will be the only earner – you understand why they moved?'

'Yeah – I get it.'

'And Charlie's grandparents…'

'Okay – Eliot was diagnosed, and so Jos and Gussie decided to send Charlie off to a mean school?'

'It made things easier, yes.'

It's hard to take all this in. They've all been talking, and they've solved two problems, and they've decided to let me know all the changes, now they've done it. 'Does Zoe know all this?'

'Some of it.'

'It saves them, you said.'

'Eliot won't be able to work much longer. Shaz will be entirely responsible for – everything, and she may have to give up teaching yoga and go back to occupational therapy. She's looking at jobs.'

'Right. That's what she did before? Okay. Thanks for telling me all that.' My feelings are all jangled. Yes, Charlie's news is terrible, but why didn't they tell me earlier, why was I treated as too young to know? Please not 'because you were doing exams'! I just say 'Can I — take this bag of shoes down to the car now? Or put it in the hall, ready?'

Later, after dinner, Dad asks me if I want to practise some of our violin pieces to play for the ceilidh at this Mullins family gathering thing, and when I say maybe not now, he starts playing the *Farewell to Stromness,* making mistakes and muttering at himself. I'm feeling what I thought Charlie would. My throat is lumpy and stiff. That music doesn't help. I kind of cry, a bit. I am so sorry for Charlie, but I can't make it right for her, and I'm the wrong kind of friend.

I look across at Dad, who's now played that sad, slow music through without the wrong notes, and at our violins stacked as usual on a shelf of the bookcase. 'Maybe now, if you've finished?' I say. And we take out our fiddles and practise.

End of Part 3

Part 4

Chapter 44

LEAVING FOR THE NORTH

It's Friday, early morning. We're packing the car under a louring, deep grey sky, when my phone dings: *'Okay Al, you'll be pleased to know they cancelled Truck! Site underwater! Cx'*

I'd forgotten completely that it's the day before Truck begins. I read the text twice, instinct says delete and ignore, then I find I'm not breathing properly. A couple of days ago I'd have shot back a nasty reply. But now I know about her dad, everything's changed and I understand why Mum wanted me to get friendly with her again. But I wish they'd allowed me to know some of it sooner. How complicated life is when you get old enough to be a sort of in-between person, half adult, and they don't let you in on things like this until they've kind of sorted it into a tidy message. A message which covers all the objections, and makes you feel a bit shit about having resented something.

That sarky text wasn't necessary though. Unless she feels so miserable that she has to get at me, 'cos I've got healthy parents.

I shove my phone into my pocket and go back into the house. Mum hands me the cold bag, inside is our picnic for the journey. 'Can you put that where it's easy to grab, without having to scrabble around and unpack things?'

I nod, turning to leave the room, but my nose is tickly, I sniff. She's alerted. Not sure I wanted that, but maybe. 'Alice?'

'Yeah, me,' I say, taking another step. Then, I think, why not share it? 'Charlie sent a text. About Truck being cancelled, not necessary, as neither of us is going.'

'I'm sorry she did that. Was it horrible?'

'Bit vindictive!' I say, dropping the cold bag and reaching for my phone. I open it to show Mum: as she takes it, her arm goes round me, and that makes me almost, not quite, cry. 'Okay, I see what you mean. That is horrible,' Mum says, 'and unnecessary.'

'Yeah.'

'Makes it hard to be kind to her?'

'Yes.'

'No need to reply now.'

'S'pose.'

'A postcard from Northumberland maybe? See how you feel. Or maybe a text better?'

'Whatever. Hi from the frozen north!' We hug. I break away, I can't stay and relax myself into Mum like I'm still a kid.

I shouldn't need Mum really, just for helping when I feel awkward and sad. I wish she was Fabian... but that's crazy.

Mum says, 'I'm so sorry for both of you. She's terribly hurt by what's happening, and throwing her hurt onto you won't change that. Probably best to ignore it, not get into a fight.'

'Yeah. What I thought,' I say. Mum hands my phone back, I close it down and tuck it away.

'Or you might send a straightforward response, if you could. A soft answer turning away wrath, as they say.'

'It's not wrath, exactly, is it?'

'No, but it's similar. Up to you!' says Mum. 'Really not my business!'

She reaches for a cloth and starts wiping the breakfast crumbs off the kitchen table, symbolising 'over to you now, Alice,' and I pick up the cold bag and take it to the car. I sort the luggage in the back and make sure the bag is easy to find. My feelings about Charlie wanting me to be around in her life gradually change: from a prickly consciousness of the unfairness of it, to wondering if it isn't actually flattering, in a weird way, as she must have other friends. Maybe she was really upset by me disappearing off to South Africa from primary school and not being her *best mate* any more? I suddenly remember that Shaz always called us 'best mates'.

I suppose the party was some kind of pathetic compensation for knowing her dad was going to become more and more helpless, and then die, probably not even knowing who she was. She must have been genuinely disappointed when I declined the invite to her sweet sixteen river party. And I was mean, but, how could I have known? My eyes and nose get all tickly again.

I take out my phone and type a message, *'Sorry to hear that, tho' Mum reminded me yr family is off to Cornwall (not yet underwater!) Enjoy my Gran & Grandad's gorgeous house. Ax'*

As we drive north the grey roads, grim towns, dull green fields, some waterlogged, all under a heavy grey blanket of cloud, look more and more sad and defeated.

The music playing in my ear buds is Haydn's *Creation*, so I'm reminded again of that evening at the Sheldonian when Charlie bounced up to me and Fabian. The little girl with the spangly trainers and the pencil with a bit of pink feathery fluff on its end, now grown big and curvy and dressed in black. At least I now understand why she's attached herself to me.

I picture Charlie, on the beach at Sennen, in two-piece swimmers with string straps. The bottom is tiny. She wiggles her way down the beach...

Actually, that's mean, she's in a hard place right now. Whatever boys she attracts can't change what's going on in her life.

Chapter 45

FIRST AFTERNOON AT THE MANSE

Grey, cool, and not raining right now, Northumberland! At the Manse of First Truly Reformed Church, square and grey, home to Pastor Ian Mullins and family. Here we are parked on the gravel drive, beside the bit of carefully shaved lawn where Granny Fee used to grow roses. We've just climbed out of the car and begun hauling our luggage from the boot. I think: mustn't refer to it as 'all that shit we brought along', meaning books, sketchbooks, cameras, violins, spiced raisin buns Mum made and butterfly cupcakes Zoe made, Dad's binoculars, and Mum's laptop 'cos she's always got some article or whatever on the go. The air is cool and fresh. The colours round here are grey, green, and if the cloud lifts, blue. I'm just stretching and adapting myself, when up rushes a male relative, eyes bulging with welcome.

'Alice and Zoe, lovely to see you!' exclaims Uncle Ian. He's the slimmer one of Dad's twin younger brothers, athletic looking, floppy blonde hair. My free hand is seized in a vicelike grip, all my fingers are crushed together, and up and down we go, like a pump, until he releases me. His hand's sweaty, and now he's transferred that to mine. Ugh. He's puffing and panting and has obviously been rushing about, probably playing some ball game: I can hear shouting from the back lawn.

Surreptitiously, I wipe my hand on my jeans-clad behind, while turning my head towards Zoe, who was standing right next to me —

but she's vanished! Silent escape. So nice to be the 'and' person, the younger sibling, who can slip away, in a place like this! 'And you've had a birthday!' Oh gosh, Uncle Ian's still there, exclaiming stuff, embarrassing me. Like, everyone has birthdays. And I'm not a child! 'Great to be sixteen, is it?'

'Yeah, I turned sixteen,' I say, feeling my face glow with the embarrassment of being picked out of the family like this. Where's Mum and Dad gone? Where is Zoe?

'So, you're sweet sixteen! Have you had a party?' Uncle Ian asks, grinning like a maniac. Ugh, that label! Icing sugar, Charlie's party!

'No, 'cos it was in the middle of exams,' I say. 'GCSEs. But my other granny had us both over for a weekend, and we saw a show. *Mamma Mia* – great music, have you…' I fade out, it's unlikely isn't it. They wouldn't go to London for a show.

At this moment, a small boy, sort of primary school age, wearing that ghastly shiny football clothing they love, rushes up and grabs Uncle Ian's arm, and kind of tries to swing on it, 'Ouch! Iso, this is your cousin Alice from Oxford – Uncle Max's family have arrived.'

'Hello, Al-*lice*!' He mangles my name into a joke, and giggles. While I wonder what 'Iso' can be short for. Of course — he's *Isaiah*!

Uncle Ian persists with the birthday theme, shaking off his son and then pushing back his blondish fringe, which flops back into his eyes again, 'and we know what we have for Alice, don't we?'

Oh my God, what? Some present I'll have to thank them for? A book I'll need to read so I know what to say? A cake. Maybe just a complicated, iced and named, cake. That'd be okay. We'd eat it up and my name in pink icing would be gone.

'Party!' Iso shouts, jumping up and down. 'We're giving Alice a party! Alice is ten years older than me, and we're having a party!'

My heart sinks into my trainers. This is awful. Did Mum and Dad know? It's the worst thing, putting me in the centre, when we were told the deal was that Granny Fee was throwing a celebration ceilidh to say bye-bye to the old Manse. I can't turn and run, because Uncle Ian and 'Iso' are grinning at me, expecting excitable thanks.

'That is incredibly kind...' I stumble out, voice very peculiar. I swivel my eyes to try to locate someone to rescue me. Nobody else here on the drive. Where've they all gone? Abandoned to the most difficult relatives! 'I mean, we've really come for the, like, family retreat and for Dad to visit his old home before it gets pulled down... and I didn't think it had anything to do with my birthday...' I am dying inside, from being featured at what was supposed to be a retreat, 'and it's – unexpected – it wasn't on the invite...'

'Well, we thought you'd like a surprise – much more exciting!'

Now Uncle Ian gives Iso a little push forward, 'Oh, by the way, this chap's Isaiah. I don't think you've met — he can't remember you!' Ah, the three-year-old in the buggy last time we were here? Since then, we haven't actually stayed at the Manse.

Isaiah (what a name!) adds, 'We've got balloons with your name on. *Alice*, and *Sixteen*, and some other balloons which are the numbers, a big silver *one* and a *six*! My Mum made the cake! And we're having a bouncy castle!' he adds, jumping about to illustrate the point.

Oh no! More jolly ideas. Noisy stuff with me as central feature.

Uncle Ian seems to have reached the end of his announcements. He just adds, as if he hasn't really upset me, 'Well, won't hold you up, can I carry anything in for you? Aunt Sue's put you in the tiny bedroom, along with your sister.'

So, Zoe and me are squashed into the tiny spare room. That'll be the one over the front door.

'I'm okay with my bag, thanks. I know which room you mean, I can find it. And...,' But thankfully, the two of them are already moving off, Iso making imaginary football moves.

As I go in, cross the hallway and mount the stairs, I can hear yelling and laughter coming from the back garden. Sounds of preparing something to eat come from the kitchen. Someone's doing piano practice, hesitantly, with repetition and wrong notes: one of Uncle Ian's enormous family, I suppose.

I am furious with this party plan, which nobody told me about. Did they consult Mum and Dad? Did they plan it with Mum and Dad? Or only with Dad, because he's a Mullins born and bred, and he's always nice to people? It's like when he put David in my room....

So, here we are, first floor, bunkbeds, separated, one against each of the side walls, small area of brown carpet between them. About enough space for our bags. Window looks down on the driveway. I dump my bag and stuff on one of the beds: I don't care which bed I have, they're identical, with matching duvets and pillowcases. Pink girly picture on them. Matching pillow with same flowers!

The pale sun casts a shadow of the window on the carpet. Maybe the weather is improving?

When I get downstairs again, there's Zoe. 'I was looking for you, where were you?'

'Caught by Uncle Ian, the one with lots of kids. And Iso, the one in football strip.'

'There's only Becky, Martha, and Isaiah — oh, but Aunt Sue's pregnant.'

'Anyway, where were you?'

'Bathroom. Escaped him. Then talking to one of them – Becky.'

'Trust you.'

'I was bursting. After the drive. And she was next in the queue.'

'In the queue?'

'Only one loo. Millions of people here, and someone's malicious toddler's blocked the proper upstairs one by throwing the toilet roll down it. There's tea and cake now, though. Outside. Come on.'

'Wait, listen, I'm furious, they've turned this retreat thing into a sweet sixteen party — for me! With an effing bouncy castle. Where's Mum and Dad gone off to? I want to know if they knew about it.'

'Ooh, I quite like the idea of a retreat with a bouncy castle, it might cheer things up a bit.' She drags at my hand, 'come on, let's get cake. You can see them after.'

'There'd better not be a birthday cake there.'

'There are six cakes, none of them's got candles on.'

Granny Fee's cakes are always worth eating. I'm faint with hunger, I could eat a whole cake.

Zoe hurries me through the family room at the back of the house, and out through the open patio doors onto the concrete terrace. Where five or six kinds of cake are arranged on a table, with two piles of plates, all separated from one another with folded paper napkins And two huge teapots, and an army of mugs. And they've put out Mum's raisin buns and Zoe's butterfly cupcakes there as well.

The main cakes are Granny Fee specials: lemon drizzle, chocolate layer to die for, Dundee with almonds on top, Victoria sponge with cream as well as jam. Huge relief: no pink birthday cake — unless of course someone appears with it suddenly! Zoe homes in on the chocolate cake at the other end of the table where several kids are busy helping themselves. I take a slice of lemon drizzle and another of the Victoria sponge. It turns out to have sliced strawberries folded into the cream, instead of jam. Oh yum! I start on that one, the strawberry juice is sweet and sharp on my tongue.

Then I spot Mum, approaching the cake table from the end of the garden. She's changed out of her old leggings and a tunic into her new smart jeans and a white shirt, tucked in, with a wide belt, and actually looks rather stunning.

I swallow what's in my mouth to hiss, 'Mum! Where'd you go? And, for goodness sake, why didn't you tell me they were planning to make this retreat into a birthday party — for me?'

She turns, holding a cake slice with a piece of Dundee cake balanced on it above a plate. 'Because I didn't know...' She dumps the piece of Dundee cake onto the plate, and replaces the silver slicing thing on the table.

And a little breeze blowing gently across the garden suddenly gusts, and the paper napkin that was on Mum's plate takes to the air, and flies across the garden. 'Damn!' she exclaims, rushing to rescue it.

I grab her by the back of her shirt, and the tail flaps free of the belt and waistband, as I say, 'It's supposed to be a *ceilidh*, Mum. But Uncle Ian caught hold of me with his sweaty paw, and said it was a party *specially for me, for my birthday* – which might've been a nice thought, but if you and Dad knew, why did you say nothing about it? I was, like, stunned. I thought, how hateful to do a party here, with all the rellies, and without my friends!'

'Oh Alice!' She pulls the shirt free all round, so it hangs over her jeans (which I think looks much better, and less like Granny Caro's style). 'Could you be careful? In what you do and what you say? Now, tell me — you enjoy a ceilidh, so what's the real problem?'

'What's the *real* problem? Can't you imagine? Can't you even think?' The ground doesn't open. It should, to swallow me up. I know, I'm aware, I've bellowed at Mum and it's making a scene, or it will in a minute. Mum takes me by the arm, and I try to pull away, but my cake fork topples onto the grass. At least my pieces of cake don't. We both bend down. 'Okay, let me pick it up, right?' I hiss, 'it's mine.'

She'll call me her best putting-down phrase now. I'm *being a right cow.* Yes, I know.

Only she doesn't. She says, before we both stand up straight again, 'Ally, I understand. We should've discussed this with you, and found out how you felt about it. And now, I am really sorry Ian did that. Let's sort this out, but can we do it quietly?'

'Let's. Where?'

'Will the veggie patch do?' We walk up the huge garden to where Granny Fee used to grow beans, and lettuces, and raspberries in a net cage. Twists my heart to remember being a kid helping her pick lettuces and beans. Remember finding a huge caterpillar among the leaves of a vegetable – a lettuce? Or a cabbage? Aunt Sue has a marrow growing here, its long stalk, huge leaves and big yellow trumpet flowers wander across from one side of the veg patch to the other.

'So,' Mum says, 'you talk, I'll listen.'

'So, okay. Why wasn't I asked? Or even told? I could have said no, please not. I could have had a chance to say what sort of party, to advise... I mean, did you, like, know anything? Did Dad know? Did he collude with his family, did he tell you?' Mum looks frowny, she looks, I don't know, stunned, that I think Dad and his birth family would leave her and me out of planning this. She moves her slice of Dundee cake around on the plate with her fork but doesn't break a piece off to eat. She sniffs, and adjusts her glasses.

'No, he didn't do that, love. He wouldn't. We... I'm afraid we were caught up with trying to help Shaz and Eliot.'

Oh bugger. I choke back a surge of anger with the Parker Pollards for invading our lives. Their thing has to take precedence. As of course, it should. 'So you did both know – or you didn't? And you were too busy with Shaz and them – but why forget about me? You do remember your work, and those people in your lab you spend so much time with. So, is your work more interesting than us – me and Zoe?'

'Is that how it feels? You have your own lives...'

'Don't we! School and... Remember, when we were left when you went to America, and Dad was away as well? Remember we had Ruth the childminder come to stay in our house?'

'You children were what, five and three? Was it awful, with Ruth?'

'No. It was – we missed you – and Dad.' I feel sad for my small self, but self-pity isn't what this is about now. 'But, we had a great time at Daze's Fun Day making animal masks with Etta – who turned out to be Daze's mum!'

'You didn't guess back then, about Etta and Daze?'

'No – but later I wasn't surprised. She'd have suited Daze better than Granny Caro, to grow up with!' Mum smiles at that. We go silent. We try to peacefully eat cake. Maybe she'll listen to me about the party now?

I look towards the house, where cricket is being played enthusiastically. A figure in black jeans wearing wraparound shades runs up from the house end and expertly bowls. David's here, hum! Uncle Ian, who's batting, wallops the yellow tennis ball they're using, begins to make a run, slides on the damp grass, falls to his knees, drops the bat, and rolls over.

He lies there a moment, then struggles to his feet, and looks around for the bat. But a plump girl in a sundress, has caught the ball. Becky, who Zoe was chatting with?

She lobs it to Dad with remarkable skill. Uncle Ian is still struggling to his feet. Dad expertly throws the ball and it hits the wicket.

'Howzat!' everyone shouts. Then they slow clap Uncle Ian as he brushes down his now grass-stained pale chino trousers and seeing that he's out, defeated by Dad and David, goes off reluctantly, trailing his bat, then turns to wave. Everyone cheers and laughs. Including Uncle Ian, after a moment's thought.

Mum and I grin at each other, and we move a little further into Aunt Sue's marrow patch. Mum forks in a bit of cake, swallows it down, and speaks. 'We – me and Dad — were sorry we didn't arrange anything special for your birthday, except that meal out. We were going to try to do something more when your exams were over, and then it was Granny Fee who suggested a ceilidh during the family retreat. And then Granny Caro booked seats for the show, and that was her present for you.'

'And when we were at the flat, she gave me a talk about contraception!'

Mum makes a dismissive noise, part laugh, part snort. 'How like my mother!'

'It felt so intrusive. It wasn't her business. It could've been yours, if she'd left it, and if you thought it was necessary.'

'You're right there. I'd have told her off if I'd known. I suppose we can't blame her - your great-gran being a campaigner for women's rights – but, typical Mum!' She laughs.

'I don't really think it's funny,' I say. 'Could you tell her to butt out of my —relationships?'

'Sorry, love. We got it more than once, the three of us. Daze took no notice, Harriet and I felt spooked about it. But what was really on our minds was escaping rural Cornwall and seeing the outside world.'

'So, we all knew about the ceilidh – but what about the party being for me, Alice at the centre of everything, and the stupid bouncy castle? Why not just have the ceilidh for fun, and say nothing about it being for anyone?'

'Oh, I see! We didn't know about any bouncy castle, that does sound grim – but it will be for the little ones, won't it?'

Saying that, Mum breaks off another piece of her Dundee cake and pops it in her mouth. As if she could simply dismiss the school-fete feel of the planned party. I correct her, 'No, it won't. It'll be because student balls and stuff have those – you must know that – you've been a student, you probably did lots of May Balls or whatever Cambridge called them.'

'May Balls they're called, but they're in June. Yes, there were discos and we had a fire-eater once...'

'Them. So I'm the centre of the party — and, listen, I haven't even got anything suitable to wear.'

Does Mum look guilty? Has she brought something secretly for me to wear? The look turns into a smiley face, 'Well, it will be fun for everyone. I'm sure they won't make too much fuss of you.'

'How can you be? You didn't hear Uncle Ian – gloating, making me feel embarrassed.'

'Okay, let's have a word with Granny. Dad and I really didn't think it all out properly, did we?'

'Like with a lot of things. Like with my A-level choices.'

'I'm really sorry about that now... and the party,' she says. 'Sorry I didn't think everything out more, and share their ideas with you, and ask them not to make a big fuss.'

'Maybe you should think more, about us as well as whatever is happening at work? And be less random about telling us things you've arranged?'

Mum doesn't seem to know what to answer. There's no more cake on her plate to eat while she thinks. 'Oh, come and have a hug, love. I'm so sorry Ian caught you like that. I can't take his style either!'

'It's gross. But if it's going to be some full-on ceilidh, and my birthday party, I haven't got anything half decent to wear. I was just going to wear jeans. So maybe, you should be a bit more practical?'

'Yes, maybe. I was being practical about helping the Parker Pollards, and about getting some funding for our post-doc from Finland to stay another year... I'm so sorry... Suppose I *had* brought you a couple of things you might wear? Could you....'

Total surprise: 'What? You *knew* and you brought stuff?' She at least looks shifty about this. 'God, Mum...'

'*Alice*—'

'Okay, language, I get it — sorry – but...'

'Maybe just take a look and see if you – might wear one?'

'I'll *look*,' I say. 'If there's something half decent... And you and Dad – maybe share a bit more with us – well, with me, now?'

We're both a bit teary, and we hug, but awkwardly. That was a lot of stuff to process. I need to think about it. To be on my own with it. I'm still carefully holding a plate with most of two slices of cake on it, and I walk slowly back towards the house. The cricketers try to draw me into their game, but I wave my fork at them to indicate that I'm too busy eating cake. Funny how this family are so keen on organized games.

Chapter 46

So now, after tea and cricket, I'm off to chill in our room.

Only halfway there, I meet Granny Fee coming out of what used to be the 'spare room' with a pretty, striped box, a bit larger than a shoe box. Have I seen this box before? 'Alice, pet!' Granny exclaims, 'you must remember this?'

'Mm, I do: my memory box, I gave it to you to keep, after primary school maybe? It had stuff I thought I'd grown out of!'

'And there are some other things you've grown out of since, and passed to me when I was visiting, to put in the box!'

'Can I look?' She lifts the lid: inside are my old ballet shoes, very worn, but wrapped carefully in tissue paper. And the headband I used to wear. 'Both pink, of course!' I say, and she smiles. I love Granny Fee's smiles, they are so lovely and real. What else? 'One of those paper puzzles, like Origami – a fortune teller! Two friendship bands! This one's from Nina, we met at the scholarship exam for Headleigh Park school, we both passed, and we're still friends! That one Charlie made and sent in an envelope when I was eleven. We'd kind of lost touch as they'd moved away… I think I never thanked her for it…'

'But you wore this one, look how that tassel on it has been rubbed and well, it's a bit grimy isn't it! But precious, as well?'

'Goodness, my old stuff! Yes, I s'pose.' I have a sudden, ingenious thought, 'Granny, let's look at this again, another time, and I may have something to add? And can we have a quick cuddle?'

'Of course, pet. I'll remind you before you go home.' I take the box, and put it on the floor. Granny is so small, now: I remember when she was bigger than me, now I'm huge and she is, really, quite tiny. I'm careful not to crush her. Once released, Granny Fee says, 'Thank you, Alice. I do miss cuddles. And now,' she says, as I gather up the box from where I put it on the floor, and hand it back, 'I'm going to have a little snooze, before our welcome dinner.'

I still have a big silly grin on my face when — my phone pings. Oh, please not — Charlie! *Hey I joined Surf School and met a great crowd!! XXCharlie.* Humph. Think of my chat with Mum this morning and squash sarky reply. I know she needs something to take her mind off... her Dad's illness.

I open the door of the tiny front room, and there's my sister, standing at the very small shaving mirror on the window sill, admiring herself. She's wearing a gold and black striped party-type dress. It's made of some stiff, slightly shiny, kind of fabric and has a pinched-in waist, a big gathered sticky-out skirt, and a lowish neckline. It's a dress I've never seen before.

'Hey – Mum bought us stuff to wear at the ceilidh!' she says, spinning round, 'And it fits. And I like it. What kind of amazing Mum is that?'

'One who shops in her lunch hour?' That was pretty nice, I think, feeling embarrassed now, that I was so mean to her in the garden.

'Beyond nice, it was amazing! Party dresses. Mum only *bought us new ones!*'

'It was – hope mine fits!' All I can manage, with a lumpy throat, and picking up the dress that's mine.

I hold it against me, then turn it upside down, to look for the label. Right size, posh shop, *Phase Eight*. Black – no, navy... More Mum's type of clothes than mine... I hold it up again, looking down at the layers of see-through fabric frothing slightly over the inner lining. It has thin straps over the shoulders. I'm worried if I'm curvy enough up top for the straps not to fall down.

'Wow. Hey, that's cool,' says Zoe. Why don't you try it on?'

'Okay: I'm going to. It had better fit.'

'It will.'

I try, and it does. It sits beautifully where it's meant to, which is the most amazing thing about it. We twirl, we run into the bathroom to see ourselves in the long mirror, and back in our room we're just about to take pictures of each other on my phone when someone bangs on the door. 'Alice!'

'Yep? Dad? Seen these?'

He puts his head round, holding the door handle like a person ready to close it and retreat again.

'Did you know about these? Mum bought them,' says Zoe.

He takes a step into the room, and surveys us, breaking into a big grin. 'Mmm, she does appear to be a good — personal shopper, is it called?'

'Oh Dad, yes it is! Mum personally shopped these for us, wasn't that beyond – beyond being just a mum?'

Dad and I laugh. I say, with what I hope is a sly smile, 'And of course, beyond being a *Principal Investigator*!'

'So, admire us, then!' adds Zoe.

'I do admire what mum has found you, and now, I need Alice, please! Uncle Ian is waiting to start a rehearsal.'

'Aw, he doesn't understand we're busy here!' My sister has grabbed me around the waist.

'Yes, but I need Alice now, please. Zoe, can you let her go?'

'He can't bully us,' I say. 'You're his much-older brother for f...'

'Don't say it!'

'What?'

'You know what you were about to say...' Dad says, my reminder not to use what the relatives would call foul language. 'Listen, Alice,

Ian's not bullying anyone. Let's try to fit in, and keep everything peaceful here.'

Then he grins, and says 'Remember, we're in a different country: the First Truly Reformed folk have their own customs, as well as their own rules about language. So, Alice, pick up your violin and walk.'

'Two minutes, while I go back to being a pumpkin?' His face is a question mark. 'Get changed?'

'Two minutes – then see you in the family room.' He goes, closing the door like a conspirator.

'Okay, you're taking a photo of me first, because he'll skin me alive if I'm late! Right? To send to my friends?'

'To *Fabian Russell!*' she giggles, poking me lightly in my stomach. 'Stand still, look sexy.' I stand like a model, my chest out, my back straight, my face sideways to the camera, one hand holding up my hair on top, a bit like Mum wears hers at work.

Zoe says, in an irritating voice, as she clicks to take two shots, 'You'll wow him. He'll come back all the way from Italy to get you.'

Ignoring this, I take my phone back, rapidly snap Zoe in a series of what she thinks are alluring poses. Then I pull off the dress, and shrug into board shorts and a T-shirt. Grab my violin in its case from under my bed.

Dad and I, and Uncle Ian's band spend an hour or more in the family room, working away at reels and other Scottish things, Ian directing. The band is a couple of middle-aged guys from First Truly church, Matt with what he calls a squeezebox, and Phil with a violin, and Uncle Ian, with, of all unlikely things, a flute. Just as I'm about to escape, Mum appears with a load of tartan fabric in her arms. 'What's this for?'

'Sashes. Worn by women at a ceilidh. Maxwell or Guthrie tartan? There's either.'

'Guthrie — it won't clash with my dress. Will you wear Guthrie to assert your identity or Maxwell to show loyalty?' Mum doesn't look impressed. 'Sorry — and thank you, it's a great dress. Nice and plain and swirly. It is really, really nice.'

'Thanks, love. I'll show you how to wear the sash. To answer your question — I'm going Maxwell with Dad — their green one.'

'He'll like that.'

Chapter 47

Even though it's clouded over, and we all need to put on jumpers, Aunt Sue announces 'It's going to be a squash around the table, so children over six, and teens, please take yours in the garden, and eat at the picnic table.'

I help, like Dad asked, struggling with moving the awkward picnic table nearer the house, and laying up on the celebratory cloth, weighting the flapping, papery thing down so it won't blow away. Dinner is actually a delicious buffet, so me and Zoe load our plates and manage to enjoy the meal, despite the silliness of the younger kids, basically Uncle Ian's lot, plus one of Uncle Alex's, a six-year-old girl called Lily.

Iso says 'I'm the only man here, so I'm going to say grace. All hold hands!'

Lily makes a 'don't want too' noise and puts her hands under her armpits. Iso looks poised to use force, but Zoe, of course, knows what to do. She and I get on either side of Lily and just touch her small protruding fingers, while Iso practically shouts 'Thank you Jesus for all our lovely food Amen!' and promptly puts a whole cocktail sausage in his mouth.

Really thankful, now we're finished. Kids are allowed ice cream in cones, and they wander around the garden, sucking and slurping, while everyone else, indoor and outdoor eaters, marches to the kitchen carrying their empty plates and all the dishes and stuff, like a small army.

Once they've done that, nearly everyone moves to the family room, because, outside, it's begun to rain.

Zoe and I bring the stuff from the kids' picnic table into the kitchen. I'm surprised to see David packing the dishwasher. He squats beside it, receiving crockery and cutlery like the King of Grungy Plates, saying 'thank you, cheers' as each piece is handed over.

The rain patters loudly, blown against the kitchen windows. I whisper to Zoe, 'So, what about the bouncy castle? You can't bounce in the rain, can you — it would be too slithery. Surely they'll have to cancel if it's raining like this tomorrow!'

Zoe whispers, 'S'pose they could put it in the church.'

'Wouldn't that be desecration or something?'

'Base Camp had trampolines inside Headleigh Parish last year.'

I roll my eyes.

Uncle Ian appears at the kitchen door. 'Entertainments in the family room, hurry up now!' he calls. Zoe allows herself to be herded off and disappears. David nods at Uncle Ian, 'You go and join them, mate.' And turns to me with a smile, 'Alice is helping me, we're coming in a mo.' He adds a surreptitious wink, as Uncle Ian departs.

Slightly disconcerting. Is he on my side or something? Does he have any reason to be? I hand him the bowl that held the cold pease pudding (a dish that they love and I don't), and a couple of serving spoons. As he takes it, he looks me in the eye with a serious expression. 'Listen, Alice. We got off on the wrong foot back in May, when I used your room. Your Dad was just turning the house upside down and couldn't think where to put me, but I might have had more consideration too. So, my apologies, and can we shake on it and start again?'

He gets up and quickly cleans his hands, then extends his right hand. I'm a bit embarrassed, but actually it's a quick, thankfully dry, firm but not crushing shake, and I give him a smile.

He asks, 'Surviving the rellies?'

Hum. What'm I meant to say? Should I be honest, or better to pretend?

'Yeah, a bit,' I say. 'We don't see Uncle Ian and Aunt Sue family, much. We live so far away. Last time was maybe three years ago, they were going to Devon for an event and came to us to use the loo and eat cake!' He laughs. 'They can be a bit much sometimes,' he says. 'but anyway, for me this is really a party for Aunt Fee. It must be tough to see the end of the home where you brought up your family. Not sure how long I'll last though.' He grins.

'I think that's really why Dad wanted to come, to say goodbye to the old Manse, and help Granny.'

The dishwasher's rammed full, so we're nearly finished. I'm kind of surprised that I'm enjoying this chat with David. I look for something to wipe the counters, or whatever I can do to continue the conversation before I have to buzz off to play music in the family room.

David says, 'I was hoping to grab your Dad and spend some time walking at Hadrian's Wall, tomorrow, to get a bit of headspace. I used to go up there a lot, alone or with him. But he's made your Gran a promise that he'll help her with some clearing-out, stuff she left in the attic here'

'Sounds like a Dad idea,' I say.

'So – anyhow – I thought you girls might like a bit of — time out?'

'We might.'

'So how about it – you up for a walk on the Wall?' he says, closing the dishwasher and setting it going.

'And avoid jigsaws and competitive Scrabble? I heard someone talking about a tournament.'

'That's what they've always done. Spot of time off from the gang sound better?'

'Much. I'll ask Zo-zo. We'll have a think.'

'Yeah, let me know at breakfast? Or rather, after breakfast, I'm at the B and B with your folks.'

Now it's Dad who appears at the kitchen door, 'Ally, everyone's asking for some music. Could you fetch your violin, please?'

Galloping up the stairs and along the corridor to get my violin, I pass Zoe giggling with Becky on the landing. I am the oldest grandchild here. I wish my older cousins, Cameron and Chloe, had arrived today.

Seeing Zoe swinging between being a child and being an adult, I see myself doing that as well, though over more grown-up things. Sixteen's not 'sweet' at all. Either I'm furious or ecstatic. 'Get down or they'll come up to find you!' I throw over my shoulder at my sister, as I practically leap downstairs with my instrument.

The living room furniture's been pushed back, and the telly banished to a cramped corner. Great-uncle Euan is enjoying a whisky with Uncle Ian's twin brother Alex: they seem to be doing a jigsaw! Uncle Ian's band members are already busy noodling on their instruments: they look like the sort of men who would help with Zoe's Base Camp at Headleigh Parish Church.

We begin to play. I love playing music with other people. It's kind of better than listening to other people playing music. Well, it's different.

And it's crazy and almost fun when some people get up and practise Scottish dance moves, out in the hallway and the living room. Dad leaves the band to join in, he and Uncle Alex look absurd with Becky and Zoe as dancing partners! Looks like David's slipped away…

Chapter 48

DAVID AND I GO TO HADRIAN'S WALL

We're upstairs, getting ready to sleep in those narrow little bunk beds. I ask Zoe how she feels about a walk on Hadrian's Wall. 'Becky said there's competitive Scrabble, and I wanted to do that,' she says.

'Oh, c'mon, I know why, you're wanting to beat the others, and you know you can! But that's halfway to doing school type stuff: come for a walk, and have some time off from the regime here, why don't you?'

'I actually think I like Becky. We might be friends, and – write to each other or something after this.'

'Really? Is she your sort?'

'She might be. You don't know her.'

Mmm, I think, picturing small plump Becky, her hair in bunches, and a pink, blue, and pale green striped sundress, worn with a cardie. Isn't she a mini version of Aunt Sue? 'What does she like doing?'

'The usual things. Reading, puzzles, learning the piano? She's on her school under-13s swimming team, but not super sporty... They have guinea pigs, she'd like them to have a dog. She doesn't have to be the same as me! Why shouldn't I like her?'

'Just thinking: is she a replacement for Annalise?' As soon as I've said that, I realize how thoughtless it is. Zoe gives me a contemptuous look, but I think she's a bit hurt.

'Oh, ha ha, that's big sister talk, isn't it? I can make friends with who I like!'

'Yeah, you can. Just saying, don't jump into anything...'

'I'm not! She doesn't have a pet toad, or live in a — weird old house!'

'She is a bit churchy though: her dad's a pastor! Like Grandpa Alisdair?'

'Yes, and our dad's a pastor's son, so what does that tell you?'

'Okay, I admit, nothing. He was a rebel, an exception. So, what about a lovely outdoor walk on the wall, with David?'

'I'll think. About it. But we're here to be with everybody!'

There are rumbles of thunder and flashes of lightning that flicker and keep waking me up overnight. First time I review David's offer: if Zoe decides she definitely wants to play board games with the cousins, will a morning with the Reverend David Robertson be more fun, or should I make an excuse? Am I happy to go with him, alone? Maybe Zoe's persuadable: though she parroted that wonderful parental phrase, 'I'm thinking about it'!

Then, after a particularly bright flash and rumble sequence, I remember how Mum very sneakily admitted she'd bought us those party dresses to wear at the ceilidh, without sharing with us the information that the relatives had decided that ceilidh was also, or even only, a sixteenth birthday celebration centring on me! Why not just be honest about it? Were they afraid that we – or at least I – would refuse to come? Because, in fact, I wouldn't do that, as it clashed with Truck and gave me the perfect excuse to tell Charlie I couldn't go with her.

Our tiny room is dim and stuffy, but the next time I wake up, it's morning. Zoe is a hump in her bed, her back to me. I'm taking a moment to think about Fabian with his family in Italy where the sun's shining. Suddenly there's the deafening sound of a bell ringing. Somebody walking about ringing a hand bell! Like this is school! Zoe turns, and sticks her head out from under the duvet. 'What...?'

On cue, Uncle Ian's voice calls up the stairwell. 'Breakfast in ten!'

'Boarding school!' I groan, duvet over my head. 'I am not Charlie!'

'D'you think he does that every day? I mean, every ordinary day?'

'Probably. He's a pastor. Rules go with the lifestyle, especially about time and all doing things together!' Screeches and exclamations come from other rooms, feet pound overhead and down the staircase. 'We'd better get up.'

I throw aside the pink and white duvet, with its picture of a long-haired girl carrying a basket of flowers, and its pink italic lettering, 'Little Princess'. No comment. I riffle through my bag, hunting for walking-type clothes. With Zoe and I sharing this kind of cupboard with a window, there's hardly space for our bags and stuff except the floor between the beds, and now she's up as well we keep bumping into each other.

'Why d'you say, 'cos he's a pastor?' she asks, her head emerging from a T-shirt with a huge star on the front.

'Control? Anyhow, where's my other jeans? My old ones? What about the walk? You coming with us to Hadrian's Wall?' I ask as she adjusts the T-shirt, so the words 'Base Camp Star' can be read, right across her boobs. 'Is that advertising?'

'For Base Camp, isn't it obvious? And nope, I've got a game of Scrabble to win against Becky and them,' my sister says, cheerfully, 'probably a whole Scrabble competition. Yay!' She punches the air.

Heart sinks. 'Okay, Miss Queen of Spelling Bee!'

'He only asked. I can say no, can't I? And Becky asked first!'

'You can, and beat them all with your dictionary mind. Go Zo-zo! But I'm walking, okay? Even if it rains.' Something, probably a mixture of curiosity and claustrophobia, has convinced me to go. I might even find something about the woman I heard about from behind the utility room door.

We're both decent, so I pull up the blind. The sun blazes in. Drops of water sparkle like jewels on the leaves of a climbing plant that seems to be trying to get in the window. Clouds are skittering across a deep blue sky, the blinding sun slyly glittering between them. As I turn to Zoe, there's a bright template of the window slanting across the thin strip of brown carpet between our beds. 'Look, sun's out! Blue sky! Walking with David might even be interesting!'

'But I like board games.'

We run downstairs. Breakfast begins. Nine of us round the table: Uncle Ian, Aunt Sue, three kids, Zoe and me, Granny Fee, and Uncle Alex, whose family went home but are coming back later. No surprise: there's a school-type prayer, before boiled eggs and home-made brown rolls are passed around. How strange: all of us are related, but we know the rellies less than we know our friends. Feel we must behave properly.

I ask Uncle Alex – politely – as we chomp through the slightly heavy but nicely flavoured brown rolls, 'Do you know if David's coming over soon?'

'Should be here, in about thirty minutes. Do you need him?'

'He asked me and Zoe whether we'd like to walk on Hadrian's Wall. I thought I'd go.'

'I'd advise you to stay and join in the indoor games,' says Uncle Ian, 'wouldn't be canny, would it, to get soaked out on the Wall.'

'Oh, I don't mind, it's fine to walk in the rain, in the right clothes, it's only harmful if you get cold,' I say. 'I've got walking boots. And a cagoule, and over-trousers, the lot. For going to the Scottish islands. I brought a fleece, and two jerseys, and thick socks and stuff. On our geography trip, we got wet most days! Nobody died of pneumonia!'

'Well, I leave it up to you,' he says, hands in the air like someone surrendering, 'and to your parents, of course,' he says, and shoves back his chair. He turns to Aunt Sue, 'Going to write my...' he leans in further towards her, dropping his voice, 'upstairs, away from the chaos.'

She stands, but doesn't push her chair back. They lean across the table and just-about kiss, as if he's going off to work, not just upstairs. Becky and Martha grin and titter (inward squirm from me and Zoe as we catch each other's eyes — hard not to roll them!).

After breakfast, and what sounds like competitive teeth cleaning between Becky, Martha, and Iso, Uncle Ian's family get busy setting out the Scrabble and Monopoly boards. Granny Fee swings into action with a loaf and the bread knife, cutting slices to make sandwiches. She and Aunt Sue argue about letting us go off on what might turn into a thundery day. She points out that if it rains there must be a plan made about the bouncy castle. Aunt Sue says 'I rang them in the week, when I saw this forecast. They'll cancel if it rains, but it would be a shame.'

'Could you not hire a marquee, or something? Pitch it on the grass?'

'I thought of that. Ian even measured the height of the church hall. Though it's not the same, is it?'

David arrives and Granny Fee hands us her carefully packed sandwiches (cheese and pickle, and lettuce and pease pudding, which is like a far-Northern version of hummus). Walking boots, over-trousers, cagoules, and cameras are stashed in his white Renault Clio.

We set off for Housesteads (such a weird name for somewhere Roman!). David chats about how often he and Dad used to go there as teenagers. I tell him 'Yes, Dad's said a bit about that. He doesn't talk an awful lot about growing up here. Mostly he tells us about Grandpa Alisdair's regime, learning psalms as a punishment, that kind of thing. I think Grandpa was a bit too – you know, serious about stuff?'

'You mean, grim and judgmental?' David says. 'He was a bit, unimaginative, I'd call it. He meant it all positively, to teach us to live the Christian life, but – unimaginative is the word, really. Not much positivity there.'

'And the times we've come here, we haven't done any touristy stuff. Long drive, short visit. Like Dad doesn't want to hang about?'

'Yeah,' David says, like he knows things he won't tell me. 'that's kinda sad. There was fun as well, though. I remember it.'

'Yes, I mean, Granny Fee's lovely. And the food, and her baking. But what else did she do? I'd like to know more.'

'Typical pastor's wife stuff. Lots of cakes and lots of kids. Wives' groups and baby and toddler groups, all that kind of thing.'

'Oh, right.' I'm a bit shocked.

'You wouldn't want to do that?' he shoots a look at me, and grins.

'Absolutely I wouldn't.'

'So, what are your plans – for after GCSE – anything in mind?'

I decide to try him out. Watching his face (he's watching the road, but I'll get an idea), I say, 'A-levels, of course. I haven't chosen those yet. I mean, we're a science sort of family, but I wanted to think a bit more, not commit to doing exactly what school and the parents expect.'

He doesn't frown, or laugh, or look shocked. He grins, and says, 'thinking for yourself like your dad, then.'

Gosh, at last someone gets it! I think.

'I wish Dad would see into that. I wish I could trust him to let me. I did think of one thing, but he's not very convinced.'

'How – not convinced?'

'That it's much of a career? Not for me, because, he says, I could do better. Like being a psychiatrist. But I want to do something hands-on but not medical.'

'Mmm. That's interesting.'

What does he mean? Why doesn't he ask what it is? I change the subject, to my sister's ambition. 'Zoe thinks she knows what she'll do, because climate change is the most important thing. I mean, so do I, but...'

'So, she's indicating she's into the science side. Why not you?'

'Complicated,' I say. How do I explain what might sound like a craze, or a ducking-out thing, into easier subjects, or being influenced by my friends?

There's the sign for Housesteads. In a few minutes we're driving into the carpark. Thankfully. Though I might tell him, later, about art therapy.

David says, 'Maybe we can come back to that subject – if you want to – later on?'

'I might want that, yes. Maybe.' This makes me like him: that he hasn't pushed me to say more, but he's left the subject kind of hanging, open to more, or no more. And my decision.

As I get out of the car, the cool breeze lifts my hair, and blows it across my eyes a moment. But the sun's still shining. And there are only a few small, scattered clouds. Across the grass, further on, groups of people are already making their way up towards the Wall. Dabs of bright blue, orange or red and black, with sticklike legs. 'Like Lowry's matchstick people, enjoying a bank holiday away from their factory lives,' I say. 'I wonder whether they ever did?'

After a moment of quiet, David simply asks me, 'You like Lowry's work?'

'Sort of. We have reproductions at school, in the corridors. I think they're – clever – I think the style he uses to paint the people is, maybe, to show how they're – like a... machine for production, like all inter-changeable pegs or something? But in reality, they had lives.'

David responds to my ideas. 'Yes, good point,' he says, 'so, would you want to take that sort of analysis further?'

'How d'you mean?'

'How might it affect your career choices? Is it the art, or the social history, that grabs you?'

'Could be both of those!'

'Well, you've definitely got something there. The challenge is boiling it down to a choice of subjects, isn't it?'

Wow, at last somebody who understands the problem, I think.

With the hatch of the car open, I use the luggage area to balance on as we change into our walking boots. 'Good make, those boots,' David remarks.

'Yep, Dad made us look for them, and actually that was one time he did talk about walking, you and him, here, and I think the Yorkshire Dales?'

'We did a fair bit of walking. Maybe when we were a bit older than you are.'

'And he told us that you and he and some other friends had walked the Cornish cliff path before he'd met Mum or visited our house in Sennen, and Mum said he'd never told her that!'

David laughs. 'Well, it was just after A levels. He brought along his current girlfriend. Maybe that's why he didn't mention it!'

'Oh wow!'

'Really. Annie-Marie was someone he grew up with on the RAF bases when your Grandpa Alisdair was a chaplain there. They met again and formed a folk group with friends, including me, but we kept it a bit quiet from our parents. We did a few gigs in the Cornish pubs. There were five of us. Annie-Marie was the vocalist. She had a nice voice, did lots of sad Scottish songs. They seemed to connect pretty well with fishing life in Cornwall!'

'Oh my God! Dad has never talked about that!'

We finish tying our bootlaces and stow Granny Fee's sandwiches and our rain gear into our backpacks. Fortunately, it isn't looking like raining. Not yet.

I'm still processing this new information about Dad. It certainly explains that he'd escaped his strict religious upbringing well before he and Mum met.

'Maybe your Dad would tell you more about his younger life now, if you asked him?'

'That'd be so cool. We kind of need to re-connect, after – well, after I tried to talk to him about my future studies. He acted like he'd never thought I might want to do anything other than STEM subjects and go off to Uni to become a clone. Of Mum, if not of him.'

'You can blame me, if you need to, for letting out the memories.'

'Wouldn't he mind me knowing, though? If he's kept it quiet?'

'Well, I suspect your Mum knows a lot more than she's told you? You could try approaching the subject? Maybe the subject could come up out of you both playing for the ceilidh.'

'Yeah. Maybe. Maybe I'll try.'

The air's cool and clear, the sun's still shining, there's a few wispy clouds but nothing ominous. I pull on my cagoule, put my camera carefully in the central pocket, shrug on my backpack. Imagining how I might approach Dad. While we're still here?

This family retreat's proving more interesting than I thought it would. Like a window into family history, and hardly a word about religion.

David's just showing me stuff on his large-scale Ordnance Survey map, heads bent, each of us holding one of its sides, when some other visitors arrive and park alongside us. From the corner of my eye, I catch two women in the group gawping at us. I kind of turn and grin at them. I get a horrible feeling that they think he's on a date with an underage kid. Obviously, they can't know that he's my Dad's cousin!

As we set off, David says, 'Of course, I like to imagine the Romans living up here, and what kind of people they were. Daily life in Vindolanda?'

'We did Hadrian's Wall as a project. I was Zoe's age. That's probably most of what I know about this place. I mean, about what went on here, why they built the Wall, how and who lived here. Army base. I suppose no chaplain though!' David grins.

On the Wall at last, we walk, we stop to use our cameras: we talk landscape and photography. David tells me that, on their visits here, he and Dad discussed their careers. 'Both our fathers were keen for us to follow in their footsteps — I think I heard you call it the dynasty thing – that is right, isn't it?'

'Yeah, and like I said, Dad didn't get it that I'm like a person with my own ideas. He even told me this weird thing, that Grandpa Alasdair said medicine was *God's second best* for him. What a putdown, you'd think Grandpa would've been pleased! I mean, it's prestigious, isn't it? So, because your dads were trying to organise you, did you guys keep your ambitions secret? I never expected that my dad and mum would try to organise me like Grandpa did!'

First, he laughs, sympathetically. Then, 'Well, obviously being a minister of the gospel was the highest calling, in your Grandpa Alisdair's book. But I also think he wanted your dad to take over his pulpit, in order to maintain his vision for his church. He'd made it into a successful Christian hub, to use language Alisdair wouldn't have used! He believed it was a sacred trust to be defended.'

'So everything was all about dynasty. And he called it God's first choice, but how could he know? Surely he was using God to endorse his own ambition, what he, Grandpa Alisdair, wanted. Anyway, I don't think God actually does plan out all our lives individually, with all the details.'

We've stopped in our tracks, while we let several other walkers go by. 'I quite agree with you,' says David. 'But it's helpful to look at it from the viewpoint of your Grandpa's theology. He believed that God has a plan for everyone's life. Even when we were teenagers, we were all taught to seek God's guidance for our careers. It's... simplistic. It can go horribly wrong. It can work, but it can also be very manipulative.'

'So, it's like God writes out a plan for each of us – including a second-best choice? And neither one is our choice? I've not heard that before... It's insanely patronising!'

'But you've also got to take into account your Grandpa's personal feelings. He really wanted this for Max, so he was convinced that Max would come to see that this was God's plan for him. And pretty much told him so.'

'So he thought he knew what God's plan was for Dad even though Dad was supposed to find it out for himself! That's — weird!'

'You're right — his hopes actually got in the way of his theological beliefs. And you can imagine that he was rather stumped when Max announced that he thought God was actually guiding him into medicine! And for his part, Max was pretty disappointed by his father's opposition, because he expected that he would respect this guidance.'

'That figures.'

'By contrast, my dad — your Great Uncle Euan — wanted me to take over his medical practice, and he made it clear this was his expectation. Nothing much to do with God.'

'So he was a bit controlling too, but in a more ordinary way. So, how come you didn't do what he wanted?'

'Well, the church's "guidance" idea influenced me too, but not in quite the way my dad might've expected. I simply left home, to escape it – and possibly God —'

I stare at David, imagining him feeling he had to escape both the church's God and his dad — thinking for himself, but still inside their church's box.

'What did you do then?'

'Well, I scarpered, went backpacking to Australia with the intention of never coming back. And my parents were very hurt, of course. They felt betrayed and confused, but more than that, they were afraid for me. I'd walked away from God, which was disobedient and even dangerous.'

'Blimey. That's beyond manipulative.'

'It's what we were taught.' David gives a shrug. 'We tend to believe what we're taught when we're kids.'

'I don't think I'd believe it. Not without proof.'

'You haven't grown up in an extreme church environment like this one. The irony is, Max and I swapped places: he became the doctor and I became the minister, which our parents could've accepted as showing we'd become thinking adults. Actually my Dad sort of transferred his ambitions to Max: he really hoped he would come and work with him as a GP up here, or go and be a missionary doctor.'

I try to imagine growing up in the north. And then I try to imagine Dad as a missionary.

'It's all a bit bonkers, as Zoe would say.'

'Well they did all come round in the end, it just took a long time. When I came back to the UK, as a priest in the Anglican church, my folks first had to cope with what they'd call my apostasy, or something.'

'Some of my friends think that religion messes people up.'

'It's more the way people, even well-intentioned parents, try to use it to control other people. But non-religious people have their own ways of being controlling too.'

I think of Mum, who's not very religious, making me befriend Charlie.

'I think even kids have to know why they're asked to do something. Earlier this year Mum got me to be friends again with someone I knew in nursery. It was awkward and embarrassing. When she told me the reason, that changed it, like totally.'

'I'm glad she told you.'

'Yes, it was because her dad has a neurological illness, and everything is changing in her family. I think Mum believed it would help Charlie to have a friend from way back. Somehow.'

'Shame she couldn't have told you before. Sometimes a person can't, and the other person has to trust.'

'Yeah, well – would've helped me if she had explained as much as she was allowed to!'

Oddly, that makes David go quiet, and indicate we should move on, before more walkers catch up.

Chapter 49

WE RETURN FROM HADRIAN'S WALL

The beliefs of the First Truly church are more extreme than I knew. Granny Fee never seemed to want control our lives like this. I see why Dad left. And why we only make short visits to Uncle Ian's family in the Manse.

So, I've told David about Charlie. Might he be deciding to tell me about the woman, or at least about coming out as bisexual? Dad knows. Does Mum know yet? Would he tell all of us together?

No, he's still on the same subject. 'Speaking as a priest, I do think there's a way that God might prompt us, without us needing to believe he has a detailed plan. If we try to get to know ourselves, that helps us discern what we might do, using our abilities, concerns, interests, and so on. This seems to me more like how God would work.'

'Can you give me an example?'

'Well, let's take the Lowry paintings: what struck you about them? It was the visual impact, and that led on to whether the workers ever got time out to enjoy the countryside. Through art to social conscience. So, it's not only about people with strong religious beliefs trying to influence your decision making. Really, when anyone tries to tell you they know you better than you know yourself, by suggesting a certain career is the right one for you, you need to question them. But also, explain your own perceptions.'

'Mmm,' I say. 'That sounds like if I have an idea myself, I don't need to feel it's a stupid waste of my brain not to have the same career as Dad – or Mum. Though now I feel that my other Granny is trying to influence me in a kind of weird way by giving me her mother's ring. Her mother was a scientist when it wasn't normal for women. But I don't really know what she's trying to do.'

'Want to talk about this? We could take a break and eat those sarnies.'

The relief of this suggestion bubbles straight to the surface. 'I'd like to study art and design or photography, something like that, I sort of find those things cool – I mean, interesting, something people need to be human? Is that weird?' Feel my mouth go into a silly smile, like when I was small and asked for something I really, really wanted, but didn't think they'd allow.

David doesn't react at all. That is, he doesn't do a grown-up horror face, 'I can't imagine why' style. He says, 'Look, let's stop and take out the food, and let's just settle down where we are?'

We settle. It's not, like, comfy, but it does give my feet a rest from the heavy walking boots. Granny Fee's egg and tomato sandwiches are wonderful, and it makes me laugh that she's managed to pack bottles of ginger beer, 'Like in those old adventure story books we found in the attic room, by Enid Blyton?'

'You found those?'

'Dad was poking around looking for an electric socket to plug in the heater, when Zo-zo and I slept up there on a visit. The books were in a box marked 'Charity'. Of course, we read them!'

'Right. I shan't ask what you thought! Back to A levels. I really think your Dad should give you credit for having a real interest in something, even if it happens not to be what the family expect. I'd not be disappointed if I were him. You mentioned the people who looked like a painting by Lowry: not everyone would see the scene that way.'

'I'm not, like, certain my drawing would be up to fine art – I only want to – do something practical, interesting, like design or photography... spend a few years studying and creating, I suppose. Sometimes my head's too full of facts.'

'And what do you do with it then?'

'Bang it on the wall? Tell it to shut up? Not really. I go over to my friend Nina's and we mess about with crayons and paint and stuff. We sketch each other or just do weird designs. I don't play my violin when my head feels like that, music's too, like, structured.' Chewing the last sandwich in my packet, I study David's face. With his shades on (the sun's got very bright in a blue sky with a few grey clouds), he looks thoughtful, eyebrows together.

'Your best idea,' he says, slowly, 'would be to gather up some prospectuses of places you might apply to, find out some details about the courses, compare them, have a bit to say about why you might choose those places. Also look into what careers could follow the degree course. School isn't going to condemn you for having your own ideas, they might even be helpful?'

I'm taken aback that I've even told David my problem, but even more that he hasn't just told me to go with what my parents think. I mean, when the teacher told me to look at prospectuses, she just seemed disappointed and not really supportive. 'That's – so amazing! You're the first person I've told who's been encouraging! I started doing the prospectus thing, and I told Mum and Dad, but — they were so quiet, they looked so disappointed, and we haven't really talked again. Actually, I want to apply for art therapy — which they should respect, surely — and they just went on saying I could do better. Like they meant, don't fool us: you could do med school rather than some pointless therapy course.'

David says, 'If you've finished your sandwiches, how about we get going again?' Once we're on the move, he goes on, 'I'd say, if I was them, that you're right about what we need to be fully human, you've discerned something rather special, beyond the way subjects are taught at school. You've realised that we're more than just the scientific or even the creative brain, the part of you that gets top marks in physics or whatever, which teachers or parents often use to push kids into places they think they should go next.'

'I know a lot of people who think arts subjects, especially the more practical ones, are for the kids who can't achieve anything better. I'm afraid my parents are worried that I haven't got ambition, that I don't want to aim high enough. It's what I meant by the dynastic thing, like they're kind of hoping for the next generation of us Guthrie Mullinses to become top this and top that in life science. Really, they're a bit like Grandpa Alistair, or at least your dad.'

'So many parents feel like that. It's certainly not exclusively religious thinking.'

'You see – in the Easter holidays, I was staying with Daze — you know, Daisy, mum's stepsister?'

David throws me a quick glance, before replying.

'Of course. I've worked with her. Remember the labyrinth and the Fun Day when you were a kid? But you said you wouldn't choose fine art as a career.'

I find I've stopped walking. I need to tell David more about how Daze has influenced me. He stops too and we step a bit off the path so as not to make an obstruction.

'No, but Daze is an example. She's an intelligent person, hugely creative, but she can do all sorts of different practical things. I don't think Granny Caro ever really understood Daze. She didn't see the talent, she only saw - you-know— a step-kid, someone she could, like, mould? So that all her girls were successful? Anyhow, I've seen this incredible picture Daze painted, when she was maybe fifteen? It's actually of Granny Caro, though I didn't realise that till I thought about how it was for Daze growing up with Granny as a step-mum.'

'Mmm. Can you describe it?' David sounds really, really interested in this. His eyes (behind the shades) are definitely on me, he's totally concentrating as I explain the picture.

'It's a crucifixion, only the cross is a woman, and the crucified person is a child. It took me a time to realise that the woman is Granny and the child is Daze!'

He lets out a long breath, like a 'phew!' of amazement. Then for a moment he says nothing.

'I tried to find out some more from Daze, but all she said was that she got the idea from a book, but she hasn't said what book.'

'That is remarkable,' he says. 'And — I think I know the book she means.'

'This is partly what made me think about art therapy, because the painting must be expressing Daze's feelings. I mean, it's extreme, but I think I understand why she did it. A child is feeling destroyed by the ambitions of other people. And is that what's going on in the book?'

'Pretty much. You should read the book. I might even have a copy. It's called *My Name is Asher Lev*, and it's about a very strict orthodox Jewish family. No spoilers! But I think you'd find it very relevant!'

David understands the feelings behind the picture. Right at the start he got what I was saying about the Lowry paintings. I've found someone I can relate to, and he's part of my family! And maybe even, I'm on the right track thinking about art therapy.

It really hits me now that Mum and Dad, while of course not *destroying* the inside me, have made my decisions about my subjects really difficult, because it feels like silent opposition to the real me. If I was in art therapy I'd draw this as being torn in half. Suddenly there's a lump in my throat. I swallow hard. 'School was worried, Mum said. About Daze I mean. Back then. They thought there was child abuse going on. I don't think Mum understands the painting at all. When I said I'd seen it, she told me that the painting got Daze into a prestigious art school later.' I'm struggling not to cry, managing it so far.

'But you saw into it. That's also worth saying if you get an interview for an art course... paintings, also other media — music is one, drama — can make a shocking indictment of society. They're saying what needs to be said. I wish I could've painted something like that – for my Dad.

There were things about me he could hardly accept, and didn't for a long time. But, otherwise he was a kind person, an admired doctor. Your dad, Max, acted as our go-between...'

I'm hardly hearing what David's saying. My throat is having another try, my nose is running, I feel so torn: grateful to David, disappointed about Mum and Dad. I don't really know what I'm doing, and I don't want people to see. 'It's been a horrible term. Wanting them to want the person I am, not the me they've created in their own heads. Like Dad being intended to – be someone else – he should've understood!'

Stupid to cry on Hadrian's Wall with David. But now I don't care. 'It's like being made from someone else's template, isn't it?' My voice comes out like a harsh whisper. I'm sniffing, wiping my eyes, fumbling in my pocket for a tissue.

'I'm sorry, I've opened something up.'

'No, it's okay,' wiping my eyes with my hands again, sniffling, 'totally okay. I needed to tell someone – someone in the family.'

He hands me a clean, nicely folded, tissue. I unfold it, and sort myself out, nose blown, eyes blotted, smile attempted. 'Are you okay — with a hug, or not?' David asks.

'Very okay, I am so – grateful!' Inside a very nice, not too squeezy, embrace, I ask, 'Could you, maybe, tell Dad a bit? Maybe that would help them see it's a serious idea? I only need to do art as a fourth subject.'

'I don't mind paving the way, but I think you need to talk to him properly again.'

'He might still be disappointed.'

'I don't think so, necessarily, if he sees how serious you are. And Daisy — you and she get along?'

'Yes, though sometimes she can be quite sharp.' I notice that David smiles at this. 'Being at hers is such a contrast to being at home. When I was there at Easter I really enjoyed watching her work, she's got such skilful hands, and I even helped a bit with Rothko's egg costume.' David's continuing to grin.

'I also had this idea that maybe my friend Nina's mum could help explain things to Mum and Dad, as Nina's going to art college, but perhaps that's silly.'

'Well, it's a good idea to explore your ambitions with Nina's family, and with Daisy. But really, you won't need somebody else to help to talk to your Dad. You won't get the response I got – your Dad is going to listen.'

'So you mean I won't have to go to Australia to be a surfing instructor!'

'I have a feeling you may not find that necessary. One last thing about vocation – I've always been fairly certain that, if he hadn't grown up in First Truly, your dad would've chosen to study music and make that his career.'

'Really?' I realise it's getting quite dark, under some grey clouds that have gathered while I have been inside my feelings. We agree it's time to go back to the Manse.

'Your dad had the ability for music. But he also had the ability to study medicine, including all that anatomy and surgery, which I really didn't want to know anything about. And to end up where the Reverend Alisdair Mullins could be proud of him...eventually! So, think broadly into the vocation you might take up – or defer going into more study straight from school?'

'And keep playing cricket with my cousins?' I say, throwaway.

'Yes, or Monopoly. Maybe not Monopoly!'

'Never Monopoly!'

The sun is gone. But I have a feeling like the sun's shining inside me. The banked-up clouds are turning purple, and joining together. It's getting darker and darker. David removes his shades and stashes them into a pocket inside his cagoule. A growl of thunder echoes around the landscape.

We march single file at a good pace back along the Wall, then as we're nearly at the car park, the rain really comes down. We run. Not easy in heavy boots! David opens up the vehicle, we fling ourselves inside, pulling the doors shut.

'Damn!' he says then. 'My shoes are in the back!'

Stupidly grateful as I am, I offer to slip out and fetch them. 'Nope – my mistake!' He goes. I switch on the car radio to find a music station. David returns, his hair dripping, with my trainers as well as his. We shove off our cagoules and boots. David has an awkward few minutes getting his ordinary shoes on in the cramped driver's seat.

On the drive back to the Manse, David asks, 'Where to after the reunion? Your dad said a road trip around the north?'

'Edinburgh first. Mum's Aunt Val, the weaving and knitting one. Daze lived with her when Rothko was small.'

'Uh-huh.'

'I'm looking forward to seeing her again. She must be pretty cool if she had Daze living with her. Of course, she came to that Fun Day that you and Daze organised.'

'So just think, there's a lot of what makes people human in your family. Maybe less reason to worry that they'll force you into a research lab or a doctors' surgery?'

I realise he is probably right. I know a little more about Dad now as well.

Lightning flickers, there's a roar of thunder, a quiet moment, and then, huge drops of rain mixed with hail.

'Pity we didn't get further along.'

'No, it was fine. All of that was good. I feel much better about next year.'

There's something else I want to know. In case Charlie asks me, I'd better ask. 'You know Hildie's, where you used to work?'

'I do.'

'When you stayed in our house, back when I was away for half term?'

'Yes, I was teaching a lecture series for a course there. When I had your bedroom.' David says with a smile.

'The thing is, I wondered, my friend Charlie's mother, Sharon Parker Pollard, brought me back home after I'd stayed the weekend with them, because she was going to St Hildie's that day. That's the friend I told you about that Mum wants me to be friends with.'

'Yes, I know Sharon. She's one of the regulars.'

'So was she on your course?'

David glances at me. 'No, not on my course. But there was a poetry workshop running, and I guess she might have been on that. I know she's interested in several of the Hildie's activities, so our paths have crossed. She's a popular yoga teacher in Oxford, isn't she?'

'Yeah, Mum goes to her classes. She and Mum are friends, but I'm not sure me and Charlie are really – compatible, now we're older.'

I'm thinking this is all I'll hear about Shaz. It's probably enough. The thunderstorm cracks and booms. But my emotions don't mirror it any more, as we drive in silence through the dimness and the rain. It was great not being treated like a small young relative, and I've learnt some family history.

Then as we turn into the Manse drive, and I'm wondering what's happening about that bouncy castle, and whether the ceilidh will be okay, even fun after all, David's voice gives me a start, as he says,

'Another thing, Alice, we've talked a bit about the culture of your Grandpa Alisdair's church, with its rather limited lifestyle and all that...'

'Oh, sorry, I was somewhere else, wondering about the party and the bouncy castle – hoping it's cancelled!'

'You don't like inflatables?'

'Not much. I mean, being sixteen is, like, being a bit beyond kiddie stuff... like still too near it to want to pretend for fun?'

'Yeah, I get that. But what I was going to say was: as your Dad and I have both discovered, there are other ways of having faith. Your Uncle Ian does give the impression that his interpretation is the best one and all the others are inferior, but really there are a lot of other options, if at some point you decided to look into it.'

'More like St Hildie's, you mean?'

'Yes, that's one option. The key thing, I think, is to keep an open mind to the possibility of faith.'

Ah, I think, he's giving me the godfatherly advice, but it's OK, not too heavy. We've stopped, parked, the handbrake's on, but we've not moved to get out.

'Just one thing I thought might be useful. The base line isn't keeping old traditions and laws, it's much more about positive things, things we need to do in order to live together as human beings. Even the Old Testament says that God isn't interested in us giving up good things, and making ourselves miserable – sacrifices, which back then meant killing and burning up your cattle, part of your source of income, in effect. It's about how we live – doing justice with mercy – which is, really, an extended form of kindness – having compassion — helping people – which is what both your parents do. Living a generous, caring sort of life. Where faith comes in, is that I wonder if without believing in someone higher than myself I could do that, consistently.'

'How do you mean?'

'What do you think?' He gives me a look, like he's trying to see into my mind through my eyes.

'Crikey, I guess, if there was just me to decide, I'd – probably just think how – you know – stuff like how if I ate all the cake there'd be none for anyone else. That kind of thing. But I mightn't do it.'

David takes off his seat belt and opens his door. I do the same. 'That's exactly the point. What helps us do it.'

Chapter 50

A CHAT WITH GRANNY FEE AND ZOE IS UPSET AGAIN

The bouncy castle was intended to go on the big front lawn, where Uncle Ian let the grass grow over Granny Fee's rose bed. I step out of the car and grab my belongings from the back of the car.

'No sign of the bouncy castle. Hope it's been cancelled!'

David says, 'Hmm. Ian may have swopped the big one for a smaller size!'

'Aw – I suppose he would! Smaller will only suit the kids though, so, where'd it be?'

'I've no idea. In a far corner suit you?'

'Totally.'

There's a rumbling behind us. I turn round and see that a lorry's appeared on the drive. 'Hey, look what's come! Ryan and Jones: Marquees and Inflatables!'

David responds with a groan, and then a laugh, 'How did I guess?'

We wave to Aunt Sue and Auntie Cait, who are busy putting up a huge banner over the front door. 'Welcome to the Mullins Family Retreat!' it says, in slightly wobbly painted letters. I guess it's the work of Ian's Isaiah and Alex's Lily. We go round the side of the house and as we reach the back door, I spot a huge marquee already on the back lawn.

'So, let's hope Ryan and Jones are putting up a smaller one for the castle, out front, and this one's for dancing?' says David.

'Oh, please let them be!'

Carrying my wet cagoule and over-trousers, I head into the kitchen, where Granny Fee's standing at the table, making scones. 'Hello, pet, how was your walk? Ooh – were you were caught in the rain?'

'We were! Walk was fine, till the rain came down. Then we had a massive thunderstorm! Didn't you have one? We had to run through puddles in the car park!'

'Well no — we saw some threatening clouds but they blew over, may've been quite localised? Now, what about your waterproofs you have there? You can hang them in the lobby – out by the washing machine? There's a line – well, a piece of string really...'

'I see it!' This lobby, as they call it, has everything to do with laundry, including the airing cupboard, and is really quaint, like houses must've been before — well, before. A shame the old Manse is being pulled down and all the little pantry-rooms and cubbyholes lost and forgotten. I s'pose this is what Annalise's house was like, and maybe even why Zoe liked going there. I throw my cagoule and over-trousers over what Granny called a line, and glance out of the door into the garden. That marquee's deffo huge, enough to contain a party. Surely that's for the dancing?

'So, you managed to eat the lunch I made you? Before it rained? Would you like a bit more to eat, maybe?' Granny says, 'there's a ham we had for lunch, you could have a slice?'

At the far end of the big pine table, there's half a joint of home-cooked ham on a plate, under a net cover. My mouth waters. I tell myself that sandwiches weren't quite enough lunch, and we did a lot of walking (and talking heavy stuff) this morning.

Granny cuts me a thick slice of ham, finds some leftover salad in the fridge, and traps it all between two slices of her home-made bread. She knows I like it with a slather of mustard, which she also adds. This is like one of Daze's 'doorsteps'.

Granny chats about her frilly lettuces, while she fetches a plate for the sandwich. 'I don't grow those anymore, pet,' she says, 'that one's come from your uncle Alex's garden...And the tomatoes and onions... Ian says he doesn't have time to grow vegetables. Now, there you go, pet,' she says, handing it to me, and going back to her baking.

Granny Fee's giving me some of those feelings I get from Daze, but in a different way. She chats about times we spent when Zoe and I were little, while she rubs the fat into the flour. Things that happened when even I was quite small, and my sister was still almost a baby. She reminds me about holidays which she came on with us. Not just the narrowboat holiday, but one year when she came to Chapel House with us, and we saw a play at the Minack theatre, 'Maybe you remember that? Do companies still perform plays there?'

'They do. It's beautiful isn't it, how you can watch the stage with the sea behind it?'

'It is. It's lovely.'

My phone pings: instinct kicks in, heart beats faster: who? Fabian? No, realistically, Mariam, Nina, or — oh please not Charlie!... I stop myself looking, shove it back in my pocket. Can't be exam results, nothing else is urgent. 'Sorry. I shouldn't... we're talking.'

'Oh no, you'll want to speak to your friends, won't you?'

'I s'pose,' I say, pulling it out again: on the screen, 'FabRuss89' Yay!

'Of course you will. Friends are very important,' Granny says, as I shove the phone away a second time. I'll save it for later.

'Nothing that can't wait.'

'And now you're so grown up – but, well you're the same person as we can remember about all those years ago.'

'Maybe.' I don't want to disappoint Granny Fee, but I feel like inside I may not be. She might not like everything I am now. 'I don't know if we could take you to Chapel House again, because Granny Caroline's talking about leaving Cornwall. She wants to retire to London!'

'Oh my! Why'd she want to do that?' She seems genuinely shocked, and then, I realise, she tries not to be critical. 'Well, I shouldn't question her taste. I expect she likes the excitement of the place. I was never one for the bright lights. On the other hand I do enjoy a good ceilidh – with people I love. We're all different.'

'Mum's mother inherited a flat in Baker Street. You know, that's the street where Sherlock Holmes lived?'

'Well I never! Anyways, I'd better not hold you up, I expect you'll want to find your sister, and if you want to look canny tonight, you can ask your Aunt Sue about using the hairdryer or anything like that, you know? This is your home for the weekend. You only have to ask!'

Now I'm being politely dismissed, so Granny can do her work. 'I'll leave my empty plate by the dishwasher, shall I?'

'That's right. Of course, your dad's somewhere around. Your mam's in the study, she had a phone call.'

'Thanks, Granny.' She's beginning to roll and cut the scones out with a frilled-edge cutter, and lay them on three baking trays. Beatrix Potter's Mrs Tiggywinkle, all busy in her kitchen. Only here it's hot with baking, not ironing. I'm really fond of Granny Fee, and I love listening to her accent, not completely Scottish, not totally Northumberland.

Then as I move off down the passage, Aunt Sue comes the other way, carrying a huge cake tin above her baby bump. 'Hiya, birthday girl!' she calls, in her Essex voice, very different from Granny's. She flashes me a huge smile. 'Happy birthday to you!' she sings, as she joins Granny in the kitchen. 'See you at the party!'

I pick up my backpack, sling it on one shoulder, and start upstairs, worrying whether inside that tin there's a birthday cake with pink icing on it. And, how nice it is being alone, sometimes, even if it's in that tiny bedroom. I want to absorb more about my discovery that David supports me, and takes my ideas seriously. How can I use that to talk about my future plans like an equal with Mum and Dad and with school?

This makes me think about David again, and I wonder whether it was coming out as gay, which unsurprisingly he didn't mention to me, or not following his dad into medicine, that upset Uncle Euan and Aunt Margaret more. So if he now reveals that he's seeing a woman will they and the rest of the family sort of collapse onto the floor with shock, or will they congratulate him on being healed, or saved, or whatever they think has happened?

Remembering what David told me I decide to text Charlie: *My Uncle David was lecturing at Hildie's and says your Mum was on a poetry workshop, so nothing doing there! Alxx.* There's no reply, but I imagine she's too busy to be bothered.

On my way up, on the curve in the stairs, I hear Mum coming out of the study, phone call obviously finished.

I hang over the banisters, 'Hey, Mum, we're back from the Wall!' She comes upstairs behind me, and I suddenly have a bad feeling that she's going to say *Very sorry to miss the celebrations but been called back to Oxford* so that the three of us will have to continue the holiday without her. 'Was your phone call from the lab?' I ask.

'No, love, it was Shaz, and then I had to give Daisy a quick call.'

'Shaz? Daze? Why?'

'Oh, Shaz was only calling to tell me how their holiday's going, but she also particularly wanted me to thank Daisy for asking Evie, the neighbour, to get milk and bread and stuff in for them, and I managed to get through to her, which isn't always easy. Don't worry, had nothing to do with Charlie. But you might be pleased to hear that Daisy says that she's up north and she and Rothko might come to Edinburgh to call on Val when we're there.'

'Really? That would be brilliant!' Suddenly the holiday looks a whole lot more interesting.

'And how was your walk, love?'

'Good. Though it ended with the thunderstorm you didn't have here. David's okay, isn't he? We talked photography and stuff.'

Mum beams like the sun on a proper summer day. 'Good. I'm pleased you're getting to know him. One of the bet— best Mullinses.' Nice one-to-one chat with my godfather. I have passed some coming-out-as-adult test! She gives me a quick hug, unusual for Mum. 'No rain at all here. You'll still get your outdoor party.'

On cue, a rumble of thunder, and raindrops the size of pound coins blown against the window by a sudden gust. We laugh. Then I say, 'What I am worried about is what's in that massive cake tin I saw Aunt Sue carrying just now.'

'Birthday cake. But no name or embarrassing messages on it, I checked. Grab a bit of time off! I think Zoe went up to read, away from the preparations!'

I'm still a bit curious about what's happening on the Parker Pollards' holiday, and whether Eliot's developed more symptoms. Would Shaz phone Mum on holiday just to tell her they were enjoying themselves and to send thanks to Daze?

Then I remember the text from Fabian I had when I was with Granny and managed to ignore. *Wet all thru France, ground soggy! Better here. Amazing frescoes. Keep smiling. See you soon. XXF.*

Why are boys so terse in texts? And why, why underline that my holiday is cold, wet, and about to be embarrassing? Though of course, my heart dances, regardless of Fabian's inane message. *See you soon* is good – Yes!

I open the door of our bedroom: 'Hey you, it's me...' Zoe, on her bed, on her front as usual, is reading. There are several paper hankies, screwed up, on the floor, and although she seems to be wearing her jeans and a Breton long-sleeved T-shirt as she was earlier, she's got the duvet tented over herself. 'Harry Potter? D'you want me to leave you two together?'

'Whatever. Before you ask, I nearly won the whole Scrabble competition. And then, I didn't.'

'How? How didn't you?'

'Don't ask. I've changed my mind about Becky.'

Ah: the tissues and the duvet mean trouble? At least they don't mean a cold, more sadness about Annalise, or anything worse. 'Okay... only tell me if you want to.'

'Maybe I do. Basically, to be totally basic, she's such a prude! Deffo.'

'She's just an Ian Mullins kid.'

'Yeah, and I'm a Max Mullins kid. Older brother an' that?' She pushes off the duvet and swings her legs down, so she's sitting on her bed, sniffly and pink in the face. 'Makes no difference, irrelevant to the argument.'

'Right. And? The argument was about?' I'm sitting on my bed now, elbows on my knees, looking at my sister. She has post-crying eyes behind those big glasses.

'Look, I was nearly there. And there's this word I had, which if I added a certain other word which I'd realised would fit, with the tiles in my tray, and the ones it'd attach to, I'd have a triple word score for the new one. It was bothering me, 'cos it isn't like a nice word. But it's just a word, right? And it wouldn't be totally obscene — like – say if I put down penis, or poo, like Iso had tried... and Aunt Sue an' Mum told him off...'

'So?'

'I sort-of gambled, I thought: the parents say it when they're really mad or they break something — so, I put it down. And Becky went like beyond insane – she leapt across the board, sent all the tiles everywhere, and pulled at my hair – she said, not to hurt me, but to make me look at what I'd done!'

'Oh my God! What was the word? Would I know it?' I say, amazed at Becky's violence.

'Only *bugger*. It was *bugger*. They do say it, don't they?'

'Not a lot. But yes, when they're very cross. Or, that kind of stuff. But Mum was there?'

'Mum and Aunt Sue. Arbitrators apparently. I think Mum capitulated? She let Aunt Sue get away with it. She did tell Becky her behaviour was inappropriate, but she also said, *that is not a nice word, and I think we should agree not to include swearing when we play word games.* Something like that.' A late escapee tear slides down Zoe's cheek, as she says, 'Becky really hurt me, and my glasses had fallen off, onto the board, so I couldn't see if I'd wanted to!'

Chapter 51

CEILIDH AT THE MANSE

So, by four o'clock, the time the party begins, we're all in the garden. It's all mums and girls in dresses with tartan sashes, dads and boys in kilts. Except tiniest boys, in shorts. You'd think we were all Highlanders. Sun's been out for a while, the midges are already dancing at their ceilidh, the sky's blue and cloudless. Because the grass is still wet and slithery, the marquee is going to be used for both eating and dancing. It's quite pretty, really, with fairy lights, and those silver helium balloons Isaiah told me about when we first arrived: a sixteen in silver and another balloon-shaped one with *Happy Birthday dear Alice!* Shrieks, oohs, and aahs come from the front garden, where Uncle Ian's being health and safety supervisor for the little ones who evidently couldn't wait to get on the bouncy castle. Which has its own marquee – and which I shall steer very clear of! Let him not offer me a go on that thing — wearing my elegant dress!

I pick up my violin, and follow Dad and the other two musicians (Matt and Phil) to play together for the first half of the ceilidh. There are calls for the MC to kick off the proceedings, so Uncle Ian appears from the front garden, trailing my small cousins, Iso, Uncle Alex's Lily, and a couple of her tiny siblings, one in the arms of Alex's partner Auntie Cait. Alex and Caitlin haven't had a wedding, but apparently it's OK for them to participate. I wonder if Ian thinks this ranks above or below the awfulness of being gay.

'Welcome, everybody to — Alice's party!' Uncle Ian bellows.

'Oh, bugger!' I whisper into Zoe's ear, and she sniggers.

'Happy sixteenth to Alice!' he shouts and starts clapping. Everyone arranges themselves into a semicircle, and they start clapping and shouting 'Happy Birthday Alice!' And now they're all singing that inane song *Happy Birthday To You*. So embarrassing! I'm feeling hot all down my back.

I catch the eye of my cousin Chloe, who arrived this afternoon and is now on the end of the line, next to her brother Cam. Can't stop myself, as the banal song goes into a second round, I scowl, mainly as a message to Chloe, who understands exactly, and rolls her eyes, satisfactorily, as our Uncle invites me to 'come round to the front garden and open the ceilidh with a solo bounce on the castle...'

No, no, no. Desperate not to. Anyhow, the kids have been on there for at least half an hour while Zoe and me were glamming ourselves up for the party, so how would this be opening anything? How'm I going to respond? I look back back at Chloe. What's she doing? Up to something. Arms go up, knees bend slightly, just enough. Ha! I get the message.

As the clapping quietens down, I step forward, put one foot behind me, sweep my arms up and outwards like Chloe did, and drop as elegant a curtsy as I can manage many years after leaving ballet class.

As I rise, I thank the Manse family for giving me this chance to enjoy their lovely ceilidh, and politely refuse the bouncy castle offer (groans from the local rellies), and 'Mind if I don't?' I say, indicating my dress, 'it's new, I don't want to crease it – how about I come and watch how beautifully Iso, and Lily...'

'And us!' Becky and her not-much-younger sister Martha chorus.

'...Can bounce!' I add my bright idea: 'I'm giving my turn to whichever young cousin wins the race...about to begin...' (Cheers and whoops) 'Wait, wait – let me tell you the course...! Twice around the Manse, ending up in the front garden, where you must not get onto the castle until Uncle Ian arrives, but you must stand right beside it, touching it with your left hand – you know which your left hand is?' (Chorus of waving hands like they're doing a spelling test and know all the answers.) 'Are you ready? Get set... Go!'

As they all tear off, yelling, I take up my fiddle, and play twenty seconds of a reel I learnt for my last music exam, really fast. When I finish, the adults all gawp and clap. Chloe comes over, we hug. 'Oh, thanks be to whoever...' I say, sweat pouring down my back under my posh dress, 'saving me the indignity of bouncing in front of the family!'

And so it goes: squeals from the littlest ones, me busy in the band, the family – all sorts in sizes and ages, dancing – some galumphingly, others elegantly, kilts and tartan scarves flying, inside the marquee on the big back lawn, until suddenly Granny Fee appears, ringing that bell Ian uses at breakfast time, calling us to eat.

Tables on the patio, under the awning to keep off the drizzling rain, are being piled with plates of finger foods: sausage rolls, egg sandwiches, slices of pizza, cheese scones, strawberries, ice cream to eat in wafer cones. It does all look rather nice, rather fun – I imagine for a moment Fabian being here with me, then wonder if he'd make some cut-it-down-to-size remark, because it is a lot like something from the 1950s in a church hall. Or a Ladybird book. Which actually makes it rather cosy. Despite the chilliness of that drizzle, and the squelchy feel of the short walk from the marquee to fetch our food and take it back in there to eat!

All settled, Granny says, 'Euan, would you do the honours by giving thanks for us?' And then, getting no response, she bellows it, using her hands as a megaphone (I'd never have expected that!). And then she sends someone small indoors to find Great-uncle Euan, who comes out saying 'And behold, I was awoken from a deep sleep behind my newspaper, by a very small person, in order to bless our food today... In view of the importance of the occasion I've chosen the Selkirk Grace' (laughter) 'and I invite you all to join in.'

A chorus of voices (they all know it, of course) chants:

Some hae meat and canna eat,
And some wad eat that want it,
But we hae meat and we can eat,
Sae let the Lord be Thankit!

And that's about it, for a beginning: most of it fun, but every now and then, there's an embarrassing moment. Zoe offers her hands towards Becky for the very first dance, but Becky turns away, acting out a huff as she marches off. Dad and Mum keep putting their heads together and talking between dances, so that the band can't start playing, and people get cross. Aunt Sue's trying to stop Granny Fee hovering about looking anxious.

After supper Uncle Alex and Auntie Cait take their two sleepy toddlers home, leaving Lily to the excitement of a sleepover. The bouncy castle has been declared closed for the night, so Uncle Ian isn't needed to supervise health and safety, and he's back playing in the band. I'm released from playing and join the dancing. I have a terrific time being whirled around by my sexy cousin Cameron, then dancing more elegantly first with Dad and then with David, and managing to avoid partnering any of the women. Maybe this is the real party?

The rain's stopped. It's almost ten o'clock. The light stays so long in the north, and now the clouds have parted, and the sun's setting behind the church, orange, gold and shimmery. But the party's not over yet. 'Say, where is that birthday girl, Al-ice?' comes Uncle Ian's cheery voice. And a hand takes my shoulder, turns me around, gives me a little push (on my bum of all places!) towards the front of the assembled family. The dreaded cake moment has come!

Enter Granny Fee carrying on a large dish a giant pink and white iced cake, sprouting (obviously) sixteen pink candles. Cheers and whistles, shouts of 'We love Alice!' I can feel my entire body blushing. If only the ground would open. Instead, a small table (like the ones at weddings) has appeared, and Granny reverently lowers the cake on to it. More shouts. I haven't been part of this stupid birthday cake ritual since I was about ten, but can't chicken out. Step to the table, deep breath, blow like crazy. Thank God, they've all gone out. More cheers and then they start singing *Happy Birthday To You* as if we hadn't had it earlier. Granny hands me the knife — this is even more like a wedding — and I make a cut, then hand the knife back to Granny, who gets busy dividing the cake up. Everyone crowds around to get their slice.

I'm just getting ready to melt back into the crowd with my slice, when Uncle Ian steps forward again, raising his hands. 'And now for the presentation!' he announces. My heart sinks. He's got a parcel, obviously a book, wrapped in white and silver birthday paper and tied with pink birthday ribbon. What sort of book could it be?

'Alice! We shared our thoughts, and we prayed about this, and your Aunt Sue came up with something we hope will partner you through these important years. From school to college. From college to beginning your life's work. A book to accompany you on that journey…'

He hangs on to the parcel, as if it's too good to give away, holding it in both hands and jerking it up and down to emphasize his points.It's like school prize-giving, but worse. He keeps going, talking about the journey from teenage to adulthood. I try not to listen. My face burns with embarrassment, but also with anger. How can relatives, who hardly know me, have decided what book I need as a guide for life?

Uncle Ian's voice drones on and on, like a sermon, while people finish their slices of cake and sidle away from the untidy circle of listeners to find somewhere to put their plates, trying to go on looking interested. Dad's crossed his arms and is frowning at the ground. David, who looks up as I look at him, very subtly just about rolls his eyes. This gives me a warm feeling. Good I decided to go to Hadrian's Wall and we had our lovely walk. My ally in the wider family.

Maybe giving helpful religious books is done for everyone in this kind of family? A rite of passage, the instructive book? Of course: finding the plan for your life, which David explained to me on our walk! I get it! They think the book will help me discover the plan for my life. Well, I don't.

Finally, it's handed over. It feels hardcover and expensive through its wrapping of birthday paper. Have I got to unwrap it in front of everyone? Thankfully Dad's voice breaks into the silence, suggesting that it'll soon be time for some of us to go to bed. 'So we'll bring this ceilidh to an end by joining hands and singing. And the obvious choice for all of us, including Jenny who, after all, is a Guthrie,' (laughter, as Dad makes the point that Mum is really as Scottish as the Mullinses) 'and of course our absent family members who've had to take their tinies home for bedtime, is *Auld Lang Syne...*' Thank you, Dad, for taking the collective attention away from me!

Though I have never heard Dad so sentimental. He rambles a bit about Robbie Burns, till finally we begin bellowing out the song. Some of us know all the verses, or think they do. Once the song is done, Uncle Ian's band starts up again, and we don't quite stop, we spontaneously dance the *Gay Gordons...* And then, it really is over.

So, I've dumped the book somewhere, and sung a New Year's song, and whirled a few times more galloping the *Gay Gordons* (I had to dance with Becky, of all people, though it's clear we have different opinions!), everything slows down, we pack things away, turn off the fairy lights. We leave Zoe, Cameron, and Chloe helping the younger kids, who were allowed to stay up for the grown-up part of the evening, to quieten down in the now dimly lit marquee. Matt the musician spots my book and hands it over, 'Don't forget your present!'

I go into the middle of the lawn. Light is streaming out of every window and there's a clattering noise as, in the kitchen, the women clean up (note, the women! I even heard someone pushing David and Dad out, on grounds of gender!). I look up at the attic bedroom: Dad's bedroom when he was growing up. The light is on in the room behind the window. That window is a photo must-have. It will look atmospheric, in this late evening twilight.

Five minutes later, I've fetched my camera from the family room (putting the present in a far corner), and I'm back outside, carefully focusing on that window. Then I go slowly back across the patio, and into the house, through the sliding doors of the family room.

Someone – maybe Dad? – is softly playing the piano in here. It's almost dark except for a dim streak of light from the hallway. Definitely Dad, he's playing *Je te veux*. I creep up on Dad, and then notice there's someone asleep in the winged armchair. Is it Mum?

No. It's Granny Fee, sleeping in the big chair which used to be Grandpa Alasdair's. One hand rests on her lap, grasping a checked tea towel. That's so like a painting, someone should take a photo. Do a portrait.

I wait. Dad plays the last chord, looks round, sees me, and nods towards Granny, warning me not to wake her. He adjusts the piano stool, and begins the *Farewell to Stromness*... I creep away as far as the top of the stairs. From there, I can see into the room Zoe and I are sharing: the light's on, but the tiny room is empty.

Suddenly the whole thing's too sad. My knees kind of fold my legs without thinking, and I sit on the top step. Being here, knowing this house will be pulled down, the memories will be obliterated. The *Farewell to Stromness* seems like a *farewell to the Manse*. Although Uncle Ian is carrying on the tradition, it won't be the same in a modern house, no history, nowhere Dad and his siblings slept and ate and played and did their homework.

I imagine more: remembering all the stuff I've been told about their family life with Grandpa Alisdair. And I can now add: Dad and David walking on the Wall and talking about how they can do what they want with their lives. The two of them founding a folk band. His girlfriend Annie-Marie. Was she was like Mum at all? What did Granny Fee think about Annie-Marie and the folk group?

I let all the feelings come, the tickling in my nose, the lumpy throat. I want to cry about my family and how it was, long ago when I wasn't here to think all this.

And my past life's gone too. So much has changed this summer. I think of Charlie, Mariam, Annalise, even Zoe. I suppose it goes with being sixteen. It's farewell to fifteen.

I'm still sitting here when I hear two voices of people coming upstairs. Uncle Ian, who's speaking in a low but rather sharp voice, and Iso, who's kind of whining, that it's not fair that he has to go to bed and not the girls. Uncle Ian nearly treads on me in the dark, and apologises rather abruptly. The altercation continues up the next flight of stairs. I realise my feet are frozen and my thin dress isn't keeping me even half warm. I unfold myself and creep towards our room. I suppose Zoe's still in the marquee, so maybe I can have a nice hot shower to warm up.

But, it seems that someone has nicked the bathroom. I hear the key click in the lock.

Whatever... Zoe's bed has been sat on and looks rumpled. I get into PJs with a jumper and woolly socks, wondering how much colder than back home it really is here. I suppose all the rain, and storms, and damp chilliness is climate change setting in, and there won't be any more proper summer? I'm a bit worried about Zoe, if she's unhappy somewhere because of the row with Becky. Should I go and hunt for her?

But now there's the noise of voices and feet, coming up the stairs. I move to look over the banisters: the light's been switched on, and here comes a procession, up the stairs, led by Dad carrying a large book, followed by Becky, eyes down, hair over her face, stamping her trainers against the stairs, followed by Zoe, still in her ceilidh dress and ballet pumps. She gives me a grin and a little wave.

Dad spots me, and gives a quick thumbs-up, unseen by Becky. I move silently back to lurk in the shadows, further along the passage, and watch as he hustles the two girls into our room. I must have a big question mark on my face, because, as whoever it was exits the bathroom and stumps off upstairs, Dad descends on me, seizes my shoulders, turns me around, and says, 'Grab that bathroom, Ally, before someone else does!' He throws my towel after me, then goes back into the bedroom, and closes the door.

Relief. Dad is in control of that stuff. I can lie in a deliciously warm bath. Only it turns out to be a small, almost-tepid bath, because the hot water is mostly used up. The window, usually open, has at least been closed, rain has started throwing itself against the glass, and the outside is totally dark. But, at least a tepid wash doesn't take long, and knowing that Dad is sorting Becky out makes up for this. How? Will she cry? She looks a bit of a toughie to me. How long until I can access my bed?

Back from the bathroom, sitting with my back against the wall in the passage, I think maybe I should have brought my present with me. However awful that book is they'll want to know what I think of it, and be properly thanked.

With nothing else to do, I scroll through the photos on my phone, select the best one, type Fabian's number, and press send. While the voices murmur on behind the bedroom door, and the rain beats against the landing window. Then, Dad's voice goes more formal, sounds like he's reading from the Bible. That must have been the book I saw him carrying. Then there's movement, feet, shifting about. Hope they're coming out soon?

A text pings. Fabian's seen the photo! *'Just wow... enticing! Fx'* He liked me in the dress! Then more: *'frescoes we've been looking at today & the skyline... Don't you wish you were here? Hot, sunny, and flowing with wine. XXF'*

Is *enticing* okay? Is it really good – or is it like, too distant? Thinking about me, anyway. *XXF*. So, lots of good things. Fabian, Haydn's *Creation*, staying with Daze at Easter... It's just a wet summer. I text back, sending the one photo of Hadrian's Wall I took on my phone. Wish they were all on there, easier to send! And there's a fourth good thing: David's encouragement...

Laughter behind the door, hopeful sign. Dad comes out first. Thumbs up again. Here come the others, their faces shiny and pink. They've been crying. I jump up to give Zoe a hug, and something prompts me to give Becky one as well: she hugs me back. Seems she means it?

Zoe says, 'Dad told us about the frog on his pillow. Mum was staying with them here at the time, she told him it was a toad!'

'And my Dad and Uncle Alex put it in your dad's bed!' squawks Becky, bending over to laugh. 'He was asleep, and it walked on his face and woke him up! Ugh!'

'Because he'd made them learn a psalm...'

'Because they'd eaten up all the angel cake Granny Fee had made!' She pauses. 'And your Dad apologised to me that he uses that word Zoe put on the Scrabble board...'

'Yes, it is rather naughty of me,' Dad says.

'Would've got me a triple word score!' says my sister.

Zoe, happy after whatever Dad said to them, goes into the bathroom, comes out, falls into her bed, and is asleep. I'm under my duvet, using my breath to warm the air inside the tent it makes. I still haven't unwrapped that book.

Chapter 52

The wind's blowing the rain against the window again: at first, I heave the duvet up over my head. Then, I wonder what we'll all do today. Okay, last night I counted four good things about these summer holidays, even if it's not the weather we wanted.

I remember the book. It'll look a bit rude of me if the present is still sitting there unopened when they all come down to breakfast. I slide out of my soft warm cave. Zoe's asleep. I open the door and listen. No voices or movement. I creep downstairs and into the family room. It's full of things from the party lying about. There are a couple of small glasses: did some adults have a late-night dram? I grab the shiny parcel and hurry back to bed with it.

Undo the ribbon, carefully unpick the sellotape, the paper's very thick and doesn't tear. Here's the book... On the hard cover (there's no dust cover), photo of a path going through pretty countryside towards distant hills. Title: *Finding Your Path*. In smaller writing: *For Girls* (is there a version *For Boys*, I wonder?). *Includes journaling pages*. What are these? In a printed book? I flip through. Each chapter ends: *Things to think about. Note down your thoughts below*, with a couple of blank pages. The chapter headings slip past my eyes... *Friendships... School subjects... What kind of person are you... Relationships...* Embarrassing, deffo not me, sounds like Base Camp stuff — Zoe might like it — could pass it on! Inside the front cover, in Uncle Ian's writing, a Bible quote, and *Always in our prayers, growing up is a challenge!* Gosh, how'm I going to say thank you politely?

Oh, and there's something else, a pink envelope, what's inside? Ah, relief, a John Lewis voucher, wow, £50, also a bit embarrassing, but at least, like, normal. Inside, Aunt Sue's handwriting (I guess): *Have a fun day out shopping with a friend, Alice!* So, OK, they are human.

'Not yet morning...' From the bed opposite, about a metre from mine, comes Zoe's sleepy voice.

'What?' I lean under my bed and drop the book and the token on the only spare bit of floor.

'Not yet morning.' She turns her back.

'Yes, it is,' I say. 'What's gone wrong with summer?'

'Climate change of course, stupid.'

'I *know*. This weather should convince some of them how totally wrong they are, the people that think global warming means more dry, hot weather.'

'They don't care. We have to make them. I tried to tell Becky that, but she didn't really listen.'

'Hey, Dad didn't give you both a psalm to learn, did he?'

'What? No! What he did was...'

She doesn't say more, as suddenly both our phones ring, together. I open mine, a text from Nina: *'On amazing art course near Brighton. Yes! Met a girl. C U soon, hugz, Ninaxx'*

Gosh... So Nina's found somebody, away from school, which was what she wanted. As I try to imagine this properly, suddenly Zoe's out of bed, seizing my phone, shaking my other arm for attention, hissing, 'Are you *listening? Earth to Alice!* like Dad says... *Listen to this*: Rothko – he's sent me a weird text. Want to hear it?'

'Is this some game you're having?'

'Alice! I think it's important. He's not stupid.'

'No, but he's an eight-year-old boy. He was into knights and battles when I stayed with Daze.'

'Well this is what he says: *Hiya Z, What's your hol like? It's like in a movie here — something horrible's happened, but Mum won't tell me more. Tell your Mum 2 call mine? Rx.* What do you think? Should we tell Mum and Dad?'

'Why?'

'Because he says something horrible's happened? Like, to find out if they're okay themselves?'

'I can't see why. It's probably road accident or something. But he doesn't say, *happened to us*, does he?'

'Well, no. But he might mean it. Why tell me, otherwise?'

'Because he needed something interesting to say? Because he's a kid with a big imagination? I didn't know you texted with him.'

'I don't think it's about his pretend knights. I think it's all real.'

'I think you're wasting time. We need to get up.' I am totally unconvinced it's more than a game.

'Where are they, Alice? Are they on holiday somewhere?'

'I think they're in Scotland, 'cos Mum had a quick phone call yesterday with Daze and she said that they might go to Edinburgh and visit Aunt Val, maybe when we're there.'

'Oh, thanks Alice. Nobody told me that.'

'Well you know, all sorts of stuff was going on, like you and Becky...'

'Yeah well, anyway, the point is, he wants us to get Mum to phone...'

'Oh, come on, he's a bored kid who lives with his Mum, it's school holidays and if they're at Aunt Val's – well he thinks she's a boring old lady who teaches knitting and weaving. He's trying to engage you in his fantasy game.'

'How do you know that? Suppose there's been an accident, like to Aunt Val or something.'

'Oh, all right then, show the text to Mum and see what she thinks.'

That's that settled then. As we follow the scent of coffee and warming croissants downstairs, I'm thinking about Nina: *people like me* she says. Lots of women who like women? After the exams, Nina began making these big hints about her sexuality. Has she now come out, to her family? To her friends? To people at this art camp she's on? What about Jack, her boyfriend?... Is Nina bisexual? If so, I know two. And it's more common than is talked about. It's, like, becoming normal. Maybe it always was – only people pretended?

Downstairs, Granny Fee spots me, 'Oh there you are, pet!' and gives me things to do like table laying, and making more scotch pancakes (the scent wasn't croissants after all, though I'd prefer them!) 'How many of us today?' I ask her, 'I mean, later on? Is everyone coming over again?'

'Alex'll bring his family later, I expect.'

'What about – Uncle Euan, Aunt Margaret, David?'

'Euan and Margaret will be here.'

Uncle Ian and Aunt Sue are coming down the passage, talking. They drop their voices as they enter. Then Becky, Martha, and Iso burst through the door and get into trouble for pushing each other.

Is the dreich weather making everyone cross? It's a lot nastier than yesterday's sun and sharp showers. Or maybe Ian and Sue are annoyed that our Dad dared to admonish their Becky for upsetting our Zoe? That's more likely.

We sit down to eat, Becky and Zoe sitting together, looking happy, drizzling maple syrup on their pancakes, trying to write their names. 'S'not fair,' Becky giggles, 'your name's too short!'

'Okay,' Zoe says, and she takes more syrup and goes on writing.

'What's that?'

'Changed my name – look!'

It looks like a mess but Zoe tells us '*Zoella*, will that do?'

Everyone laughs. Finding something everyone can laugh about and change the mood is so like this family. The nice side. Whatever, I'm happy that Dad got them to be friends again: that's two good things he did: that and saving me from Uncle Ian's embarrassing speech. David's not here though: I didn't see him go, I don't remember seeing him after the party. So what does that mean? I'd like another chat, maybe to hear more about when he and Dad were growing up. Also, if we're all expected to attend church at First Truly, whether maybe he's going somewhere else and I could go with him? What I won't do of course, is talk about Nina, and ask about how bisexuality works! Though it is an intriguing idea: how can a person be attracted to both men and women, how do they choose which to settle with?

'I – wonder – d'you know where David is today? I had a question I wanted to ask him. Is he coming over later?'

'As far as I know. But David is his own person,' Uncle Ian replies.

'Oh, okay.' Odd description: *his own person?*

'Can I help? I hope you'll be coming to church with us?' says Aunt Sue, leaning across the table.

'Oh no. I mean, it's okay, thank you!' They give me a look. I didn't say no to First Truly, did I? Should've made that clearer! I said no to the help. Though I'm not that keen, probably better not to try to explain. Anything. But what did Uncle Ian mean, David is his own person? Makes his own decisions? Doesn't tell other people what he's doing?

Aunt Sue smiles across the table: as I try to grin back at her, she's already turning away, the smile gone.

What did that mean? Like, was it meant to be a message? What sort of message? A 'Don't ask about David' message? No, it was a 'What about the present' message!

I quickly say, 'Thank you so much for your present. I opened it this morning, in bed. It was such a lovely parcel, I hardly wanted to undo it!'

'Oh, so glad you loved the paper! I got it from a new stationery boutique in Hexham. They sell beautiful notebooks, great for journaling,' Aunt Sue says, the smile back on her face.

'I'm really thrilled with the token, incredibly generous. Oh — and the book looks very interesting!' I'm trying to apply David's thoughts about family culture here, but hoping that this won't lead into a discussion with Uncle Ian. Fortunately he seems a bit preoccupied this morning. Uncle Ian and Aunt Sue can look quite bored, or cross, if you catch them when they don't know you're looking.

Chewing on a Scotch pancake, I have this creepy feeling they disapproved of me going on Hadrian's Wall with David. They may think he's a bad influence, but it's not their business.

Outside is looking brighter now. The rain's stopped, the wind's blown the clouds away, and the sun's out. Dad arrives, with a Sunday newspaper. The three adults begin to discuss whether and where everyone's going to attend church. Dad's explaining that Mum is going to 'do something with Erin this morning', and this remark is obviously reflected in Ian's disapproving silence. How can he be so different to Granny Fee? How could Granny Fee have been married to Grandpa Alisdair for so long? What's so wrong about a walk and a coffee on a Sunday morning? It's a holiday, they're all staying in the same B and B, and they get along. The grown-ups don't say it, but they make it very clear when they dislike one another's choices. Bit like when cats don't fight, but sit very still, staring, and making growly noises.

Breakfast over, the group's breaking up: Aunt Sue herds her kids out to clean their teeth and get ready for church. Uncle Ian's disappeared to do whatever pastors do. Dad's forced Granny to sit down and chat, so she's perching sideways on her chair, like a bird about to fly off, and clutching a jar of marmalade. I pick up the newspaper: the headline reads *widespread flooding*, and details reveal *including Oxfordshire*, but not exactly where. Could a really big flood make the canal overflow Fabian's garden? Then I see, in a corner of the page, there's a story about a family on holiday 'found unconscious' at a property in Cornwall... sad... I think of Charlie at Chapel House and wonder if they can really forget about Eliot's illness.

Aunt Sue appears from the hall, with raised eyebrows, and addresses Granny Fee: 'Are you coming to church with us today? Iso's class is doing a song.' Granny says 'I'll just need ten minutes, pet. To get ready. And I thought I'd stack your dishwasher. You're not going straightaway are you?'

'Oh Mam, you don't need to!' says Aunt Sue, shaking her head.

And before any more argument, Dad springs into action, grabbing plates and cutlery off the table, 'Mam, you go! Alice'll give me a hand and we'll clear up... go, or I shall change my mind.'

Granny hesitates. I'd better show willing, hadn't I? Gathering plates and mugs, opening the dishwasher. I wonder where Zoe's disappeared to. The churchgoers have finally sorted themselves. Ian and family are taking Granny Fee to First Truly. Dad's off to Hexham Abbey, taking Zoe who wants to see something historical in the crypt there, and as he says, 'Anyone else? There's room in the car for four more!'

And I'm free. The sun's shining, the garden is sparkling outside, it's a perfect day to take a few more photos of the Manse before it's pulled down. Once the kitchen's tidy, I'm off to find my camera. Then I prowl around, looking at this squarish, granite-built house (even the building looks disapproving), moving up and down the garden, considering the best angles and how to use the sun to give the whole composition a bit of a lighter feel. My trainers squeak on the wet grass, birds arrive to peck for worms, I wonder if I'll be here all morning on my own?

While I'm focusing on the tree house (nice that Uncle Ian kept it for his kids – makes me feel he is human after all) another text arrives on my phone. This is from my cousin Chloe. Cameron and Chloe are planning a walk in the gorgeous Northumberland Country Park, and maybe a drink afterwards. I'm invited. Yes!

Cameron drives us. It's a bit damp and windy, but we do a bit of a walk and then find a village pub, and talk about the family. When we get back to the Manse, Cam goes off to the kitchen and makes what he calls his 'famous Turkish coffee substitute' (instant coffee made very strong indeed, and served in Granny's smallest tea cups, with brown sugar and a glass of water) which we elegantly sip, to dispel any wooziness (I slightly regret my glass of cider). We devour left-over nibbles from the ceilidh feast, perched on garden chairs in the big marquee.

I say: 'Do you know where David is? I had a really helpful chat with him about careers and stuff, and he talked to me like two grown-ups having a discussion not like a teacher. I was hoping to go on a bit with it today.'

'Good,' says Chloe, 'he's actually great at that kind of thing. Far as I know he was still at the B and B when we left, not sure really.'

'Doesn't he have a sister? Chrissie, isn't it? I don't think I've ever met her. I wonder why she's not here. Do they all get on?'

'She couldn't make the date, 'cos she's like a high-flying lawyer with some international company, and she's in Hong Kong or somewhere. But she sent one of her super bouncy messages of good wishes and stuff. Ian stuck it on that noticeboard he has in the hall, "Family News and Views"'. Cam makes a face.

They exchange glances, and then Chloe, having casually taken a bite of a cheese scone, asks, 'Did you know that David's bisexual?'

'Er... I overheard something, but I wasn't sure,' I say.

'You can be sure,' Chloe says, mysteriously.

'Okay! And one of my friends thinks she is...'

Before I can ask, why is it necessary for me to know? Zoe appears through the flap of the marquee, looks around, spots us, and disappears a moment to yell, 'They're here!' back towards the house. Then coming back again, she says, 'And, you'd better be quick, it's roast beef with Yorkshire pud!'

On the way in, Chloe says to me: 'By the way, in case you didn't know, Mullins family gatherings pretty well always end up with a prayer meeting, compulsory attendance. It's a bit grim, but it shouldn't last long.'

'We all have to be there? What are you meant to do?'

'Nothing. Keep your head down, and think of England,' says Cameron.

I wish David would come back, he made me feel better during that awful present-giving.

Chapter 53

PRAYERS AT THE MANSE AND ANOTHER WEE CHAT

Lunch is absolutely classic: made by Granny Fee and Aunt Sue, who put a joint of beef to roast before leaving for church, then dashed back from church and did the Yorkshire pud and veggies. Mum and Erin (who doesn't let us call her 'aunt') complete their contribution — an angel cake — while each have a glass of wine, from yesterday evening's leftovers. Great-uncle Euan and Aunt Margaret arrive, but no David — I'm a bit disappointed.

After this huge and satisfying meal, at which everyone seems really relaxed (perhaps because they've done their duty in church?) there's a ritual washing-up, apparently a family tradition. No dishwasher, the whole family join in, men do the wet part. Dad, sleeves rolled up, is at the sink, and there's a crowd of tea-towel wielding women and teenagers, Mum and Granny, Chloe, Cameron, and me (they seem to want to make sure they know where we are!). Uncle Ian, Aunt Sue, and Iso, meanwhile, have disappeared.

Becky, Martha, and Zoe are 'putting away' the plates and cutlery, even though Zoe doesn't know where anything lives. In between trekking back and forth to the cupboards, with dinner plates, veg dishes, and cooking equipment, Zoe's full of chatter about the Roman Crypt at Hexham Abbey, where there are inscriptions! And about how she's going to ask Uncle Alex, who's a science teacher, about studying environmental science when she goes to Uni. 'Which isn't for at least four years, but I've decided to do that,' she says. Okay, A level decisions made, well in advance, by my sister!

The front door's opened by someone arriving who has a key: it's Uncle Alex with his family. So Zoe can have her chat. But still no David, so I can't have more of mine. All the family are here now, except David, his sister Chrissie, and Dad's sister Kirsty and her partner and family, who apparently never come to anything.

Children, those under about eleven, are hived off into a creche: Becky and Martha in charge, surrounded by toys and with a kiddie video, in the family room. Uncle Ian directs everyone else into the smart lounge, stuffed as we are with lunch, to find seats. I go for a dining chair (there isn't any choice really, looks like younger ones on the floor or the dining chairs, specially moved in for the occasion). I find Dad's grinning across at me from the armchair which was Grandpa Alisdair's, which he's brought in from the family room.

Everyone suddenly goes still and incredibly quiet, all of them looking at Dad. What for? Uncle Ian calls for complete silence for one minute, to settle ourselves. Then he says 'Max?' And then Dad's voice – *Dad's voice?* kicks off the proceedings by *saying a prayer*.

I can't believe this. I die inside. I gaze at the floor, sweat prickling all over me, wanting to disappear. He piles it on, asking for 'God's blessing on this time, in view of the great changes in many of our lives'. I wish my ears had flaps to close them.

But it's also fascinating, in a creepy way. It's not an act — he means it.

Then the door slides open a crack, making a soft swooshing sound on the carpet, and I glance up to see Zoe shimmy through, closing the door quietly behind her. She creeps across and sits at my feet. I touch her shoulders. I whisper. 'Thought you were doing creche?'

'Nope. Just sorting the video for Aunt Sue.'

Everyone's head is bowed. Dad so obviously knows how to conduct a prayer meeting. I wonder why they got him to do it, since we're not really okay with God as far as they're concerned. Maybe simply his position as eldest son of the pastor? But, people's spontaneous prayers are so embarrassing. They're going up like incense at the St Hildie's Easter service Dad dragged us along to. Like letters someone's thrown on a fire, twirling in the smoke. Are we a great big extended family wasting our time on a sunny afternoon, talking into a void? Or – is someone really there?

Does Mariam take her religion seriously? *We're very liberal...* that's all she said about her family's beliefs: but then they've all had to give in to her uncle, or whoever it is, organising her sister's wedding overseas...

Sneakily, I text Fabian: *we're having a prayer meeting here —!* He responds straight away: *Wow. I guess no Hail Marys though! FXX.*

As I drag my brain back into the room, someone's praying for the wrecking crew who'll pull down the old Manse, and the builders who'll construct the new one. There's a long prayer about all us young Mullinses and our futures. Good idea: if God is really here, he might listen to my problems... I wish I knew... Finally, Uncle Ian thanks God and all of us for blessing his ministry (did we?). And Dad wraps it up, by getting everyone to join in the *Our Father* prayer.

Everyone now looks up expectantly as Dad goes through to the family room, where he pounds out a hymn tune on the piano loud enough to hear through the wall. *Great is thy Faithfulness,* which is sung loudly, with lots of enthusiasm, as if we were a football crowd! Apparently it was Grandpa Alisdair's favourite hymn, and it always makes Mum catch Dad's eye, and they smile, though of course today they're in different rooms and can't. And though we ask, they never share the joke with me and Zoe. I gently nudge my foot against Zoe's bum, and she looks up, and we smile, anyway.

'God, that was creepy,' I whisper to her as everyone is yawning and stretching, chatting and moving towards the door.

'Which bit?'

'All of it!' I say, with emphasis. 'Dad playing the pastor role?'

'I didn't think Dad was creepy. It was like Base Camp, only more so.'

'Blimey!'

I find Mum next to me, and I say quietly: 'Mum, why do you and Dad always laugh about that hymn?'

Mum whispers back: 'Grandpa Alisdair had a habit of ringing up at a particular time of day, about the time that Dad had got in from work, which annoyed him, 'cos he was tired. There's a line in the hymn, "O God, my Father", which Dad used to find himself spontaneously quoting when the phone rang at that time.'

'Didn't he think that was irreverent or something?'

'Well, yes, I suppose so, but that was part of the joke.'

We then realise that there's some shushing, and as everyone falls silent and stops moving about, Uncle Ian announces: 'Time for a breather, everyone. Alex is organizing outdoor activities for the bairns, followed by story time in the marquee with Sue and Caitlin and I believe Jenny has kindly offered to help. Margaret will lead a walk around some of our favourite family landmarks for the grown-up folk, ending back here in time for those involved to attend the Manse business meeting — you know who you are. Tea at six o'clock!'

Faint applause greets this, and once again I think what a weird culture they have. And that Uncle Ian has reverted to the northern way of calling the evening meal 'tea'.

Uncle Alex, in teacher mode, gathers a crowd of younger cousins who've been released from the creche. Everyone from Martha and Iso, to Uncle Alex's little girls in their pink and white organza princess outfits, and including some neighbours' kids. 'Well, now,' (rubbing his hands together) 'any of you bairns for croquet?'

We're all stuck in the passage between the front and back of the house, squeezing past the staircase while someone in front is shimmying in though the half-open door to the understairs bathroom, and several kids at the back start pushing.

'Move along there – keep the team together! Everyone into the garden!' Uncle Alex calls, supervising the crowd.

As we reach the family room, we fan out towards the garden. Becky and Martha carefully carry out the croquet kit, one each end of the long wooden box, onto the lawn. They begin setting out the hoops on the bit of grass not covered by the marquee. A cloud of midges is dancing in the sunshine.

I'm wondering how to escape being corralled into helping with the 'wee ones' (I notice that Zoe's enthusiastically unpacking mallets), when there's a touch on my arm. I look round and it's Chloe, who says, 'Quick, let's go up the tree house and get away from everything!'

We creep away round the back of the marquee, past the veg patch and the compost heap, and quickly climb the ladder and get comfortable, hidden from everyone.

'Why were you so keen to tell me that about David?' I ask.

'Well, you may as well be prepared — if you meet him somewhere away from the family, *she* might be with him. But there might be problems in the family about it, so she's had a low profile so far.'

'Do you know who it is? Have you met her?'

'No, sorry! But there seems to be a bit of gossip that she's not at all conventional. Hence the low profile!'

This makes me feel even more positive about David, as well as confirming my guesses from behind the kitchen door.

'I wanted to talk to him about something else. My Mum kept trying to make me be friends with someone I knew at nursery.' I explain how it all happened. 'It was awful because Mum didn't explain the reason — and it was, like, a really serious reason — until just before we came here, and this friend, Charlie, isn't my type at all. But now I know the reason I feel bad about trying to put her off all the time. Like, this weekend there was a music festival she wanted me to go to, and I was *so* relieved that we had to come here.'

'Your Mum really should have told you about it from the beginning.'

We talk about this a bit more, and then we chat about university life, friends (including boyfriends — she's with someone called Andy), and stuff like that for ages.

Suddenly there's a rustle of leaves and we realize someone's standing under the treehouse. 'I had a good idea you girls might be up in the treehouse and not on the walk with the oldies! I'd like Alice to come and give me a spot of help with tea — I don't need the both of you, Chloe,' says Granny Fee's voice. Chloe says, 'Crumbs, what's the time? I'm supposed to be texting with Andy!'

I scramble out of the tree house, and Granny leads the way into the kitchen. The table is covered with plates of 'finger food', but there's also something else there: my memory box. Of course, she said she'd remind me about it.

'I'd like you to help me with the cakes, but Aunt Sue has made some savoury things and a salad for tea, so before she comes through from doing story time with the bairns, can we have a talk about your memory box? I've remembered you said you might have something else to put in it, and I wanted to give you the opportunity while we've a quiet moment, and maybe have a wee chat. Or would you like to take the box home with you now?'

'Can you keep the box for me a bit longer?' I ask. 'And I have got something I'd like to put in it, for now.'

I dash upstairs and run down with my cross-body bag, where Ianthe's ring, in its box, has been ever since the weekend in London. Feeling so unhappy with the idea of being part of a dynasty of scientific women, I don't really want to wear it like I've agreed to be next in the line. It'll be safe with Granny Fee, and if I feel differently in a few years, I can get it back and wear it. I hold the ring out for her to see, and explain what it is.

'It was lovely of her to've left it to me but I don't think I'm quite ready for it, somehow. And we're not really allowed to wear jewellery at school.'

Granny smiles, 'Oh, the famous great-grandma? The suffragette?'

'Not quite – a bit later than them! But she was an innovator and she specialised in women's health.'

'Well, that's all right then.'

I put it back in its small box and hand it over. Granny says, 'I'll look after your box, for now, and take it to my lovely new bungalow. And you let me know, if you want to wear the ring later. I had thought you might want the box for your own memories, not my ones about you!'

'No – please keep it for now. Maybe I'll want it all when I – leave school or something?'

'Well, you can have it any time, pet.'

'I mean – I'd like to think of it being up here, with you?'

'Well, thank you,' she says. 'I'll keep it safe and you let me know…'

The box is put aside, and I feel relieved not to have that responsibility any more. Now Granny switches to her practical voice. 'I'd like you to cut up the cakes, please, and slice the scones for me to butter. You've such neat hands. Like your mam.'

I take the silver cake knife from the dresser drawer. Suddenly I see in my mind the drawer cast aside as builder's rubbish — or the whole old-fashioned dresser, 1930s at least, carefully taken out, and sold as vintage kitchen furniture to a family in Newcastle. 'Thick slices, thin slices? Eights maybe? More than that?' I say, feeling the tension, the sort you have when you're scared or sad, in my bum, and the backs of my legs. Even I shall miss coming to the old Manse!

Granny advises on how many slices I should make from each cake. The Dundee, full of fruit and laced with alcohol, goes into twelve slices, the sponges into eights. I halve the scones, and Granny does the buttering.

That's not all of it. As I carefully work on the baked eats, Granny constructs one of her wee chats. First, we exchange the facts: yes, I am thinking about my future, and yes, I may do science A-levels and follow Mum and Dad to Cambridge. And yes, I do have some other ideas. 'And what are those, pet?'

'I'm not really quite sure… We haven't made the tea yet, should I put the kettle on?'

'There's plenty of time. Come here, Alice…' We hug, Granny, scented with the smell of baking and lavender fragrance, is smaller than me, and gentler. When I was little her hugs were great big strong squeeze ones. We sit, or rather we kind of *stumblify*, onto two kitchen chairs, at the big pine table.

'Och, I remember you as such a wee thing, when your Daddy brought you here for your Grandad to do the baptism... you know you're a baptised Truly Reformed Presbyterian don't you?'

Of course, I don't remember that happening, but the story's been told and told. Mum and Dad have an album of pictures from back then. Me and Zoe both, wearing white baby dresses with bonnets and shawls like little old lady babies, traditional as fairy tales, for our initiations. David is my godfather, and Alex is Zoe's. We have godmothers: Dad's sisters Erin and Kirsty.

'God doesn't give up, even if we give up, or choose to ignore him a while. I'm praying you girls will both come to know him. And then, listen to this, Alice,' (says Granny, as I'm trying to remember when we last saw Kirsty and her family — she must've noticed my inattention — how?) '...your calling will be clearer to you. For now, whatever your next step is, he will be guiding you... he can use everything if you... if you are willing...'

This isn't the same as Dad taking charge of organising the family prayer meeting, using those weird special prayer phrases. This is like a whole different scenario, like everything works via God in Granny's world. And it's not about generations being different, it's another culture. Is faith in God – real? Am I being asked to do faith seriously?

Far too difficult. A tear splashes down. Guess Granny spots it, though I hope her eyes aren't good enough. I rub it into the polished boards with the toe of one dusty, grass-stained trainer. Yes, she'd probably prefer me in a nice dress and white sandals, but it's 2007. And I know she'd like me and Zoe to share her faith.

Granny now gently ends the hug. I turn away towards the table. For now, we've closed down that solemn, difficult conversation, so we dry our eyes and complete the food preparation. Before we take the big trays out, Granny adds, 'You must know that verse which says, *My grace is sufficient for you?*'

And then she leaves a second for that to sink into me, and as we pick up the trays, says firmly, 'Right, here we come, everybody!' as Mum appears through the door Granny was about to go out through.

'And here it comes, the rain!' says Mum, 'I'm so sorry, Fee – can I take that tray from you? Where are we transferring to, for tea?'

So we're all back to the family room. Immediately Great-uncle Euan and Great-aunt Margaret appear, evidently hunting some tea. Followed by Aunt Sue talking about pushing tables together to make a buffet. The small kids are coming in through the drizzly rain. And Granny's organizing Great-uncle Euan to say family grace before tea: 'Will you do the honours for everyone? Using that Selkirk Grace again?'

Chapter 54

BAD NEWS

Tea is arranged on two tables pushed together, and we all take what we want and pile it onto our plates.

Zoe comes rushing up to me, trying to show me her phone in one hand, while balancing a huge pile of food on her plate in the other hand. 'Look at this – Alice! This could be urgent – another text, look…!'

'Is it Rothko again?'

'Yes, just look!'

'What happened about the first one?'

'Oh, Dad said "If it's really important he'll send another one". And then I turned my phone off in church and I've only just turned it on. Just look, can you!'

Zoe's holding the phone in my face, by now. I try to hold it still, while balancing my plate of food. The text says: *'didn't you tell your parents? yr Mum shd phone mine. it's urgent, pls tell her!'*

'OK, maybe it's like Dad said, and it is important, or anyway we have to do something about it. Let's show it to Mum then.'

'Finally!' Zoe says.

We find Mum among the massed crowd around the tables. Zoe gets her attention and shows her both Rothko's texts. She looks more concerned than I expected. She extracts herself and her plate of food, leads us out to the hallway, and motions for us three to sit down on the stairs. She then says, 'Zoe, can I read those again, love? I couldn't really concentrate back there.' Zoe hands her phone over, and Mum reads Rothko's texts, aloud.

Zoe dumps her plate on the low windowsill beside the stairs, moves in close to Mum, and hangs over, so she can see the screen, gazing at the text. 'So, are you going to phone her now? Daze? Please? He's sent two texts so it must be important!'

'Mmm. Can I keep this?' Mum says, and as Zoe nods, she slips Zoe's phone into the pocket of her jeans. But she doesn't look as if she thinks phoning Daze is urgent.

'I talked with Daze yesterday and nothing was wrong.... I'll call her after tea,' Mum says. And if I can't get her, I'll call Val, assuming they're at hers.'

'Please,' Zoe says, her hands in tight fists and looking desperate, 'please? He's sent two like that today. Anything could've happened. Do it now!'

'Yes, shouldn't we give Rothko a chance, and look like we believe him?' I add, 'he thinks it's important, whatever it is.'

And, with what I'd call an indulgent smile, Mum pulls Zoe's phone out of her pocket. Just then Granny emerges from the family room with a teapot, on her way to refill it in the kitchen, and Mum waves the phone at her: 'Just calling my sister, Daisy – shouldn't take long...'

'Of course — use the study again, Jenny pet, away from the noise!'

Mum slips into that grim front room, now Uncle Ian's book-lined study, which I remember as a scary place when Grandpa Alisdair was alive.

She comes back quickly, 'Daze's phone is turned off: so I called Val. I'm afraid she said they're not coming to her, they told her they've had a change of plan.'

Not coming to her? My stomach drops. 'Shucks,' I say, remembering halfway through not to use a word the Manse family wouldn't like. So disappointing. 'I had things I wanted to chat with Daze about.' Which were, of course, questions about that strange, powerful painting.

'Sorry love,' Mum says. 'Was it urgent?'

'S'pose not, really. Only about her work?'

'Can't you keep trying Daze?' Zoe asks, almost jumping up and down.

'Look, let's have our tea, and then, I'll try her phone again.'

'Bet she forgets,' Zoe murmurs at me, as we eat, still sitting on the stairs.

'We'll remind her. Let's get some cake before the gannets snaffle it all up? And maybe we should stay in the family room, so they don't come and ask if we're all right?'

After the tea's all cleared away, and after several tries, Mum finally catches Daze. We hear her voice, on speaker phone, 'Oh Rothko did – well, really, no worries. Nothing you can do – get on with your holiday. I'll deal with what needs doing.'

But then, as everyone's sorting themselves out to find indoor things to do, Mum's phone goes again, and Mum talks in a low voice, walking up the stairs so that nobody else hears, but I can tell it's Daze on the other end.

She's away a long time. Everyone starts arguing about whether to have some dancing in the marquee again. Then Mum comes back down. 'I'm looking for Dad, where is he?'

Dad, who was just going to get his violin from the B and B so that he could play for the dancing, reappears at the door.

I watch her showing him the text on Zoe's phone. He stares at it a second, looks round and says, 'Sorry all, I won't be free to help with music tonight, Jen and I've got something to sort out.'

Mum and Dad hurry off, Mum saying 'I tried my mother – it went to voicemail – thank God I remembered she's in France...'

I reach out to stop them, 'Please...?' but they shake me off. So now it looks certain that whatever's happened it's seriously important. But why bother Granny Caro – unless it happened at, or to, Chapel House?

I start following after them, towards the study. Mum's saying '...she's with friends — a kind of college reunion with – I think my father's there

369

as well…' and Dad interrupts and says something like 'not worrying Caro at this stage'.

The door closes behind them and I turn away: jumping to conclusions isn't a mature attitude. Though this sounds like there's some trouble at Chapel House, so is it about Charlie and her parents?

That cold feeling creeps down my back, and settles in my bum and the backs of my legs: suppose Charlie's dad has – collapsed or worse? That could happen, couldn't it?

Though if that's the scary thing, Rothko wouldn't understand it.

Maybe, I think, they are the *family found unconscious in Cornwall?* Wasn't that what the newspaper said?

Mum suddenly opens the door, puts her head round and calls to me, 'Where's Zo-zo? Can you find her?'

'What's going on?'

'Tell you later. Can you find Zoe for us? And bring her upstairs?'

'If I know why.'

Mum beckons me in, and pretty much hisses at me that we need to have a family conflab – whatever that is – and Zoe needs to be there too. That cold creepy feeling slinks back up my legs. Looks like we're having to leave the chattering, laughing party atmosphere where the worst problem is about who can play reels along with Uncle Ian on flute! I go to find Zo-zo, while Mum and Dad climb the stairs to our bedroom.

'I told you!' says my sister, when I find her in the marquee, along with Becky and Uncle Alex and Aunt Cait, and we hurry back through the rain and into the house.

'Yeah, you were right, okay. I hope they've got in touch in time, whatever's going on.'

We sit on our beds, me and Mum, Zoe and Dad. The room's so small, our knees all almost connect across the divide.

Even so, Dad leans forward to speak, rather quietly, 'Well you've been given some idea of the seriousness of this, by Rothko, who seems to be a very astute wee boy,' he says, sounding far more Scottish than he needs. This usually highlights what's coming isn't going to be fun.

'Your Mam's been in touch with your aunt Daze, and it seems we've a problem with our holiday.'

Mum leans forwards, 'Oh, do get on with it, Max, they already know something's up, from Rothko, now they need some facts!'

'The facts are — well we don't know many facts yet, but what we do know is worrying enough that we – your Mam and I – need to suspend our holiday and – go down to Chapel House and see what's actually happening and be there for Daze – and of course for the Parker Pollards.'

Zoe draws in her breath noisily, and *'What?'* she says. 'What scary thing was it then?'

'He means we have to go now, without visiting Val or the Western Isles,' Mum says, 'there's no other choice – so...'

'So you don't know – but we'll be dumped here till you get back or what?' Zoe says.

'No love, best thing is, we all go back...'

'What, back home? And then – your leave will've run out so... what about our holiday?' Zoe practically shouts, but I interrupt:

'Hang on – Daze and Rothko are in *Cornwall,* I thought they were in Scotland, I was looking forward to seeing Daze... so are you saying – did whatever it was happen to Charlie's family?' I see a surfing accident, I see a power boat mowing down surfers, I see Charlie arsing about with a boy she's met and falling over the cliffs onto rocks... I do not want to see what the newspaper referred to. 'Are they, are they okay?'

'It's not Charlie – it's not only Charlie...' says Mum.

'It's not clear exactly what happened,' says Dad.

'The neighbour found them all...'

'What? *Found?*

'In Chapel House, then, it happened in Chapel House, didn't it?' Zoe's angry, or, or heartbroken, or something. 'It's *our family's* house... *What did they do? Why did you let them stay there?'*

'Ssh,' I say, 'Mum told me a few things,' I look over at Mum, 'shall we?'

Mum doesn't answer. She crosses over to where Zoe is, and she puts an arm around my sister, which leaves me stranded, heart in mouth, pictures of disasters buzzing round my brain. I say:

'I saw in the newspaper: *A family was found unconscious at a house in Cornwall.* That was them, Charlie's family, wasn't it?'

'It was.'

'Nobody would be staying there except us, if Granny Caro hadn't started to make plans – remember she wants to sell it... why's Daze gone there? What – what caused...?'

'Daze went down as soon as she knew.'

'Wait – why? What knocked them out? Carbon monoxide? But Granny's got alarms all over the place! Doesn't she have – inspections or whatever?'

'Alice, we don't know much yet. It's early days, Charlie and her mum are in the ICU at the Royal Cornwall – I've talked to the consultant. They have a good chance...'

'And her dad? I mean, the things you said – he's like, not well — was he there, in the house?'

'He – didn't make it, love.' Mum's hand is on my knee. As if that helps. I say nothing. What can I? 'It's a lot to take in,' Mum says. 'For all of us.'

Zoe has begun to cry. I'm shaking, I feel like I need an extra jumper, I wish I had my fluffy winter slippers (which I left at home) on my feet, which are now frozen. Dad quits sitting on Zoe's bed, comes across to me, opens his arms, and I fall into a huge hug. I cling to him, shamelessly, and bury my face in his shoulder, inhaling the disinfectant scent of the bar soap Uncle Ian's family use in their bathroom. 'Oh, poor Charlie, poor Charlie... it's not a holiday, it's all awful...'

We all sit silent, Mum hugging with Zoe, me hugging with Dad. Suddenly knowing I love my family very, very much, and we're all together inside this horrible thing, I'm crying too. Just a bit. Well, more than that. And I've been a terrible friend to Charlie – that's what's making me cry.

Well, Zoe and I quieten down, and mop ourselves up. Dad makes a silly face and says, 'And Alice has drenched this sweater through to my shirt!', so I take off my jumper and drape it rather solemnly over his shoulders, 'Aw, Dad, I am *so sorry*, please take mine...' Which is meant to be being light-hearted and makes us all laugh. Then the parents, of course, have to go downstairs to let the other adults know we'll be leaving in the morning.

While they're doing that, I say to Zoe, 'Let's go and find Chloe and Cam and tell them this horrible news.'

I can see they're shocked, but they let me talk about Eliot being ill with this auto-immune thing, and how awful I feel that I really didn't want to re-friend with Charlie who I hadn't seen since nursery. Zoe sits quietly beside me while we talk. I think maybe she is experiencing a big step up towards the grown-up world, that moment when it hits you that people, sometimes people you know, do things like – whatever has gone on at Chapel House.

I say, 'We don't know exactly how this happened, but it looks dodgy to me, if Granny Caro has all the right alarms set. And if she didn't, then she's in trouble. No way someone didn't do something stupid or wrong or both.'

Cameron looks thoughtful, and then (unhelpfully), adds that 'What is wrong or stupid to some people may not look that way to somebody else. And right and wrong are archaic concepts in today's world.'

I snap back, 'Well that's totally idiot crazy, how do we decide on anything then? Can it be right to steal or kill people?'

'In a war, people who kill people come back as heroes,' he says, and he looks straight at me, in my eyes. With such a satisfied face. I feel ready to kill him – or at least his argument.

'Yeah, and people who kill people not in a war are in trouble,' I say, which really means nothing, and I wish I'd not said it.

Zoe curls her feet underneath her in the armchair she's sitting in, and almost sucks her thumb, but doesn't. Chloe says, 'Don't listen to my brother being clever. I promised Iso and Lily a bedtime story, could you two help me?'

'Haven't the Uncle Alex family gone home?'

'Nope – they'll go about ten I think. I guess there'll be another prayer meeting, for your friends. Then there'll be supper – Northern style. All the kids – Iso, Lily, her little sister, and Iso's big sisters, are all in their pjs and snuggled up together in Becky's room.'

At least this gets us away from Cam's philosophy or whatever it was. We, Chloe, Zo-zo, and me, go upstairs and read them Thomas the Tank Engine stories, taking parts, which the kids really like.

After that, when we hear everyone else out in the hallway talking and moving about, Chloe and I run downstairs. Just as Chloe guessed, the Mullins family have got prayer high on the evening's agenda, now that they know what's happened. They want to pray, but they argue about what kind of prayer. Erin's keen on something called Compline, an evening service they say in convents and monasteries. I agree with her, since, even though I don't know what Compline is, it sounds like something that'd be okay for all of us. Uncle Ian wants a mini version of the afternoon meeting. Dad tries to forge a compromise: 'Well, time's getting on for Alex's wee bairns to go home, maybe we just need to commit this to the Lord together, and say a blessing?'

He wins them over. As heads bow I look round and realize that Zoe isn't there. She must've stayed upstairs with the kids? Or gone into our room? I bound upstairs. Inside our room, Zoe is a hump of jeans, jersey, and hair on her bed, her face on a book. She's asleep. The book's open, I glance at what I can see of it: it's that birthday present they gave me at the ceilidh. The chapter she's sleeping on is called *Relationships*, a subject we know Dad gives talks about to children at schools we don't go to, and thankfully not to ours. His talks are on the physiology of human reproduction, how our hormones try to take over our feelings, and how to resist the strong urges we feel and get on with our other interests!

I creep away: then hear her calling me back, 'Alice? What's everyone doing now?'

'Praying again. Then Northern supper – snacks and hot drinks. Thought I'd let you sleep. What're you doing with my book?'

'Reading about sex.'

'Why? You know everything we're told.'

'Because I ruined the holiday!'

'What? How?'

'I was the person who got those texts, and I told Mum and Dad? I thought your book might help – relationships — but it's only how to always be good, so no help at all. Why's sex coded as 'relationships', like *always*? And the difficult parts of relating – like telling people awful things without feeling you're soiling their fun, there's no guidance about that at all?'

'Soiling? You mean spoiling?' I laugh a bit.

'Yeah, 'course. Don't *laugh* Ally, I'm being *serious*.'

'You are. Answer, I don't know. D'you want to come down? Nobody's angry with you because you were the one who told us. Just think, you were the person Rothko felt he could write that to. Not to Mum or Dad. That's – oh come down, anyway. Or shall I bring supper up to you?'

'I'll come. So they all know, now? Can they not talk about it – it's too sad.'

'Maybe. We can ask them.'

It's evening. In the family room, Mum is busy, sat in the big armchair where Granny was asleep after the ceilidh, with her laptop. She looks up as we walk in. 'Thinking about trains,' she says, 'I need to get down there, support Daze, see what's happening with Shaz and Charlie.'

'Okay – can I come with you?' I wonder where that came from? It jumped out like I hadn't really thought about it.

'Oh – I thought you —'

'I could maybe see Charlie – if she's – okay?'

'Mmm – let me think about that,' Mum says. 'Here's a train, goes direct, takes about ten hours.'

'So?' I sit on the chair's arm, leaning over to look at the railway timetable.

'I'm not sure you'd be able to see her so soon.'

'Would you be able to see Shaz though?'

'I don't know.'

'Why rush there, then?'

'Because I feel I want to be near her, as a friend, in case I can help, in case I'm allowed. Just, as a friend?'

'That's why I do. I wasn't the best friend before, maybe I can be, now?'

'Oh, Ally,' Mum says, and she gives me a big hug.

Dad is on the sofa, with Zoe and Becky. They have a jigsaw out and are doing it on a tray, the tray's balanced on Dad's knees. Everyone else has left us alone: there's the sound of someone in the kitchen, and quiet voices, and there's a CD playing; I recognize some of the songs, because Zoe learnt them at Base Camp.

I say, 'Dad, don't you think I should go to Cornwall with Mum tomorrow?'

'We'll see,' he says. 'See what tomorrow brings?'

'Can it bring anything we don't know?'

'Well, that's what we don't know, isn't it! We may have more information.'

This is hugely frustrating. How can anyone think about a jigsaw (two horses in a field, with trees, some cottages, and sky beyond, one thousand pieces) when they've let down a person who had thought that they were a friend?

'Something we do know is that the neighbour who found that the family were in trouble is a nurse, she had an idea what the problem was, and called the ambulance. She'd met Shaz earlier in the holiday and had a chat with her about yoga over a coffee.'

'And?'

'If you can wait, I think we'll know more tomorrow. And then I'll let you know. Is that okay?'

'No. Well, it has to be!'

'Good. Now, who can find these pieces of sky and complete the border for us?'

I leave them to their jigsaw and go to find Chloe. She's helping Granny Fee putting out snack food on the table 'so anyone who wants can have a bite to eat,' she says. 'Is your friend...?'

'Dad says more news tomorrow.'

'Hard not to think about it.'

'Yep.'

Anyhow, today's supper is left-over scones, tea and coffee, and the whisky's brought out for those who drink it — the Uncles (including Great Uncle Euan), Dad, and Cameron (only of all of us grandkids). Everyone's very quiet.

Aunt Erin's family are going home straight after breakfast. Chloe says stay in touch, and we exchange mobile numbers and e-mails. I hope she remembers to friend me on Facebook. We hug a long time. Cameron gives me a short hug and a quick kiss, 'Hey, cousin Alice, promise me you won't try to be too good!' and after the door closes behind them all, I feel something's been torn off me, I've made and lost friends, we're, like, going to be the next generation of the family. What'll we all do, will we keep in touch?

Last thing, Dad's back playing the Maxwell Davies *Farewell*, again, softly, and that feels just awful. I want him to stop, but I also want him to go on.

Chapter 55

LEAVING THE MANSE

Monday morning. Soon as my eyes open, Charlie's in my head: I can't get her out. I wonder if she's yet conscious. How she feels. How awful it must be, being Charlie right now.

And for me, there's no chance of more holiday, Edinburgh and the islands. Even if the weather dries up.

Zoe's bed's empty. So I go down, in pjs and a jersey, to be with people. Granny Fee's making tea, Uncle Ian's brewing his own coffee, Aunt Sue's fussing around her kids with a cereal packet, and they all stop to look at me with a kind of question mark on their faces. Like, 'Is she upset and needing comfort, or should we talk about something else?'

Anyway, as if by thought transference, they all decide to talk about something else. Except that Uncle Ian says, 'I think your Dad's going to take you girls home today, while your Mum goes down to Cornwall on the train, is that right? Sorry that your holiday's been cut short.'

I swallow hard, so as not to argue with him. I am not going home: I need to see Charlie, Charlie will need me… Whatever I last said or did… Zoe is nowhere, nor Becky either.

So, Monday breakfast. I eat coco pops (Aunt Sue's left the packet on the table) and toast. The chosen topic is the new manse, and they talk colours and curtains and decide Dunelm is quite okay for house linen.

Granny Fee gets up to refresh the teapot, and I get up to go, and she comes across and gives me a big hug.

'Thanks, Granny,' I say, 'I needed that.' And Zoe walks into the room, looks round, and says, 'Sorry I'm late,' to Uncle Ian. She has on her pyjama top (strappy camisole, in pale lime green) and a denim mini skirt. Granny gives her a hug, and Zoe immediately begins to cry, her face buried in Granny's navy cardigan.

'I know, pet, I know... you've lost your holiday and your Mam and your Da are worried about their friends.'

'And Alice's friend, Alice knows Charlie from nur-sery,' wails my sobbing sister, centre stage and so embarrassing. Charlie and her family weren't even her friends.

Upstairs I find that Mum's grabbed all our stuff and packed it – without asking! I sit on my bed, take out my phone, and begin typing a text to Nina and Emily. *'Our hol cancelled: a family we know were staying at the Cornish house & something awful happened.'* Staying at the Cornish house: I can't type its name... What happened there? And what has this done to it? I start another text, to Fabian, but I can't find the right words, I can't express all the thoughts and feelings in a way that sounds sensible, so I delete the rubbish and lie on my bed, head under the pillow, and think.

I can't think. Suppose they're all – suppose Charlie... Last time we texted I wasn't feeling friendly. And they were staying in Chapel House. What went wrong? Hopefully Dad will have those details today? I think: carbon monoxide poisoning? Will Granny Caro and Des be in trouble?

I get dressed – jeans, T-shirt, jumper — what I wear doesn't feel important today. When I go back down the family are all gathered around the table, praying for Charlie's family — even Uncle Ian's younger ones are. Zoe (with Granny's navy cardie draped over her back) is praying with them. And Dad. And even Mum... 'Oh God,' I say in my heart, 'Let them wake up, Shaz and Charlie – *please, please, let them wake up...*' And my throat catches, and I sit down plonk on the floor, at Granny's feet.

I feel a soft hand take one of mine, and know that's Granny Fee. She squeezes my hand, and I squeeze hers back. I don't wail, though, I bite my mouth shut and let a tear just squiggle down my face. And I wipe it away, and sniff.

Before we finish, Dad does his taking-charge thing again, 'Let's wrap this up with the Northumbria Community's grace before travelling, shall we?'

Everyone who knows it (and most of the northern rellies seem to) says it together:

> *'May the road rise up to meet you.*
> *May the wind be always at your back.*
> *May the sun shine warm upon your face,*
> *the rains fall soft upon your fields,*
> *and until we meet again,*
> *may God hold you in the palm of his hand.'*

Then everyone quietly shuffles out to begin their day. I grab my camera, which someone's put on top of our suitcases in the hallway: I need a last, proper, photo of Granny Fee with the old manse as the background. That feels important. Aunt Sue comes by, 'Your Dad really knows how to bring people together,' she says, squeezing my elbow annoyingly. Before I think, I snap back, 'Yeah, he probably gets it from Pastor Mullins!'

'I suppose I meant, he knows what to say when,' says Aunt Sue, with a smile in her voice, and tinkles a laugh to end the sentence. She turns to go upstairs, humming, and gathering her pink cardie around her baby bump. I catch Granny outside, hanging washing, with Becky helping. Zoe comes across the grass with scissors and a bunch of sweet peas. 'I'll put the stems in wet cotton wool, and some foil,' says Granny.

'Can I have a photo? Just quickly?'

Granny Fee moves away from the washing line, and gathers the two of them into a bunch in front of her, and I take three shots from different angles, all showing the house. 'I hope those come out well,' she says.

'I'll show you now, see?' I hold my camera out, and Granny adjusts her glasses. 'Oh yes...'

'I love it that we can see if they're okay right away: it must've been frustrating having to wait for your pictures to be developed!' I say.

'Delayed gratification!' she says, giving me a smile I like a lot more than Aunt Sue's. We hug.

Soon after that, we're all packing the car. Mum and Dad want all my and Zoe's stuff in there. Zoe screams at Dad because he shoves her copy of *Lord of the Rings* into a basket that's stashed away in a corner, 'I'm reading that! Why don't you just *ask me* about my things? I say where my book goes!'

Dad looks shocked. Zoe (looking at the ground), says, 'Okay, sorry,' and then (head up again), 'But I've been texting with Rothko about *The Hobbit*, and telling him he has to try *Lord of the Rings* now – although,' she says (head on one side, gazing straight at Dad), 'maybe, maybe now I can go and queue for the new Harry Potter? I *was* going to go with Annalise...Waterstones or Blackwells, which do you think?'

What a time to ask! Utterly irrelevant, stupidly off-topic, mood wrong! My turn to yell. 'For God's sake, Zoe, shut up behaving like a kid!' I shout.

'Alice...' says Dad in his low, quiet voice. I hear my words repeat, in my head.

'Why don't I take Alice with me?' Mum is the voice of reason. She's understood that's what I want. 'Yeah,' I say, 'so if Charlie wakes up, I...'

'I think we'll wait to know...' says Mum, interrupted by Dad who adds 'But you'll have things to do down there she won't want to be part of. I'll have things to do and I can't leave Zoe on her own for hours... it would be easier...'

'No, I think Alice has a better reason...'

I watch them, parrying each other's arguments, as a light drizzle begins. Dad tries to shove a large suitcase into a space too small, and Mum pushes her hair back as it falls out of the combs holding up the chignon. Tense, maybe as shaken up as I feel? Definitely as shaken: why wouldn't they be?

Finally Mum says, 'Well you can hardly think you're simply going to go back to work, can you? Sticking your head in the sand isn't like you. This is our holiday, booked months ago, and nobody's going to thank you to come charging into work messing up the carefully organised rotas – are they?'

He moves a couple of plastic bags bulging with shoes, and succeeds with the suitcase. Then, 'You're right of course. If we all go to Cornwall, the girls can find something to do there. Hang out at the beach... Though where we'll stay...'

'Oh, there'll be somewhere. Or we'll put up the tent!' she laughs. We all laugh at this idea in such a wet summer. 'So, Alice, you and me on the train?' Mum says, 'Dad and Zoe can follow on slowly, with the luggage. Quick, you can put a few of your things in my bag for tomorrow – pjs, underwear, and your bathroom stuff,' she says, unzipping the bag, which is already bulging.

'I never thought you'd offer,' I want to say. Better not. Their dynamic is interesting: I'd expect Dad would, like, seize control as it's going to be about medical stuff and an inquest and people – but he seemed to want to disappear into his work... 'Okay, and when do we leave?' I say, and, after a second, I offer Mum a hug. Mum's so often head-down in her work, she's surprised me.

But I suppose Shaz was, actually, a closer friend than I knew?

Granny and Aunt Sue have made sandwiches for our journey. Then the Northumbria Community's Grace is said again, out on the drive.

Uncle Ian, of course, has to correct Dad, and says 'It's a traditional Irish prayer, Max, not Northumbrian.'

And Dad says, 'Sorry, Ian, I'm not as precise as you at these things. The Northumbria Community is where I met that prayer...' He says this in a way that I know means he's not *that* sorry.

'As long as your prescribing is as precise as my knowledge of the things that matter in the church...'

'The practice of medicine isn't always a precise art,' says Dad, and he grins, and rattles his car keys. 'Anyhow, thank you, everyone for the hospitality, and now, we must away.'

And we get in the car, and they all wave... and we wave... and it is all the saddest thing, the saddest way to say goodbye to the Manse before it's pulled down, on our way to the dreary impersonal train station.

Chapter 56

EVENING AT THE COTTAGE

At last, the train is gliding past the sea... slowing as we arrive at Penzance. I normally love this bit, first sight of the sea... but today... we're gathering our bags, I'm feeling sad with butterflies in my stomach about everything. I've been worrying whether Daze is going to be angry about Dad and Mum suggesting Charlie's family as house-sitters while Granny Caro and Des are away, instead of us, or about the fact that the house is Daze's inheritance, not Mum's, so she should say who stays there. But Mum has told me that she and Daze 'worked stuff out' last night, and, that they agreed to insist to Granny Caro that *all's under control, no need to spoil your holiday by leaving early...*'

Daze has also told Mum that Grandpa Guthrie is there in France with Granny Caro and their friends from college days... 'Why?' I asked. 'After they've been divorced forever?'

Mum shook her head. 'He'll have a reason.'

I wonder? What reason?

We're off the train and walking through the station: there's Daze outside in her signature skinny black jeans, with a white shirt and a gorgeous purple, orange, and brown waistcoat. She's leaning kind of relaxed against her van, parked opposite the exit, and that might mean, she's gonna be okay with us.

She's waving. She doesn't come over, but she's smiling. A bit. And Rothko is hanging out of the van, also waving. He looks okay. Maybe it'll be all right?

When we reach the van, Rothko jumps out and gives me a hug, 'Hiya, Alice!... Mum — *Day-zee!*' he yells at her, 'You didn't say, fetch Jenny *and Alice* from the train station!'

Daze gives me a thumbs-up, and then, a big warm hug. My legs almost go weak with relief. Didn't know I could be so amazingly nervous of her. Of her and Mum's relationship. Daze and Mum hug – which is unknown. Then Mum is texting her lab about something (when doesn't she?), and Daze doesn't talk about why we're here, she's telling me the incredible waistcoat is made out of boiled wool. 'Gosh, can you boil wool?'

'To make it change like this, yes. You boil it after making the garment, or if I'm doing bags, I do it before using the cloth.'

'I've never seen it before, I thought that was felt, when you were making those bags before.'

'Feel it,' says Daze, with a grin. It's soft.

We put our things in the van and rattle off. When we get to the other end it turns out to be the same cottage that Daze was house-sitting when I came down at Easter: it feels like years and years ago...

As soon as we're indoors, Mum texts Dad to ask when he and Zoe are likely to arrive. Daze unwraps the sweet peas from their foil and wet cotton wool and finds a vase for them. She puts the vase on the table, and looks out of the window.

Someone arrives just then, lets themselves in with a key, and almost bumps into Daze. 'Whoops!' says a male voice. Lots of *Sorry, sorry...*' and laughter follows, then Daze says, hurrying to the kitchen area, 'Yep, they're here! We should cut that saffron cake...'

The person is David — *David?* What on earth? Last time I saw him, he was at the manse, and now he's here in Cornwall, visiting Daze and Rothko! David looks a bit surprised to see me, but he also looks pleased. 'Hi, Alice, don't suppose you expected to see me here! Sorry we never really finished our discussions at the manse, I had to rush off urgently. Hopefully we'll have some time soon.'

'Yeah! That would be great if you're around for a while.' I'm not really sure what to say.

'It's dreadful news about the Parker Pollards. You remember I mentioned to you at Hadrian's Wall that Sharon was a regular at St Hildie's events, so I got to know her situation quite well. Hopefully I can help out a bit when she comes round.'

If she does, I think grimly. OK, so perhaps he was Shaz's sort-of counsellor, so if and when she wakes up, he'll talk her through it all? That must be it.

There's no further explaining about why he's here. Talk is about whether Dad and Zoe will arrive today or tomorrow, and Mum saying that we had Grandpa Guthrie to thank for Granny's non-interference. 'I do wonder if it was him, and not you and me, Daze, or Max, who persuaded Mum she didn't need to dash for the Eurostar and come flying to anyone's rescue here. I guess he turned on the charm. I suspect she wanted to remain there because of him.'

'Well nothing she can do. She agreed to it. Whole thing's a mystery. I've coped with worse.'

'Yeah,' Mum says, looking at her plate. She cuts her slice of saffron cake in two. 'You really have, Daze. And now, suppose I cook supper?... Or at least, I help?'

David suggests to Rothko that they go and play cricket outside. I wander out, feeling a bit like I don't have a part in this crazy play we're all in. I watch the cricket game in the long thin garden at the front of the cottage, where there's a washing line, and veg plants, and grass. David and Rothko get along with each other quite well. In fact, they're absorbed: so I go back in, and wander round the cottage. It feels familiar and strange at the same time.

I look into the bathroom, which is downstairs. There's a wet suit hanging on a rack over the bath. At least there's not a piece of seaweed floating in the bath! Beyond the bathroom, in the utility room, there are surf boards stacked carefully. Three of them – no, two, and a body board. Several pairs of flip-flops. The floor's all scrunchy-sounding with a small scatter of sand from the beach. There's Rothko's bucket and spade and a net for looking in rock pools, and a row of shells on the window sill.

I go upstairs. Daze has taken the big front bedroom again, and piled sketch books and art books by the bed. There's a mattress on the floor, and on that some half-made Lego trucks and stuff, and what look like small boy's pyjamas thrown on top of the covers. Rothko's place. This looks like a couple usually use it: big bed, built in wardrobe (shall I look inside? Maybe better not). Books. On sailing. And novels. Shells and pebbles arranged on the windowsill. I look out of the window at David and Rothko. And you can just see the sea, a dazzling strip of sun on water, far away. It's so holiday here, I'm washed over with sadness, like a wave breaking on the beach. Get a grip, a phrase I've read in books: we're not here for that.

So, as the sun's shining (it really is sunny here) and it's actually warm, I may as well change into something holiday to suit the place. My stuff that Mum took in her bag is on the bed in one of the two small rooms at the back. Next to the narrow bed is a blow-up mattress, (Zoe can have that, she's a bit smaller!). Mum's suitcase is on the double bed in the other back room. If she's been really kind she may've put me a change of clothes in there.

I undo the zip, and take a look. The clothes inside smell of home. Really, of our washing powder: another wave sweeps over me. Sitting back on my feet, I wonder why Dad was so keen, so insistent, to go back to Oxford before coming down here. And moody. And poking about among the clothes, they're all mixed up, his with hers, and somewhere there's a glimpse of blue denim, and I pull out a pair of cut-off dungarees, which are definitely mine. Then I try to tidy up the mess I've made of the stuff in the suitcase.

When I go back down, Mum's admiring Daze's waistcoat. They've gone to the kitchen-living room front window to look closer at the fabric, then they turn back and notice me, and drop their voices into a whispery conversation. I watch them, my ears tuned in to hear, but they're half turned away, backs to the window now, their faces in shadow. The talk is about Shaz and Charlie being taken to the ICU at the Royal Cornwall, which is in Truro, and how the neighbour (called Evie) found them.

'Thank God for that ruddy cat of Evie's, getting into Chapel House as usual, and Evie coming to look for him, and when there was no answer going inside,' says Daze.

'And thank God Mum leaves a key with her,' Mum adds.

So that's the cat I put over the wall. Evie went looking for him – and found – them all. Nobody has properly told me the details. I mean, bare facts, but not – enough. How did it happen? I go outside. My arms hugging my body. Because really picturing it, I feel shivery, like after you cry but I haven't been crying – only inside, where nobody sees. Maybe wearing cut-offs was a mistake even here with the sun on a lovely Cornish evening.

David and Rothko's laughter suddenly cuts across my mood, and then they see me, and they make gestures like I should join the game. If David's trying to help Rothko cope with the tragedy he knows about, well, Rothko's only eight, and he's easier to help? There is no help when you're not a child and not totally grown-up – and a person you decided you could do without in your life might have... too awful to think about!

'Alice! Ball – didn't you see, can't you catch?!'

Bugger the cricket ball – tennis ball – whatever... it rolls all the way to the garden wall. I plod after it. Tennis ball. Yellow. Soft and light in my hand.

'Aren't you fielding? Don't you know...' Rothko shouts, then stops and does a few overarm moves without throwing anything. He looks like a crazy windmill. 'Haven't you ever played cricket?' he yells. David hands me the bat, he tries to teach me how to hold it properly. We play: I wallop the ball into the neighbouring garden. Because I'm not concentrating. I want to know how Charlie is now. I want to see if my meanness earlier – which of course didn't cause this – can somehow be turned around so I can be a proper friend. I want to know she's woken up, and she's, like, normal, how she used to be? That weekend at the Spa's so vivid in my mind now: Charlie and me waiting for our massages, in that room, and laughing about the hole 'to breathe through' in the couches. Charlie's royal blue satiny shiny thong.

At supper, the grown-ups all drink beer from bottles. At the end, David leaves promptly, 'See you all tomorrow!' (I wonder where he's staying?). I've never seen Mum and her step-sister so fond of each other, clearing up after, hugs, touching, memory-talk, then with mugs of coffee and squares of chocolate, looking up mobile numbers and addresses. They discuss how and whether to contact Daze's Dad, Mum's step-dad Des, who's somewhere remote in Wales running a water-colour course for wannabe artists.

When Rothko goes to bed, I go to bed too, because I'm too tired to do anything else. I lie awake a bit on the narrow kiddie bed, in my sleeping bag bought for our abandoned camping holiday, with the book the relatives gave me. It's really not my kind of book. Nothing about now is like my usual life. I read about how girls like Becky might decide their futures, looking for God's plan. And I contrast that with what David said at Hadrian's Wall about focusing on what I love doing, looking at college prospectuses and at what careers the courses lead to. Because? Because God may create us, but he doesn't control us like we're drones! I end up head on the book like Zoe was, but not asleep. Then Zoe texts from the car: she and Dad are on their way.

Daze and David seem very comfortable together, except they also behave as if they need to be very polite and watch what they say. When he left, Daze waved, from the sofa, 'Okay, see you!' as if he's a casual friend. Then she broke off a couple of squares from a chocolate bar they were all sharing, passed one to Mum, and said something like, 'It's supposed to be good for depression – ha ha!' I try to figure all this out, but somehow, I'm asleep when Zoe comes up to bed. I wake in the night, and turn over. This room, someone's study, is lined with books, and there's no blind or curtains. There's an Anglepoise lamp on the desk and the moon is giving it a weird shadow. The moon is an intruder.

Chapter 57

I'm woken up by blinding sunshine from the curtainless window. Down on the floor beside my bed is my sister, on a mattress, in a blue sleeping bag. Lying on her front, reading *The Lord of the Rings*...and biting her thumb. Seagulls cry overhead, but the house is quiet.

'When did you and Dad arrive?'

'Eleven, 'bout. You were asleep,' she says. 'What's this place like? I was soooo tired...'

'It's a very old cottage. But there is a shower. And a loo, obviously. And, the weirdest thing, Uncle David turned up yesterday! I think maybe because Shaz has been seeing him for counselling.'

Doors are opening, feet moving about, voices beginning in the next room, then moving off downstairs. We venture down in our pyjamas: Rothko is stirring chocolate powder into a glass of milk, Dad is pouring coffee into mugs from one of those metal jug-like things you boil real coffee in. The smell reminds me of staying with Grandpa Guthrie in America: what was it Mum said? That he's in France on holiday with Granny Caro and her friends? Bit unexpected!

Daze is eating muesli. Mum is eating toast. Toast, and coffee, would be nice. 'Dad, enough for me?'

He adds another mug, and I signal *lots of milk*. The flagstone floor's icy cold under my feet as I walk over to fetch it: forgot to put slippers on!

Breakfast is silent, adults busy eating, sipping coffee, and not catching anyone's eyes. Rothko then loudly asks Daze, 'Can I do my holiday diary all in cartoons?'

Daze says, 'No, but you can put in as many illustrations as you like.'

'But I don't want to put all this in the diary. Is that okay?

Adults all chorus, 'Of course it is! Just put in all the highlights, your own ones.'

His teacher will know this happened anyway. The story hit the headlines in the *Western Morning News*.

Mum gets to her feet and starts gathering things off the table to put away. Zoe snatches back her plate, 'Isn't there more toast? I hardly ate yesterday, I'm starving!'

Daze fetches paper and a pencil, and begins a shopping list, in her wonderful italic writing: 'Eggs, bacon for carnivores, bread, fruit, veg, wine – anything else?'

'Meat for carnivores?' says Dad.

'Cheese? Coco pops, ice cream?' says Rothko, hopefully. 'Pizza?'

'I can make you pizza,' Mum says, 'put flour on the list, Daze!'

'And Cornish cream and — yogurt?' Zoe suggests. 'And can you make a cake as well?'

We're all avoiding talking about why we're here. Instead we're planning a trip to buy groceries in St Just. We leave Dad behind, making phone calls. I glance back before I get in the van, and he's by the window, on his phone, looking earnest. I wonder if he's talking to some medical person about Charlie and Shaz...

As we drive through the lanes, the foxgloves, scabious, some rather small yellow flowers — quick flashes of colour — and glimpses of the sparkly sea, lift me up, in spite of what has happened. The landscape's so beautiful when the sun's out. It's good to be back.

On the way into St Just we stop briefly to drop Rothko off at his friend's house. We park in what Zoe calls the ugly square (I suppose it is ugly, with those boxy flats looking down on it?) and walk up the road. The grey stone-built shops match the flats and the little miners' cottages.

All of it reminds me of the old manse, and the pulling-down, leaving only grim, heavy, blocks of stone. So are they all from the same rock?

We go to the family butcher to buy meat for carnivores, and the baker for bread, Cornish pasties, and saffron buns. Walking round the square, where most of the shops are, Daze grins and calls 'Hiya!' to about half the people we pass, like she knows almost everyone who's not a tourist. So, does she come down more often than we know? Suppose that's not our business. Although she did tell me all the disadvantages of living here, when I stayed in the Easter holidays. And how come her friends' cottage was conveniently free for us to stay in at a moment's notice? Interesting...

We move on to the Co-op for everything else on our list, where I stand in a corner and google the rocks in Cornwall and Northumberland: I'm wrong about them being the same, around Penzance, the rock is granite, and Northumberland is sandstone. It must be the architecture then that makes the buildings so similar. That and something about terraced cottages and occasional huge grim municipal buildings, and Methodist churches which remind me of the manse. It's a town built to accommodate people who spend their days underground: mining tin, or mining coal, both must be grim, dreary work. Like in those mills, where Lowry lived and painted.

Last stop is the pharmacy, where Mum buys paracetamol, insect bite cream, and toothpaste. Also, a couple of those soap and stuff presents in pretty boxes. Maybe for Charlie and Shaz, if they've woken up? Does she know they have? I turn to ask her, but she's met someone she once knew at school, and they're chatting, as matey as if they'd kept up and remained friends forever. I instinctively stand back so as not to have to be introduced, grin, and make conversation about GCSEs or some other inane subject. Zoe is spinning the stand where they hang things like hair slides and Alice bands, hair brushes and nail scissors. Then she trots up to the counter with what's called an Alice band, and pays for it. 'For Becky, we decided we'd write,' she says, joining me in the corner where the shampoo and shower gel are displayed.

'You're proper friends again, then?'

'Why not? You're friends with Chloe!'

Ignoring her, I look beyond the counter, to where they keep the drugs. I wonder about Eliot, whether there were any drugs to help his illness? I guess not, if it's genetic? But what do I know?

Daze takes us to a cafe we all love, called the Cookshop, for tea and cake. Zoe looks around, and having finished her chocolate milkshake, she says, 'Mum, can we — me and Ally — look at the books upstairs?'

'Don't be long. Daze and I have somewhere else to go.'

Upstairs, there are connecting rooms stuffed with books of all kinds. We love browsing here. I've always liked looking at the special editions, arranged in showcases, especially imagining the Edwardian children these belonged to. There's a wonderful fat copy of the two Alice books – *In Wonderland* and *Through the Looking Glass* – but Zoe pulls me away from gazing at it. 'Listen, I got us up here so's I could tell you something. Okay?'

'Okay, I'm listening.'

'In here,' she hisses, holding my arm, and moving us into the next room, away from two women browsing by the window.

'Right. So, what's it about?'

'About where Dad and me went on our way down. Why we arrived so late.'

'Well, why did you?'

'We went to St Hildegard's, I had to sit and read in their visitors' lounge while Dad talked to Elaine, you know, that woman priest who runs it now. She gave me tea and a plate of ginger biscuits...'

'Did you hear anything they were saying?'

'No, I was downstairs and they went up to her office. I ate all the biscuits, and read a lot of *The Lord of the Rings* and got them all – not Frodo and Sam or Gollum – the others — into a huge battle at Helm's Deep. But what I was going to say was, I was hoping — d'you think it could have had anything to do with Stacey — and Annalise?'

'Well, maybe — I don't know... Or d'you think it was all connected to Charlie's family, and why we're here?'

Zoe does a huge shrug, 'Oh, okay. I s'pose it could be, 'cos this old couple, in smart clothes, came into the lounge, and Elaine and Dad came and met them and they all talked in low voices, not taking any notice of me, and then they all went off to the office. So I read a lot more of *The Lord of the Rings*. I was just hoping, about Stacey, you know...'

She looks as bit crestfallen, as if she had really hoped that Dad might be doing something about Stacey's situation.

'Yeah, I get it, it would be nice to know what's happened to them. But David says that Shaz used to go to St Hildie's for lots of stuff — he said this yesterday, and he was Shaz's counsellor, at least I think he was, they had meetings at Hildie's. So maybe the older couple were Charlie's grandparents, Jos and Gussie, I've seen them! What did you do next?'

'Well, we went home and left some of the luggage. Like all the party clothes, Mum had put them together in the big suitcase. I said don't leave Ally's violin, I thought you might want it. We had boiled eggs and toast and bananas, and we got back in the car and came here. Dad put music on, said we wouldn't bother chatting, and drove like the clappers except when it was raining, and we hardly stopped. He said, "Okay, we need to get there, no breaks except toilet ones", and we whizzed along in the fast lane, with Bach on a CD. But it was only to get here before midnight or something.'

'Why?'

'Just because he was fed up and wanted to get the journey done, I expect.'

'Was he fed up?'

'Well, he was, like, silent. Maybe just sad.'

Mum calls up the stairs, time to move on. Out in the road, Daze takes us along to the craft co-op shop, which I feel really happy to see again, and Zoe admires the clothes and bags, and pottery things, and paintings, through the shop window. 'Could we, like, just go inside a few minutes?' she asks Daze.

Daze and Mum glance at one another, and Daze says, 'We'll come back another day. If your Mum's busy I'll take you.'

Mum adds, looking at Daze, 'Today quick lunch, then the house?'

The house? *The* house – where this all *happened?* 'Could I – if that's Chapel House – could I come with you? I'd – like a walk...'

Daze does a thumbs-up, but Mum says, 'Maybe next time? We'll be going again.'

Dad's left a note (why didn't he text?): he's gone to Truro, to see Shaz and Charlie's consultant. After lunch, David and Rothko invite Zoe and me to join them on the beach. Mum and Daze are walking to Chapel House, mostly along the cliff path, and I really want to go with them. But, I'm counted with the youngsters, told to hire a wet suit, and enjoy the surf. I feel that the adult world has drawn a dividing line, and left me on the wrong side.

Once Dad's back, I hope at least he'll tell me how Charlie is. They must know that's important to me – it was them who wanted us to become friends again!

'Great weather for surf!' says David, as we pull up in the beach car park right next to the surf board shop. Changed and ready, Zoe and Rothko rush off down to the beach with their body boards. David's brought his and Daze's surfboards.

I say, 'I'm not sure how confident I feel about surfing. I don't think I can concentrate.'

'No worries. Let's just stroll.'

David and I clatter over the shingle and along the wet sand, the lacy tongues of incoming waves licking our feet. The sandy beach is well full of holiday families with windbreaks, buckets and spades, and picnics, and we have to step aside into the sea a moment, to avoid a group playing Frisbee. A lifeguard vehicle trundles by. Very quietly, the breeze blowing my words out to sea, I say, 'D'you know any more? About Charlie?'

'Your Dad's the one who'll know, I think he's waiting for more, then he'll tell us. You and Charlie — I remember you said it wasn't easy to be friends?'

Too right! I feel dreadful about how I treated her, before I knew about Eliot.

I glance at David, he looks back at me. 'You're finding it hard. Only talk if you want to...' he says.

'We were friends up to age five. We were at nursery together, then, remember, our family went to South Africa for two years 'cos Dad had that sabbatical. While were there Charlie's family moved away. Then we had nothing to do with them for ages. Charlie just turned up again, at a concert... and she saw me. You have to understand, it was a first date, and she came slinking up in the interval, and I was, like, not very nice to her.'

'Oh, no! Of course, you weren't ready to re-meet under those circumstances! It must've felt very awkward!' says David.

'Exactly...'

'It wasn't just an interruption, it was a sort of challenge: would he look at Charlie and think, wow, look at the friend!'

'Yeah, and think he'd like to know Charlie better? Or Charlie might think I didn't deserve him?'

'And on a first date – you were getting to know each other, wondering if there'd be another time like this.' David smiles. 'It's totally forgivable!'

'And, you haven't seen Charlie!'

'She's...?'

'Very sexy. Now. And, we – me and Fabian — were having fun, because we both love music, and Fabian, who knows more about it than I do, was telling me useful interesting things about the piece, and... d'you know Haydn's Creation?'

'Not as a musician would – but, translating that into riding the waves... I get your point...'

'Yeah, well, we didn't need an invasion by a Miley Cyrus fan whose grandparents had dragged her out to be indoctrinated with high culture... Sorry, but that's kind of who they are... And Mum had joined this yoga class and it turned out that Shaz was the teacher. They seemed to get very close suddenly, and Mum started pressuring me to be friends with Charlie. But I just felt she was totally not my type.'

'I get it. I totally understand how you felt when Charlie invaded your space in the concert interval... And friendship's not something you can just create out of nothing!'

Thanks, David, for getting it again. After a silence he says, 'And, by the way, I find this waiting frustrating, just like you do. But, here we are, at the beach on quite a nice afternoon, with about the right kind of surf out there, so... maybe it's time to get some relaxation and forget about our worries for an hour or two? And, it's actually quite hard to talk about, wouldn't you agree? How about we go back for the boards?'

'Yeah. It actually is. I – think you may be right?'

I gaze down the beach, allowing myself to accept that David's idea for the afternoon is actually a good one. A long way down, thankfully between the red and yellow safety flags, I can see Zoe and Rothko messing about in the shallows. 'Hey, they're enjoying the sea... maybe I could...'

'Sorry — where?' David asks.

'There,' I point. And then, I realise suddenly that Rothko isn't there now. He's nowhere, I can't see him at all. Zoe seems to be jumping up and down. What's happened? I get a sick feeling, and start to run towards her.

David must have had the same fright. He's running too, though running on smooth wet sand is slow. As he passes me, he yells, 'God, where's my kid? Bloody hell, what's happened?'

'What?' What's he mean? Did I hear right? It's not the swearing — it's *my kid*! I'm dodging around paddling toddlers and collapsing sand castles, my mind half on what's wrong and half on processing what he said. Have I found the missing piece, and *David* is Rothko's father?

'Hey, brilliant!' yells Zoe, 'hey, did you see that?'

I skid to a stop. David is on his knees in the surf, giving Rothko a hug. He's perfectly fine, he's trying to demonstrate how he rode the wave, and Zoe is blathering on about how brilliant it was and she couldn't do as well.

And I'm putting it together: David is the mystery man I was curious about, the guy who Daze found to have her kid with. And Daze is the mystery woman, David's new partner. That overheard conversation whizzes through my brain.

David and Rothko still have their heads close together and the likeness hits me in the eye. They smile the same smile, the wetsuits outline that they've got the same build... Rothko's got more hair, and it's a paler blond, but it's so alike... I am stunned. Then a warm feeling comes over me: Daze and David — my two fave rellies!

Chapter 58

SECRETS ARE REVEALED

'He's *your kid*? Yours and Daze's?' I say in a sort of choked way. 'That's like, amazing!'

There's a moment when no one speaks. A microlight drones over-head. Rothko points at it. 'Hey, cool! I'd like to do that!' He rushes off up the beach to watch it.

David's grinning, a bigger grin on his face than I've ever seen. He puts a finger to his lips. '*He doesn't know yet!* Keep it under your hat for a bit, if you can! Daze and I — well, it was all going to be explained in Edinburgh, at your great-aunt Val's. Then — this awful thing happened, so...'

'Oh, so you came down because Daze is here.'

'Not only that — remember, I know Sharon — and her story — from St Hildie's.'

Zoe's face is like a question mark. 'What are you two on about? What about Daze and you?'

'David, can I tell Zoe — and make sure she keeps quiet?'

'Wait till you get back to the cottage, can you? Bit complicated to discuss here with *him* buzzing around! But, look, soon we'll all have a proper talk — no more secrets then!'

I can see Zoe's bursting with curiosity, but just then:

'Glad I caught you!' We all jump. Dad's appeared from nowhere, in shorts and a t-shirt, with a broad smile, as if we're here as a nice group of family out for an afternoon, not people wrestling with a tragedy and a massive surprise. 'Mum and Daze not here yet?' Dad asks cheerfully, though it's self-evident they aren't. 'You want to hear the good news or the good news?'

Zoe shouts, 'You mean they're both okay? Dad? They're totally okay?' She throws herself at Dad as if he'd worked a miracle.

'Whooah, Zo-zo! Yes, they are – they will be, physically. They're both very shocked, quite stunned and – they do need lots of peace and quiet at the moment. But we'll be allowed to visit tomorrow – I think, Alice, and Mum first though. One visitor each?'

'Where?' My mind flipping back from my incredible discovery, back to Charlie. 'At the hospital?'

'Possibly there – if they're still waiting to leave. They're going to be discharged to a convalescent place. And when you go, Alice... Alice, something wrong?'

Gosh, what's my face doing? Trying to handle too many happy feelings at once. 'No! I'm really, really happy for Charlie. And some other stuff!'

'How's that?'

'Ask David! Anyhow, I'm so happy I can visit Charlie!'

This is turning into a very odd afternoon. We all understand there are secrets – or at least Dad, David and me understand this, Zoe probably does as well, but does Rothko? Dad and David walk a few steps away up the beach, but keep distant from a large family with two windbreaks and a blue tent forming a blockade around themselves. Then they literally put their heads together a few minutes, while the rest of us – Zoe, Rothko, me – stand about at the edge of the waves and I try to keep the other two from interrupting Dad and David by asking them the details about the surf school and how Rothko rode that wave so perfectly a few minutes ago. Then Dad and David call us over. They're saying obscure things like 'Well there are a few matters to sort out,' and 'Rather you than me!'

Obviously, Daze (and I suppose David), had decided that when we all met up at Aunt Val's they would tell us that they were an item, and that David was Rothko's dad. That makes me think how brilliant it is that it all came out in this weird messy way — it'd have been dead embarrassing all sitting round in Aunt Val's flat having a formal announcement or whatever.

'So, all meet up tomorrow, then?' David says, and he and Dad step apart, and he calls Rothko over and says they need to find Mummy up at Chapel House. He gathers up the surf boards and they set off, heading towards the ice cream shop on their way back to the car.

'Hey Dad, what does he mean tomorrow? They going somewhere?'

'Yes, they're away to David's friends in Marazion, where he's staying just now. The general feeling is that the cottage is a wee bit crowded with all of us, and his friends have got a barn of a place. They've things to sort out, and we've got your visit tomorrow, so we all need some space.'

Ha! They're an item then, even if Dad's trying to imply that everyone will have their own room at David's friends' place. I have a secret inside smile. Anyway, that kind of ends our beach afternoon. There's not much to do except playing with a slightly battered orange Frisbee which Dad has brought from the cottage. It's turned grey and chilly and there's a fresh wind, so when you throw the Frisbee into it, it comes back to you like a boomerang. After a bit Mum turns up, from whatever she's been doing with Daze up at Chapel House, and we go back to the cottage for tea indoors with saffron buns and plum jam.

By now, I'm wondering when something's going to be said about David and Daze, and Zoe looks like she's about to explode. So then Mum looks around at us three sat at the kitchen table, and says 'It's time to share a secret I've had to keep for much longer than I've felt comfortable about.'

Zoe says, 'I think I know what it is!' And I say, 'I definitely know what it is!'

Mum's expression is a bit like a punctured balloon, so disappointed that the news isn't going to be a big surprise. But I still want to know how it all happened, I mean, could they have had an affair eight, nearly nine years ago? And what about whatever is special about priests – they can marry, but wouldn't an affair be just terribly wrong? And, of course, we all thought he was gay back then: but now, I know he's bisexual since I overheard that embarrassing conversation in our kitchen.

'Rothko,' Mum says, 'knows his dad was a sperm donor – what he didn't know was that the sperm donor was much closer to him and his Mum than a stranger. He was Mum's friend Uncle David!'

'Yay!' says Zoe, punching the air. 'I guessed right didn't I? Like David said *my kid,* didn't he? I heard him.'

'People should be careful what they say around you, then!' I say.

'– and so now,' Mum continues, 'they're at David's friends' house in Marazion, getting used to being a family – which is how they're going to live from today! Isn't that wonderful?'

We're all grinning like loons by this time. Zoe turns to Dad and asks if he also knew before. 'I had a strong suspicion,' Dad says, 'But obviously I couldn't say anything.'

'How come all of this?' Zoe asks, 'I thought – I mean, Uncle David's gay, isn't he? Does he want to be a family with – well, you know...'

'David came out as bisexual,' I say, 'Isn't that how? He, like, found himself attracted to Daze, but I guess he had to work out what that meant? Like, was this real?'

'I think he took some time to feel confident about it, yes,' says Dad.

'I think that could feel weird,' says Zoe.

'It probably did,' says Mum. 'But, it's such a happy thing.'

'It really is,' says Zoe. 'Hey, they've got to have a wedding, haven't they? Are they going to? I mean, David's a priest so he must want a wedding.'

I say: 'You just want to be a bridesmaid, don't you, Zozo!'

Mum says; 'Well, you know Daze, everything a bit throwaway, but I think she did mention the W word briefly!'

There's a pause while Zoe starts on yet another bun. Then I say, 'Listen, Mum, you and Daze were at Chapel House today. Is it okay? What's gonna happen to it?'

'Yes, it's okay. Once the police are finished with it, they can get the cleaners in...'

'And then? Is Granny Caro still convinced about selling it?'

'Yes, she is...'

'Oh, no,' goes Zoe, 'what a —'

'Wait Zozo! David and Daze are going to buy it. They're planning to run a sort of arty retreat centre.'

'Oh, wow, brilliant! Daze gets to keep it! It'll be like St Hildie's at the seaside! But what happens to Des?'

'I think he's going to have a little flat there. They'll have to make some alterations.'

'So is Granny Caro going to live happily ever after in Baker Street then?'

Mum laughs. 'Well, you know, a rather sweet thing has happened, though it's a maybe a bit ironic from my point of view, and Harriet's.' Mum's looking a bit pink.

'What's that about, Mum?' Zoe asks.

'It's about Grandpa Guthrie...'

Dad interposes from the corner. 'It seems that, having met up again with your Granny at the college reunion, he's taken a fancy to a wee apartment in the West End of London and the lady that goes with it!'

'Oh Max, he is going to pay off the inheritance tax!'

'Only joking. She sounds very happy.'

I try to imagine Granny Caro secretly having a thing for Grandpa Guthrie all these years, even after he'd walked out on her and Mum and Auntie Hattie.

Chapter 59

MORE REVELATIONS

It's into mid-morning the next day when we begin to make arrangements to visit Charlie and Shaz. We check whether they're still at the hospital, and find they're now at the convalescent place, but that's also in Truro. A text arrives: ping! Fabian... oh how much I have to tell him... but not now, not by text... And thinking of Charlie, and that I have a half-Italian boyfriend... I put my life and hers into perspective... and feel kind of, what is it? *Humble* is a funny word to use: outside the Sheldonian I was, like, terrified of Charlie just taking Fabian off me. Was that all that stopped me wanting to be her friend? What kind of a person... 'Alice! Lunch before we go – to Truro, to see Charlie and Shaz?'

'Uh?'

'You'll need to get changed,' Mum says. 'And we'll have a quick lunch — Daze has left soup we can warm up.'

'What?'

'Soup. Vegetable soup. And brown rolls.'

So, we eat, and after lunch, I put on my skinny jeans and that top I wore for punting. And eye shadow. Mum and I drive to the convalescent place. We hang about in reception while someone works out the best place for us to go to see Charlie and Shaz. Mum's brought the soap and shower gel gift boxes she bought at the pharmacy, wrapped in gold paper. I can't sit and wait on the chairs and sofa supplied, I have to walk up and down the corridor. There's a door open and as I saunter past I glance in, and stop in my tracks. There are easels in there, with paintings on them — some people are quietly painting. Group art therapy! I get a warm feeling.

Then I'm back thinking of Charlie and Shaz. Will they look different? I mean, not physically, but somehow, changed by the truth, whatever it is? Will Charlie want to talk about it? What do I say? I mean, really my family, and my whole life, are fine compared to hers.

My thoughts are somewhere far away, a long time ago when I was five and we four went shopping in a big store, and Charlie decided she and I must hide amongst the furniture and give our mums a scare... I hid in a wardrobe, like Lucy in Narnia...

'They've been given a lovely room,' Mum says suddenly, giving me a jump.

'I hope Charlie doesn't mind sharing – with her Mum.'

'Well, that is a thought,' says Mum. 'anyway, there she is – you go down and say hello and I'll see if Shaz is in here,' and she knocks quietly at the door.

Charlie's a few steps down the corridor, with a nurse, waiting, in a wheelchair. And I'm hugging her, somehow folding myself over the horrible chair, 'I'm sorry, I'm so sorry,' I'm saying, while Charlie's saying, 'Alice! Hey Alice...' and we're crying all over each other.

The nurse waits, and then says, 'Let's take you outside, there's a visitors' garden.' Or something like that.

The nurse stays, she sits on a bit of low wall, and I sit on a bench next to Charlie, and Charlie holds onto my hand. 'This is nice,' I say, as the sun warms me. Nice? Stupid thing to say. It's horribly sad, being here...

'It's a physic garden, all herbs and stuff that has a good smell,' says Charlie. 'Actually, see that one with the little red flowers? It's sage, and if you crush the leaves in your hand, they stink like cats' piss.' And she laughs a bit, and so do I, because the old Charlie is still here. 'I like your top,' she says.

'This? It's an old one, but I like it...holiday clothes.'

'Our holiday,' Charlie says, 'was so good until Friday night happened. I mean, Dad was like, let's do everything, let's visit the vineyards and buy wine, go to this and that garden, and eat dinner out lots, and – everything. We drove about looking all over. We did the Eden Project on the way down — it's awesome! We were supposed to take a boat trip on Sunday. We were planning to go to Lanhydrock, which is an amazing house with everything Victorian, kitchen, nursery, that kind of stuff, on the way back. We looked at where this writer who's called Daphne du somebody...'

'Du Maurier?' I ask, because Mum bought some books by her when we visited Fowey once.

'Her,' says Charlie, 'and Mum bought a whole stack of books she wrote, and we went to Tintagel which was King Arthur's castle, we went to the museum in St Ives to see Barbara Hepworth sculptures...' She's sniffing and wiping tears away with the back of her free hand by now. The nurse comes over and gives her a bunch of tissues, and goes back and sits. She doesn't talk.

I start to say to Charlie, how lovely, and does she have photos, but then Charlie says, 'And then, we had dinner at the Old Success Friday night, with lots of wine and... we came back and... I woke up in the hospital, and so did Mum a bit after me 'cos she'd drunk more wine... and Dad was... you know...' Charlie has to grab her other hand back from me, to cover her face.

And, Oh God, I say inside, *do something*... So, what actually happened is about to come out? And what'll I say when it does? I don't have to wait: Charlie uses all the tissues up, and then she blurts it out – most of it. 'He said he didn't want me to have to go through what he had... he wanted me to die, Ally – my Dad wanted... in a note he put that...' She sniffs a few times, 'he's got what he wanted... for himself... and we didn't want that... we weren't *asked*...'

I'm totally stunned by this. Eliot tried to kill his family deliberately? Can I imagine this thing? How – how, I need to know. A thousand confused thoughts. Like, *how?*

The nurse is really nice to me, and she sorts Charlie out, and brings us some tea. She sits with us, talking about a yoga retreat place Shaz and Charlie are going on to for a few weeks. *Weeks.* And asking how long we've been friends. We end up talking about visiting Daze's narrowboat, on the Oxford Canal, when we were kids at primary school. 'I loved your aunt. I want to see her again now!' says Charlie. 'I – went in the art room today, and the therapist woman said what had I planned to do and I said my friend was coming to see me. We talked a bit, and she said why not draw something about your friend, something happy.'

The nurse takes Charlie back into her room. Charlie is swivelling her body round as far as she can in the chair, and telling me, 'Please come again, Alice! Please come and see me again! And bring Daze, can you bring Daze?'

'I'll try!'

Yeah, I'll defo bring Daze, I think to myself, and I'll have some amazing news to tell you, now it's all out!

I'm left on my own, outside the room where Mum and Shaz are talking. Suddenly, through the door, I hear Shaz's voice, almost shrieking, 'And it was all a big mistake, because he isn't her Dad at all – as you know, Jen...'

What? I'm stunned again.

♥   ♥   ♥

So, Mum's told me. She came out of Shaz's room, and she could tell I'd heard it. We go for a cup of tea and some cake, and she fills me in, talking like adult to adult. Such a relief not to be treated like a kid who overhears something and has to be fobbed off.

'Yes. It was quite early in their marriage. Eliot was working all hours as a newly qualified junior doctor. Shaz was at a yoga weekend, met some guy who found her attractive, and impulsively had a fling. Then, she found she was pregnant. She immediately regretted everything desperately. She couldn't bring herself to tell Eliot.'

'And so now… if she had…'

'As she never did, I suspect she thought she'd spare Charlie hearing about the affair… But, as she kept it secret, and Eliot knew that any child of his would have had a fifty percent chance of inheriting Huntington's — his degenerative disease — he felt the only thing he could do was to make sure Charlie didn't survive to the age where she could develop it.'

'And it was all for – nothing… How – how awful…' I feel stunned, all over again, like I've stopped breathing.

'Yes,' says Mum.

We sit silent, obviously both unable to speak. I feel oddly joined to the grown-up world, where terrible things absolutely can't be undone. I realize that Shaz will have to tell her, now, to reassure her she's safe. How awful. Her dad is not her dad, her dad tried to kill her… I look at my slice of cake. Poke it with my fork. Lay down the fork again.

'Yes,' Mum repeats, and she takes a deep breath. 'What a mess.'

Mum takes off her glasses, rubs her eyes, sniffs, and put the glasses back. 'He must have felt such despair. He must've – I don't know — Shaz said she hopes it wasn't planned, it was an impulse…'

'How did he do it?'

'Injection. He gave them an overdose of insulin. It makes you unconscious. It's fatal if the dose is big enough.'

'How did he get it?'

'They don't know. But — I can't see how it can have been an impulse, he'd have to have planned how to obtain it somehow, you can't just get it over the counter.'

I'm kind of frozen hearing this. It's like a crime story, but about people I know. I suddenly remember the conversation about muckraking in Shaz's garden.

'Hey, is this connected to Eliot investigating his family history?'

'Yes, exactly. Eliot found all this out when he discovered his birth mother. It was a terrible shock. The symptoms begin in early middle age, and Eliot was forty-four when he found out, and that would be about the age it could strike.'

'So, I guess he began watching out for symptoms... That would creep me out — what does it do – what causes the symptoms?'

'The disease causes a breakdown of nerve cells in the brain.'

'So – kind of generalised?'

'I think it begins with difficulties concentrating. Then depression and memory lapses.'

'And that's why – why he gave up...'

'Clinical medicine? Yes. You can't...'

'Yep. I get it.'

'And other things. Physically, someone would have difficulty with their balance, and walking would become difficult. Swallowing too, as the illness progresses.'

'Gosh, horrible.'

'This is why I do the work I do – this is why research is so important... And of course knowing what genes – which precise chromosomes – are affected, and testing, that's only the beginning of possible prevention...'

I wrap my piece of cake in the paper napkin it came with. We leave the cafe. On the way back, Mum says 'You can't tell Zoe all this. I'll tell her the outline and that'll do for her.'

So, I'm included among the adults who know. But why did it have to be something as awful as this?

Chapter 60

AT THE BLUE LAGOON

Going back in the car, Mum and I are silent, in unspoken agreement. I'm thinking about fathers, and how much power they have. The unimaginable thing Charlie's dad did. Annalise's dad, beating her mum up, and terrifying them. Grandpa Alisdair telling Dad that God wanted him to be a pastor and marry a girl they'd picked out. And then Dad acting like Grandpa when I said I wasn't sure about science. And Mariam's dad, making Dina marry his friend's son. And Uncle Ian lecturing me about growing up. Grandpa Guthrie wanting to get back with Granny Caro — after how long? And goodness, Derek Bradfield, he wasn't a dad at all, just an *inseminator* (where did I learn that word?). Which makes me think of David: he seems to care about Rothko, but can that change? Like, they must all start off caring... And what would Fabian be like as a dad? *That* gives me a weird feeling.

Back at the cottage, everyone's a bit quiet. I mean, it's fantastic that Shaz and Charlie are OK, but the other stuff is pretty shattering, even for Mum and Dad. David, Daze, and Rothko are not there: I guess they're considerately keeping out of the way.

Now I know what I need to do: share it all with Fabian. I text him about everything weird and awful and brilliant that's happened since Sunday. I end up by saying 'Now I realise what Charlie and Shaz were going through before, and what they're facing now, and I'm really sorry.

I'm going to try and somehow be a better friend to Charlie. Maybe all this has changed her too...'

And then, after a bit there's a phone call, and I hear Dad talking, evidently to David. It sounds like he and Daze, who aren't so affected by what's happened to Shaz and Charlie, want us all to celebrate their news with a dinner out. I hear Dad say that there's a good reason why we might avoid the posh restaurant at the Old Success hotel. He comes off the phone a minute and asks Mum for suggestions. She says, and we all agree, that the amazing fish and chips at the Blue Lagoon in Sennen Cove would be perfect for a celebration dinner. We'll meet them down there.

The Blue Lagoon's got a drinks licence, and Dad pushes the boat out so that right at the start a lot of bottles appear. I gulp down a glass of wine on an empty stomach, 'cos they're taking a long time to fry fish and chips for seven people. Then I start on another one and Mum and Dad don't notice, as they're knocking it back like there's no tomorrow. Even Zoe has a glass (she makes 'not sure' faces, but it's getting emptied) as well as something fizzy. I even get a third one, which I don't finish...

I'm feeling super relaxed when Daze and co. appear. Then there's a bit of an embarrassing moment when we're all adjusting to them being like an actual real family, which they sort of have been all along in secret. We're all being polite and saying 'where would you like to sit?' and stuff. Then suddenly everyone jumps up and starts hugging and kissing each other. Zoe and I even kiss Rothko! Everybody has been completely strung out with stress for days and something has just gone snap.

Mum and, I think I notice, *even Daze*, are actually crying a tiny bit, and David and Dad are sort of braying away about something, possibly bishops and religious stuff, and guffawing and waving their arms. I just overhear David saying something like 'Yes, it was totally out of line, even the C of E says it should be within a marital relationship...' This must surely mean him being sperm donor? Then they do some murmuring, and I catch the names of Great-uncle Euan and Great-aunt Margaret, David's parents, so again I stretch my ears. 'Of course, it's all

OK in their eyes now, now there's going to be a wedding…' and he and Dad laugh and give each other knowing looks.

Rothko keeps jumping on David shouting 'David-Dad! Dad-David!', which would really annoy me if I wasn't half pissed. Zoe's all excited, blathering stuff to me about surfing and the Hobbit, or maybe, would hobbits have done surfing if the Shire had had a beach, and I'm not listening, but she doesn't mind and carries on. For some unknown reason my mind jumps to the day when Daze and I were leaving Chapel House and I discovered that painting. I gather my fuddled wits together enough to say to Daze, 'Hey, you've got to tell me about the picture, you know, the crucifixion one! David told me which book you got the idea from, and he's going to lend it to me.'

Daze says, 'Yeah, *Asher Lev*, that's where I got the idea. The guy in the book did a painting of himself like that, and I kind of borrowed it for how I was feeling, a bit trapped like, but nothing like him. You should read it.'

'I will. It's kind of the key to what I want to do.'

Dad's sitting just by me and I grab his arm. 'Listen, Dad. You can help people who are depressed, or they have other mental health problems, through expressing their feelings and problems visually. There's an art therapy room at Charlie and Shaz's convalescent place. I looked in. And there was a painting drying on a table near the door: Me, Charlie and Daze on the narrowboat when we were — maybe — five? Weird Charlie thought of that! I *know* I that's what I want to get involved in, kind of hands-on healing stuff.'

'Och,' says Dad, 'I suppose you'd better give it a wee try?' I think the wine may have got to him.

'Look, of course I'll do relevant A levels: psychology for one, obviously. I think with one science, which'll be chemistry, and art of course. Even, s'pose I could do four subjects and manage physics? Or maths? Whatever.'

'However'd that help?' Dad says.

'Make you happy!'

'Och...' he says again.

'I think you then have to do a master's in art therapy. It's like four years. It's not nothing. Okay?'

Daze is watching us. She joins in. 'Come on, Max, give the girl a break. She needs to follow her dream,' she says, giving him one of her looks. And that's the subject closed. Daze starts offering the wine bottle round again. 'Drink up, Father Dave, you're way behind!', she says, and empties the bottle into David's glass.

I belong to a really, really weird family! Not just the northern rellies, but the Guthries, and Daze and David, are totally eccentric.

Quite honestly the other people in the Blue Lagoon must think we're all round the bend, and it's surprising the owners don't ask us to leave. Anyway, we eat our fish and chips, which are sooo delicious. Eventually we do leave, and have a lovely walk (me kind of stumbling along in a complete alcoholic haze) in the dark along the promenade and then all the way up the sandy stairways to the carpark on the cliff. I feel I'm asleep before I get into bed...